Crucible of Faith

CRUCIBLE OF FAITH

VERN PACE

iUniverse, Inc.
New York Bloomington

CRUCIBLE OF FAITH

iUniverse books may be ordered through booksellers or by contacting:

iUniverse

1663 Liberty Drive

Bloomington, IN 47403

www.iuniverse.com

1-800-Authors (1-800-288-4677)

ISBN: 978-1-4401-5550-5 (sc)

ISBN: 978-1-4401-5551-2 (ebook)

ISBN: 978-1-4401-5552-9 (dj)

Printed in the United States of America

iUniverse rev. date: 7/2/2009

Although from a different time and circumstance, the words of Winston Churchill aptly apply to the pioneers on the Mormon Trail—

"Death and sorrow will be the companions of our journey; hardship will be our garment; constancy and valor our only shield. We must be united, we must be undaunted, we must be inflexible."

CHAPTER 1

James and Amanda Weston stood silently on their porch gazing at the horizon as they pondered the consequences of a major, life-altering decision. It was 1841, in Double Springs, Rutherford County, Tennessee. Thirty-year-old James Weston and his family owned, worked, and lived on a large and prosperous tobacco farm. This well-to-do, educated family enjoyed an enviable lifestyle as successful farmers, respected members of their community, and mainstays of the local church. Despite these idealistic circumstances, the Weston family was on the verge of walking away. Amanda would be a reluctant participant in this venture.

With a sigh, James broke the silence. "God knows we've enjoyed a bountiful life here, Amanda. The choice to leave and start all over is not an easy one." James, a tall, big-boned, powerfully built man, was at one of those self-made crossroads that men sometimes find themselves. His knitted eyebrows reflected his torment. The normally determined set of his strong mouth sagged from fatigue—a tiredness that comes not with physical labor, but rather with deep, prolonged, and serious thinking. James's downcast, worried eyes gradually regained their focus—their resolute, penetrating blue stared intently at his wife's gentle, round face and sad eyes.

"But the Lord is pulling strongly. He calls us to follow in the footsteps of Brother Smith and his church in Nauvoo, and I believe we must not pass up this opportunity to save our immortal souls." He pressed his beloved wife to his chest and wrapped his strong, reassuring arms around her tiny frame.

"I know, I know," Amanda whispered, burying the side of her face into his chest. In her mind's eye, this quiet, gentle woman conjured up the turmoil to her happy, healthy, comfortable, little family that would result from such a decision. Although the children had no choice, ultimately, she knew they would be the ones affected most.

James married Amanda in November 1832; he was twenty-one, she but seventeen. Their first child, a son they named Jeremy, arrived nine months later in July. Clara followed in January 1835 and Christine in August 1838. The children were now respectively, eight, six, and three. They were, indeed, vulnerable to any decision that would uproot their known world, especially for anything as incomprehensible to them as religion. It seemed, to an indifferent Jeremy, that one church was as good as another; he didn't much like sittin' in any of 'em.

This new religion had a strong and growing hold on James. He and his older brother, William, decided to join the Mormon Church, and their wives would follow. Ruth, William's wife, did so enthusiastically. She was an intense individual who never did anything halfway. Religion was a passionate part of her personality and once committed, she threw herself into the conversion wholeheartedly.

Amanda, on the other hand, accepted her husband's decision with disquieted resignation. She had no strong feelings one way or the other about the specifics of worship. The existence of God was not in question. Church was a social, not ideological thing to Amanda. She was not a good candidate for any zealous religious movement.

The message of the Mormon missionaries appealed to many people who were uncertain in their beliefs during a period of political and religious change just before the Civil War. This change, called the Second Great Awakening, saw an enormous expansion of the Baptist and Methodist churches, and the creation of many new sects and denominations, including one by Joseph Smith. In the case of the Westons, two dedicated young missionaries spent many hours with the brothers discussing and explaining the positive aspects of the Church of Christ, better known as the Mormons.

Life for James and William in Double Springs was ideal. Though they owned slaves, the reality of slavery tore at their souls. This was the paradox of living in the South during these times. The brothers also disliked the lackadaisical, mechanical attitudes of the locals toward religion. Besides, the urge to try something new provided fodder for many of the brothers' conversations long before the missionaries came to town. They were ripe to hear of a religion that promised everything the Baptists did and more. The Mormons dreamed of a new country and life—a divine reordering of the affairs of the world—a Kingdom of God on earth. The young men of God pandered to the pioneering yearnings within the brothers and to their hope that God would have direct intervention into their daily lives.

Mormons believed in many of the religious rites and philosophies the brothers already accepted: total immersion baptism for remission of sins, seizures, the gift of tongues, and the promise of the imminent Second Coming. The more novel ideas, though often only half understood, like the precepts of *The Book of Mormon*, contemporary divine revelation, the beginning of a millennial reign, and the return to pure Christianity, appealed to restless people like the Westons. In 1830, a questionable self-styled Prophet named Joseph Smith in Palmyra, New York, founded the Church of Christ. It was a new religion for a constantly changing population and was, in many ways, in tune with mid-nineteenth century America. Some people saw the forceful communal concepts of Mormonism as attributes needed for the vagaries of frontier life. Most people, especially those who knew the Westons, believed these ideas poppycock. The Saints' beliefs and practices often seemed downright dangerous and seditious to those who lived face-to-face with large numbers of them.

William married Ruth, a local girl the same age as Amanda, seven years ago. She was his second wife. He married his first wife one year after arriving in Double Springs, but she died of scarlet fever nine months later. In Ruth, William found an ideal partner. She was a plain looking woman with a sturdy frame and a strong personality; a trait William admired. Deeply religious—almost fanatically so—she had no truck with dishonest, lazy, godless people. Her stern face and serious nature cast a no-nonsense aura that only a village idiot could misread.

William and Ruth committed their family to move to Nauvoo, Illinois. Nauvoo was a new Mormon settlement founded on the banks of the Mississippi river. Here, with their two children, Mary who was six and Edith, now five, they planned to gather with a multitude of others of like mind. Once there, the Prophet, Joseph Smith, would lead them to their salvation. William's decision put greater pressure on James as he usually followed the example of his older brother. Both men were strong and ethical in character, hard working, determined to succeed, and inseparable. They were independent by nature but had always stayed together, seeking each other's counsel, and defending each other, whenever there was trouble.

The Westons could trace their ancestry back to the Jamestown Settlement in Virginia. Starting it all in the New World was a man named Thomas Weston, who was born in 1702. Old Thomas lived to be seventy-three-years old. That was quite an achievement in those days, considering the countless skirmishes with Indians, rampant diseases, and many other disasters that befell those early settlers. He set the pace for a sturdy stock of descendants that all lived long lives, unless cut short prematurely. For example, old Thomas's grandson, Jeremy, died at the age of thirty-six, leading a charge in the Battle of New Orleans. Though short-lived, this war hero managed to leave behind six children to carry on the genes—one being the father of William and James.

William was born in Richmond, Virginia and James in a small town southwest of Richmond called Farmville. Their predecessors, after migrating from Jamestown, became tobacco farmers, and prospered doing so. Unfortunately, tobacco was an enervating crop that bled the soil of all nutrients. Farmers knew little of fertilizers and crop rotation in those days and merely packed up and moved to a new location when the soil gave out. There was, above all, plenty of land.

Ten years ago, William, who at the time was twenty-three and James, a mere twenty, decided to move to Tennessee where the land was rich, fertile, and plentiful. Striking out on their own, they left the family farm in Virginia to Thomas, their elder brother. They were rich in cash, ambition, a willingness to work hard, and a desire to succeed. And succeed they did. Both brothers separately developed businesses over the years that included significant tobacco crops, many slaves to work those crops, and big houses. Well-liked in the community, they had the reputation of being honest, hardworking, religious men with good families. Their crops in Double Springs did not have the problems of soil depletion as in the past. The brothers and their neighbors learned to let some acreage lie fallow for a year or so to regain strength.

Based solely on a perceived spiritual need, the call to move this time transcended family historical rationale. So it was, after many sleepless nights and much soul searching, James and Amanda decided to move to Nauvoo. This meant selling their house, most of their possessions, the Negro slaves, and considerable farmland. In this way, they could join the Prophet Joseph Smith and the main body of Saints. Like William and Ruth, James truly believed this to be the road to salvation. Amanda? Well, she always stood by her husband.

"My land, Amanda, fer the life a me, I cain't figure out why ya'd run off with this here Smith and his bunch, leavin' behind such a wonderful life."

That was Sarah Perkins talking, as she pursed her lips and shook her head gravely from side to side. She had been Amanda's closest friend for the past ten years and always had a genuine concern for her little Amanda's well being. Sarah, who was five years older than the twenty-six-year-old Amanda, looked into her friend's eyes. She knew that Amanda, though barely five-feet-tall and slight-of-build, was, nonetheless, strong-of-character and body. My goodness, she thought, whatever is ta become a this darlin' little child?

The Weston's decision confounded their friends and neighbors in Double Springs. These reactions were nothing new. Throughout history, similar decisions produced comparable results. As the Westons soon found out, joining seemingly radical political or religious groups always caused people, friends and foes alike, to shake their heads in disbelief and detach themselves to avoid contamination.

"I know, Sarah. This wasn't an easy decision for James and me. But our minds, hearts, and souls tell us it's the thing we've got to do," Amanda said. "Now don't you never mind, we'll get along just fine.

God in his infinite wisdom and mercy will guide and protect us." She spoke with conviction and resolution, despite nagging concerns.

"Well, God's gotta be a heck of a lot more generous than smart and merciful ta help ya folks out. Besides, them Mormons always seem ta be a movin'. Don' stay in one place long enough ta plant roots. I hear tell they's lookin' fer some land a Zion clear outta the States. Good grief, girl, there ain't nothin' out there but savages and wilderness."

"I don't know about any land of Zion. All I know is that we're goin' to Illinois to be close to the Prophet Joseph Smith. All will be well, Sarah, you just quit your worryin', ya hear?"

"No, I won't quit worryin'. But God bless an' protect ya, Amanda Weston." Sarah, some eight inches taller and twenty pounds heavier than her friend, leaned forward and gave Amanda a kiss on both checks as tears clouded her eyes. Amanda slowly turned and headed for the two-wheeled shay. There, her faithful old horse, Gus, stood in front of the white picket fence. Climbing into the carriage, she took the reins, snapped them once, and with a wave of a white hanky at her friend standing on the porch, rode away. The shadow of her bonnet hid the tears sliding down her cheeks.

"Damn fool nonsense," Sarah muttered bitterly to herself, dabbing her eyes with a handkerchief. She felt an ache in her heart and a sinking in her stomach as she watched her dear friend's buggy disappear behind a dusty bend in the road.

"Lord, I'm gonna miss that there woman," she sighed.

It took more than a month to dispose of all their property and the other holdings that could not go with them on the journey north. James and William were smart businessmen, but they knew that they were selling out under less than desirable conditions. Local farmers, bankers, friends, and others that were familiar with the situation, knew that the Westons were going to sell, no matter what. Their offerings were cut-rate and often downright criminal. Those caught in the buying frenzy whispered that the Westons were crazy to leave their lucrative operations for such an idiotic idea. Nearly everyone reckoned that the Westons did not deserve anything but rock-bottom prices. The thievery became so widespread it almost bordered on a conspiracy.

"Might just as well get used ta being takin' advantage of," said the local banker. "From what I hear, them Mormons get their asses kicked from one end ta the other all across the country. Yes sir, they might just as well get used ta it," he concluded to his small circle of cronies.

"Way I look at it, we're doin' 'em a favor," chimed in a prosperous farmer from the south of town. "Sort a like breakin' em in early," he chuckled.

"Well, certainly I'm not for takin' advantage of any livin' soul," the town's Baptist minister, arrogantly added to the conversation. "But, maybe this is Gawd's way of warnin', yea even punishin' them, for goin' off an' joinin' that bunch of morons ... I ... I mean, Mormons." He feigned embarrassment at his own tasteless joke. The cluster of men rewarded him with raucous laughter and approving slaps on the back.

Both Weston families felt the sting of disapproval from all corners of the community. It was their first taste of prejudice, and it angered the adults, while confounding the children. One of the foundations that built this country was religious freedom, but as the Westons were finding out, it all depended on what religion one chose. The situation deteriorated quickly, and then got worse. Hostility and greed took turns battering the hapless families. Finally, it was over and one early July morning, the two Weston families—nine persons in all—boarded their large, heavily laden Conestoga wagons and pulled slowly out of town.

Even though the caravan consisted of only two wagons, it was still a remarkable sight. The Weston brothers had spent a substantial sum of money buying and outfitting these wagons, often called prairie schooners. Each large, heavy, boat-shaped wagon bed had an underbody that was fourteen feet long and painted blue. The red painted upper body stretched out to nineteen feet. Easily, the most recognizable feature of these wagons was the enormous white canvass covers. Suspended high on the ends and lower in the middle, the covers stretched over a skeleton of wooden bows that made them look like giant sails. The covers had been soaked in linseed oil to protect the travelers from rain. The front and rear entrances could be drawn shut with ropes, giving the occupants both privacy and protection from the weather.

Axles, attached to four spoke wooden wheels—the front two smaller than those in the rear—supported the giant wagon beds. It was relatively easy to remove and repair the wheels. A toolbox, located on the side of both wagons, held the wrenches, hammers, and other tools needed for almost any situation. Hanging from the rear axle of each wagon was a bucket full of grease to lubricate the wheels. Wide wrought iron tires encased the wheels to reduce wear and breakage.

James and William reckoned they left with less than a third of the cash they deserved. Their concern then was to protect what money they had accumulated, for not as much as deserved or not, it was still a considerable sum—over twenty-five thousand dollars. Since paper money, notes, or scripts were unreliable and difficult to redeem, the brothers had all their money in gold and silver coin. They hid these heavy coins in specially designed, hollowed-out compartments within the wooden flooring of the wagons. The brothers had no delusions about the less desirable members of society who would strip them of all their possessions, given the chance. To ensure that did not happen, they brought with them two Hall breach-loading rifles, four Colt revolvers, and two Bowie knives, all newly purchased. The brothers each wore one holstered Colt and they placed the other two under the seats of both wagons. They also had an old family flintlock smoothbore musket. James and William displayed these weapons openly as they rode out of town, putting potential robbers on notice.

Practically everyone around viewed their departure, lining the streets as if a circus were passing through town. It was a rare sight, as Double Springs seldom saw these large, lumbering covered wagons roll through town. The slowly turning wheels and the shuffling feet of the giant, dapple-gray horses—six to a wagon—generated lazy clouds of dust off the dry, rutted road. Two tethered milk cows brought up the rear.

"Look at them horses, Gram Pa," said a boy standing in the group. "They sure is big."

"Yep, I heard them come all the way from Pennsylvani," answered the old man.

They were big—sixteen-hands-high. They were powerful, too. The giant draft horses came from Lancaster County, Pennsylvania (very near where Amanda had lived in Millersville) and purposely bred for the job of pulling heavy loads. Amanda's uncle helped James select the teams and negotiate the purchase. James had stayed with Amanda's relatives during the buying process. He bought all twelve horses all the same color and rigged them with ornate gear. Trimmed with shinny brass, each heavy harness had a hoop of six tinkling bells, and a stiff brush called a Russian cockade that stood straight up from the horse's forehead. The Westons may not have left town under the best of circumstances, but they definitely left in style.

James and William, armed with their Henries slung over their shoulders and their pistols by their sides, walked alongside their lead horses until they reached the outskirts of town. They then mounted and rode the left-hand wheel horse of their respective wagons. All during the slow but short procession, only one person waved goodbye, Amanda's tearful friend, Sarah Perkins. The rest, including children influenced by the adults, stood dispassionate and dumbstruck as their friends, associates, and classmates quietly left the home they loved.

CHAPTER 2

It would take over a month to reach Nauvoo. The small caravan could travel about twenty miles in one day if all went well, which it seldom did. All kinds of natural and manmade circumstances, some near disastrous, conspired to keep them from their goal.

The Weston wagons avoided Nashville. Being country people, they were uncomfortable in larger towns. For them, it was better to stay in the open country, using whatever roads were available so as not to trespass on obvious private property. Tennessee and Kentucky folk, with their long reliable rifles, short tempers, and distrustful ways, were not to be disturbed.

God tested their resolve. They were four days into their journey, just outside Clarksville, Tennessee, where they had decided to cross the Cumberland River. James, riding his horse with the lead wagon, was lulled into a listless reverie. The now familiar sensory inputs provided by the wagons, horses, and surrounding environment, were but a subconscious blend of background noise and movement as his mind wandered aimlessly. Gradually, unfamiliar subliminal sounds and motions began to eat at the edge of his awareness.

The leaves on the trees and bushes began to rustle impatiently. The animal world was coming alive. Birds flew faster, flitting here and there. Rabbits, squirrels, and other assorted ground-level creatures scurried out of bushes and from behind rocks. Two deer bounded from the underbrush and ran across the road. All these creatures raced in one direction—the northeast. Next, James noticed his horses' steps were livelier, their heads up, nostrils flared, and they snorted repeatedly. The horses' ears all pointed up and forward, their wide eyes darted about nervously. Like most animals, they sensed change long before humans did.

Then, James saw it. In the distant southwest, a flash of lightning and a lagging roll of thunder. His head jerked up and to his left. Before him, advancing quickly, were huge black, billowing clouds. Streaks of lightning and increasingly louder claps of earth-shaking thunder accentuated the churning, ominous mass of gray and black. The rest of the sky gave off an eerie yellowish cast.

James experienced only one tornado in his lifetime. Double Springs was lucky back then as the full force of that funnel struck two miles south of town. Although his farm was in no danger at that time, the sight of that whirling dark twister and the roaring noise left an indelible imprint on his brain. The next day, he and William rode to the site of the tornado's path and were astounded at the destruction left behind.

William came running up to the side of his brother. "You think what I'm thinkin'?" he asked. Serious concern spread across his face.

"Yep." James viewed the tongues of flashing lightning that split the clouds. A definite dark twisting funnel erratically headed their way.

"Quick, ever' body get down and go into that ditch yonder," James turned, pointed, and bellowed. "Lay flat an' cover up your heads."

Amanda and Ruth gathered the children about them, their long dresses flapping uncontrollably in the increasing wind. The ditch James pointed to was a foot or so deep, two-foot-wide depression in the ground running parallel to the road. The women hurriedly placed their small children under each arm and lay face down in the ditch.

"Come on, Jeremy," James yelled at his son. "Do as I say." Jeremy stood stunned with his mouth open, taking in the rapidly forming spectacle in front of him.

"Jeremy!" snapped his father. Jeremy shook his head as if getting rid of a bad thought, and then ran for a spot in the ditch.

James and William anxiously unhitched their horses from the wagons and led them toward a nearby gully. They hoped the twelve-foot wall of the small ravine, leeward of the approaching tornado, might give them protection. Getting the excited horses to the site was difficult. The large animals were on the verge of bolting. The wind ripped off the men's hats, hurling them to God knows where. Pieces of hail began to fall, stinging their heads and shoulders, and making the wide-eyed horses almost uncontrollable. In the ditch, the children screamed as the hail rained down upon them and began to pile up around their bodies.

The brothers reached the gully just before the full force of the winds struck. Leaves, twigs, branches, and debris swirled about their heads and bodies as they tried desperately to keep the horses together. Each struggled with the reins of six horses, while dodging flying fragments and the huge hoofs of their terrorized stallions. For what seemed like an eternity, the noise of the wind and the shrieking horses deafened their ears; dirt and debris blinded their squinting eyes. A large branch struck one of William's horses on the flank, causing him to jerk free and sprint off into the blackness.

As quickly as it accumulated, swirling, surging winds sucked off the hail from the women and children. Tumultuous winds alternately pushed down and then pulled upward on the huddled, frightened families. The force of these motions almost tore the clothes from their bodies. The stronger the winds blew, the tighter the mothers held on to their screaming children. The tornado's roar absorbed the screams as if there had been no sound at all. Jeremy was lucky. Left to fend alone, he found a large tree root bridging the ditch, and he held on to that tenaciously.

Then, the chaos stopped. The black funnel shifted away as quickly as it came, forming a swirling waterspout on the surface of the angry river. Both brothers stood in semi-shock, barely breathing, their hearts thumping wildly. The horses stomped their huge hoofs nervously and swung their heads from side to side, wide-eyed, nostrils flared.

"You all right, James?" asked William, taking his first deep breath since it all began. He saw that James had superficial scratches about his neck and face. Some were bleeding slightly.

"Yeah, yeah," James replied, unaware of his slight injuries but noticing similar abrasions on William. "And you?"

"I'm fine," William said, flashing one of his broad grins.

"Whoa, boy. Shh, shh," both men repeated in variation as they stroked their horses' necks one after the other. Sensing the danger had passed, the agitated animals began to settle down.

"Everyone all right?" William shouted at the family members. The stunned mothers and their brood rose from the shallow ditch like spirits from the grave. The children sobbed uncontrollably and looked about with wide frightened eyes as their mothers inspected them for injuries. Little Christine had both arms wrapped so tightly about Amanda's left leg she could scarcely move. Ruth's youngest daughter, Emma, had a small cut on the back of her head—nothing serious. Jeremy remained seated upright in the hollow looking like some abandoned war orphan. He was disoriented but aware enough of his surroundings to be in awe at the dislodged debris he saw all about him. They were all dazed, dirty, and disheveled, but everyone managed to escape serious harm.

Now, strangely, everything was the quiet. The only audible sounds were the departing tornado's muted roar and the ebbing sobs from the children. The rest of the immediate world was silent. The bright sun and a gentle, warm breeze announced that it was all over. It would take a few seconds more for all living creatures to accept that truth.

William was relieved when he saw his errant horse standing about fifty yards away amid a pile of forest rubble. The horse was bewildered but appeared to be unharmed.

James walked over to his son, still sitting in the ditch. He dragged the boy to his feet. With kind and gentle hands, he examined his face and head, and then his body, to make sure he was not injured. "You all right, son?" he asked with loving care as he brushed off the dust and dirt that encrusted the lad's clothing.

"Yeah, sure, Pa." Jeremy was still feeling a bit confused.

"Why don't you go fetch Uncle William's horse over yonder, so he doesn't wander off?" James thought that giving him something to do might help clear his son's confused state. He patted Jeremy on the back and pointed at the horse.

Jeremy looked at the animal and began walking toward him, picking his way through the littered landscape. "I'll get 'im, Pa," he said.

"Oh, Bill, our wagon," Ruth said as she viewed their overturned Conestoga. The large wagon lay on its side, its blue underbelly exposed and vulnerable. Everyone started to gather around and examine the wagon as if it were some dead beast. William and James inspected the wagon from one end to the other, paying particular attention to the undercarriage and the wheels. They found no exterior damage. The cache of money was intact. Those Pennsylvania craftsmen make one heck of a wagon, thought James.

"Looks worse than it is, dear," William reassured his wife. "Once we get 'er upright, we may have to tidy up a bit inside, that's all. That ol' canvass top hung on, thank God, so everything stayed inside." No tellin' what we'll find when we see inside though, he thought to himself.

Somehow, James and Amanda's wagon remained upright, though skewed about forty-five degrees off the path, some fifty feet from where it was before the storm hit. Jeremy returned with William's horse and left the subdued animal with the rest of the group. The horses bunched together nearby, quietly grazing on the abundant grass and drinking from the many pools of water as if nothing had happened.

Everyone first set about unloading Ruth and William's overturned wagon. They took everything out and placed them on the ground. Ruth found one broken mirror and a number of dishes shattered. Later she would find other damaged items, but for now, considering what happened, she felt quite lucky the loss was so slight.

After everything was out of the wagon, William took two horses and, with long ropes tied to the one side, gently righted the wagon. It flopped into position with a loud clatter, wobbling back and forth before settling down. The motion made the wagon look like some giant dog shaking to rid itself of dust and dirt. The women and children clapped and cheered seeing the wagon upright.

Ruth and Amanda were beginning to feel the effects of the near calamity. Fatigue from the stress was setting in. The women talked briefly and then suggested that they stop for an early lunch, and that the children take a nap. Everyone agreed.

William, increasingly the religious leader of the group, asked that they first thank God for their good fortune. As all knelt in a circle with hands held and heads bowed, William prayed. "Oh God, thank you. Thank you for saving us from that storm from hell. We know that without your heavenly protection, we would surely have perished. This storm was but a test of our resolve. Our deliverance only makes us more determined to reach our goal. We know you love us, Lord. Amen."

"Amen," intoned the group. Seems to me he'd show he loved us more if he didn't let it happen at all, thought the ever-skeptical Jeremy. The boy was young, but he had old thoughts.

The hair-raising morning had whetted their appetites. Dining on cold beef, biscuits, and apples, and drinking many cups of water, the group soon sated their hunger and thirst. The children quickly fell asleep, bundled together on a tarp under a nearby tree. Touching one another seemed to reassure the children that they were safe again.

As the children slept and the horses grazed, the weary adults reloaded the empty wagon. They also inspected the rest of their equipment for damage and put everything back in its place. William and James examined their beautiful horses carefully for any cuts or bruises. They were astonished to find nothing except for a large scratch on the rump of the horse that had broken away. By the time all had finished, it was almost four o'clock and they were very tired. They decided that their hectic day should end here.

That evening, in contrast to a few hours earlier, the sky was clear and the temperature mild. A tender breeze brought the sweet smell of maturing corn from nearby fields. One major benefit was that the usually annoying mosquitoes were no longer around. The tornado had dispersed them to wherever, and nobody cared. It seemed Mother Nature was at peace with herself again. The Westons sat around the campfire excitedly telling and retelling their thoughts, feelings, and experiences during the horrible tornado. Like Mother Nature, they took a respite and before retiring for the night, in solemn prayer, thanked God again for saving their lives. As usual, James and William split the night, two hours on, and two hours off. Someone always had to be on guard.

The brothers were a good team; they thought, acted, and looked alike. William's jaw line was set a little stronger, his eyes more determined, and his hair more unruly, but both men were six feet tall and had strong, powerful bodies, weathered and developed by years of hard work. James respected William, not just because he was older, but also because he had that extra something in his character that made him special; something men sensed that commanded respect—he was a natural-born leader. "Ol' Bill" was always getting James out of trouble when they were growing up, not by fisticuffs, but by mere presence. When William showed up, even larger boys and men seemed to back off. He had won many a wrestling match held in the Rutherford County Fourth of July celebrations. William was a man's man.

A distant rooster crowed raucously as the sun's rays crept over the trees. The Weston families stirred; stretching and yawning to shake off the much-needed rest they had enjoyed. They surveyed the surrounding evidence of yesterday's storm. It took a moment for them to realize where they were and what had happened. The morning was crisp and clear, and they had a long way to go. William, who stood the last guard shift, had previously rounded up the horses, and was hitching them to the wagons. Soon everyone was busy getting ready to continue the journey. James told the excited children that they were going to ride a ferryboat across a river.

Later, as they approached the river crossing, they were dismayed at the number of wagons lined up to make the crossing. One large Conestoga wagon like theirs, two buckboards loaded with supplies, one buggy, and four smaller covered farm wagons waited patiently in an untidy row. The ferry was on the opposite side of the river. James groaned. He reckoned it would be noon before they could cross. Resigned to their circumstance, the brothers pulled their wagons into line. They left their families and sauntered down toward the debarkation point.

As the brothers approached the Conestoga wagon that was to be loaded next, they saw a large, overweight, scruffy man, who was obviously the ferry proprietor, arguing with the wagon owner. The one word that described the ferryboat owner's rumpled clothing and wide-brimmed, floppy hat was, filthy. This man's coarse language and complete disregard for his patrons was exceeded only his obnoxious, unkempt appearance and foul-smelling cigar.

People had to use his service, and he knew it. Oh, there was a cheaper ferry about three-quarters of a mile down river, but in this man's mind, that sorry-assed competitor was just tryin' to horn in. The competitor's ferry was smaller and it didn't connect to a road. Anyone using that boat had to board in the middle of nowhere and disembark in the middle of nowhere. As a result, the man at the better location charged what he wanted and took no truck with those who objected.

James and William came in on the end of what had been a very intense argument between the ferryman and the wagon owner. "Don' give a damn what I charged that last bunch. For you it's seven dollars, fifty cents, an' that's final. You don' like it, don' use it."

Red-faced, with temples pulsating, the wagon owner had been protesting vigorously. He knew the ferry delivered a wagon about the same size to the other side for $2.50. "Bein' charged three times more'n the going rate," he complained under his breath. Judging the demeanor and words of the dreadful man standing before him, the wagon owner realized further protest was useless. He reluctantly paid up.

"I hate them damn Mormons," the ferryboat owner growled as he stomped past James and William, counting his money and heading toward a small wooden shed he called an office. The brothers glanced at each other as they walked up to the still fuming wagon owner.

"Havin' some trouble, brother?" asked William as they came near.

"Might be," replied the wary man. His long beard, hollow cheeks, and sad eyes seemed to reflect his predicament. He was, by appearance and speech, a mountain man.

"What seems to be the problem?" William continued.

"Don' know it's any a yer business," the man said. His drawl definitely established his origin as Tennessee. Then, softening his attitude, he said, "If ya fellers be Mormons, don' tell that savagerous pig. He'll charge three times the goin' rate an' take glee in it."

"I'm sorry for your situation, brother. We'll learn from your experience. And where might you be headed?"

"Nauvoo."

"That's where we're goin'," James said.

"Well, don' tell that blackguard scalawag 'cause then he'll know yer Mormons an' hornswoggle ya like he did me."

"Maybe we'll run into one another at our journey's end. God be with you," William said with a nod of his head and a nonchalant two-finger salute from his hat brim. The man nodded his head in return. No one shook hands.

As predicted, it was noon when James pulled his wagon in line. The ferryboat owner approached their wagon. The scowl on the proprietor's unshaven face had not changed all morning, nor had his manners. He gave the wagon an overall look and then leered up at Amanda sitting next to the children on the wagon seat. Blood rushed to James's temples, but he remained outwardly calm.

"Where might ya folks be gittin' to?"

"Saint Louis and points west," James calmly lied. He felt his face flush. He was not used to lying. His children lowered their eyes, for they had never heard their father tell an untruth. Amanda continued to stare straight ahead with her lips pursed. Inside, she was seething.

"Mighty big rig for travelin' west," said the man, eyeing James suspiciously.

"We like traveling in style. Any law against that?"

"Nope, guess not. Two dollars fifty of any kind of money that ain't continental," said the ferryman, holding out his fat, dirty hand. It was usual to trade in a variety of types of coins in the 1800's. The owner had used a commonplace word for long devalued and worthless paper money issued during the Revolutionary War, called continental money.

"That seems like a lot just to cross this little ol' river."

"Don' give a damn what it seems. This ain't no donkey cart ya got here an' that ain't no little river. Pay up, pull out, or swim. Makes me no never mind."

"All right, don't get your bowels in an uproar," James said, handing the man a Half Eagle. He felt good about taunting the bully just a little.

The man carefully examined the gold piece and then, satisfied, stuffed it in his trousers' pocket. Counterfeit coins were common and this smart businessman was not about to be taken. "Be about twenty minutes afore yer loaded," he grumbled, squinting as he glanced out over the water at the approaching cable and scow ferry. He trudged off toward his dismal shack, black, smelly fumes emanating from his well-chewed, cheap cigar, commonly known as a long nine.

It was well after three o'clock by the time both wagons had safely crossed the river on the rickety ferry. The large wagons were so top heavy James thought they would surely tip over. He did not appreciate how many hundreds of wagons as large as his had made the journey without mishap. After everyone talked about how horrible the ferry-boat owner was, the brothers headed their wagons on a course that would take them into Kentucky, north of Lake Barkley. They still had at least three more hours of the day left to put them closer to their goal. No one mentioned James's lie to the ferryman.

CHAPTER 3

Fragrant tobacco leaves swayed gently in the warm summer breeze. Amanda was on the porch ringing the dinner bell. She had just fixed a hearty dinner of roast chicken, noodles, mashed potatoes, green beans, and spicy applesauce. The aroma made her mouth water as she summoned her family to join her. However, though she clattered the triangle loudly, no one came. Frustrated to the point of tears, she began to notice a faint sound in the background. A familiar voice tugged at her consciousness. She awakened from the dream and became aware of Clara sobbing in a corner of the tent.

"Mommy, Mommy," Clara blubbered.

"I'm here, sweetheart. What's the matter, little one?" Amanda asked as shc snuggled next to her daughter in the pale light of early morn. Clara had always been a serious child, as if carrying the weight of the world on her shoulders.

"Mommy, I miss my home. I miss my friends," she cried, huge tears filling her eyes and running down her fat little cheeks.

"I know, darling. So do I." Amanda cradled her daughter's head and wiped away her tears. "So do I," she repeated.

"Can't we go home, Mommy? I don't like bein' way out here. I feel scared all the time."

"Now there's no need to be frightened, darling. We're all here together. Daddy won't let anything happen to any of us, you know that."

Amanda wondered when the excitement and newness of the journey would wear off. She was not surprised that Clara would complain first. The child had always been sensitive to change. Jeremy probably would never openly grumble—he would just become more sullen and silent. On the other hand, to Christine, the world was just one big adventure. The three-year-old reveled in every experience, adding to her store of knowledge about the world around her.

Amanda was dreadfully homesick herself. She didn't miss the comforts of living in a fine home as much as the stability of daily living. She pined mostly for lost friendships and community standing. These are important to virtually all women and particularly to Amanda. Her entire life had been lived and based on the values concomitant with where she resided and with whom she associated. The sudden separation from those values greatly affected her emotional well-being. It caused her to wonder about the wisdom of what they were doing. Of course, she kept these feelings secret from all those in the wagon train, especially James. After all, she told herself, they were only two weeks out.

The journey had fallen into a routine. At sunrise, all awoke to tend to their grooming needs, cook and eat their breakfast, and strike their tents. At noon, they would stop to rest and tend the horses, eat lunch, and give their weary bodies a respite from the constant jarring of the wagons, chaffing of the saddles, or plodding footsteps. About an hour later they were on the trail again, horses and migrants resigned to another four or so hours before the evening break.

Every rest period the horses required feed and water. This was no small task considering, the number and size of the beasts. Fodder was not a problem as rich, lush grass covered the roadsides and adjacent fields. Water was the challenge—rivers, lakes, streams, and ponds seemed not to care about measured miles. Looking after the horses was a priority; the success of their journey depended on these magnificent animals.

Most of the time, dust from the roads and trails swirled up from the horses' hooves and enveloped everything in, on, and around the wagons. There were days though when heavy rains caused delays. The wagon wheels, supporting their massive loads, would sometimes sink into the mire. Extracting the heavy wagons proved to be a major challenge for the Weston brothers. Even when the wagons weren't stuck, the thick mud slowed and tired the horses. Every day seemed to present some new challenge.

When the small convoy finally stopped for the day—usually an hour or so before dark—they reversed the morning routine. Whenever possible, William or James would approach nearby farmhouses and buy fresh fruit and vegetables. The locals were glad to exchange their goods for cash money and often visited with the Westons. They were rightfully curious about these nomadic people with their large wagons and beautiful horses. Despite being cautious about saying they were Mormons, the Westons never lied if asked. They sometimes met skepticism, but so far, no open hostility.

Visitors or not, the Westons had to do their chores. They put up their tents, cared for the livestock, made their fires, and cooked and ate their dinner. Only then was there time for singing, story telling, and readings from the Bible, often continuing into the late dusk. Sometimes the local visitors joined in, happy to be a part of the camaraderie. When it was all over, it took little coaxing to convince the weary children to retire for the night. James and William took turns guarding their precious cargo throughout the night.

The little band of neophyte Mormons began their fifteenth day on the road, knowing they were about 250 or so miles from their destination. Maps given to them by the missionaries pointed out not only the best routes to take but also the distance between points. The late July days had been hot and muggy, sapping the energy of horses and humans alike. The nights were not much better, with temperatures in the mid-seventies and mosquitoes by the hundreds. Tempers and tantrums flared in direct proportion to every degree rise in temperature. William reminded everyone, after a particularly cantankerous day, "God is testing our strength and resolve. We cannot ... we will not, fail Him." To cranky children, this admonition went in one ear and out the other.

One day, only an hour out of camp, the horses plodded along with heads already sagging from the heat. As they came around a bend in the road, the lead horses pulled to a stop. There, directly in front of them, a large tree trunk lay across the road. The dense forest and many large boulders lining the road made circumvention impossible.

"What's the problem, William?" James shouted from the rear. He couldn't see past the lead wagon.

"There's a tree lyin' right across the road," answered William, as James came frontward to investigate.

"How the devil did that thing get there? We haven't had any storms or high winds in this area."

"That's why," William said, pointing to a freshly cut stump next to the base of the hewn tree. "Somebody's makin' sure we don't pass easily." He looked worriedly from side to side.

"Jus' stay rat where yer at, mister," a large unkempt man said, stepping from behind a dense bush. He pointed a long menacing rifle at the brothers.

"Hold it," said William, the hair standing straight out from the nape of his neck. "We've got women and children on these wagons and we don't want anything to happen to them." The brothers held their hands shoulder high, palms out, as if such a stance would ward off any harm.

"Ya know, I don' much give a damn what ya want. Now, one at a time, real slow like, with yer left hands, drop them pistols from yer holsters ta the ground. Ya first," the man said to William as he gestured at him with his rifle. William's pistol hit the ground by his feet with a dull thud and a puff of dust.

"Now ya," he pointed at James. "An' kick 'em guns way off'n the road." The brothers booted their weapons out of the way.

"What do you want?" William asked, as if he didn't know.

"What do I want?" said the man, scrunching up his pocked marked face in an expression of contemplation. "Well, now, let's see, from the looks a it, yer some a them Mormons that's been comin' through here as a late. Them fancy horses tell me ya ain't exactly travelin' light with cash. Now, it's simple; gimme yer cash money or I won't care nothin''bout makin' them kids a yer's orphans."

"Don't shoot 'em, mister," said a woman's voice from the rear wagon. It was Amanda. "I got the cash box back here," she shouted.

"Amanda, what are you doing?" yelled James, his eyes wide with concern; tension and surprise etched his face. The brothers exchanged worried, quizzical glances. They knew there was no cash box.

"Ya two stay put," the robber said with a scowl and a threatening thrust of his rifle. "Seems ta me the lady's got a lot more sense than ya do. Yer just stupid. Billy, watch 'em while I go fetch the cash. If'n they move, shoot 'em."

That was the first time James and William were aware of a second robber. He had been standing quietly behind them. Both men glanced over their shoulders. William, his hands still held high, slowly turned to face Billy. This man was worse than the first; his eyes were wild and crazed. His head canted to one side and his chin jutted out sporadically with a nervous tic. William sized him up instantly as not mentally sound and, as such, very dangerous. Meanwhile, James watched helplessly as the first man headed toward the rear wagon, leering up at a terrified Ruth as he passed by.

"Now ... now, don' cha move none," slurred the second villain. Bits of saliva seeped from the sides of his mouth. James turned to see the threat from the rear. "I'd love ta blow ya ta kingdom come," snickered the man, his finger dangerously flexing on the trigger of a shotgun. The brothers stood dead still.

"So, my pretty little lady," sneered the robber as he approached the rear wagon, "what cha got fer me?"

"I've got the cash box right here," said Amanda, her voice tight with tension and her mouth bone dry with fear. She pointed to a spot behind the wagon seat.

"Well, don' dilly dally. Git it out," the man scowled, motioning at her with his rifle. The man craned his neck back toward the front wagon. "Billy, ya watchin' 'em two?"

"I got 'em, Jeb," Billy shouted back.

Amanda turned and drew out a wooden box.

William and James still faced the half-crazed Billy standing before them. All three men froze when three rapid shots rang out. James went blank with paralyzing fear. There were screams and crying from the children.

"You bitch, you rotten bitch!" The shots and the man's screams unnerved the horses. They stomped their huge hoofs, jerking their harnesses in opposite directions, snorting and whining.

As soon as he heard the man's screams and saw that the half-wit, Billy, was distracted, William jumped him and wrenched the weapon from his hands. Within seconds, the man was on his back and William had the shotgun pointed at his face.

"One move an' you're a dead man," he threatened, meaning every word of it.

James raced back to his wagon. The robber, covered in blood, lay on the ground writhing in pain. Amanda sat in the wagon seat sobbing uncontrollably, a six-shooter hanging limply in her hand, the barrel still smoking. She had retrieved the pistol from the box under the seat and shot three times blindly at the man in front of her. It was a miracle she hit him at all.

James picked up the wounded man's rifle and climbed in the seat beside his frantic wife. He put his arms around her, whispering softly in her ear. "It's all over, Amanda. It's all over. Everything's going to be all right." The terror of the moment was beyond her experience or imagination. She had never even fired a weapon before.

The crying children emerged from the back of the wagon, numb from fright. They clutched at their mother and father as if the closer they got, the safer they would be. Jeremy kept peeking around the huddled group at the man prostrate on the ground. Curiosity overcame fear. Never before had he seen anyone shot.

"Everything all right?" William breathlessly asked, shoving the robber's feeble-minded accomplice in front of him. Ruth followed close behind, the children tightly hanging onto their mother's skirt.

"Jeb, Jeb," the man blubbered, as he knelt down beside his companion. He stared at the two bloody bullet holes, one in the right shoulder and one in the left arm. The third shot had gone wild. The wounded man lay quietly now, in shock.

"Everything's all right now," James reassured everyone. "Seems like our brave Amanda saved the day."

"Oh my God," exclaimed Amanda, "I can't believe what I've done. I shot another human being! I actually shot another human being!" she cried hysterically. She felt sick to her stomach. Quickly she climbed down from her perch on the wagon and vomited on the side of the road. Her head was reeling and she nearly fainted. James was instantly by her side steadying and consoling her.

"You, sit down there on the ground!" William commanded Billy. Billy meekly sat next to his wounded companion. All the fight left him as his brother lie bleeding beside the wagon wheel. Irrational as he was, he knew he had no other option.

"Ruth, see what you can do to stop the bleeding." William removed a knife from a scabbard strapped to the wounded man's leg. The robber was no longer a threat—his strength was ebbing quickly and his complexion was pale from the loss of blood.

Ruth bent over, examined the man's wounds, and then ran to get some bandages. Amanda was slowly regaining her composure, although she would not look in the direction of the man she had shot. Even though it was only 9:30 in the morning, William and James knew they had to take a break. Everyone needed to calm down. Besides, they had to figure out what to do with the two villains. Ruth had extracted the slugs, stopped the bleeding, and bandaged the wounds. The would-be robber was lying in the grass in a painful daze. His brother sat next to him like a frightened, whipped child.

Amanda was composed now. She kept sneaking glances at the wounded man. She still couldn't believe what happened. It was all like a dream until she looked over and saw the results. No matter how often anyone else told her that she had no choice, she couldn't understand how she managed to pull the trigger—not just once, but three times. She slowly realized that her actions were a direct response to a situation endangering her family's life. She had found out that in a crisis, she was strong enough to meet the challenge. Amanda did not know that about herself before. It would be beyond her comprehension to know she would have to call on that trait more than once in the coming years.

"What the heck are we going to do with these two scalawags?" asked James.

"One thing's for sure, we can't leave 'em here." James and William were busy chopping away the tree trunk lying across the road. Ruth was sitting back on a large rock, rifle in hand, keeping an eye on the two robbers. William continued, "The mean one needs to see a doctor and the nitwit can't make it on his own. We have to take them to Mt. Vernon. I think it's about ten or fifteen miles up the road."

"I agree. I hope the law won't hold us up for any kind of hearing. We're losing a lot of time as it is."

"I think everyone's calm enough to continue, don't you?" William asked as they cleared away the last of the tree trunk. It was about eleven o'clock. "I even heard Amanda giggle a bit a while back. That's some woman you got there, little brother."

"You can say that again," James replied proudly. "I knew she was tough but I guess I never knew just how tough until today. Remind me not to make her angry," he concluded with a snicker.

"You got that right, my man," William said, laughing aloud.

CHAPTER 4

The sheriff in Mt. Vernon was most helpful. "Them's two genuine bad eggs," he said. "They been pullin' that crap fer some time now. Ya folks are the first ta make 'em pay. Just sign these here complaints an' ya can be on yer way. No need ta hang around 'cause they confessed ta what they done ta ya— an' ta a bunch more folks, so, far as I'm concerned, ya can skedaddle, with my thanks."

The Westons drove their wagons hard after leaving Mt. Vernon. They had to make up lost time. Their goals were to reach Highland in three days, Litchfield in two, Springfield in another two and Quincy five days after that. Finally, they expected to reach Nauvoo in only three or four days after stopping near Quincy. Although barely half way through the journey, the Westons, nevertheless, felt rejuvenated after coming as far as they had. Breaking down the trip ahead into specific goals helped make the task less daunting.

By now, the sights, sounds, and smells of being on the road permeated the very fiber of every Weston. They all had their own thoughts and interpretations of the events thus far. James began to enjoy the harshness of what they were doing. It was cathartic. Besides, he knew that every step he took placed him that much closer to Nauvoo and to his salvation. He was beginning to walk in the shoes of a dedicated, religious man, and he liked the feeling.

All the same, as he walked mile after mile, or rode astride a horse, his thoughts often turned to Tennessee. At first, he missed the routine and the feeling of accomplishment that he got from running the farm. After being on the road a while though, he felt the pressures of his back-home business slowly ebb from his mind and body. A big plus was that he did not have to worry about his slaves anymore. Yes, James and his brother had both owned slaves, but deep in their hearts, they opposed the practice. They were kind and generous owners and their charges respected them. The idea that one man could own another was anathema to the brothers. They discussed the possibility of freeing all of their slaves instead of selling them. But that was not a wise thing to do in Rutherford County—the brothers wanted to leave of their own accord, not be run out of town. Both brothers made sure their slaves ended up with men of character, known to them as having similar views on treatment and use of these unfortunate chattel. In any event, James didn't miss the responsibility and accompanying culpability associated with that unseemly practice. Since leaving the farm, he was beginning to feel like *he* was the freed man.

Amanda had a different perspective from that of her husband. She missed having a roof over her head, of course, but she loved the outdoors. Amanda and nature were as one. She observed everything and took great pleasure in her heightened sensory awareness. There was the endless creaking of the wheels, the clopping of the horses' hoofs on the dusty roads, and the constant jarring of the wagon as it traversed rocks and ruts. The smell of the horses' sweat mingled with the leather harnesses, and the odor from their urine and manure, was ever-present. Even the jingle, jangle of the harness bells, annoying at first, became a part of the cacophonous background. The screech of a hawk or eagle high in the sky, or the sight of a deer running through the woods made her feel good. Equally pleasing was the smell of food cooking over the campfire and the sound of the children playing nearby. Amanda lived for the moment. Unlike the other adults, religious fervor was not her motivation.

They were one day out of Highland and the small caravan was idle—resting for the nooner—the noontime break. All were quietly eating their lunch, the horses and cows munching on the surrounding grass, swishing their tails and stomping their hoofs endlessly to rid themselves of bothersome flies. Jeremy heard it first. The plaintive howl was weak, but distinct.

"Listen, Pa! What was that?" Jeremy turned his head in the direction of the sound. "Listen, there it is again." The lamentable wail came from the right of the lead wagon.

"Sounds like some animal to me," answered James. "Whatever it is, it's hurt."

"Sounds like a dog to me. Yes, sir, that's a dog if I ever heard one. Pa, it's right over yonder in the trees. Can I go check it out?"

"Not alone, you can't," commanded Amanda.

"Not sure we should, son. We've gotta be movin' on. Don't have time to be messin' with any side show right now," James said.

"Ah, please, Pa," pleaded Jeremy. "It's not far off and it sounds hurt."

"Go ahead, if you want," William nodded. "We've got another ten or so minutes before we start up again."

"All right, let's check it out," James gave in. He picked up his Henry Rifle. Jeremy was already at the edge of the woods heading in.

"Jeremy, you wait for your father," shouted the always-cautious Amanda. "Ya, hear?"

Jeremy ignored his mother's plea. Everyone knew Jeremy was a true animal lover. Actually, he got along better with animals than he did people. He always had an assortment of birds, rabbits, snakes, mice, and so on that he took care of back home. His mother never knew what to expect next from her somber little boy. All sorts of varmints showed up in his pockets and he had staked out as his, a section of the barn loft to care for all these critters. To his sorrow, he had to leave all that when they headed west.

"Pa, look!" Jeremy pointed out as James came through the tree line. It was, indeed, a dog, and in woeful condition. A trap savagely held its leg. "Ah, Pa, look at that poor thing," sobbed Jeremy.

"Careful now, son," cautioned James. At the sight of the two humans, it was all that the animal could do to muster up a decent snarl; he was so weak from the trap. "Never get too close to an injured animal. They don't know what they're doin' and'll bite ya ever time."

Jeremy fell down on both knees a few feet from the dog. "Shh, boy," Jeremy said soothingly. The dog stopped snarling and began to whimper, looking soulfully into the boy's eyes. That magic Jeremy worked on so many animals seemed to have an instant effect on this creature. Jeremy inched forward slowly and kept up a quiet, comforting tone. "Good boy. It's all right. Good boy. You're goin' to be all right," he whispered repeatedly, getting ever closer to the now quiet dog. Finally, he put the back of his hand to the dog's nose for the animal to smell. Then, sensing acceptance, Jeremy began gently stroking the injured dog's head. "You poor thing."

"Pa, we gotta get him out of this trap," said Jeremy, his voice distraught and his eyes watering in empathy. "Look, his leg is hurt, maybe even broke. We just gotta get him out. He needs water too. I can tell he's very thirsty." It was as if Jeremy were reading the dog's mind and relating his every need.

James laid the rifle on the ground and came ahead cautiously. The dog gave him inquiring looks but didn't seem to mind his presence as long as Jeremy was close by. James surveyed the trap. It was not a big one but staked well so the dog could not escape. He saw that it would not be difficult to free him but worried about the injured animal's reaction to the pain in doing so.

"Don't worry, Pa, he ain't goin' to do anything. I'll hold him while you get it off." That'll be some doin', thought James. The fawn-colored dog with the sad eyes was big—eighty or so pounds—even though they could tell it was still a pup. James couldn't figure out what breed of dog he was, but he had a set of jaws as big as he had ever seen. James was anxious, but he had seen his son work miracles with all kinds of animals and trusted his skill now. Slowly, he moved to spring the trap open. When the trap opened sufficiently, Jeremy tenderly pulled the dog's leg free. The trap slammed shut; Jeremy startled, held the dog even tighter. The animal hardly whimpered throughout the whole process. Once free, the dog began to lick his wound. As Jeremy got up from the ground, the dog jumped to his feet, keeping the injured right rear leg hiked off the ground.

Jeremy rattled off, "See, he's gonna be all right. We gotta fix that leg an' get him some water an' somethin' to eat. Poor fella, he's been there for quite some spell. He just needs some fixin' an' love an' he'll be all right."

Jeremy and his father headed slowly toward the wagons, looking back every now and then to check on their new friend. The injured dog hobbled along behind, wobbly but determined. All of the other children came running forward as they saw the threesome emerge from the woods.

"Careful," warned James. "He's been injured and no tellin' what he'll do. Just keep your distance until Jeremy gets him settled. Amanda, get some bandages so's we can fix him up a bit. Jeremy, can you tell if it's broke?" he said pointing to the dog's injured leg.

Jeremy examined the mangled leg carefully. "Don't think so, Pa. This fella's got one powerful strong leg. But it's goin' to be mighty sore for a while."

"Here, boy," Ruth said, putting a bowl full of water before the dog. His great jowls and tongue flapped noisily as he lapped up the water. He then attacked the scraps of meat and other leftovers Ruth placed in front of him. Back he went for more water when he finished the meal. His tail was wagging—he had all but forgotten about his injured leg. All the children crowded around the big animal, stroking him on the head, fondling his ears and patting his back. The grateful dog licked the children in the face one after the other with his big, sloppy tongue. They giggled and laughed as they tried to fend off the animal's rejuvenated exuberance. He obviously was no stranger to children.

Amanda had been standing by with the bandages. The dog jerked its leg once as she began to bandage the wound. Beyond that, he remained perfectly still, his sad eyes searching Jeremy's face for consolation.

"Good boy, good boy," Jeremy kept repeating until the job was done.

"There, almost like new." Amanda stood beaming down at the boy and the dog. She sensed the immediate bond between the two.

"Can we keep him, Pa?" Jeremy begged. "Can we, huh?"

"Yes, yes, can we keep him?" chimed in the rest of the children.

"Whoa, steady," James warned. "That dog belongs to somebody. We can't just up and haul him off. Wouldn't be right."

"Well, they sure as heck didn't care much about him," Jeremy lashed out. "He's been out there at least two or three days. Why didn't they come an' help him?"

"Yeah, they must not a loved him very much to leave him out there all by his self, hurt an' everything," added little Clara, her hands on her hips in a display of indignation.

"I know, and I feel the same way, but that doesn't mean we can just ride off with him. Besides, I reckon he's still just a pup. Look at the size of those paws. When he grows into 'em, he's going to be a monster and will take a lot of care and feed." Before them stood a fawn-colored bull-mastiff pup with a black muzzle and sad, beseeching eyes. Full-grown, he would weigh 140 pounds.

"Course, he could have been a big help back there with those two that tried to rob us." That was William talking. He had been standing to one side quietly watching the scene unfold. "Dog that's going to be that big could cause a genuine ruckus, that's for sure." Both Amanda and Ruth nodded their heads in agreement.

James knew the argument was over and that his objections had been overruled. "OK," he sighed with resignation, "but if someone shows up and claims him, back he goes. Understood?"

"Understood." Jeremy beamed. He knew he had a new dog. His old dog lived with them for five years and it broke Jeremy's heart when he died last spring. He had been lost without that old friend.

"So, Jeremy, what are you going to call him?" asked William.

Jeremy pondered for a moment and then shyly said, "I think I'll call him Jake. Yeah," he said with more conviction, "I'll call him Jake."

"Sounds like a fine name, son. Jake it is." Everyone nodded their heads in agreement.

All of the adults knew the significance of the name. Jake was Jeremy's best and only true friend back in Rutherford Springs. They had been pals since they were about three years old, going everyplace and doing everything together that their parents allowed; and some they didn't. When the Westons announced that they were converting to Mormonism, Jake's father forbade him to see Jeremy ever again. Of course, neither Jeremy nor Jake understood why and James and Amanda were at a loss to explain it to their son. This sort of prejudice was new to them, as well.

CHAPTER 5

The Westons felt that God was surely beginning to bless their quest as no major problems had befallen them for days. James's wagon did break a front wheel spoke on a large rock just south of Litchfield. The brothers were prepared to deal with such a situation, and they replaced the wheel within two hours. All the Westons were in high spirits as they pulled into a small town called Fall Creek, south of Quincy, Illinois.

Quincy and the surrounding area was a haven for beleaguered Mormons, who called themselves Saints, during their flight from Far West, Missouri during the winter of 1838-39. Previously driven from their homes and Temple in Kirtland, Ohio, the wrath of the non-believers now made Missouri persona non grata to all Mormons. Plainly put, the edict was, leave Missouri, or die. Fortunately, Illinois was a friendly shelter lying immediately across the river from the decidedly very unfriendly Missouri.

Joseph Smith, the Mormon Prophet, and four other followers were in jail in Liberty, Missouri awaiting a trial for treason. During this time, his wife, Emma, and their children crossed the frozen Mississippi in mid-February of 1839. Joseph's family was but three people of about three thousand Mormons who took refuge in the Quincy area by early spring that year.

Much to the delight of his followers, Joseph Smith and his fellow prisoners arrived in Quincy in late April. The authorities in Clay County, Missouri had turned their backs and let the small band of Mormons escape. They wanted to avoid a malicious and unpopular trial. It was from Quincy, during the following summer, that the Smith family journeyed fifty miles north to settle Joseph's new Mormon citadel, Nauvoo.

In Fall Creek, thirteen miles south of Quincy, near the roadside by where the Westons intended to camp for the night, was a small clapboard farmhouse nestled among the trees. Two buckboard wagons stood in front of the house. A swaybacked horse, two oxen, and three cows grazed nearby. People milled about leisurely packing various items into the wagons. Laughter and idle chatter floated from this cheerful group of adults and children toward the Weston camp.

As the Westons prepared to encamp for the night, the children from the house came running toward the campsite. They surrounded the Weston children and peppered them with questions. They were happy to learn that the Westons were Mormons.

"Pa, these here people's Mormons goin' ta Nauvoo, jus' like us," the oldest boy shouted back to the group at the house. The adults stopped what they were doing and moseyed toward the Weston campsite.

"Any problem with us spendin' the night here?" William asked the group as a whole.

"Nope, yer welcome, brother," replied a tall, thin man who came forward and shook William's hand. "I'm Brother Anthony Adams an' this here's my wife, Sister Annie. We own that there house, such as it is," motioning with his thumb over his shoulder. Annie nodded her head and smiled broadly. There were many teeth missing in that smile.

"Name's Thomas, Brother Roy Thomas," said a big, burly man displaying a full, unruly beard stained about the mouth with tobacco juice. He lumbered forward with a noticeable limp and thrust out a huge hand to William and then James. "This here's Sister Amelia, my wife, an' them there's the Jessups, Brother Joshua an' Sister Prudence." The Jessups stood back a little from the group. Joshua nodded and gave the Westons a faint smile. Prudence, a large-boned plain-looking woman with curly blonde hair nodded as well. This woman had all her teeth—too many and too big.

"'Course, all this bunch is our kids," Thomas continued, spreading his right arm in a sweep that covered the ragtag cluster of children, ages one to twelve. "Eight a 'em's mine an' Sister Amelia's, two's the Jessup's, an' them two belong ta the Adams's. Everbody but me an' Sister Amelia's a bit slow in producin' God's children," he concluded. Anthony, Josh, and Annie laughed; Prudence blushed.

William introduced the members of his group. It was the first time William used the designations of Brother and Sister. Best become used to it, he thought. The adults shook hands all around, nodding their heads and smiling broadly. The children intermingled; they were excited to meet new people. The closest boy near Jeremy's age was nine-year-old Mark. Jeremy was reluctant at first to mix with the rest of the children but soon found a kinship in the affable Mark, who was almost twice Jeremy's size.

Most of the folks the Westons met along the trail were just like them, newly converted Mormons on their way to salvation. However, this group was different. These people were true, tested Mormons. They had survived the Mormon War in Far West, Missouri back in '38, barely escaping with their lives from that unhappy place. Leaving with only the clothes on their backs, they made their way to the Illinois border after many harrowing experiences. For the past two years, these religious refugees had been staying in Fall Creek with the Adams family. Anthony was Amelia's cousin and offered them a safe haven. It was here that they healed their wounds and were able to save an adequate amount of money to buy wagons and supplies. Now, these families wanted nothing more than to start for that blessed place of refuge, Nauvoo.

The Westons, being new converts, were both fascinated and aghast as the stories of persecution unfolded from their new friends. The determination and courage of this group of poor farmers impressed the Westons. It was their first encounter with the reality and consequences of the decision they had made. Apart from for the poor treatment they received when they left Rutherford County, which they attributed to ignorance and greed, and the meeting with the despicable man at the ferryboat, which they ascribed to a miserable and immoral personality, they met no outward prejudice along the trail. The robbers didn't count, as they would have gladly taken money from anyone, Mormon or not. It was incomprehensible to the Westons that people lost their homes, and in some instances their lives, just because they were Mormons. Downplayed by the missionaries and, in their zeal to convert, ignored by the Westons, these facts had not been absorbed previously.

"Yep, mighty near lost it all in the Battle a Crooked River," Roy Thomas reminisced around the campfire. He had a deep booming voice and a rather crude, frontier-like personality that somehow came across as likeable. "Apostle Patten an' a bunch more was kilt, but we kicked them Missourians' butts that day anyway. Excuse me, ladies, don' mean no disrespect," Roy apologized. "But jus' six days later, they caught up with us at Haun's Mill," he continued. "That there was a mean bunch. They kilt seventeen a our brothers an' wounded fifteen more. That's when I darned near lost this worthless stick." He slapped his stiff, mangled left leg. "Them Mormon Eaters near blew my lag away."

"Ol' Brother Josh, here," he said, patting Joshua on the shoulder, "well, a mob in Far West slapped him up side the head so many times they darn near kilt him. We all met up in February a '39 when Sister Prudence was a pullin' Brother Josh in a hand wagon at the Mississippi crossin'. He was so beat up he couldn't raise his head an' didn't know where or who he was most the time. Yep, the Lord sure does ask a lotta us Mormons."

"My land," gasped Amanda, "whatever got those folks so riled up? I never heard of such goin's on among God-fearin', Christian people. Why do they dislike Mormons so much?"

It was Roy's wife, Amelia, who answered, lips set in a straight line, determined and uncompromising. Her steel-gray eyes shone with the conviction of a true zealot. This obese, unkempt woman was the epitome of the radical converts who were the backbone of the followers of the Prophet, Joseph Smith.

"Them unholy Gentile pukes had no cause ta do what they done ta us. Hate made 'em burn our farm an' take ever' thin' we had. Same thin' happened ta other Saints all 'round us. After Crooked River, some a us families holed up at Haun's Mill, thinkin' we might be safe. But, a whole army a them Missourians come on us shootin' ever which way. All us women an' children ran hard as we could fer the woods. Ever' one was screamin' an' cryin' while we was hidin'. They shot Brother Roy three times. The worst one was in his knee; near blew it off. Some a the wounded men an' older boys hid out in the blacksmith shop." Amelia's body was trembling as she relived the horror. Tears started to form in her eyes, but then abruptly stopped. The hard, determined look returned as she fought off the tears, regained her stoic composure, and resumed her story.

"But them cowards stuck their guns through the cracks a the shop an' fired ag'in an' ag'in. After they thought they kilt everbody, they rode off laughin' like devils. All us in the woods was scairt as could be, but soon as they left, we come a runnin' ta see what happened ta our men folk. It was horrible—blood was ever' whar. Found Brother Roy here in the bushes all shot up an' passed out. When it was all over, there was seventeen dead an' the rest was all shot up bad. All us women was so scairt we didn't know what ta do. We thought they might come back so we didn't have time ta bury no bodies. We jus' dragged all the dead 'cross the yard an' tossed 'em down a well, thinkin' we'd come back later an' git 'em. Weren't possible though. After that, all us walked ta the river crossin', havin' ta carry most a the wounded. Believe ya me, that's a day none a us will ever fergit." Amelia sat drained after finishing her story.

Amanda sat stunned. The dark cloud of reality hovered over the decision she and James had made. My God, what have we done, she thought. With a sudden wave of guilt, she glanced over toward the children playing in the ring of light from the campfire. Looking at James, she saw that the story also disturbed her husband. His look was one of growing animosity and determination. She knew her husband well and the unjust treatment these people received only steeled his faith. This desire to look adversity in the eye and gear for battle to right all wrongs was a characteristic Amanda did not understand in men, including her husband. She sat silently and trembled, longing for what was lost and dreading what was to come.

Had Amanda talked to Mrs. James Benson, back in Far West, she would have been even more disturbed. Mrs. Benson was a widow with quite a different point of view than that of the Thomas family. She too lost her husband, her farm, and all of her belongings. The most painful loss though, was that of her only child. The feared Sons of Dan, a secret band of Mormon avengers who retaliated in kind for the abuses heaped upon their people, victimized this hapless woman. It was on a warm, quiet August night in 1838 when her world came apart.

Mrs. Benson never quite understood the intensity of the hatred her husband and neighbors felt for the Mormon people. She knew they were pushy and arrogant in their beliefs, and very clannish. Nevertheless, before that terrible night in August, she also saw them as clean living and industrious. She didn't know, nor did she really care much about the god they believed in or their political ideas.

Her husband, on the other hand, had spoken about the Mormons with fire in his eyes. He ranted often about how the Mormons thought God chose them above everyone else and how their political unity was a threat to the local community. "Nobody knows what despicable acts go on inside their houses an' temples," James Benson had said. He believed and repeated every bad rumor he heard, especially since that "fire-breather" Sidney Rigdon, a staunch Mormon advocate, had made a taunting speech in Far West on the Fourth of July. "That Satan dared us ta do somethin' about it if we didn't like it. By God, we're gonna kick their asses out a Missouri. That's what we're gonna do. We don' want them sanctimonious sons-a-bitches tellin' us nothin'. Yes, sir, we're gonna kick them bastards clean outta the country." Mrs. Benson was upset at the time because her husband used such bad language. He only swore when he talked about the Mormons.

Perhaps because of Benson's angry talk, the Danites selected the Benson farm for retaliation. When the raid was over, Mrs. Benson found her husband shot in the head, the house looted and burned, the livestock stolen, and the barn destroyed by fire. She couldn't remember if the raiders knocked her unconscious, or if she fainted. When she came to, the horror of what happened was all around her. It took a while for her to shake off her confusion and realize that the barn she had sent her little daughter to hide in, lie in a pile of smoldering wood and hay.

As in all wars, large and small, long or short, the Mormon War had horrors on both sides. Of course, both sides viewed and interpreted the very same atrocities differently. Done to friends, it was a terrible tragedy, but inflicted on the enemy, it was justifiable cause for celebration. An unbiased individual would view the acts of both sides as despicable and unwarranted. Such was the view of Amanda Weston at this point in her life.

CHAPTER 6

It was a beautiful mid-September afternoon in 1841 when Nauvoo abruptly materialized before them as they rounded the bend and came out of the woods. James, in the lead wagon, pulled up short on the reins. "Whoa," he commanded the horses. The animals willingly came to a halt, accompanied by a discord of snorts, shuffling hoofs, swishing tails, and blinking eyes all mixed with the creaks and groans of the wagon settling to a standstill. Dust from the commotion drifted upward as similar sounds of stopping rippled backward through the small wagon train.

Eyes wide and mouth agape, James gawked at the scene spread before him. Amanda sat silently in equal astonishment. The girls peered from within the wagon over their mother's shoulders.

"Wow, would ya look at that," said Jeremy, standing beside the wagon.

The sounds of many voices talking, laughing, and grunting from labor reached the ears of the travelers. Axes, hammers, and saws assaulted wood each in their own particular way. The resultant din and the smell of fresh-cut lumber blended into a pleasant impression. The place was a scene of controlled chaos. From the number of buildings in various stages of erection, this activity had been under way for some time. The buildings, many hand-hewn log cabins, called blockhouses, a few substantial brick buildings, and countless frames houses, spread around the limestone flat in an orderly fashion. They numbered in the hundreds.

William and his family, and the families from four other horse-drawn wagons that had been following the Westons up the road from Quincy and Fall Creek came forward to see what was causing all the commotion. There was a collective gasp as they took in the scene spread before them. They had heard of the wonders carved out of the wilderness all along the trail, but the actuality far exceeded the dream. Built at the edge of the frontier, such an advanced city was awe-inspiring. There was little doubt in their minds they had made the right choice to come to Nauvoo.

Joseph Smith named this bustling city, located on the banks of the mighty Mississippi River. He called it Nauvoo, claiming it was a transliteration of the Hebrew phrase meaning "beautiful place." It was beautiful only in the eyes of the visionary Smith at first, as much of the acreage was a wilderness thick with marshes, trees, and underbrush. Much of the land required drainage before they erected any buildings during that first miserably hot summer of 1839. Overlooking the flatland to the east was a domed-shaped hill, long used by red men and white as a landmark. It was atop this hill that Joseph decided to build the Temple so that his people could receive the endowments of salvation—a ritual drama re-enacting the scriptural narrative of the creation and the fall, and pre-enacting the safe return of the faithful into God's presence. William and James, with an arm interlocked on the shoulders of the other, beamed as they viewed the hectic activity before them.

"This is it, little brother," William smiled broadly at his sibling. "This, indeed, is what God has called on us to be a part of. I just knew it had to be something big. I just knew it."

"Come on, let's get to it," exclaimed an excited James. All the travelers raced back to their wagons and the small convoy began to move toward the bustling throng in front of them. As they approached the first group of people, joyous cheers, and much hat and hankie waving greeted them.

"Welcome friends," shouted one person. "Welcome ta the city a the Lord," shouted another.

"Thank you, thank you," voiced James. "Where do new people go for information?"

"Yonder," replied a man on top of the roof of one structure under construction. "Thar, on Water Street. Jus' foller that there road ta the left past the stables ta Brother Smith's homestead," he said pointing westward. "Folks'll tell ya whar ta go."

"Much obliged," said James.

The wagons moved slowly down the road and turned left on Water Street. The travelers were amazed to see streets laid out in orderly fashion and flourishing fenced-in gardens everywhere. They passed a stable on the left and continued across Main Street. Then, again on the left, the train came to a substantial log cabin. Behind the fence and standing outside the cabin door was a group of men in animated discussion. William dismounted his horse and walked toward a man standing near the hitching post. "Where do we find out about land and housing, friend?"

"Right there," the man pointed toward the group of men. "Jus' go right on over an' Brother Smith'll take care a ya," the fellow said pleasantly. "I think it be best if ya go in as families and not all at once," he continued, as he strolled away and down the street.

"Did he say Brother Smith?" James asked in astonishment. "Surely it is not *the* Joseph Smith himself."

"Don't know," William said, "let's go over and find out." He shouted back at the others in the wagon train to wait until they found out what to do. No one questioned William's authority.

With hats in hands, first William and then James entered the gateway. William approached a man standing on the periphery of the group of twenty or so men who milled about, shuffling papers, pointing, talking, laughing, and arguing. "Where might I find Brother Joseph Smith?" he asked.

"Over there, friend," came a smiling response. He pointed to one man who was the center of the commotion and obviously relished being the eye of the storm raging all about him. There was little doubt he was in control. Slowly, his head emerged from the gaggle of bodies and he looked directly at William and James. He broke away from the group and headed toward the brothers, walking with a slight limp, the result of a serious leg infection operation when he was eight years old.

The impressive man was six feet tall and of stocky build, weighing about 220 pounds. He had a large head that supported a shock of light brown hair, a prominent nose, and an engaging, open smile. Dressed in a black coat, blue trousers, black boots, white shirt, and a full, white cravat, the man strode confidently toward William and James. William averted the approaching man's eyes long enough to notice the large gold ring dominating his left ring finger.

"Welcome, friends. You have the look of the road on you. Have you just arrived?"

"We have," William replied. For the first time in his life, he felt intimidated. The gaze of the approaching man mesmerized him.

"I'm Joseph Smith," he said proudly, proffering his hand first to William and then to James. His handshake was firm and confident. Piercing light blue eyes surveyed the two men before him and, glancing over their shoulders, appraised the beautiful rigs and horses parked outside on the road. No poor dirt farmers, these, he thought.

"I'm William Weston. This here's my brother, James. We've come all the way from Tennessee."

"God bless you, my brothers, and welcome."

"We're here to start a new life in your holy Church and to save our souls. We trust you'll show us the way." William mustered as much respect as he could. "There's four more wagons beside ours waitin' as well," he added. "All of a like mind, I reckon."

Smith beamed. "Well, you've come to the right place. You and your families must be tired. Pull your wagons around to the field just west of the house over there," he pointed, "and camp there until you're settled. Soon as you can, come back here and we'll see about getting you all something more permanent."

"Thank you, Brother Smith. You're more than kind. Excuse us and we'll tend to our families." William and James nervously fingered the brims of their hats and backed away. Smith smiled, nodded, and then returned to the boisterous group in the rear.

The brothers were ecstatic. They practically stumbled over one another getting back to their families and the other fellow travelers assembled by their wagons.

"We talked to the man himself," James blurted out.

"Joseph Smith?" a man asked, incredulously.

"Yep, Joseph Smith," William confirmed, his tone conveyed a feeling of being an insider that had experienced something the rest had not. "Brother Smith asked us to pull our wagons in that field yonder and make camp." His extended arm and index finger pointed in the direction of the nearby location. "Once you're settled, the men should come up here and talk to Brother Smith about more permanent arrangement for your families." No one had appointed him the leader, but William naturally fell into that role. The families hurriedly returned to their wagons and followed the Westons single file into the adjacent campsite.

By the time the Westons arrived in the middle of September of 1841, Nauvoo was a city of considerable size and sophistication for a wilderness community, and growing daily. Although estimates varied, there were around 3000 residents within the city limits and many hundreds more in the surrounding area. Estimates also varied on the number of houses that existed in the city at that time, but 800 or 900 were reasonable numbers. Some of these homes were nothing more than log cabins, but a growing number were wood frame and red brick (the preferred material if, one could afford it). The year 1841 saw a great influx of new converts, many immigrants from England. At the height of the inflow, families usually lived in tents for a time, until they found better housing.

The streets were wide and straight, and the lots, for those with sufficient cash or credit, large enough to hold a good-sized house, a small garden, a pair of milk cows, a horse or two, and a stable. Considering that just a few short years ago the land occupied by the city was an unlivable swamp covered by trees and underbrush, the transition was astonishing. Non-Mormons living in the area were shocked, bewildered, and jealous that vast change of such quality could happen so quickly. This was a common reaction to any place created by the Mormons.

William and James pooled their buying power to purchase two large city lots at the intersection of Ripley and Granger Streets, one block west of Main Street. Together they also purchased an established two-hundred-acre farm two miles south and east of Nauvoo. A split rail fence, also known as a zigzag or worm fence, surrounded most of the farm property, excluding a large wooded area. The farm had plowed fields suitable for growing corn and wheat. It had a sizeable wood frame house, pigpens, pastureland for livestock, a vegetable garden, and an orchard.

Since they no longer had use for the large Conestoga wagons and most of the beautiful horses, they sold them. They kept two of the horses to work the farm. To add to the menagerie brought from Tennessee, they also purchased the horses, cows, pigs, sheep, and other farm animals already on the farm.

The brothers bought the farm from a man whose wife had died and who had decided to move back to upstate New York where he was from originally. The man had witnessed the sudden encroachment of the Mormon's all around him. He personally had nothing against these hardworking, industrious people; however, he foresaw the many problems that lie on the horizon from his friends and neighbors who had difficulty accepting the influx. The opportunity and the price were right, so he packed up his few items and headed east. Paramount in the decision to sell the farm to the Westons was that they could pay in gold and silver coin.

The Weston brothers bought a going operation because, as they looked about for the right opportunity, it didn't take them long to figure out that starting a farm from scratch would be time-consuming, backbreaking work. They were used to being "gentlemen farmers" and though they worked hard physically everyday back in Tennessee, their slaves did the most of the difficult manual labor. Besides, they had the money to start at a much higher level than many of the poor souls that arrived with the clothes on their backs and little more.

Numerous converts who came to Nauvoo were people of means and, like the Westons, invested heavily in their newfound home. The effects of the tithing and other donations extracted by the Church were not lost on these people. Logic dictated that it was better to sink most of your money into a revenue-producing enterprise and pay such donations from the monies earned rather than from the principle you owned. Of course, everyone also had to donate time and talent in public works projects, especially the building of the Temple. They also were expected to help their neighbor whenever and however possible. This combined effort helped ensure that those who arrived with nothing could soon prosper as well. There was plenty of work for all in this communal environment. It was through this method that the Mormon settlements grew so fast and did so well. This highly organized combined effort had a synergistic effect that produced wondrous results.

"Are you sure that Ruth will go along with this arrangement, William?" James asked. The brothers decided that James and his family would live in the farmhouse during the construction of their Nauvoo homes. William and Ruth were to move their family into a tenement house.

"No problem. It won't be ideal conditions for either family but Ruth so loves being in the city with all that's going on with the Church activities that she prefers it. We've already talked about it. Besides, you don't think I want to be out there where all that work has to be done, do you?" he taunted his brother. Actually, since William had to work the farm everyday as well, coming back and forth between the city and the farm was more trouble than staying there all the time. A key factor for having one of the brothers live in town was to keep an eye on the construction of their new homes. William was ideal for that task.

Therefore, James, Amanda, the three children, and Jake moved into the frame house on the newly purchased farm. Amanda was delighted. Unlike Ruth, she needed a little breathing room before living among the enthusiastic crowd of fervent converts. Being somewhat isolated from the hubbub of the city definitely appealed to her. It would give her time to get her family back into a more normal, stable routine. The house needed a massive amount of work to meet their living standards. During this renovation, the many chores associated with running the farm went on unabated. It wasn't until she made a list that she realized how much of the mundane work the slaves did back in Tennessee. This place was much smaller though, so she didn't see a problem getting everything done. The work was actually cathartic after the routine of the road. For the first time since they left Double Springs, Amanda felt a calm come over her soul. Perhaps, she thought, everything will be all right after all. She had no idea that most of her neighbors around the farm were grumbling among themselves about the invasion of yet another bunch of Mormons.

Jeremy began attending a school founded by Joseph Smith located on the southern edge of the town. Every school day, starting after the harvest in the middle of November, he rose before dawn, completed all his chores, and climbed on a pony for the forty-five minute ride into Nauvoo. Even though Clara was old enough to attend, Amanda felt the daily trip was too demanding. There would be plenty of time for Clara to attend after they moved into town.

From the beginning, it was a fruitless battle with Jake, who persisted in following Jeremy to school.

"Jake, go home!" Jeremy would shout, repeatedly jabbing his finger in the direction of the farm. Jake would lower his head, stop, and sit, his sad eyes beseeching his master for understanding. As soon as Jeremy turned in the saddle, Jake would follow at a discrete distance. If Jeremy turned to look back, Jake would stop, sit, and timidly wag his tail in the dirt. It didn't take long for Jeremy to realize he was fighting a losing battle and soon, the big dog was trotting along the side of the boy and his horse or charging ahead happily barking at anything that moved. The truth was, Jeremy didn't care if Jake came along. He liked his dog's company. Amanda had expressed her displeasure more than once and Jeremy felt that at the least, he had to put up a front to assuage his mother. After a while, even Amanda gave up. As usual, with his master's collusion, Jake pretty much got what he wanted.

There was a bit of a concern at school. When the weather was comfortable, Jake would lie out under a big tree, loll about, and fall asleep, belly up, legs akimbo—dreaming about whatever dogs conjure when they are content. When the weather was bad, Jake would crawl in through the doorway, slinking into a corner hoping the teacher would not see him. That technique didn't go far as the schoolroom was too small and the dog too big. Repeatedly, under the glare of the teacher, Jeremy ordered Jake out of the room. A chorus of whining objections from the children accompanied each ejection. In the course of time, Jake got his way again and soon became a permanent fixture at school.

After school, Jeremy would mount his horse with Jake happily trotting alongside, and return to the farm, often after it was dark. The school day lasted seven to eight hours, but Jeremy didn't mind—only the harshest of weather or illness kept him from going. Jeremy performed this routine until mid-April when the weather improved and the farming began in earnest again.

His teacher was James Monroe, who had somehow found the balance between the harsh discipline so common to schools in those days and the kindness that fostered learning. Brother Monroe was typical of most pioneer teachers: underpaid, overworked, and subjected to an abysmal teaching environment. Sitting behind a small wooden desk and armed with a blackboard and inadequate textbooks and supplies, he would try to maintain order with a commanding voice, a noisy handheld bell, and the ultimate threat—expulsion. Often he had as many as forty-five to fifty students crammed into the one-room schoolhouse.

The children, ages six to sixteen, sat on wooden benches and worked with their copybooks on separate writing tables. The girls sat on one side of the room and the boys on the other. That line blurred on very cold days as the students tended to meld together in order to sit as near as possible to the centrally located stove. Because the school days were long and the curriculum of memorizing and reciting long lists of facts so boring, a typical day could seem like an eternity to student and teacher alike.

Jeremy, the quiet, somber child, did not make friends readily. His size, excellent physical condition, and good looks kept him from being a candidate for hazing by those children who had territorial rights because of longevity. Joseph Smith III, the Prophet's son, sought out Jeremy after the first day. Generally well liked, Joseph treated everyone with respect and readily accepted the mantle of leader due to his father's position within the community.

"Hi, I'm Joe Smith," he said as he offered his hand to Jeremy.

"Name's Jeremy, Jeremy Weston," replied Jeremy. Joseph was almost a year older than Jeremy, but he was not as tall, nor did he possess his father's athletic figure. He was, in fact, rather chubby with spindly arms and legs. Still, he had a presence that commanded respect.

"So, you going to be coming to school everyday, or just now an' then?"

"Far as I know, ever day 'til spring," was the reply. Jeremy took the measure of Joseph and intuitively liked what he saw. "My folks are strict about schoolin'," he added.

"Yeah, mine too. Where do you live anyway?" pressed Joseph.

"A couple miles south."

"That's too bad. Makes getting here kind of hard, doesn't it?"

"It's not so bad. I've only done it for two days, so I guess I really don't know."

"Where you from?" Joseph continued his line of questioning. It was a very logical question—everyone in Nauvoo was from somewhere else.

"Tennessee. What about you?"

The group of children standing around and listening to the dialog chucked and laughed at Jeremy's question. They all knew the story of Smith's expulsion from everywhere the family went.

"Well, it's hard to say. I'm from Missouri the last time I checked. My family's been run out of so many places; I'm not sure where I'm from. Guess I'm from Nauvoo." Joseph's rundown didn't seem to bother him much so Jeremy just accepted it at face value.

"That your dog? Sure is a big one." Joseph pointed at Jake sitting just outside the doorway looking in.

"Yep," Jeremy said proudly. "Name's Jake an' he's a real good friend."

"Ahem,"—Brother Monroe, cleared his throat to get everyone's attention. "Everybody take their seats, please." He jangled the bell a few times just to add emphasis.

"See you later, Jeremy," Joseph patted Jeremy on the back and headed for a seat.

"Yeah, yeah," replied Jeremy. He really liked Joseph. Later, when he told his folks about his new friend, they were delighted.

During the winter of 1841, work at Nauvoo progressed steadily—homes and businesses were erected and the Temple continued to advance. Like beavers building a dam, the Mormons pushed forward, no matter the obstacles in their path. Joseph Smith consolidated his hold on the Church and was involved in every aspect of city's religious, social, political, and commercial progress. To Joseph, the Church and the city were the same, and he made sure that he had sway over all. For the most part, his progressive ideas and dominant leadership greatly benefited the city. However, there were those who began to grumble that he profited financially more than he should.

The first winter in Nauvoo was an experience like no other for James and his family. True, an occasional snowstorm would hit Double Springs, maybe even an ice storm to make things interesting, but such conditions were few and nothing like that experienced in Nauvoo. The ice and snow didn't bother them—it was the cold. Bitter winds roaring down from Canada chilled them to the bone. Fortunately, the tightly built farmhouse managed to keep whistling winds and raging storms at bay. The family took great comfort in the security afforded by their warm and cozy home.

Despite all precautions that first winter, it was impossible for James's family to avoid the common cold, called catarrh by most folks. It seemed that someone had a cold at one time or another throughout the long winter. Fortunately, because they lived in relative isolation from Nauvoo, exposure was less and they contracted fewer of the ailments that plagued most of the city dwellers. For example, the winter fever, the flu, ran rampant through William's family, but never touched James, Amanda, or the children.

Fortunately, the Weston children were all in excellent health when they arrived in Nauvoo and, therefore, stood a better chance to combat diseases and survive those they did catch. Many destitute families, especially from England, were in poor health upon arrival and contracted almost everything in the new environment. The child mortality rate in Nauvoo in those early years was abysmal—about sixty-four percent. The Westons had learned long ago to rely on good old Tennessee herbal and common sense solutions to cure their ailments. Doctors, with their bloodletting, ingestion of poisons like calomel, picra, and paragoric, and other practices of quackery, caused more deaths than cures.

The only consistent complaint James's family had during this time was Jake's smell. He loved the outdoors. Whenever released from the confines of the house, he would run helter-skelter, barking wildly, and plowing through snowdrifts and mud puddles while chasing rabbits and other creatures (including Amanda's chickens on occasion). Of course, he managed to become totally soaked and filthy in the process. When he came indoors—as Jeremy insisted he must—he would plop down by the fireplace and steamy, odoriferous fumes would roll off his heavy coat of fur. It was not pleasant and the girls complained bitterly. They would just as soon have Jake stay in the barn with the rest of the smelly animals.

There were plenty of things to keep them busy during the long winter months. Besides the regular household chores, there was the livestock to water and feed, repairs to harnesses and other equipment, and, weather permitting, trips to town—to buy staples, to work on the house, to assist in volunteer work on the Temple and other communal structures, etc. In addition, of course, Jeremy had to trudge through all kinds of weather every weekday to attend school. During particularly harsh weather days, the family did find time to sit beside the warm fireplace and participate in communal reading and games.

Because the masonry had been mostly finished before the cold weather hit, work on the brothers' homes in Nauvoo progressed well throughout the winter. They were able to move their families into almost identical two-story brick structures by mid-March. The lots had cost only $500.00 apiece, so the brothers could afford to spend more on construction. Both buildings contained eight rooms—a large living room, a library (doubling as a sitting room), a dining room, and a kitchen were located downstairs; four bedrooms upstairs. While the homes had large fireplaces in the living room, they used cast iron stoves as supplemental heat upstairs and down. Both homes had basements, which helped keep the houses warmer.

Outside, the land sloped slightly to the rear, where each house had a privy. Also in the rear, the families shared a stable and buggy shed. They likewise shared a well for water located in front of James's house. There was still adequate room on both lots to have a good-sized vegetable garden in the back, a small flower garden in the front, and a number of fruit trees scattered throughout. A white picket fence surrounded the properties. The new homes for the Westons were inferior in size and quality than what they left in Double Springs; nevertheless, they were better than the majority of houses built in Nauvoo at that time.

Furniture and household items were sparse, but they were available to those with sufficient cash to purchase them. The Westons were fortunate enough to be in that position and soon the few items they brought from Tennessee were supplemented by chairs, tables, beds, pots, pans, buckets, dishes—mostly locally made—and the many other things that make a house a home.

One item that Amanda was proud of was a cast iron stove that had come all the way from the manufacturer in Philadelphia. This stove put her ahead of most of her neighbors, many of whom still cooked over fireplaces. Gradually, more and more of these stoves became available to the homemakers of Nauvoo. Nevertheless, the task of being a homemaker was daunting, indeed, with all of the many never-ending chores, like cooking, cleaning, gardening, etc. There never seemed to be enough time, especially completing the time-consuming and demanding work of making soap and clothes.

William and James still had to go back and forth to work on their farm. However, in due course, they were fortunate; they found a full-time tenant farmer to run the place. An immigrant Welshman, named Jeremiah Johnson, and his wife, Mary, were delighted to live in the farmhouse and manage the daily operations. Recently converted to the Church, this couple, with their two strapping teenage sons, Tom and Jeff, were honest, hardworking, religious individuals who knew how to run a farm, and were efficient and effective in doing so. For their labors, the Johnson's received free room and board, food from the farm, and a share in the profit from the crops. All families involved in the arrangement felt blessed.

The bright sun glistened off the late snow that fell shortly after Amanda had moved into her new home. Like her neighbors across the street, Fanny and John Martin, Amanda was clearing off the latest accumulation of snow on her front walkway. Pausing for a moment to give her back a rest, she shaded her eyes from the reflecting sun and peered down the street toward an oncoming commotion. She heard people murmuring, babies crying, horses snorting, and wagon wheels crunching through the hard rutted road. The assemblage came her way and would soon pass in front of her house.

As the group trudged nearer, Amanda saw desperation and sadness in the faces of the men, women, and children walking beside and riding on the slow-moving wagons. There were so many and they seemed so depressed.

"Where you suppose all these poor people are coming from?" Amanda called across to the Martins as she scanned the approaching column of shabbily dressed families with so few possessions in their wagons.

"They're from Iowa, Sister," replied Fanny. Both Fanny and John crossed over to stand beside Amanda.

"What in the world happened to them?"

"That's a long story, Sister Amanda," explained John. The Martins had lived in Nauvoo two years longer than Amanda and were her source for what was going on in town. "It all has ta do with that scalawag Isaac Galland. You ain't been here long enough ta know, but he's the cause a all their problems."

"And who, pray tell, is Isaac Galland?"

"Well, at one time, he was Brother Smith's chief land agent. Don't know all the details, just rumors. Seems he sold a bunch a land ta about 250 families over in Iowa. Trouble was, it was Indian land, an' the deeds was forged. Half-breed lands they called 'em. Anyhow, these here people just lately found out an' they been evicted. Had ta pack up an' come here. Broke, most a 'em."

"My word, what are they going to do?"

"Oh, I suppose Brother Smith will find a place for 'em somehow—with all our help. Ya gotta wonder sometimes, though. Brother Smith let ol' Galland back in town even after he cheated the Church. Heard tell that Galland stole a bunch of money that was supposed ta go fer land-tradin' deal back East. Again, I don't know the details but he sure must be a smooth talkin' son-of-a-gun. He's walkin' around town like nothin' ever happened. Don't seem ta care what people think about him—an' that ain't much."

"You don't say," Amanda mused. Seems like Brother Smith and his cohorts somehow always manage to make money off this whole settlement thing; and not always to the betterment of the Saints, she thought. Why is it, in a community where everyone is supposed to be equal in the eyes of the Lord, some are more equal than others are? Nauvoo doesn't seem any better than the rest of the world in that regard.

The destitute families continued to file past, bundled against the cold as best they could. They headed toward Brother Smith's place. Amanda pursed her lips and shook her head as she returned to her doorway. The complexities and harsh realities and disparities associated with creating such a place as Nauvoo were lost on Amanda's simple world of equality and justice.

Chapter 7

In 1840, Joseph Smith received a charter from the Illinois legislature granting implicit autonomy to Nauvoo and the right to form a militia. The militia, called the Nauvoo Legion, grew quickly. In his mind, Joseph was not going to allow the local non-Mormon population to inflict on the Saints the humiliating and devastating conditions they endured in Ohio and Missouri. Eventually, this well-equipped militia became a formidable force that served its purpose well. They proudly performed their drills at virtually every public occasion. To the chagrin of many non-Mormons, the Illinois legislature even appointed Smith a lieutenant general in the militia and Commander of the Nauvoo Legion, a position he relished.

Mirroring the actions of their fathers, the boys in Nauvoo, some 500 strong, formed their own military unit. Joseph Smith III was a charter member of this organization by the time Jeremy arrived. Soon Jeremy was beseeching Amanda and James for permission to join this elite organization. Young Joseph himself had asked Jeremy to join in the fun. Amanda wasn't so sure.

"But, Ma, almost every boy in town belongs. Pa and Uncle William belong to the Legion, why can't I join up too?" That William and James had no choice was lost on the boy. Every able-bodied man between the ages of eighteen and forty-five were required to join the militia and heavy fines imposed for failure to appear at a parade. By vote, Church members showing leadership qualities became officers and the Weston brothers had both been so selected—William a captain and James a lieutenant. Thus, Joseph Smith assembled a fighting force of 2000 men by 1842.

"I thought this was supposed to be a religious experience," Amanda said sarcastically—more to James than to Jeremy.

"Amanda, the Bible is filled with stories of how the true believers were constantly forced to defeat an enemy in order to protect their beliefs and way of life. And *The Book of Mormon* says repeatedly how we have to be the defenders of our faith," James rebutted, with a slight show of impatience. "Brother Joseph is making sure we are in a position to do just that. Teaching our sons this principle from an early age only makes sense. Why do you have to challenge everything?"

"Joe Smith belongs and you know his mom's not too keen on anything military," Jeremy begged. "Besides, I like the motto: 'Our fathers we respect; our mothers we'll protect.' " Jeremy wasn't stupid. He knew that Amanda would fall for his motto ploy. How could she not?

"All right," Amanda sighed. "I guess there's no harm." She knew further resistance was fruitless, but it seemed to Amanda that the Legion was just a little too aggressive to her liking. She heard that the non-Mormons in the area were alarmed at the size, attitude, and armament of the Legion. It did seem out of proportion to the threat. On second thought, considering the many terrible things that had happened to the Saints, maybe such a force of defenders was understandable. It was just that Jeremy was so young for such things—*too* young from a mother's point of view.

Thus, Jeremy enthusiastically joined the boys' troop, to the delight of his friend Joseph. Armed with wooden swords and a banner with their motto proudly displayed, the boys were involved in many military festivities. Brother Smith liked what the boys were doing and enthusiastically helped them organize their activities.

Just who came up with the idea is lost in history, but once germinated, it took on a life of its own, and creative and mischievous ringleaders of the troop soon finalized a plan. The boys watched their fathers, uncles, cousins, and others old enough to belong to the Nauvoo Legion, parade many times to the cheers that stirred the heart and were jealous of the approbation received by the soldiers. The boys often marched behind the Legion, but the respect and adoration for their ragtag bunch was missing. They usually solicited "oohs and aahs" from approving mothers and titters and snickers from sisters and other children. Hence, they decided to do something that would command respect. On this particular day, the horse troops and the Nauvoo Legion Band were practicing for the upcoming annual Saturday parade in May.

The plan was simple: attack the troop of parading legionaries and see if the boys could disrupt their precision marching and superior attitude. They had witnessed previous sham battles between the infantry and the horse troops on the parade grounds located east of the Smith homestead. Perhaps that's what gave the boys the idea. Emboldened, the boys—some two hundred strong—assembled out of sight behind a bank of trees and a grassy knoll. The weapons of choice were wooden swords, sticks, and tree branches, along with an assortment of pots, pans, bells, and other noisemakers.

Down the parade grounds, came the twenty-eight-man Nauvoo Legion Band playing a loud and lively march. The legionnaires, astride their strutting horses, sat stiffly at attention. The uniforms of the men in ranks were somewhat mundane (whatever they felt like wearing) but the officers displayed colorful sashes, plumed hats, brass buttons, and shiny swords hanging smartly at their sides. Many of the men wore pistols, as well. Lieutenant General Joseph Smith sat proudly atop his large horse at the head of the body of troops. Smith loved this militaristic display.

The usual crowd of enthusiastic onlookers lined the parade grounds, clapping and cheering as the parade passed by. The Saints had seen this troop parade many times before, of course. Nevertheless, they loved their Legion and never tired of the feeling of pride and the sense of security their "Army of the Lord" brought them. The sun shone brightly upon this great display of military might. Surely, God was pleased with what he saw.

Unexpectedly, from behind their hidden assembly point, the boy's legion sprang forth in a burst of energy and raced across the field toward the mounted militia. Waving wooden swords, shaking tree branches, banging on metal objects, and blowing horns and whistles, the boys created an alarming hullabaloo that took both the Legion and the crowd by surprise. Jake was ecstatic as he ran from one end of the charging boys to the other barking wildly. About forty other dogs of every description followed his lead.

Initially, startled like the rest, General Smith soon recovered and wheeled his horse around and took charge. He ordered Company A of the militia to charge and disperse the boys. Although the troopers were willing, their horses went but a short distance and began to balk in disarray at the loud and noisy approaching enemy. Amused but disgruntled, Smith then ordered Company B to thwart the attack. The result was the same; disorder among the frightened horses. The boys' rout was a clear success.

It was then that the leader took control. Smith charged and dispersed the boys. What was the secret for his success where all others failed? Brother Smith's horse, Charley, was nearly deaf and was not the least bit intimidated by the boisterous brouhaha. Everyone cheered as their leader chased one group boys and then another off the field. Put down in this way, the "rebellion" was the subject of discussion and laughter for years to come. Deep down, Smith was proud of the boys. They showed initiative and guts, traits needed in the tough times ahead. Victorious in defeat, the boys knew they had caused a moment of chaos within the celebrated Legion. All the participants had bragging rights the rest of their lives.

Despite the serious nature of the Nauvoo Legion, that is, to defend the Saints from aggressive action from without, the blatant militarism displayed bothered many Mormons within the community, especially the immigrants from Canada and England. It most assuredly disturbed the Gentiles. Emma Smith was one of those who disapproved of the perceptible war-like attitude of the Legion. As one subjected to some of the worst kind of prejudice and hardship from non-Mormons, she all the same felt the Nauvoo Legion went too far. Shortly after the mock battle, she convinced young Joseph to leave the organization; reluctantly, he obeyed. His father and Uncle William remained staunch supporters and members of the Legion, but Jeremy's interest waned with time. There was never another "attack" by the Legion's boys.

In March of 1842, Joseph Smith installed a Masonic Lodge in Nauvoo with the headquarters upstairs in the big room of the newly built Red Brick Store. The rituals associated with Masonry intrigued Smith. Shortly after the installation of the lodge, in a secret meeting, he instructed seven of his closest men in the rituals of anointings, washings, endowments, and communication of keys. All of these adopted rites were to become the principles and order of the priesthood performed in the Nauvoo Temple.

The lodge itself became very popular and soon boasted 286 members. Both William and James became members. This display of solidarity and explosive growth, typical of everything the Mormons did, alarmed the non-Mormon lodges who had a membership of only 227 in all of Illinois. They felt the selective membership process associated with Masonry had been totally degraded. It was just one more burr under the saddle as far as the local Gentiles were concerned. The cycle of mistrust and condemnation continued to grow. Somehow, the Mormons failed to understand how their never-ending successes alienated and angered everyone else.

Young Joseph and some of his playmates watched from the sidelines as their fathers joined this elite group. The rituals of brotherhood associated with the Lodge, with all of its obvious intrigue to outsiders, fascinated the boys. They decided to form an exclusive brotherhood of their own. This band of boys was a source of great fun for Joseph and his friends. Jeremy Weston was a member of this group and, unofficially, Jake was their mascot. Not interested in the intellectual precepts behind the degrees of Masonry, the boys developed elaborate initiation ceremonies that, typical of the male species, evolved into physical hazing. In addition, characteristically, some of this hazing got them into trouble with their elders. For the most part, however, this exclusive group engaged in good, clean activities—the kind that cemented lifelong friendships.

Recognized as a potential leader William was more active in all functions, increasing his stature and his presence in many of the lower level activities of the Church. With the constant urging of Ruth, William gave more hours and money than was required. He and Ruth were the perfect Saints—committed to the core. Being initially on the farm, James was separated from many spontaneous activities that could further his position within various organizations. In addition, it was obvious to many that Amanda was more reserved in her participation and acceptance of Church doctrine and affairs and, to his consternation, this reflected negatively on James.

Amanda couldn't believe what she heard.

"William has been sealed to another wife," James reported, as nonchalantly as he could; a slight tremor in his voice gave away his nervousness.

"He what?" demanded Amanda, displaying total disbelief and scorn. Her clenched hands were on her hips and her rigid body language spoke volumes on how she felt. If seen, her normally sanguine blue aura would have changed to bright red.

"You heard me, Amanda," James came back defiantly, "William has taken another wife."

"And has he managed to tell Ruth about this remarkable development?" she retorted sarcastically.

"He has, and she is in full support."

"Now, why doesn't that surprise me? She's a religious nut and would blindly kill her own children if the Church demanded it." Amanda could barely contain her violated sensibilities. Her words were sharp, clipped, and angry.

"Don't make light of Ruth just because she has a deep belief in what we are doing," insisted James. "It's abundantly clear that you have come to Nauvoo only because you had no choice, but that doesn't give you the right to criticize true believers like Ruth."

"You're right, *Brother* James," Amanda derisively retorted. "But then, we've gotten off the subject, haven't we? What on earth, or in heaven for that matter, makes the Church think they can go against the law and permit bigamy? Just who do they think they are?"

"Brother Smith has philosophical and religious reasons for promoting this idea. Ruth and William are true believers and have come to terms with all that plural marriage means—both the good and the bad."

"Is that so," challenged Amanda, "and tell me, what are these deep philosophical and religious reasons? Explain them to me so I can understand and believe."

"No, Amanda, not in your current frame of mind. Once you calm down, then we'll discuss it." James made a slashing movement with his hand to punctuate his statements and turned to walk away.

"Truth is, James, you don't know, do you?" she called out as he left the room. "You can walk away but this subject will not."

The truth was, James did not fully understand the concept, and he felt ill equipped to discuss it further. He deluded himself into believing that Amanda would calm down and be able to discuss the matter more rationally later. Another truth was that Amanda would never condone this practice, no matter how entrenched it became in the Church.

The news of William's second marriage raged in the pit of Amanda's stomach like the core of a seething volcano. She was unable to eat or sleep normally; the reality gnawed away at her inner being. She'd been able to accept, or at least go along with, so much that didn't make sense since joining the Church. Why was this particular bit of nonsense so upsetting to her? Deep down, it was the subliminal awareness that the practice could threaten her marriage. She loved James. He was a good man, a first-rate provider, a great father, and a kind and considerate husband. She knew that he loved her. That she had not fully accepted their conversion to Mormonism was an obvious disappointment to him, but despite a noticeable skepticism on occasion, she seldom made any waves and tried desperately not to cause him any open embarrassment within the flock. Amanda, however grudgingly, went along with the program. This was different.

For the next couple of days, James and Amanda elected to avoid the controversial subject. In truth, they had little to say to each other at all. Finally, on the third day, Amanda decided to go to the source to search out some answers. She would go to William. To bring the subject up with Ruth was a waste of time: Ruth's faith made her blind to reality. The Church had many women like Ruth within their ranks. They were the backbone of the movement and ready to do what was required, whether or not they understood. If Joseph Smith said it had to be, that was good enough for them. Mormon men, like the majority of men of that period, were the movers, shakers, and defenders. The Mormon women were the glue that held everything together, never wavering, forever faithful, and indefatigable—they were always there.

William, alone in the barn, was shoeing a horse. Amanda, knowing that both Ruth and James were elsewhere, chose this time to make her move. She entered the barn door and found William grasping his horse's upraised hind leg between his legs and methodically filing the hoof with a heavy rasp.

"William," Amanda spoke, after standing for a moment and watching his labor.

"Oh, hello, Amanda." William paused in his work and looked up.

"William," Amanda repeated nervously, "may I talk with you a minute?"

"Of course, what's on your mind?" He dropped the horse's hoof and laid the rasp aside. He could tell by the tone of her voice she was in a serious mood. Besides, they seldom talked alone. James told him that Amanda was not pleased with his taking a second wife and he suspected that was to be the subject of conversation. He wiped his brow with his sleeve and then motioned toward a bale of hay. "Why don't we sit down and rest our weary bones?" She sat on one bale and William sat on another, giving her his full attention.

"I'm a bit nervous," Amanda confessed, "but I have to talk to you about this second wife business."

"Oh, you mean Mary Ellen," he said, as nonchalantly as he could muster.

"Yes, about Mary Ellen." That was first time she had even heard the new wife's name. "But, what I really want to know is why you would even consider such a thing."

"Well, Amanda, I can understand why you may not approve, but if Ruth has no problem with the idea, why should you care?"

"Why should I care?" Amanda said with incredulity. "Why should I care?" she repeated. "Other than the fact that it's wrong, against the law, and will destroy your family, not to mention mine, I can't see why I should care. Flat out, Brother William, it's a sin. What possible explanation can you, Brother Smith, and all the others, give me to justify your actions?" Her voice was quivering with emotion at this point.

"Amanda, calm down. Let me try to explain to you why the Church has taken this stand. And, I might add, it doesn't apply to everyone, only those individuals who are approved by Brother Smith and who believe it is the right thing to do."

"Well, I'm certainly glad to hear that it's not mandatory," she said sarcastically. "But I can't begin to understand what reason you can give that would make it right."

"There is plenty of precedence for plural marriages in the Old Testament, Amanda, and in his fertile mind, Joseph has seen justification for a man to have more than one wife if he is worthy."

"If a man is worthy?' she challenged, "What about his wife? What about his children?"

"It a complex idea, Amanda. Joseph teaches that if a man is sealed to his wife under the new and everlasting covenant in the Temple, they will be together in heaven forever. If his wife dies and he remarries, and his second wife is sealed as well, he will then have both wives in heaven."

"I don't know anything about this sealing ritual," Amanda said, "but what you've said sounds logical to me. What's that got to do with having two wives on earth at the same time?"

"Well, the road to godhood in heaven is based on what a man learns on earth and on his good works. Man's position in heaven depends on the blessings he earns on earth—the more blessings—the higher position. The sealing of another wife, and all the children they have together, gives the man that many more blessings in heaven."

"I see then, if a man has ten wives, he has ten times the blessings?" Amanda couldn't believe what she was hearing.

"In theory, yes, but remember, the man must provide equally for all of his wives and children while here on earth. He cannot let them fend for themselves. So there is a practical limit."

"Well, I'm certainly glad to hear that. But tell me, if this is such a good thing, why isn't it legal and why doesn't everybody else do it?"

"I know you don't believe this, Amanda, but the Mormons are a chosen people. This wondrous gift can be given only to the Saints in the revelations of Joseph Smith."

"You're right, I don't believe it. This 'revelation' seems to me to be nothing more than an excuse for the male Saints to go to bed with anyone they can afford without any regard for the effect on their wives and families. I'd sooner they spend their money on prostitutes." Amanda then switched direction. "Tell me, if this is such a good thing, why is it kept so secret?"

"If I'm having difficulty explaining the intricacies of this belief to you, how would you expect those outside the faith to understand? As with many things in religion, Amanda, eventually one has to have faith in order to believe. It would be suicidal to profess this practice openly at this time."

"Maybe it is difficult to talk about because it's wrong. Honest moral beliefs are easy to understand and to explain."

William saw that he was getting nowhere. With a tinge of exasperation he said, "Look, Amanda, I've tried to explain to you briefly the concept behind what I and others have come to accept and believe. There is much more to the practice than we have discussed. You seem to have a mindset that makes added explanation a waste of time right now."

"You're right again, William. *I'm* going to have to have a revelation before accepting this one. I fear for the Saints once the Gentiles know about this plural marriage business. They'll use it as a weapon; mark my word. Brother Joseph must know that and that's why he tries to keep it so secret."

She rose from the bale and started for the door. It was obvious their discussion was over. "Thank you for your time, William. I sincerely hope that this all works out the way you think it will. I'll not cause any problems within the family, but I have to tell you, this is a very bad idea."

"I appreciate your honesty, Amanda. We can go this way because it is God's will and it is my responsibility to make it work. May I assume we part as friends?"

"William, we are more than friends, we are family. It will forever be so. I'm sorry I bothered you. Please … finish shoeing your horse," she said, waving her hand dismissively toward the horse as she turned and walked away. "Foolish nonsense," she muttered to herself as she walked back to her house, "foolish, foolish nonsense."

CHAPTER 8

Many of the Saints, in Nauvoo, including the Westons, hated John C. Bennett, Joseph Smith's First Counselor. Instead of acting as a moral compass, Bennett used his position to take advantage of residents. He cheated them in land and commerce and this left a bad taste in their mouths. Stories of his opportunistic dealings were the subject of countless backyard conversations. Many also knew that he was philanderer and an abortionist for hire. All this reflected negatively on Smith. Instead of being a buckler for Smith, he became a lightning rod of discontent. Bennett was an open and enthusiastic believer of Joseph's teachings, but there were many who wondered why Smith put up with such a person. Smith's wife, Emma, despised the man.

It was a shock but no big surprise then when Smith, finally realizing Bennett was a liability, excommunicated and expelled him from Nauvoo on June 23, 1842. The city was abuzz with implications of this action. Bennett's outing would cause Joseph Smith and his Church much pain over the coming months. Those in the know agreed with the ousting but worried about the underlying reasons. They knew others of more significance were dissatisfied with the way things were. No one seemed to have serious concerns from a religious point of view.

There were important leaders, nonetheless, who questioned the distribution of tithes and contributions. Joseph Smith seemed to be enriching himself at the expense of the Church. Besides, there were always those who seriously doubted the justification of his not so secret revelation concerning multiple wives.

One early morning in July, Amanda hitched up the shay and rode out to the Hayward's farm, located about a mile farther out from Nauvoo than the Weston farmhouse. She was in the mood to talk to her friend Betsy. William's decision to take another wife, particularly in light of the Bennett scandal, was weighing heavily on her.

Amanda and Betsy Hayward had met at the John Lyon Store back when Amanda was still living on the farm. After meeting and exchanging pleasantries, they had ridden south, each in their separate buggies, talking along the way, until Amanda turned off to head east. Over the months, Betsy had become her sounding board of sanity. She did not hate the Mormons like so many of Amanda's Gentile neighbors. Kind and gentle, with love in her heart for all, Betsy often listened to Amanda about her frustration of coping with the world of the Saints. Amanda felt comfortable with Betsy as a confidant and stabilizing influence. She always came away from Betsy's home with renewed strength and sense of purpose.

"Goodness, Amanda, what's going on in Nauvoo?" Betsy asked, once the usual banter was over.

"I'm not sure I know what thing you mean," said Amanda. What *hasn't* been going on, she thought.

"Well, I've been reading this article in the *Sangamo Journal* that John brought home from Springfield. Seems this fella John Bennett is making all sorts of accusations against Joseph Smith and your congregation. Wasn't he one of the leaders up there until recently?

"He was. But I haven't read the paper so I don't know about any accusations."

"I've got the paper right here, if you want to see it," said Betsy, extending the paper to Amanda.

As Amanda read Bennett's article, she recognized that some of the charges were outright lies and others were only half-true. She also recognized that some were factual and damaging. I knew this polygamy thing would come to roost, she reflected.

"Seems to me that this kind of stuff can't do you folks any good, Amanda," Betsy said as Amanda finished reading the article and put down the paper with an exasperated look. "I understand that papers around the country have picked up on this and the rumors are spreading and growing. I'm concerned about what will happen if this gets out of hand."

"As always, you're right, Betsy. This fella Bennett is not a very nice person and I think Joseph Smith did the right thing in expelling him from our city. Many of these accusations are outlandish and reasonable people everywhere who look at Bennett's flawed character will discount much of what he says. But, there are many outsiders that will use this against the Saints."

"As we've often discussed," Amanda continued, "Smith appears to be enriching himself at the expense of others and this business of multiple marriages—that even his wife disagrees with—is bound to cause problems someday. What did John have to say about this?" she asked.

"Oh, you know John," replied Betsy, "he doesn't say much." Betsy's husband, John, was a good man who worked his farm, never bothered his neighbors, went to the nearby Baptist church on Sunday, loved his wife and children, and seldom badmouthed anyone. Live and let live was his motto. His demeanor was slow moving, determined, and stubborn, and his massive size—six-and-one-half feet tall and weighing in around 240 pounds—were assurance that no one would bother him or his family. "He did allow that this was not a good sign for you Mormons," she concluded.

"He's right, of course," sighed Amanda. "The problem is that anytime there are attacks from outside, the Saints stiffen their resolve. It always makes them more fanatical. It's always the same. They believe that God sends these trials and tribulations to test their faith and strength. These situations always seem to harden the mindsets of both the Saints *and* of their enemies. My gosh, it gives me a headache just thinking about it."

"I'm sorry if I spoiled your visit, Amanda. I know you come out here to escape from all that, even if only for a minute or two. As most of these things do, I'm sure this will pass." Switching subjects, she asked, "How are all the children?"

"All is well, thank God. Everyone is working hard now that school is out. You know how it is with the church duties, tending the garden and livestock, and everything else. It's a busy but happy time. I assume it's the same with your family?"

"Yes, for the most part. Little Jonathan broke his index finger yesterday foolin' around in the barn."

"My goodness, is he all right?" Amanda expressed genuine concern.

"Oh he's fine. I bet he learned not to stick his finger in the bung hole of a barrel when it's rollin'."

Amanda laughed. "Why do they test us so?" she asked. The two women sat and chatted about this and that for the better part of another hour, keeping the subject matter light and cheerful.

"Well, my dear, it's time for me to head back home. Please give my best to John. She gave Betsy a hug and a small kiss on the cheek. Betsy reciprocated and they walked hand-in-hand down the path from the house.

"Oh, here, I almost forgot." Amanda reached into the buggy and brought out a jar of pickles. "I put these up the other day and thought you and John might like some." She offered the gift to Betsy with a nod of her head.

"Why thank you, Amanda, how thoughtful of you." Betsy gently took the jar and gazed appreciatively at the contents. "John loves bread and butter pickles. You take care now, Amanda. I hope I didn't upset you with this newspaper stuff," Betsy said with a look of concern.

"No, it will be all about the city by the time I return, I'm sure. I'd rather hear it from you. God be with you, Betsy," Amanda said as she climbed back into the shay and headed out the farm gate. Yes, indeed, she mused, this should stir up the Saints.

It was still early and Amanda was in no hurry. The warm sun comforted her as she let her mind meander, thinking about nothing in particular, just enjoying the peace and quiet of being alone. The horse seemed to sense her mood and reflected it by his ambling gait. Still within sight of the Hayward's farm, Amanda hadn't notice the four mounted men in the shade of a nearby clump of trees, just off the side of the road. She became aware of them only when one of their horses chortled.

She raised her head in the direction of the men. Their horses' heads formed a semicircle with their noses almost touching; the men murmured back and forth, as they looked in Amanda's direction. Curls of smoke from their roll-your-owns and cigars lazily drifted upward above their heads. Amanda could not hear what they were saying; but she sensed a tension that worried her. She nodded her head at the group and gave them a weak smile. Then looking forward down the road, she gave the horse a quick snap of the reins. Jerking its head upward, the horse awakened from its lethargic pace and reluctantly quickened its step. Amanda reined in slightly. She did not want the men's demeanor to appear to disturb her.

Surely, what she heard was not happening. The sound of horses at a lazy but determined trot wafted menacingly from the rear. Her worst fears were confirmed when she turned and saw the men almost abreast of her shay. The immediate impulse to snap her horse into a blinding gallop was only a fleeting thought; there was no way for her to outrun them. Frozen with fear, she looked straight ahead while her mind scrambled with implausible options of escape.

One man trotted forward and grabbed her horse's rein near the bit. Slowly, the horse came to a standstill. For a moment, besides the sound of leather upon leather as the men shifted in their saddles and the usual noises of horses at a standstill, there was absolute silence. Amanda sat stiffly, eyes fix straight ahead; her heart pounded visibly and her mouth became cotton dry.

"Well now, little lady, what cha doin' way out here? This ain't no place for a Mormon bitch ta be hangin' out." Those menacing words came from a man in dirty, rumbled clothes and a long, tobacco-stained beard. Amanda hadn't felt such fear since the robbery back in Kentucky. Only then, she had a gun.

She tried desperately not to tremble as she slowly, purposely moved her head in the direction of the man to her left. Lifting her chin slightly, she looked him in the eyes and said in as steady a voice as she could muster, "I've just been visiting my friends, John and Betsy Hayward."

"Yeah, we suspected them Hayward's was Mormon lovers," the man to her right sneered.

Slowly coming up from the rear and reining his horse to a stop in front of the man to her left, a lean, mean-looking man with a large scar on his right cheek, stared at Amanda with a steely gaze. He eyed her from head to toe and back, undressing her with his gaze. A fat, cheap cigar protruded from the side of his mouth.

"Seems ta me," he slobbered, "you Mormon women are getting' the short end of the stick. While yer man gets a lotta women, you only get part of a man. Don' make no sense 'cause a woman can have as many men as she wants, one rat after the other."

All the men laughed ominously. "Yeah, don' seem fair." "How about another part of a man, sweetie?" "I got a stick fer you, honey."

The men slowly began to dismount from their saddles, not one taking their eyes off Amanda. Only the man holding her horse's lead remained mounted. The man with the smelly cigar pulled himself up onto the shay and grabbed Amanda by the arm. She screamed and struck out with all her strength, knocking the cigar from his mouth and causing a trickle of blood to come from his lip.

"Bitch," he sneered, "git down here where ya belong." He jumped down with a thud and pulled her roughly from the shay, slamming her to the ground. As she lay there trembling and sobbing, two men grabbed her arms and pulled her onto her back. She lay face up, kicking at the filthy cigar smoker as he began to undo his belt buckle. "Let's see what a Mormon bitch can do with one *real* man," he snickered.

All of a sudden, there were sounds of a dull, sickening thud, followed by an agonizing groan. All of the men were intent on the action they so lustily desired and hadn't noticed big John Hayward come up from the rear with a large piece of wood. For the man with the unbuckled belt, there was a blinding flash of stars as John hit him in the back of the head with a solid blow. The man fell forward heavily on Amanda, succumbing to darkness and relief from the intense pain as he passed out. The other two men instantly released Amanda, stood up with fear-drenched faces, and upraised arms.

"Anybody else want a piece a this stick?" John asked, holding it over his shoulder threateningly.

The responses ricocheted from one man to another. "No, John. We didn't mean no harm. We was just funnin', John. We'll leave peaceful like."

"Pick that piece a garbage up an' get outta here," John snarled.

The would-be rapists needed no second command. They dragged the unconscious cigar smoker off Amanda and threw him belly down over his saddle. They then mounted their horses and galloped away in a cloud of dust. They wanted no part of a fight with big John.

"You all right, Amanda?" John leaned over and gently grasped her arm and helped her to her feet. As her knees shook and tears welled in her eyes, she straightened herself, dusted off her dress, and adjusted her bonnet.

"Thank you, John." Her lower lip quivered. "It's obvious that you did me a great service. No telling what those scalawags would have done if you hadn't come along. I'll be eternally grateful for what you did. Thank you, thank you," she said, as the words tumbled in a nervous cascade.

"It weren't nothin', Amanda. You don't owe me at all. But, I think it's best you don't come down here alone again until things settle down."

"I know, John. I'm terribly sorry if I've caused you any problem."

"Don't worry none about that. Are you going to be all right going home by yourself? Do you want me to come along?" John asked, in his deep but gentle voice.

"No, no, I'm all right. You've done enough. I won't tarry. I'll make it home. Don't you worry. And, John, thank you again." Amanda was near tears as she unsteadily climbed into the buggy, assisted by John. "Bye, John," she said with one final wave of her hand as she urged her horse toward home. Gratitude welled within her.

"Goodbye, Amanda. Take care now, ya hear?"

James, William, and two other men were in the living room when Amanda entered the house. They were in heated debate over the Bennett affair and paid no attention to her as she headed upstairs. Amanda made no mention of what happened to her outside the Thomas farm. There was too much hostility within the community as it was. She never brought the assault to light—ever.

Chapter 9

Amanda met Emma Smith briefly in Scovel's Bakery and Confectionery Shop. Hannah Thompson introduced Amanda to Sister Smith. Scovel's was a favorite place to buy bread, as well as puddings, pies, and all sorts of other sweets. Even though Amanda had seen Emma before from a distance, she had never spoken to her.

"Hello, Amanda. It's so nice to meet you."

"Thank you, Sister Smith. The pleasure is definitely mine."

The friendly tone and gentle demeanor of the serious-faced woman with sparkling hazel eyes that stood before her surprised Amanda.

"Please, call me Emma. And where do you come from, Amanda?"

"Tennessee, Emma," replied Amanda, uncomfortable with calling a woman of such high stature by her first name. "Double Springs, Tennessee."

For some reason, an aura of understanding and commonality engulfed these two women. Their eyes locked and unseen energy and communication flowed between them. Saying nothing in the seconds that transpired, each woman took the measure of the other. Though they had never met, they were one of a kindred spirit. If pressed, both would be at a loss to explain the attraction.

"Ahem," stuttered Hannah, nervously. She did not understand the situation but had no doubt that whatever was transpiring did not include her. She was also reacting to the group of women standing outside the bakery waiting to enter. Scovel's was very small and could not hold more than three or four customers at a time comfortably.

"Oh, I'm terribly sorry," said Emma, looking back at those waiting in line and sounding sincere, but not meaning a word of it. She paid for the bread she had selected and turned to leave. "Amanda," she said looking over her shoulder, "we must have tea together sometime. I'll contact you soon." She walked by the women waiting outside the door of the bakery, nodding and smiling as she went.

"My word, you two certainly hit it off," said Hannah with a slight upward motion of her nose and pursing of her lips, displaying an obvious touch of jealousy. She had known Emma for years, never once been invited to tea.

"Well, she certainly is friendly. I doubt she was serious about tea. That was just a pleasantry. Besides, she won't remember my name and doesn't even know where I live." Amanda selected two loaves of bread, paid for them and skirted around the women in the doorway. She was conscious of their questioning eyes. She smiled and nodded as she passed.

"Believe me, if she wants to find you, she will," Hannah said, strolling side-by-side with Amanda. "She's a very strong person. Has to be to live with Brother Smith," added Hannah, as if she knew what really went on in the Smith household.

Hannah was right and Amanda was wrong. In less than a week, Amanda received a note from Emma Smith, inviting her to tea the following day at two o'clock in the afternoon. Amanda was shocked. She was in a stew wondering what to wear, how to act and, mostly, what to say once she was in Emma's presence. She decided not to be too pretentious, but still selected one of her better outfits— a black velvet bodice with a long-sleeved cotton chemise and matching gray three-tiered, full-length skirt. With an appropriate bonnet, she looked nice but not as if she were going to church.

Amanda decided not to walk the eight blocks to the Joseph Smith

Homestead. The weather had been dry that last few days. Dirt and dust would cover the bottom of her skirt and her shoes by the time she arrived. Jeremy had hitched up her one-horse shay and Amanda climbed on board for the short drive.

Pulling up short of the Smith's home, Amanda climbed down from the carriage and tied her horse to a hitching post. As she approached the house, she felt nervous and self-conscious. There were many eyes in the busy street wondering what she was doing calling on the Smith's at that hour.

As she started to knock on the door, it unexpectedly jerked open and Joseph Smith, in his usual rush, came close to bowling her over. Amanda hopped to one side, her hand at her chest and her mouth frozen open from surprise. Backing away, Smith started apologizing. "I'm *terribly* sorry. I didn't mean to startle you. Sometimes I'm in such a rush I never pay attention to where I'm going."

"That's quite all right," Amanda managed to utter. "I'm sorry, I wasn't paying attention either."

"So, what brings you here, my dear?" Smith asked pleasantly.

"Oh, Sister Emma ... I mean, Sister Smith, invited me over for tea."

"Good, good. Come right on in. Emma," he shouted back through the doorway, "Sister, uh, I'm sorry, what is your name?"

"Amanda Weston"

"Oh yes, Amanda Weston is here for tea." Then as an afterthought, Smith said, "I don't think we've ever met. Are you William Weston's wife?"

"No," Amanda replied, "I'm married to his brother, James."

"Yes, yes, I know them both. Fine men, good Christians. They are a true asset to the Church. Well, I must be off. Have a pleasant chat with Emma. Don't let her fill you're head with a lot of rebellious thoughts," he chuckled as he strode quickly down the path, turning left toward the Red Brick Store.

"Thank you, Brother Smith. It's been a pleasure meeting you," Amanda mumbled awkwardly. She wasn't sure he even heard her.

"There you are, dear. Please come in," Emma gushed, as she took Amanda by the arm and escorted her through the doorway. "I do hope Joseph didn't startle you too much. He's such a bull at times."

"No, no, not at all. It was pleasure meeting him. I've seen him from a distance but actually never met him."

Like Amanda, Emma was wearing a bodice—a dull red one with soft stays to maintain support. She also wore a white cotton chemise, but only three-quarter length sleeves. Her one-piece, full-length green skirt had a drawstring waist. Amanda was somewhat surprised that Emma was dressed in color as most of the time in public she wore rather drab grays and browns.

"Please, sit down," Emma gestured toward a divan with a long low table and tea set located in front. "Joseph is not keen on me drinking tea. He considers it a stimulant. But unlike him, I need a stimulant from time to time. So, my dear, tell me a little about yourself and your family."

Emma leaned forward and poured tea in Amanda's cup. She motioned with her hand toward the cream and sugar sitting on the table. Amanda's head nodded slightly.

"Thank you," she said, adding a small amount of sugar and a dollop of cream to her tea.

For the next hour, Amanda, prodded by questions from Emma, told the story of the Weston families coming to Nauvoo. The women talked about the happenings in Nauvoo, things about their community that would interest any woman, like shopping, schools, and, of course, the weather. It was obvious that the two women were naturally congenial, as they had been from their very first meeting.

Ringed by dark hair parted in the middle and usually a serious, almost stern look, Emma's face was intriguing. Her large eyes seemed sad and betrayed the pressures of being constantly in the swirl surrounding her famous husband. Amanda sensed the emotional tribulation that such a life could have on a person. She could not possibly imagine all of its ramifications though.

"Tell me, what do you think of this John Bennett situation?" Emma asked unexpectedly.

Taken aback by the switch to a serious, political level of conversation, Amanda could only stammer, "I ... I really haven't thought that much about it, Emma. I try not to be involved in things that are above my head."

"Come now, Amanda, surely it is the subject of conversation and gossip throughout the city. What do *you* think?"

Hesitantly, Amanda offered, "From all I've read and heard, it seems a lot of lies and false accusations are being passed about. Most Saints don't believe a word of it; most Gentiles believe every bit of it. Everyone I know believes that Bennett should have been excommunicated from the Church."

"It's interesting that, so far, you've told me what everyone else thinks. To be honest, I never trusted the man from the day I met him. He was too smooth talking. I couldn't understand what Joseph saw in him. Now he's making some serious accusations. So," said Emma in her blunt manner, "what do *you* think about all this plural marriage business?"

Amanda squirmed. Everyone knew that Emma was a staunch defender of her husband regarding this matter. She in no way conceded he had anyone but her.

"Well, let's put it this way, I'm not sure what goes on in other households, but in mine, there has been and never will be another woman. One man, one woman, and that's that," she added with emphasis.

"Goodness, how diplomatic you are. But, how glad I am to hear you say that, my dear, because that is my feeling as well. Despite all that is rumored and written about Joseph, I know that he has had no other woman; especially, no other wife." The fervor of Emma's remarks, coupled with commonly accepted knowledge to the contrary within the Church and its hierarchy, made Amanda feel uncomfortable. How sorry she felt for Emma.

"And how do you truly feel about the teachings of Joseph Smith?" Emma continued on her serious vein.

"Well ... a, to be honest," Amanda blurted out, "there are times when I have my doubts about some of the things the Church stands for." Then, recognizing that she had revealed to the wife of the founder of the Mormon religion something that she tried to keep hidden from all but her family, Amanda stammered, "I'm sorry, I know that you don't want to hear that."

"Now don't you fret, dear. What you're feeling is common. Why, back in the early days in Harmony, Pennsylvania, I was very doubtful."

"Really?" Amanda asked with surprise.

"Oh yes," Emma sighed. "Back then, we were so poor and Joseph was not willing to earn a living from the farm. I was frightened then, same as now, because Joseph's preaching was greeted with a great deal of rancor. You know, I had seen no golden plates and heard no voices. It was some time before I joined the Church and was baptized."

"That must have been very difficult for you."

"Yes, it was. I was very close to my parents, and they held Joseph in such contempt, as did many of my friends and neighbors. This pressure along with living off the uncertain and intermittent charity of Joseph's friends and followers was almost more than I could bear. I felt so vulnerable. There are times when that old feeling creeps back, and I become unsure of myself again. The point is, Amanda, it is not easy to be the wife of a Saint, especially the Prophet himself."

"Thank you for being so honest with me," Amanda said. "I was beginning to think I was the only one in Nauvoo besides the Gentiles who had such feelings."

Emma laughed heartily. "Heavens no, child. Being a follower of this religion, especially if you're a woman, is not easy. Nevertheless, after all the trials and tribulations over the years, I have become a true believer in the basic tenets of the Church. With time, you will too."

"I'm sure that is true," agreed Amanda. She wanted to ask how anyone could believe in a book that purported to be the history of a tribe of Hebrews that immigrated to America before Christ was born. Instead, she said, "Goodness, I have taken up so much of your time. I really must go," she added, standing and extending her hand to Emma.

"You're right, the time has gone by quickly; and delightfully so, I might add. Thank you so much for coming. I have thoroughly enjoyed our conversation," Emma rattled on as she followed Amanda to the door. "And, dear, let's keep the thoughts we expressed today between just the two of us, as friends."

"You have my word," Amanda said convincingly, as she stepped out the door into the bright sunlight. "Goodbye, Sister Emma."

"Goodbye, Amanda," replied Emma.

Many months passed before Emma and Amanda saw each other to speak. Even then, it was only an exchange of pleasantries. Their different social circle and the seeming stream of crises that hounded the

Smith family always seemed to put off encounters that both wanted. Amanda treasured the memory of their one meeting as it gave her insight into the world of a woman more tortured than she was. How the woman survived was beyond Amanda. She often felt a sympathetic ache in her heart when she thought of Emma.

Amanda had to run an errand before she headed for home. James had asked that she buy four sets of horseshoes. Climbing down from her shay, she headed toward the blacksmith shop entrance amid the swooshing sound of the blower and smell of tempered metal. Unexpectedly, her friend Betsy Hayward exited the building. They stopped and stood facing each other without saying a word, surprised at their chance encounter.

"Betsy, my dear, how *are* you?" Amanda finally managed to say. She stepped forward and gave Betsy a gentle, loving hug.

Betsy returned the embrace and then, holding on to each other's hands, they parted at arm's length and fondly appraised the other. "I'm fine, Amanda. You look great. I've missed you," Betsy said rapidly. She was obviously pleased to have encountered her friend, but nervous.

Amanda pulled Betsy to one side of the building away from the main line of traffic. "And I've missed you, my dear friend. I'm sure John told you what happened after my last visit?"

"Yes," Betsy answered with a slight tinge of tears beginning to develop.

"Well, John and I agreed it would be best if I didn't visit any more. God knows I wanted to, but I just couldn't. Now that I see you, I know I should have at least written you so that we could keep in touch."

"Don't fret all that, Amanda. I understand, believe me, I do."

"Well, what is happening these days? Let's sit down somewhere so you can fill me in on everything," Amanda said excitedly.

Betsy's face grew solemn and she did not suppress the tears this time. "Oh, Amanda, all is not well," she said, sniffing as she attempted to find a handkerchief.

"Betsy, what's wrong, dear?" Amanda couldn't stand to see her friend so distraught.

"Well," Betsy hesitated, "a gang of men came last week and burned us out. We have nothing left. We're taking whatever money we have and heading back home to New York to our families."

Amanda became faint from shock. "My God in heaven, why?" she blurted out. "Why, Betsy, why?" she repeated in disbelief.

"They kept screaming that we were Mormon lovers." Betsy was freely crying at this point. "They just about killed John as he tried to save the house. He couldn't get to his guns because they were in the house, and it was on fire. He was in the fields when it all started."

"Oh my God, this is all my fault," Amanda wailed. Panic made her voice quiver and tears flowed from her eyes. "I'm just sick, Betsy, it's all my fault."

"No, no, no," Betsy tried to sooth Amanda by stroking her face.

"They did it just to get back at John for helping me. I know they did. They were such horrible people, Betsy. I'm so sorry," she cried. Then she gasped, "Is John all right? He's not hurt is he?"

"Oh, he hasn't got any injury that time won't heal. But, I'm afraid they've broken his spirit. He feels he let his family down. I feel so sorry for him because he's always been in control, always so strong."

"Are you really leaving that beautiful farm?" Amanda asked.

"Yes, we're worried. There's nothing for us here now. With the hatred that's all around us, we can see only more trouble, even bloodshed. We don't want any part of that."

"Is there anything I can do for you? Do you need money? What about your belongings?"

"Hush, now," soothed Betsy. "We're fine. We've got enough money to return home and start again. We still have family and friends there that can help us. Our little adventure out west just didn't work out, that's all."

"Betsy, you know I'd do anything for you and your family. I'm just shattered by what has happened."

"I know, dear one, but we've got a place to go and we are young and healthy, so don't worry about us." Then switching tones, Betsy said, "To be honest, I'm more worried about your family's future. Amanda, there are evil forces out there that I'm not sure your people realize are there. I know they've suffered before but I'm frightened to death at the hatred your way of life has created. I don't claim to understand it, but let me tell you, if I were you, I would seriously consider heading back to Tennessee before it's too late."

"Yes, I understand what you're saying. But, it may be too late for that." Amanda was somber.

"Look, Amanda, I've got to go. We leave first thing in the morning, and I've got a lot to do."

"All right, dear Betsy. Are you going to be safe traveling?" Amanda asked with heartfelt concern. "Do you want one of our men folk to see you home?"

"No, no, I'll be all right. I went to Browning's gun shop yesterday and bought two of his best rifles and a shot gun—and I do know how to shoot." Betsy tittered slightly. "The mood John is in, I feel sorry for anyone who gets in his way. He's a mild man but just don't make him mad ... and he's mad."

"I know. I saw some of that the last time I was there. Please tell John how sorry I am and how very much I appreciate his help that day. If he hadn't been there ... well, there's no telling what could have happened."

The two women embraced. Amanda whispered in her friend's ear, "God bless you, Betsy."

"And may he keep you and yours safe, Amanda," replied Betsy.

"Please write and let me know all is well."

"I will. I promise."

Amanda watched Betsy climb into her wagon. Betsy blew her a kiss and with a snap of the reins, turned her horses south, never looking back. Amanda slowly waved her hand, feeling as if she were in a trance. Flashes of the Hayward farm confrontation battered her brain. She couldn't help but feel that she was responsible for their situation.

The year 1843 was an excellent time for the Westons and the City of Nauvoo. Immigration continued unabated—the population estimated at ten to twelve thousand—and construction was explosive—more than one hundred well built brick houses. There were pleasure excursions on the Mormon-owned steamboat, Maid of Iowa. The builders of Nauvoo strictly enforced building, street, and walkway ordinances in an effort to beautify the city. The streets and roads, though, were not paved—rough and rutted in dry weather—quagmires of sticky mud when it rained. Amazingly, all of this went on despite the fact the Mormons did not consider this their permanent home. In July, Joseph Smith prophesied that the Saints would someday settle in the Rocky Mountains. To the constant amazement of Amanda, the paradox of Nauvoo was that the residents continued to plan and build their city as if it were a permanent home, when it wasn't.

The riverboats were the main means of transport for the immigrants that came up from New Orleans by the hundreds. Nauvoo was a busy river port with almost six arrivals every day. It had two landings—one at Nauvoo House located at the end of Main Street at the south end of the city and the other at the end of Granger Street in the north. During the winter, the Mississippi would freeze over. While wagons and people could cross over to Montrose, Iowa on the ice, regular riverboat travel and commerce came to a halt. During the late spring and early summer, river traffic resumed vigorously.

One irritating fact of living near the river was the annual infestation of river insects. Besides the ubiquitous and dangerous mosquitoes, there were large, moth-like flies well known in that part of the Mississippi, dubbed "Mormon flies," which often blanketed everything exposed. Much to her consternation, these annoying pests seemed particularly attracted to Amanda's bed sheets hung out to dry. There was little time for such nonsense as shaking and picking these clinging insects from her wash.

"Brother William."

"Yes, Brother Joseph."

The clouds overhead were light and fluffy and scooted across the sky as if late for a meeting somewhere far to the east. These phantom clouds barely hindered the sun's rays from heating the earth below. It was a pleasant, low-humidity day in May in 1843.

William and James stood outside the Red Brick Store, intermingling with a dozen men, more or less, all conversing on this and that, enjoying one another's company and the beauty of the day. All ears were attentive as Joseph and William spoke.

"I hear from your brother, James, that you're quite renowned for your wrestling skills back in Tennessee," taunted Joseph.

"It's true, I was undefeated among the rough an' tumble mountain men of Rutherford County, Tennessee," boasted William. The challenge in Smith's tone was not lost on William or on the crowd of men standing around.

"And do you think you could take the champion from these parts?"

"I'm not sure. Who might that be?" William knew without question, who that might be.

Smith looked at the growing assembly, puffed up his chest, stood at full length balanced on his toes, and snapped his bright colored suspenders. "And who might that be?" he shouted to the crowd.

In unison, the men shouted back, "You, Brother Smith, you!" Old timers in the group had participated in this ritual before. Joe Smith's talents as a wrestler were well known and a great source of pride and joy to the Prophet. William had never witnessed a Smith match before, but he was well aware that stories of how Joseph vanquished all who dared to challenge him had reached almost legendary proportions.

"Really, Brother Smith," retorted William in mock surprise. "And how does a man of God have the temperament to do strenuous personal combat?" By now, William had come nearer Joseph, raised himself to his full height—equally that of Joseph's—and perceptively flexed his muscles.

"Oh," Joseph's voice thundered, "it is from God that I derive the strength to overcome all challengers. His power flows through me and ensures my victory. I'm unbeaten, save one tie."

"I grant that you have more influence with the Lord than I, but surely it would not diminish your stature if God, just this one time, would give victory to a lesser member of his flock."

"Ooh," groaned the crowd as they felt the tension rising between the two men. Joseph loved it. This was his stage. "You're in trouble for sure now, Brother William," called out one man in the assembled throng.

"Good, good, I like your attitude," Smith said as he began to unbutton his shirt and take the measure of William. "Now let's see if your skill matches your tongue."

Both men were soon stripped to the waist and began circling each other, first to the right and then to the left. The combatants shook their arms to loosen muscles and stretched neck muscles from side to side to lessen the tension. Smith cracked his knuckles. Then, at the same moment, both men grasp the other firmly—one hand behind the head and one on the free arm. In this fashion, they circled one way and then the other, testing the strength and balance of their opponent. Although Smith was older, William was impressed with the firmness of his grasp and the hardness of his muscle tone. This was not going to be easy, he concluded.

Suddenly, like charging rams in mating season, they slammed into each other and grasping full-body began the match in earnest. Expressions of encouragement from the crowd matched the sounds of exertion from the wrestlers. Smith fell first, but with cat-like agility, broke free from William's grasp and scrambled to his feet ready for the next charge. The crowd cheered their approval.

Again, the combatants locked arms, this time in a wider stance. With a feint one way and lightning speed the other; Smith turned his body into William and then slammed him to the ground. Somehow, William pulled himself free. For the better part of fifteen minutes, the men wrestled back and forth, neither seeming to gain the advantage over the other. Repeatedly, they traded falls and managed to break free.

James was enjoying the match immensely, shouting encouragement to his brother, groaning when he was on the bottom and cheering when he was on the top. The majority of the crowd, of course, was cheering for their leader and local champion. A few, however, secretly wanted to see Joseph receive a comeuppance just once.

Both combatants were beginning to tire. In one final burst of energy, Smith, who was at least twenty pounds heavier, kicked William's feet from under him and then fell, full-force on top, as they tumbled to the ground. With his arms wrapped tightly around William's head, chest-to-chest, legs spread wide to form a triangular base; Smith penned William's shoulders to the ground. One of the men in the group of spectators fell to his knees and slapping the ground, "One, two, three!" counted William out. The crowd erupted in a cheer, clapping loudly—the confidence in their leader confirmed once more.

Smith rolled off William. The exhausted men lay on their backs spread-eagle, side-by-side, their chest heaving to recoup the oxygen lost. Finally, after catching his breath, William rolled to his feet, offered his hand to Smith, and pulled the Prophet to his feet. The men shook hands and then embraced, much to the approval of the crowd.

"You're one devil of a wrestler, Brother," panted Smith. "The best I ever beat."

"There's no shame in losing to you," replied William.

"Bet you could beat him at pullin' sticks too," shouted one of the spectators. Smith was also the champion at this pioneer game where two men sat facing the other, feet together, grasping a stick between them. The man pulling the other off the ground won.

"No, no, not today. One battle is enough. Emma," Smith called to his wife who was standing in the doorway watching the whole affair, "how about some lemonade for our brave warrior." Emma pursed her lips and shook her head as she turned to do as her husband asked. Why he got so much joy out of displaying his wrestling prowess was beyond her. It didn't seem to her that the leader of a religious movement should grapple in the dirt like a common stable hand.

"I thought sure you had him," James said under his breath as he and William walked away from the dispersing, murmuring crowd.

"Well, he is very good, little brother. Besides, do you really think it would be wise to beat the Prophet himself at his own game?" James didn't pursued the subject but often wondered thereafter if that meant William could have won the match and didn't.

CHAPTER 10

It was clear and warm June day. William was tending his grapevines in the rear of the house when he heard a horse coming at a full gallop. The rider, a fellow named Stephen Markham, shouted at William as he sped by on a horse lathered from a hard ride.

"God help us," he shrieked wildly, "Brother Joseph has been kidnapped by a band of Pukes"—one of the names used to describe the Saint's tormentors. "They're headin' for Dixon!" Markham, in a Mormon version of Paul Revere's ride, continued onward, sounding the alarm.

William ran toward James's house. He burst through the front door and found James sitting on the floor repairing a chair. "Saddle up your horse. Brother Markham just rode by and said they've kidnapped Brother Joseph. And bring your weapons," he shouted back as he headed for his barn.

Within minutes, the brothers headed for Smith's homestead. There, the city council had assembled and declared what amounted to martial law throughout the city. As ordered, William summoned his company of the Legion with great dispatch. Two companies, William's included, went to intercept the Prophet and his captors.

Two Missouri sheriffs, at gunpoint, arrested an unguarded Joseph Smith on a preaching tour some distance north and east of Nauvoo near Dixon. They whisked Joseph away and locked him in an upstairs room in a local Dixon tavern. Their mission was to return Smith to Missouri. Joseph's nemesis, John Bennett, had convinced Governor Reynolds of Missouri to issue a writ on a four-year-old charge of treason. Once they had him in Missouri, their intention was to try Smith for the attempt on former Governor Lilburn Boggs's life. Smith knew that if they got him as far as Quincy, it would be but a short trip across the Mississippi River into Missouri. His would-be rescuers knew this as well and, therefore, the Legion scurried to intercept them at a place in between called Monmouth.

It was here, in Monmouth, that the Legion contingent of about one hundred and forty armed men surrounded the small group holding Joseph just after they had crossed the Fox River. The ride from Nauvoo had been so furious that men's horses were near collapse, but they had rescued their Prophet. Whig Party politician and criminal lawyer, Cyrus Walker—for a healthy fee and other considerations—arranged to argue the case in Nauvoo rather than Quincy. Thus, did Joseph Smith elude the possibility of certain death, had he returned to Missouri.

The citizens of the City of Nauvoo were ecstatic. They saved their beloved Prophet from the hands of the ghoulishly, vindictive Missouri Pukes. William and James bragged that the Legion had proved its worth. Smith gave long, detailed speeches in the Grove describing his ordeal and all but challenged the States of Illinois and Missouri to recognize Nauvoo as a state unto itself. Though they averted a disaster, the signs for the Saints, and particularly Joseph Smith, were not encouraging. To a critical Amanda, Smith was getting too big for his britches. Her observation was not too far off as Joseph was becoming drunk with his own perceived political potential. In the process, he made a series of political blunders that squandered whatever advantages he had within Illinois and set the stage for chaotic retribution in the future.

During the Fourth of July celebration, the weather was hot but bearable, and a great many people from all around the city came to enjoy the one holiday the Mormons liked best. Denied basic freedoms repeatedly, it is remarkable that the Saints were patriotic at all. Strangely, despite all that had happened, these people were proud and thankful to be Americans, especially those so recently arrived from other countries. The recent deliverance of the beloved Prophet from the hands of their enemies added meaning to their celebration this year.

Like many others, the Westons assembled near the riverside for a picnic after the speeches and prayers concluded in the Grove. Joseph Smith had been particularly eloquent that day and everyone was in the best of moods. Ominous signs abounded outside their world, but for the moment, all that was forgotten and like the rest of the people of Nauvoo, James and William and their families settled down for a well-earned holiday. The air was cool and refreshing next to the water. Recent rains had filled the river to near capacity—the rushing water still carried parts of trees and other debris from up north. It was not a day to go swimming.

Amanda was getting used to having William's dual family at various events. She did not like it but accepted what she could not change. Mary Ellen, William's second wife, wasn't the brightest thing in the universe, but she was pleasant and kind and did her best not to cause friction within the Weston clan. She, like Ruth, was pregnant. Both were expecting within a couple of months of each other—Mary Ellen in October and Ruth in December. To Amanda, this situation was mind numbing, but no one else seemed to have a problem with it so who was she to raise a ruckus. It wasn't any skin off her nose or money out of her pocket, she kept telling herself. Her family unit was intact. William and Ruth had diminished considerably in her eyes, but she saw no reason to dislike innocent Mary Ellen

"Spread the blanket out here, James," Amanda said, "the grass is thick, and the tree will shade us a bit." James smoothed out the edges of the blanket. A mild breeze defeated his attempt to be neat by puffing the blanket, first at one end then the other. He put the picnic basket on one edge and a nearby rock on the other; that solved his problem.

"Jake, get off of there," James commanded, as he pushed the big dog out of the way. Jake always thought he should be in the middle of everything that was going on. The trouble was, the big dog took up too much room and left little for the rest of the family. In addition, if you let him too close to the food, he would to snap up a bite or two before anyone knew it. Sluggishly he dragged his body off the blanket, tail end last, and sprawled out in the shade of the tree, his head on the ground between his front paws, his sad eyes looking up from one person to another seeking some form of pity. This was Jake's way of pouting.

"Come on, Jake. Here, boy." Jeremy patted his knees. Jake instantly did as his young friend and master asked, jumping up, and lumbering toward Jeremy, just about knocking him over in the process. Jeremy tussled with the big head and Jake rewarded him with a sloppy kiss from his pliable tongue. Like a child, Jake needed constant attention and approbation.

William and his family spread their blankets beside Amanda's and soon an abundance of food covered all. There were many other families all around going through the same routine. Children squealed at play, grownups laughed, conversations buzzed, dogs barked and ran after one another, a musical group played in the distance—the sounds of celebration were everywhere. There was much camaraderie and fellowship among the Saints while they enjoyed a day off from the normal hardships of everyday life. This was truly a fine display of communal living in the midst of compatible people.

All of a sudden, a woman's terrified wail hushed the assemblage. "Oh, my baby, my baby!" she screamed, pointing to the water. All eyes searched the river where a small child, caught in the rushing water, bobbed, and floated downstream at an alarming rate. Men jumped up and started running down the bank trying to anticipate where the child might go farther downstream. A woman shouted, "Oh, my God!" Another cried, "Somebody do something!" There was a crescendo of screams and shouts that filled the air as various individuals became aware of what was happening. Repeated attempts by men to enter the water and swim to the child failed. The futility of their efforts was maddening.

Almost unnoticed at first, and then knocking over a few men in the process, the big body of Jake dove, front paws first, into the water. He began to paddle furiously downstream toward the child, gaining with every powerful stroke. Almost lost from sight, as he and the child bobbed up and down in the turbulent, foaming water, some of the taller men that caught a glimpse of the attempted rescue started cheering, "Come on, Jake you can do it! Go, Jake, go!" Jeremy, who was almost beside himself, led the pack of men down the bank as they ran abreast of Jake. "Do it, Jake, do it!" he screamed.

"He's got her," shouted a boy standing on the branch of a tree. "He's got her!"

Jake had somehow managed to reach the little girl and his big mouth had gently but firmly grasped the clothing around the nape of the child's neck. He then began frantically churning his way cross-stream toward the shore. Painstakingly slow, he pushed and pulled the child to the riverbank and then dragged her to safety on dry land, nearly a quarter of a mile downstream from where he had entered the water. The dog was so exhausted from his efforts; he plopped down as if he had no bones in his body and panted heavily, his big tongue lying out of the side of his mouth. Amazingly, the three-year-old child was unhurt and sat upright, spitting out water between gasps of crying.

Jeremy and the rest of the men that had been trailing along the bank came rushing toward the child and the dog. One man picked up the little girl and examined her for injuries. To his astonishment, he found none. Jeremy fell on Jake crying and hugging his heroic friend. The rapidly growing circle of people that surrounded Jake cheered his unbelievable achievement. Having caught his second wind, Jake stood up and shook from head to toe, splattering everyone around in a sheath of water. No one complained, but, instead, laughed and danced about as they all tried to pat and hug the tired but happy animal. Bursting through the crowd with her child in her arms was the formerly frantic mother, now filled with happiness and gratitude. She took Jake's big face between her hands and gave his black, wet nose a lingering kiss. The crowd cheered its approval.

The news of the rescue went through the city like a wildfire. There was little doubt that Jake was a hero. His brave action erased all past grievances—like when he had chased someone's cat or chicken, or fought with someone else's dog. Jake now could do no wrong. The main newspaper, *The Neighbor*, gave his heroic rescue considerable space. A week after the popular feat, during an exceptional ceremony at the Grove, Joseph Smith himself extolled the virtues of this magnificent animal and presented him with a cast bronze medal made in Jonathan Browning's gun shop. Inscribed on one side was the single word, "Jake," and on the other, "Hero." Thereafter, Jake proudly wore this medallion, affixed to a beautiful leather collar, around his neck. The Weston's shed tears of pride and joy. Jeremy, of course, had perpetual status as the owner of such a brave and famous animal. Much to the chagrin of his owners, Jake occasionally resorted to his old ways of chasing a chicken or two, treeing a few cats and, always, defending his honor in the circle of dogs that inhabited the city. People didn't seem to mind as much as before. There was little doubt—Jake was the top dog in Nauvoo.

The children were in bed. It had been a long day, and both Amanda and James showed the strain from the arduous fall harvest season. James heated a pan of apple juice on the stove and when it reached the right temperature, poured it into two cups. He brought one cup to a weary Amanda who sat with her elbows on the table, her head held between each hand.

"Oh, thank you dear," she said with surprise, as he set the cup in front of her. She looked into his face searching. Something's up, her woman's intuition thought. Men are so stupid. They can't seem to realize that the slightest variation in routine causes all women to sense trouble. James might ask Amanda to get him some juice but, unless she was sick in bed, he would never fix it himself. James brought the other cup to the table, seating himself across from Amanda. They sat silently sipping their juice, enjoying the taste and aroma. Amanda looked at James as he studied the rim of his cup.

"Tastes good, doesn't it?"

"Yes, very good," she replied.

"Fall seems to be coming earlier this year."

"Think so?" There was more silence.

"You know, I'm really glad we came to Nauvoo, Amanda. It's not just being here but being a part of the great movement that is taking place. Even though I know you've had some reservations from time to time, don't you feel we made the right decision to come here?"

"James, I'm at peace with our decision."

"I hope you are as comfortable as I am with the faith and all it stands for," James continued.

"You know I can't be as intense about it as you are, but I find I can live within the teachings without conflict for the most part," she parried, still wondering where all this was going.

"William says being sealed to Mary Ellen is working out well in their family."

"The answer is no," Amanda came back bluntly, with a deadpan face.

"No? No what?" James said defensively.

"No, no other woman in this marriage is what." By now, her voice was well above the conversational level of a few moments ago. "If you think I'm going to share you with any other woman, you're crazy. I don't give a damn if Joseph Smith and all the rest of the Saints in the world say it's all right to have fifty wives, it's not all right in this house." Her tone and demeanor left little doubt she meant what she said.

"All right, that really wasn't my point," James quibbled—deflated, and subdued.

"I'll go along with all this other stuff, because I have to, but not . . ."

"All right!" James shouted, standing as he pounded his fist on the table. "I said all right. Now leave it alone, woman." Seething, he turned away from Amanda and faced the hearth.

"Bring another woman in this house, an' I'll shoot her and you." Both startled parents turned and faced the voice. It was Jeremy standing at the foot of the stairs. There was an awkward moment of silence as everyone oriented themselves to the embarrassing situation.

James was the first to speak. "Son, there will be no other women in this house besides your mother. I give you my word." He then walked over to Amanda, put his arm around her and the two stood facing their upset son.

"Come here, Jeremy." Amanda stretched her arms out toward the boy. The chagrined parents engulfed him with embraces as he came forward. Amanda was very proud of her brave son. Plural marriage was never a subject of conversation again in the James and Amanda Weston household.

By the end of 1843 and the beginning of the next year, there was growing unrest in Nauvoo and in the surrounding communities. This restlessness had many causes, a lot of them due to the Prophet himself. For political expediency, Illinois's Governor Ford ignored the writs and other demands of Governor Reynolds to capture and return Joseph Smith to Missouri for a trial. The politicians in Illinois vied for the Mormon vote, as they knew it would be a substantial, unified vote. Despite their misgivings about the validity of the charters granted Nauvoo—and their desire to revoke them— they were reluctant to push the matter until after the upcoming elections.

Joseph properly assessed the situation and took full advantage the opportunities presented. Unfortunately, due to his perceived position of strength, he was blind to his weaknesses. His ego was beginning to cloud his thinking. As he charged ahead to consolidate personal gains—including even running for the President of the United States—the Gentiles began to amalgamate their fears with their hatreds, following the pattern that seemed to bedevil the Mormons wherever they settled. Experienced Mormons, who were so successful in building a beautiful city out of a vast wilderness in just a few short years, again began to worry and fret about their personal safety. William, James, and their families had never experienced these feelings before. Even though they knew the goal was eventually to abandon their homes in Nauvoo for the Promised Land, they worried that they might have to leave sooner than planned, and under duress.

With thoughts of grandeur and power virtually consuming Joseph Smith in early 1844, he, nonetheless, could not ignore the consequences of his actions, especially that of polygamy. He knew that some day he and his people would have to leave the United States. In anticipation of this reality, he sent out secret missions to explore routes westward of the Missouri River. Meanwhile, the rhetoric of the media, especially the newspaper, *Warsaw Message*, openly called for the exile and or extermination of the Mormons—every man, woman, and child. The growing animosity of the non-Mormon population surrounding Nauvoo forced the Saints into a siege mentality. Typical for the Mormons, this only steeled their resolve and the synergy of their collective strengths made them feel more secure than they had a right to be. Amanda could but shake her head and worry—worry over where this collective delusion would lead and how it would affect her family.

All of this illusion was a tribute to Joseph's remarkable personality.

Somehow, he was able to cope with the pressures of running an evolving religion and an expanding city. In a maelstrom of swirling hatred, he tweaked local, state, and even national politicians to gain favorable decisions regarding his flock. Joseph always went for the brass ring. For example, he once proposed that Nauvoo should become a completely independent federal territory. He recommended the Nauvoo Legion's incorporation into the United States Army and that he, the Mayor of Nauvoo, have the power to call out the troops whenever needed. All these far-fetched schemes merely nettled the political power structure and gave fodder to the Mormon haters.

CHAPTER 11

The January wind outside was ferocious and chilling, forcing the light snow to spin and swirl, with no chance to accumulate. Inside William's home, it was comfortable and warm, especially with the combined body heat of eleven adults and their assortment of children that had gathered socially for a winter discussion, dinner, and a prayer session. Besides the Weston families, three other neighborhood households attended. The children played games upstairs. The men sat around the living room in deep discussion, drinking hot apple cider. The women scurried about from the dining room to the kitchen and back, clearing away the remains of the large supper all had enjoyed and, all the while, keeping up a constant banter about nothing of importance.

"It's all well an' good ta keep sayin' everythin's awright, Brother William, but there's a lot a strange things goin' on makin' me nervous," said Jeffery Payne, the neighbor two houses down. Old Jeffery had reasons to be nervous. He and his wife, Sarah, had been with Joseph Smith and his Church since 1836 in Kirtland, Ohio. They had earlier suffered ignominious expulsions from Kirtland in 1838 and then from Far West, Missouri in 1839. Jeffery was not high in rank in the Church and privy to their decision-making process, but he and Sarah knew well the signs of danger that faced the Saints.

"Like what, Brother Payne?" asked William; he was considered the senior member of the group and had led them all in prayer before the meal and reading from *The Book of Mormon* afterwards. He was the highest-ranking member of the Church at the meeting and with almost rabbinical-like status, expected to interpret what was going on within the Church to the others.

"Well, like we're gittin' ready ta move God knows where west an' Brother Joseph's involvin' his self in all kinds a political shenanigans right here in Illinois. An', what's all this stuff about him runnin' ta become president a the United States?" Jeffery didn't say it but he knew that the more Smith aggrandized himself to the world, the bigger the target he and his followers became.

Just then, Amanda came into the dining room to collect some of the remaining dishes. She heard the question Jeffery posed and stopped to hear William's response.

"There's a big picture here that I don't have all the facts on," replied William, "but I'll tell you what I do know. Yes, Brother Joseph and the Council of Fifty are looking for a suitable place for our people to call their final home— a land of promise. I know they have sent people to investigate places as far away as Oregon and Texas. Nothing's been decided on yet."

William shifted in his chair and inserted a long dramatic pause as he sipped from his cider cup. "But, we must think about the here and now at the same time. We have great political power here in Nauvoo and Brother Smith is trying to use that power to gain respect for our people. There are many forces of evil surrounding us and only if we are strong, respected ... and yes, feared, will we survive unmolested until we pick a day of our own choosing to leave."

"Seems to me that running for president, when he stands no chance of winning, just aggravates the situation, and gives those who hate us all the more reason to do so."

The men all turned toward Amanda with looks on their faces ranging from questioning to shock. Amanda knew she was defying protocol by interjecting herself into the conversation of the men without invitation. She stood a little taller, raised her chin in a slight show of defiance while her steady gaze went from one face to the other in response to the stunned silence of the men. James winced—he would never understand her defiant attitude. He admired her strength but got tired of her constant challenges concerning matters of the Church.

"Amanda," James said with more than a hint of exasperation, "We're trying to have a serious discussion here, if you don't mind."

"Does that mean women can't have a serious conversation? Seems to me that the women have as much right to discuss what's happening and what's going to happen as the men do," she retorted without hesitation. "We're all in this together, aren't we?" Heads turned back and all eyes shifted to William.

"Sister Amanda does have a point, Brother James," interjected William. "Sister Amanda, why don't you invite the other ladies in? Don't see any harm in getting their viewpoints as well." He nodded his head in the direction of the kitchen, in a subtle command.

Without hesitation, Amanda went into the kitchen and began to gather up the women. Some came through the doorway wiping their hands on their aprons, some smoothed out their dresses, while others pushed strands of hair into place. All, but Amanda, were hesitant, nervous, and somewhat bewildered, not certain why they were joining the men. Nothing so unnerves disciplined groups of people as changing the routine.

Each man rose and let his wife sit in his place as William, always the leader, strode to a commanding position with the room. "Sister Amanda has suggested that the women join us in a discussion regarding what is happening these days in our community and, maybe more importantly, what will happen in the future." Then, purposely putting Amanda on the spot, he said, "Sister Amanda, was there anything in particular you wanted to talk about?"

Without hesitation, Amanda answered. "Brother Joseph is a good and amazing man; a man to be loved and a loving man but, many of us follow him too blindly. For though he may be a prophet, he is still a man—good but not perfect. It is because he is not perfect and allows imperfection around him that makes him so endearing; so human and so real."

"Sister Amanda," William said, "what you have said is true—maybe a little harsh—but what is your point?"

"Well, I have a number of points. One is that our religion is not only a belief; it is a way of life. Most people in this country believe in the separation of church and state; we Mormons believe they are one and the same. This makes many of our neighbors uneasy and gives those who don't know us reason to criticize us."

"But that is also one of our strengths. We must make the non-believers see that we have power and will not be abused as in the past," James interjected.

"Don't you mean, as Brother William said, fear us?" retorted Amanda.

"If that must be—so be it," said Tom Wilson, another member of the group.

"You're right, Brother Wilson, so be it," agreed Jeffery Payne. Jeffery seemed to be losing some of the uneasiness he had expressed earlier.

"Yes, but we'll pay a price for that attitude in the future. There are many more of them than there are of us and time is on their side," Amanda came back.

"Yes, yes, that may be true," interrupted William in a somewhat condescending manner, "but the Bible is replete with stories of the followers of God who, though small in number, defeat hordes of godless enemies. What other point did you have in mind, Amanda?" This question was actually a statement and closed the subject of church and state.

Amanda knew she was trying the patience of the men and shocking the women, who kept issuing forth small gasps while covering their mouths with their hands all during the exchange of views. She desperately wanted to bring up the subject of polygamy, but knew that was taboo and might just cause a riot. Amanda could have stood there forever outlining her concerns, but she decided it best to bring up only one more point.

"Well, now that you ask, one thing we should know that really hurts us is our self-righteous, holier-than-thou attitude toward everyone outside our faith."

"Sister Amanda!" Ruth was indignant, her eyes radiating disgust. "How could you possibly say such a thing?" Her sister-in-law's brazen, irreverent attitude embarrassed the ultra-religious Ruth.

"Because it's true," retorted Amanda. "We know we are the chosen people, but do we have to flaunt it to the detriment of our relations with people who mean us no harm, as well as those who do? We make people feel inferior. We are successful in our endeavors—we know it, and we show it. People envy much of what we do but our arrogance makes them hate us in the process. It destroys all the good we do. I see and feel it all around us."

It was then that Sarah Payne spoke up. "Sister Amanda, eventually ya just gotta have faith. I've folla'd Brother Smith clear from Kirtland an' I've seen the worst the Gentiles have ta offer. As our Prophet says, 'It's God's way a testing us ta see if we're worthy.' Yep, I've been with Brother Smith most everwhar he's been an' I'm a gonna folla him ta hell an' back if needed ta save my soul."

"Amen," the group murmured collectively. Then a smoldering hush fell over the group. All but the blind fanatics knew that some of what Amanda said was true. However, that was not an argument one could win with these people. Their leader had indoctrinated them well, and they believed to the bone in what he preached.

Breaking the quiet that had fallen over the group, William spoke. "Was there anything else, Sister Amanda?" he asked. By the tone, it was more of a command to quit than a question.

"No," Amanda said quietly. "Thank you for letting me state my views."

"You're more than welcome. Does anyone else have anything to add?" Eyes darted around the room but no one had a differing view, or was brave enough to bring it up.

Then William said, "It may be appropriate to review some of the thirteen articles of faith that apply in this case." William had memorized the principles that had become the functional basis of the Mormon doctrine. "Sister Amanda, although we may not act accordingly all the time, we believe the following things: We claim the privilege of worshiping Almighty God according to the dictates of our conscience, and allow all men the same privilege, let them worship how, where, or what they may. And we believe in being honest, true, chaste, benevolent, virtuous, and in doing good to all men; indeed we may say that we follow the admonition of Paul, 'We believe all things, we hope all things, we have endured many things, and we hope to be able to endure all things. If there is anything virtuous, lovely, or of good report, or praiseworthy, we seek after these things.' "

"Amen an' a-men," intoned the group. "Well said, Brother William."

Of course, they'd all heard that litany before. To the believers, it was welcome reinforcement. To Amanda, it was just a repetitious and often ignored doctrine.

"Well, it's late and time to head for home," William concluded. "Thank you all for coming, and may God bless each and every one of you."

The unusual conversation had taken its toll on the assembled guests. The adults gathered and bundled up the children, bowed heads as they shook hands all around, and there was a collective mummer of "Thank you," and "Goodbye," as the group slowly broke up and went out the front door. Amanda purposely stayed off to one side. With a variety of blank and quizzical expressions, the adults nodded to her as they departed. Ruth smiled broadly at the guests leaving and then turned toward the kitchen, busying herself along the way. She glared at Amanda as she went by, pursing her lips and shaking her head in disgust. Interestingly, William's second wife, Mary Ellen, smiled at Amanda and gave her a quick wink. There may be some life in that girl after all, thought Amanda.

William Law had been Joseph Smith's Second Counselor for more than two years. In that position, he had great influence and was a steadfast and honest contributor to the affluence and growth of Nauvoo. A Canadian convert of considerable wealth, he had come to Nauvoo and invested heavily in real estate. Slowly, he began to question the wisdom of much of Smith's economic decision-making, especially concerning the building of the Temple and the Nauvoo House, a large hotel project favored by the Prophet. Over time, what began as an economic disagreement, developed into a vicious and bitter confrontation that shook the foundations of the Church. Law quietly smoldered in private about the actions of his "fallen Prophet," especially concerning the growing practice of polygamy. Such affairs were like shadows in the night in Nauvoo. James caught wind of this underground conflict on an aside with one of the temple construction workers. In hushed tones, he had discussed the implications with William. They concluded that it was troubling and could become messy, but certainly out of their realm.

It wasn't until Joseph boldly hinted of sealing with Law's wife that the quarrel surfaced to full light. Caustic confrontations finally led to Law leaving the Church and, with many other influential citizens opposed to polygamy, began openly to propose reform. Their views and concerns, published in a newly established newspaper, *The Nauvoo Expositor*, on June 7, 1844, gave a restrained but nonetheless shocking account.

Smith was furious and realized the seriousness of the situation. The citizens of Nauvoo were stunned. Exposed in print was the obscure world of multiple wives. Those who had practiced polygamy feared the wrath of the outside world. Those who had not participated began to realize that the subversive gossip could well be true. All awaited the response from Smith. His answer was to repudiate such practices and, backed by the city council, he instructed the city marshal to take care of the situation. The marshal and his men then broke into the printing shop, threw the press into street (smashing it with a sledgehammer), dumped the type into the street, and burned the undistributed copies of the newspaper.

Outside of Nauvoo, the word of his actions spread quickly and the reaction changed from anger to outrage. Furious crowds filled the streets of Carthage and Warsaw while mobs began to threaten isolated Mormon families, sending them fleeing to Nauvoo for protection. Inside Nauvoo, there was confusion, frustration, discussion, and, finally, the instinctive circling of the wagons of the true believers.

Chapter 12

It had been less than six months since Amanda's unprecedented display of rashness by interjecting herself into the men's group discussion at William's house. During that time, winter had changed to spring, her children seemed to have grown out of proportion to their age, and her brother-in-law, William, sealed to another wife, twenty-one-year-old Elizabeth Granger. Elizabeth was a true beauty with a full head of blonde hair, a shapely body, and a flirtatious and out-going personality. She was also one month pregnant when sealed to William. When born, Adam would take the Weston name, even though there was always a question if it was really William's child. Amanda saw nothing but trouble when she looked at this new addition.

Elizabeth's introduction into the growing William Weston clan—Mary Ellen and Ruth had their babies in October and December of last year respectively—sent Amanda into a fit of depression. How can Ruth just turn a blind eye to this travesty, she lamented to herself. When will it ever end? What William was doing violated everything she believed. That the rest of the outside world agreed with her viewpoint only made her more heavyhearted and apprehensive.

The Nauvoo Expositor she held in her hands did nothing to improve her depressed state. It confirmed what she had long suspected. If what she read were true, the Church was in even more serious trouble than she thought. John Bennett had written extensively about some of the same things, but his ranting and raving smacked of an exiled evil man with a bone to pick. William Law, on the other hand, was a respected and godly man. His exposé had credibility and the impact of a sledgehammer blow. Restrained rhetoric could not soften the accusations of polygamy, irresponsible financial maneuvering, violation of the separation of church and state, and much more.

James burst through the door in a highly agitated state. "I can't believe this is happening," he blurted out. "This simply cannot be happening." He paced back and forth, alternately running his hands through his hair and wringing his hands.

"What is it, James?" Amanda asked.

"I just came from a formation of the entire Legion. General Smith addressed us and told of the many lies and illegal activities of our enemies. He is preparing us to defend our right as American citizens to fight for our faith, our families, and our homes. To a man, we are solidly behind him. But, the cost could be great and soon. In the name of God, we shall persevere." He pounded his fist on the table. The intensity of his fervor startled Amanda.

James was usually not passionate. That was reserved for his brother. Amanda could see the zeal grow within him from one year to the next since joining the Mormon Church. He had definitely become a staunch supporter and believer and, like all the rest, the harder the anti-Mormon community pushed, the harder he resisted. Each side hardened their positions and allowed no room for compromise. To Amanda, the Mormons were on a collision course that was spiraling out of control.

Not being totally committed to the cause, Amanda could put herself in the shoes of the non-Mormon community that surrounded Nauvoo. The shear number of the Mormons genuinely frightened these people. In their view, the political, economic, and social juggernaut of blindly led fanatics headed by the hated despot, Joseph Smith terrified them. Living among her people, she could see that much of what frightened the Gentiles was unwarranted. Amanda had labored over the idea of approaching James about taking their little family out of this growing madness and moving back to Tennessee. That, she concluded, was nothing but a dream. With each growing crises, James became more entrenched in his belief that Joseph Smith and the Mormon Church were the unimpeachable source of their salvation. What could she do?

June of 1844 was a crucial turning point for Joseph Smith. The destruction of *The Expositor* presses was the catalyst for a backlash that even Joseph had not fully anticipated. Governor Ford demanded that Joseph and anyone else implicated in the destruction of *The Expositor* come to Carthage to face trial. Joseph knew submitting to that meant certain death.

Fearing immediate arrest, Joseph, and his brother Hyrum, fled to Iowa in the dead of night across a swollen, dangerous Mississippi River. This flight to Iowa was not a solution, as there he was subject to extradition to Missouri for the old charge of treason. Also, he began to feel he had abandoned his flock. Emma and others pleaded for Joseph to return. Governor Ford assured him that he would receive a fair and legal trail, as well as protection. Urged on by Hyrum, Joseph agreed to return and stand trial, even if he felt death was a certainty.

Joseph was beginning to realize his well-organized community was falling apart. His absence had made them leaderless. Even the Legion was in disarray. Some wanted to fight to defend the city while others wanted to disband as ordered by Governor Ford. Joseph elected to disband. Secretly, though, he had all personal arms stashed in a readily available warehouse—just in case.

On June 24, Joseph, Hyrum, and others who were to stand trial with them started for Carthage. Outside of Nauvoo, a company of militia from McDonough County escorted them into Carthage. Angry troops from Carthage and Warsaw waited for them. There was a preliminary hearing, resulting in deferred charges and release on bail for all men with the exception of Joseph and Hyrum Smith. A flimsy charge of treason unceremoniously landed the brothers in jail.

William was beside himself. Giving up was just not in his makeup.

He wanted to fight, as did James. James was smoldering as he stood in the kitchen with Amanda. Amanda was frantic.

"James, we cannot possibly win under these circumstances. Surely, God has abandoned Brother Joseph and the wrath of our enemies is ready to spill into our streets. Why in God's name can't we take the children and leave?" she pleaded.

"It's true, things don't look good, Amanda. But the Saints have been through this before and somehow have survived. William says this is the time of testing to see if we are worthy."

"Worthy? Worthy of what?" Amanda's voice strained to the point she was barely able to speak the words. "William does not know everything and blindly follows whatever the Church leaders say. I don't want to prove my loyalty to God by spilling the blood of my children, do you hear?"

"You know I won't let anything happen to the children, Amanda. As you know, our strength comes in numbers and in sticking together. We cannot survive if we scatter to the winds. We have to put our trust in God. We've come so far, surely, you don't want to abandon all that we have worked for, do you?

"James, I have gone far beyond what I consider prudent. Try as I may, I cannot accept everything at face value. There are too many holes. At this point, I have only one thing that I care about and that is you and the future of my children." Amanda's eyes filled with tears.

"I hear you, Amanda, and I share your concern. I promise not to let anything harm you or our children," said James. He meant every word he said but, nonetheless, had a sense of overwhelming dread. He could see that there carefully planned world was spinning out of control. The pressure in his chest and head was incredible.

It was June 27, 1844 and at the jail in Carthage, Illinois, the local militia murdered the Prophet Joseph Smith and his brother, Hyrum. The news hit Nauvoo like a thunderclap. Those who had been with Joseph since the early days and had experienced every type of prejudice and hardship despaired at the loss of their leader. Fear, disorganization, and a paralysis-like pall overshadowed calls for Legion action to revenge their terrible loss.

The city clearly was in shock and when, on the next day, the wagons bearing the bodies of Joseph and Hyrum returned to Nauvoo, a procession of the Legion and some ten thousand mournful citizens followed in the wake. Emma Smith was beside herself with grief as she saw the body of Joseph in the coffin on view in the Nauvoo mansion.

On the next day, June 29, the mansion opened to the public and some twenty thousand Saints paid homage by filing past their fallen leader. Amanda came with James late in the day. The gory appearance of the Prophet, whose many wounds oozed fluid that seeped onto the floor, distressed her. A mixture of tar, sugar, and vinegar kept heated on the stove served to alleviate the increasing stench from the decaying bodies. She could hardly wait to leave the room. As she departed the building, she saw Emma sitting on a chair under a tree surrounded by a small group of mourners. She felt compelled to speak with her.

Amanda worked her way through the small circle and approached a totally distraught, tired, and tight-lipped Emma, who was also pregnant with the last of Joseph's progeny. Emma looked up as Amanda came near, forcing a strained smile of recognition.

"Sister Emma, I am so sorry," whispered Amanda as she extended her hand.

Emma accepted her hand limply. "Thank you, my dear. These are dire days and trying times for all."

"I know you have much support from many people but if there is anything I can do for you, please let me know," Amanda said with sincerity.

"You're too kind. We'll talk again under better circumstances, Amanda."

"Yes, I hope so," nodded Amanda. "Goodbye for now," she concluded as she turned and walked through the circle of questioning faces.

James was standing on the periphery watching all this and, as always, was amazed at Amanda's actions. As far as he knew, Amanda was not exactly included in the social status recognized by Emma Smith. He knew of Amanda's previous visit to the Smith's, but he hadn't discussed it with her, and it was so long ago he had put it out of his mind.

Many Saints attended the ceremony at the gravesite the next day and watched the caskets descend into the graves. For those who hoped for the end of the Mormon Church after the death of the hated Joseph Smith, they couldn't have been more wrong. His martyrdom only strengthened the resolve of followers like William, James, and Ruth.

Though there were many important defectors after Joseph's death, like Sidney Rigdon, one man, Brigham Young, gradually gained control. Young was born in Whitingham, Vermont in 1801. Though he was a Methodist, the *Book of Mormon* impressed him and he joined the new church in 1832. He rapidly progressed in the church and by 1835, became a member of the main governing body in the hierarchy, the Quorum of the Twelve Apostles. Returning from a successful mission in England, Young helped Joseph Smith establish Nauvoo.

After much politicking, Young became the president of the Quorum and the interim leader of the Church. The majority of the Mormons accepted this man and followed him in the years to come. Nevertheless, wresting control of the Church was not easy. Over the succeeding months, Young was able to tame the majority of all competitors with the exception of one—Emma Smith.

The beauty of October came to Nauvoo oblivious to the turmoil that consumed the city's human inhabitants. The radiant colors of crops, trees, and other flora seemed brighter than usual. Perhaps it was nature's way of counterbalancing the madness of humankind. The antagonism between Brigham Young and Emma had reached epic proportions.

Amanda knocked softly on the Smith family door. Inquisitive onlookers stared at her. She tried her best to ignore their quizzical looks, some bordering on hostility. After all this time, she had again received a note from Emma inviting her to visit. Lured by curiosity, Amanda had accepted. She made no mention of this to James. Even though he loved her dearly, he did not always appreciate her views and she was becoming an embarrassment to him. She was somewhat persona non grata among folks staunchly committed to Brigham Young, including the Weston brothers.

The door opened. "Amanda, dear, how nice of you to come." Emma was genuinely pleased to see a friend. Her face was tired and drained.

"Thank you for inviting me. It has been so long," answered Amanda.

"I know, I know. There has been so much going on." Emma escorted Amanda through the door, pausing to look out over the people gathered at her fence line and giving them a look of disgust as she shook her downcast head. "I have some wonderful cider. Would you prefer that over tea?"

"Yes, that would be nice." Amanda sat in the same spot on the couch she had occupied those many months ago. So much had happened since her last visit that she felt as if it were the first time.

Emma came in with a pitcher of cider and two glasses. First, she filled Amanda's glass and then hers. She then positioned herself as best could with her protruding stomach. "Nice thing is, you always have a built-in table when you reach this size," she laughed weakly, placing the glass atop her stomach.

"Goodness, Emma, how can you have a sense of humor with all that's going on?" asked Amanda.

"Truth is, I don't," Emma replied, "but some things go on no matter what and having Joseph's last child is at the head of that list now. I take whatever comes along. But, tell me Amanda, how are you surviving with all this nonsense? I remember you as being rather noncommittal the last time we met. Surely, what has happened has caused you an even greater concern?"

"I've always been truthful with you, Emma, and I confess, given the opportunity, I would pack up my children and head back to Tennessee tomorrow. Course, that's easier said than done, and I'm afraid I'm saddled with seeing it through."

"And your husband, has he decided to follow Brigham Young as most of the people have?"

"Yes, I guess he has. He and his brother are heavily involved in deciding what to do and how to defend Nauvoo from all the evil doers."

"Well, there are certainly plenty of people that would do us harm," agreed Emma. "In my case, I have to worry about them *and* Brigham Young. I never have liked that fellow and believe he is trying to steal the Church away from the true followers."

"I've heard stories of some of your differences, Emma, but they're just that, stories. I am uninformed of what you disagree about."

Emma gave a false, nervous laugh. "What don't we disagree about," she said. "First and foremost is the polygamy business. Nothing infuriates the Gentiles more than that issue and I must say, I don't blame them. Joseph would be appalled at the degree it is practiced. Now, they're trying to blame my dear husband for its hold on the leaders. He was true to me to end, I know it," she said emphatically.

"You may remember that we agree totally on that subject," soothed Amanda. For the life of her, she couldn't understand why Emma was so blind to the truth. Joseph Smith was a polygamist, plain and simple; no matter how often Emma denied it.

Then, as if opening one subject was an excuse to open all grievances, Emma began down her list. "Joseph and I worked hard for many years to build an estate. Now Young claims that most of it belongs to the Church. Everything is in turmoil and dispute and my family and I hardly have enough to get by. It isn't fair or just."

"I'm sorry to hear all this, Emma. I had no idea that was going on," Amanda said sympathetically.

"Oh, that's just the beginning. We also have a major battle going on over all of Joseph's papers, some of them of divine and sacred origin. I simply will not let them steal everything holy that Joseph developed through years of work and revelation." Why she was unloading all this on Amanda, who was not a close friend, was a mystery. Maybe because she needed to talk about it with someone and discovered after the last meeting, Amanda was a trustworthy confidant. "But," she continued, "I have them beat in one instance. They do not know where Joseph and Hyrum's bodies are buried, and it is upsetting them very much."

This was a shock to Amanda and her face showed it. Like everyone else, she believed them to be in the cemetery. She attended the ceremony with James. "I'm not sure I understand," she said. "I thought they were buried in the cemetery."

"No, of course you wouldn't understand, dear child. We wanted everyone to think they were buried there but, instead, we buried them secretly in the basement of the Nauvoo House. We were all concerned that angry outsiders would come and desecrate their bodies. To ensure that did not happen, I secretly had them buried elsewhere. This has not made Brigham Young and the rest of the Church hierarchy very happy. I don't care. Joseph belongs to me and our children, not to the masses. I trust this secret will remain so," she added.

"Of course," responded a reeling Amanda. First, she didn't understand why Emma was confiding all of this to her and second, although she knew there was friction and dissension between the Church leaders and Emma—everyone did—she had no concept of the extent or content.

"Emma, I had no idea all this was going on. How can you stand it? All of this must be terribly difficult for you while you are grieving for your lost husband, not to mention having his child."

"As I told you before, Amanda, being the wife of a Prophet of Joseph's stature is not easy. I know that Joseph would be terribly upset with what is going on at this time. He meant for his oldest son, Joseph, to be his successor. He's too young for that of course, but it was our intention that someday he should take his rightful position as head of the Church that his father founded. Is any of this being discussed by the members of the Church outside the top level?" asked Emma.

"My goodness, Emma, you are asking the wrong person. I have expressed my views openly too often and am not considered a part of the groups that discuss such things, including even my family at times."

"Yes, but surely you hear what's going on; you must know the local gossip." Emma was searching. What she wanted to know was what people on the street, outside her normal circle of confidants, were discussing and assuming.

"Well, yes, but I don't put much stock in gossip," countered Amanda, "so I don't pay attention."

"But what members of the Church believe is important and though it's often distorted, it usually gives one the pulse of what they want to believe. I know it may be an imposition, but is it possible for you to keep me advised of any major concerns and happenings going on within the city? Other people keep me informed from time to time but they all have some stake. I remember how objective you are, and trust your viewpoint. Is such a thing possible?" The words fell rapidly and nervously from Emma's mouth.

Amanda was speechless. Here was a woman of high position who she hardly knew asking her to spy for her. She had great empathy for her but Emma marched to the beat of a different drum, an almost fanatical drum from Amanda's point of view. Emma noted her hesitation.

"Well," said Amanda, drawing out the word, "I'm not sure I'm a reliable source for you. Of course, I have a vested interest too—my family. Everything I think about is shaped by the effect it will have on my family, especially the children."

"That's what makes your viewpoint so valuable, Amanda. Religious fervor aside, all Mormon women are driven by a concern for their families. Our women are the strength behind the Church; they are the backbone of our social movement."

"I understand what you're saying, Emma. I'm not sure what I can add, but if you think my observations will help defend us from our enemies, I will relay anything I believe appropriate." Amanda was not sure what that meant, exactly.

"Amanda, you're a dear person. We have many trying days ahead, and I pray that you and your family will be safe and realize the full and happy life that I know Joseph intended for all the Saints. And now, I've taken too much of your time." Emma wearily struggled to rise from her chair. Amanda jumped up, gently grabbing Emma's arm to assist her.

"Thank you, my dear."

"You're more than welcome. Don't see me to the door. I can show myself out," Amanda said reassuringly. "You take care of yourself and that baby now, ya hear?"

"I will, Amanda. God bless you and all your loved ones," replied Emma, as she smiled weakly and patted Amanda on the shoulder.

Amanda turned and left the house. Outside there were numerous people milling about the home. There seemed to be a disproportionate number of young men hanging around, as if they were on watch. They studied her carefully as she turned and walked down the street. An aura of tension gave her a slight chill. Soon, she was lost in her thoughts about her discussion with Emma. She was confused and not sure what she had committed herself to, if anything. She did not plan to discuss this meeting with James, of course.

As it turned out, she didn't have to. Her visit was grist for the rumor mill, and it wasn't long before Ruth conveyed an exaggerated version of the meeting to William. He just shook his head at the news.

"James," said William, "Amanda is at it again. She made a two-hour visit to Sister Emma Smith and inside sources say that she is committed to the Smith's fight against Brother Brigham. This is not in the best interest of our families. Folks are talking a lot."

"Damn, I just don't know what to do with that woman. Every time I turn around, it's something else. I'll speak to her, William," James said in reply.

"Make sure she understands that going against Brother Brigham and the Quorum is not wise. She doesn't have to believe in Mormonism, but she does have to keep her mouth shut and if nothing else, keep a low profile. People are just not going to stand for this in our hour of need. Unity is what we need, not dissension. We have plenty of enemies from without—we don't need any from within." William spoke harshly and had fire in his eyes. The brothers had never talked to each other like this before.

"I understand, brother. I'll take care of it." James stomped out of the room in search of Amanda. He found her in the barn milking a cow.

"Amanda," he said in a raised and agitated voice, "we've got to talk."

"All right, James, what's on your mind," she said warily. She stopped milking and sat on the stool wiping her hands on her apron.

"It's all over town that you talked to Sister Emma Smith for over two hours, and that you have committed to stand with her against Brother Brigham in his fight to save the Church. Just who do you think you are and what do you think you are doing?" His voice was combative and accusatory. Amanda was shocked. They seldom argued or raised their voices to the point James had just done. His words reverberated off the barn walls.

"First, speak to me in a civilized tone or don't speak to me at all. I will not lower myself to engage in such stupidity."

"Stupidity? Who are you calling stupid after what you've done?" James came back.

Amanda took a deep breath and set her jaw. Her eyes stared vacantly at the barn wall for a second or more and then slowly came up to meet

James's livid stare. Calmly and quietly she said, "I am not calling you stupid. I'm calling what you said stupid—and wrong. Where you are getting your information I do not know, but it is wrong."

"William said it is, according to Ruth, common gossip around town."

"Ruth. I should have known," lamented Amanda.

"Well, did you or did you not visit Sister Emma?"

"I most assuredly did. It was at her invitation and hardly lasted half an hour, not two hours."

"And did you or did you not commit to Sister Emma against Brother Brigham?"

"I did not. We discussed the situation. Mostly, I listened to what she had to say. The poor woman has just lost her husband, is in a late-term pregnancy, and now is in a fight to keep her dignity. She needed someone to listen. I did that, no more, no less."

Amanda was puzzled. How did all this start? Surely, Emma had not revealed their discussion to anyone. Knowing how the rumor mill worked, someone in the crowd around the Smith house must have observed her visit and started the rumor. A half-hour visit grew each time someone told the story into two hours and the obvious conclusion of someone along the rumor path was that there was no way she could spend two hours with Emma without collusion.

"You're absolutely sure?" James countered; the fire had gone out of his voice.

"Have I ever lied to you, James—ever?"

"No."

"Then why would I start now? What is being said is untrue and unfair."

"Then are you committed to supporting Brother Brigham in his attempt to consolidate the Church and to lead us all out of here in one piece?" James queried.

"I give not one wit who runs this Church and will follow anyone who gets us out of here safely. However, neither you, nor anyone else, will bully me into accepting blindly everything Smith, Young, William, or God knows who else says. Is that understood?" Amanda was adamant.

"I understand. But what *you* have to understand is that this a very tight-knit community and what you say and do reflects on your family." James assumed the role of teacher now, not preacher.

"James, think about it. Has it ever been any different? Was it not the case back in Double Springs? Everybody there was as petty as could be. The only difference between Double Springs and Nauvoo is this obsession with a religion-driven, communal life style. Sometimes it is overbearing."

"Maybe so, but this is where we live now and whether you like the rules or not, you have to live by them."

"You're right. I will try not to embarrass the family. But keep that psalm-singing Ruth out of my face. She should have enough to do just trying to find time with her husband, considering she has two prettier and younger co-wives." Amanda knew that what she said was contemptible, petty, and unfair, but she couldn't help herself. It seemed to Amanda that Ruth was taking her hostility out on her sister-in-law, instead of her competition.

James ignored her comment. "All I ask is that you don't go out of your way to cause problems."

He turned and walked toward the house. The conversation was clearly over. He wasn't sure if he had made his point or not. Amanda was getting harder and harder to read. She was obviously troubled. Blinded by his own obsession, he could not see how much she was hurting. The naturally likeable, lighthearted Amanda was turning into a quarrelsome, troubled old woman at the early age of twenty-nine.

As it turned out, this was the last visit Amanda would make to Emma Smith's house. In fact, it was the last time she would meet with her at all. Besides giving birth to a child, Emma's constant quarrels with the Quorum and Brigham Young, and near isolation because of it, left her with little time for pleasantries. With all of the work preparing to leave Nauvoo, Amanda had given only Emma passing thoughts for over a year, and all during that time, discounted the many negative rumors that swirled whenever Emma's name came up. Besides, the men constantly stationed outside Emma's home, known as the Whistling and Whittling Brigade had become more hostile toward visitors. Emma was unwelcome for anyone following Brother Young.

Chapter 13

In January 1845, the Illinois Legislature revoked the Nauvoo charter and ordered the Legion to disband—they did not. June came and went. Joseph and Hyrum Smith had been dead for one year and their killers acquitted in May. Oddly, there was outward calm between the Saints and the Gentiles, and during this lull, the city seemed to prosper. However, underneath the surface, the old concerns that followed the Mormons wherever they went, were boiling and bubbling into a future of discontent. Mistakenly, many of the Mormons had a false sense of security believing that the mobbers were more frightened of the Saints than the Saints were of them.

"Don' look like they's movin' no whar ta me," said Myra Johnson, the shopkeeper on the fringe of town. "Did ya hear all that shoutin' an' hosannain' yesterdey comin' from that temple they's buildin'?"

She was talking to one of her friends and customers. Myra was not the only Gentile in Nauvoo who was wondering and concerned. Despite the Mormons' contention that Nauvoo was just a gathering place for the big move west, to the non-Mormon population in and around the city, it looked like they were digging in for the long haul. Why else would everything appear to be so permanent?

What particularly concerned the non-believers was the beehive of activity they saw surrounding the building of the temple on the mesa overlooking the town below. There were as many as three hundred men working on the structure at times. Besides, this was no small, temporary structure. The stone and timber building was a large edifice of obvious, enduring beauty.

"I know. My husband's getting' mighty edgy. He knows quite a few a them folks an' he sez ever' one of 'em gives a heap a money ta build that there temple. They's made ta give the Church at least one dime outta ever dollar they make, so he sez," chimed in her customer. "An' they's got hundreds a people workin' on that place ta boot," she added.

"Well, my George is downright havin' a fit," said Myra. "He an' others was talkin' the other night about that there Legion they got. Sez their charter been takin' away by the gover'ment, but they ain't stopped meetin' none an' ain't given up even one rifle like they's supposed ta. Sure is makin' ever'body wonder if these crazies is ever gonna leave, that's fer sure."

Only the Mormons knew their actions belied their true intentions. However, amidst all the frantic activity, even the Saints needed an occasional reminding.

"The Temple," explained William to the Westons gathered around a family prayer meeting, "will be the gathering place where our priests will give us the endowments that mean our salvation. Joseph Smith," he read from a pamphlet, "said, 'the main purpose in gathering the people of God, is to build unto the Lord a house wherein he could reveal to them the ordinances and glories of his Kingdom.' "

"And Brother Young added, 'If you do not help build the Temple ... if you do not help to build up Zion and the cause of God, you will not inherit the land of Zion. Be faithful or you will not be chosen, for the day of choosing is at the door.' " William gazed intensely into the eyes of his small audience, "And that's why we must do all we can to build the Temple. The sooner it's built, the sooner we can be saved and move on to the Promised Land."

"Amen," bellowed Ruth with clasped hands and glazed eyes pointing toward the heavens. Amanda said nothing. She looked into the eyes of her husband and saw total acceptance of what William said. Yet another layer of concern and doubt encased her kernel of disbelief.

Like the Westons, thousands of faithful in Nauvoo who yearned for the initiation that would complete their covenant with God, watched with great zeal as the Temple rose from the ground. They knew in their hearts that they would have their endowments before winter. The officials of the Church were actually ready to issue an official letter urging all Saints in the United States to sell their property, gather in Nauvoo to receive their endowments, and then join the great migration westward. Indeed, the Mormons intend to leave Nauvoo, but without the endowments, the migration would be nothing more than flight. With the endowments, they believed that the faithful could go a saved and covenanted people. If the Gentiles could have only understood and accepted this, it would have avoided a great deal of bloodshed and tragedy. Unfortunately, that was not to be.

The people living in and around Nauvoo, who were not Mormons, saw them as a fanatical cult. With the bad points usually exaggerated, the activities of this unique religious, cultural, and social experiment were the subject of many newspaper articles and raging gossip throughout the country. Contrary to the American cultural belief in a free and independent individual—especially in the West—the Mormons believed in an obedient group. For whatever reason, Joseph Smith promulgated his revelation on celestial marriages, and tried unsuccessfully to keep that doctrine secret. It was not a well-kept secret. The practice was an abomination to some powerful individuals within the Church—like William Law—and a cause of ridicule and concern for all non-believers.

From a political point of view, those outside the Church were fearful of the Mormon influence, as their numbers, growing daily, voted as a bloc in state and national elections. This despotic approach gave them a disproportionate and threatening influence that represented viewpoints that were for the benefit of the Mormons, but not necessarily the population as a whole. Because the Mormons banded and worked together, like a swarm of insects, they had built a large, beautiful, high-quality city almost overnight. This was the catalyst for unbridled envy of those living in and around Nauvoo. But, as Amanda had so correctly pointed out in her infamous comments before William's prayer group, the most infuriating and volatile problem the Gentiles who came in regular contact with Mormons had, was the haughty attitude they displayed; believing they alone were the chosen people of God.

All of these actions and beliefs, some hidden, some flaunted, fed mountains of rumors that fostered distrust, envy, fear, and a common feeling of ill will. Ultimately, misunderstanding creates fear and fear creates prejudice. In addition, as shown in the past, prejudice toward the Mormons nearly always deteriorated into a raging conflagration that consumed everything in its path. Even a believer like James could see that in many ways, these productive, well-intentioned, God-fearing, innovative people were their own worst enemy. Could see, that is, if he wanted to.

By September, the calm that prevailed began to unravel. Violence increased on both sides. The Nauvoo Legion countered every act of violence against Mormons with swift and ferocious reprisal. Raids and burnings on both sides became prevalent. The Mormon haters—the mobbers— had genuine and justifiable fear of the Legion's retribution.

William and James became increasingly active in the Legion. In one case, they were part of a troop that had to rescue about two hundred Saints from the city of Lima and bring them to Nauvoo for protection. Then, the conflict struck home for the two brothers.

Tom Johnson, the oldest son of Jeremiah, came galloping through town and arrived at William's house in a cloud of dust on his lathered, spent horse. The lad was frantic.

"Brother William, Brother James," he screamed as he dismounted his still moving horse.

William burst through the front door. "Tom, what's wrong?"

"Brother William," repeated the breathless young man, "Mobbers have hit us. Dad and Jeffery are holding them off but there's too many. Please, we gotta go to help 'em now," the frenzied sixteen-year-old Tom was screaming as he held back tears.

James heard the ruckus and came running from the barn in the rear. Jeremy, who had been working in the barn with his father, was at his side. A small crowd instantly began to gather. William put his arm around Tom's shoulder.

"Don't worry, Tom. We're going to help." He looked up and saw James. "James, round up whoever you can from the Legion and let's head out—now!"

James headed for the barn to saddle his horse. "Come along, Jeremy and saddle up a fresh horse for Tom." Jeremy and Tom followed James. As they passed by the front door, Amanda came out with a look of confusion. "James, what is it?"

"Mobbers," he said simply. Then he added, "My rifle and pistol—bring 'em to me in the barn." Amanda stood looking, first at James, and then the crowd assembling around William. She hesitated, trying to understand what was going on.

"*Now*, Amanda. It's our place," James emphasized, as he rounded the house and headed for the barn. Amanda immediately ran inside to do as she as told, making sure that she picked up a supply of ammunition as well.

Inside the barn, James quickly assembled the halter and saddle and began to make his favorite horse ready. Jeremy and Tom did the same for the other horse.

Within twenty minutes, a band of thirty Legionnaires assembled and headed out of town at a full gallop. Unhappily, the men of Nauvoo Legion had become accustomed to these hurried assemblies. Their weapons and horses were always at the ready. They were the Mormon Minutemen.

It took the men about twenty minutes to reach the farm; their horses were exhausted from the dash. By then, it was too late. James was the first to spot the smoke in the distance and knew instantly that it was not good. Acrid smoke began to assault the riders' nostrils. As the men rounded the bend and came upon the farm, they could clearly see the farmhouse, the barn, and some smaller adjoining buildings consumed in flames. Corn and wheat fields were ablaze, as well. The Weston brothers' hearts dropped. Chickens were scurrying frantically about between the dead carcasses of pigs, cows, and sheep—all filled with blood-oozing bullet holes. There was no one in sight and the men began to frantically search about for the Johnsons. Tom Johnson was in a panic and kept screaming repeatedly, "Dad, Mom, Jeff!"

Faintly, from the distant woods, Jeremiah's voice bellowed, "Over here, son." A collective sigh of relief came from the rescuers. Jeremiah and his wife and son came stumbling out of the woods. Both Jeremiah and Jeffery were wounded, Jeremiah in the shoulder and Jeffery in the arm. The beleaguered Johnsons were distraught and disoriented, but apparently safe. Some of the Legionnaires quickly rode to their side, while others scouted the outskirts to see if any mobbers were about.

Dismounting quickly, William and then James came rushing forward. Tom was first at his family's side, consoling his mother and hugging his brother.

"I'm sorry, Brother William," blubbered a weakened Jeremiah. "They were on us before we knew it. I think I shot a couple of them but there were too many; probably, thirty or so." He was near tears as he stood clutching his shoulder and surveying the devastation.

"Don't you bother none, Jeremiah," consoled William. "Are you all right?"

It was then that Jeremiah began to swoon and sank slowly to his knees. He had lost a lot of blood and was about to faint. Mary and James rushed to his side. They laid him down on the grass and began to examine his wound. Luckily, the bullet had passed through his shoulder without breaking the clavicle. The jagged wound was large and the blood flow great—especially out the exit wound in the back. James took off his jacket, rolled it, propped up Jeremiah's head, and slowly gave him sips of water from his canteen. One of the Legionnaires came forth with a first aid kit, stripped off Jeremiah's shirt and began to attend the wound. He then looked after Jeff's arm that, fortunately, had sustained only a flesh wound. A tight bandage took care of the damage.

Seeing both wounded men tended to and Mrs. Johnson calming down, William and James mounted their horses and began to survey the damage. The blackened brick fireplace of the house stood like a lonely sentinel over the smoldering remains of the charred framework and household contents. The barn was still burning fiercely. The hay and other accumulated equipment and material were difficult to destroy. The remains of a pair of horses trapped in the structure were visible and the emanating odor was nauseating. The barn and its contents were a total loss. So too were other small structures and the crops. The mobbers also had stolen the four remaining horses. It was total devastation. The main source of income for the Westons and the Johnsons lay in ruins.

"Well," James said, trying to see some good in all of this, "we sure didn't lose much of a crop this year with all the crickets and flies." The hot dry summer had been ideal for breeding both crickets and the large black, crop-eating Mormon Flies. By now, the insect plague had cost them about twenty percent of their crop.

William reluctantly nodded in agreement.

The demoralized band of Legionnaires and the Johnson family slowly rode back into town. Everyone wanted to know what had happened. Expressions of anger, anxiety, and sympathy rippled through the crowds as they got the word. William veered off toward Brigham Young's home to bring the leader up to date. Other Legionnaires split off from the formation and headed for their respective homes. The Johnson's, who by now were showing signs of shock, were brought to James's house to collect themselves, tend to their wounds, clean up, eat, and rest.

Amanda was in a state of disbelief. She saw this as not only a tragedy for the Johnsons, but for her family as well. The loss of income and capital would have a devastating effect on their future. The threat of violence and even death suddenly became more real. If she had any idea of leaving Nauvoo with her children, that possibility was no longer viable. She felt the door of an impregnable cell slam shut. She was now a prisoner in a world not to her liking, one that drew her in inch by inch over the years. As this realization gradually took hold, she nearly hyperventilated. She felt claustrophobic and was unable to breathe. Her actions in aiding the Johnsons settle in were robotic. At the first opportunity, she dragged her weary, numb body up the stairs, entered her room, closed the door, and cried an eternity of tears. Her body shook uncontrollably as she buried her face in a pillow to muffle the sounds of anguish.

Finally, when she had not a drop of water left to shed and her body was too exhausted to shake anymore, she rolled over on her back and stared at the ceiling. Slowly, her mind began to clear. This was not the true Amanda. She had always been able to somehow make sense out of any situation and react accordingly. As a multitude of competing thoughts cascaded through her mind, she gradually began to see what she must do. If she could not extricate herself from the situation, she would then try to control it as best she could. Her naturally positive personality stepped forward. If we have to leave Nauvoo and move west with all the rest, she thought, we will do it in an efficient and effective way. She was determined that her family would suffer as little as possible. Amanda rose from the bed, washed her face in the nearby basin, straightened her clothes, and resolutely strode out of the bedroom and down the stairs. There was a mountain of work to do.

The Weston farm was but one of many confrontations between the Saints and the Gentiles. In one episode, Porter Rockwell—a Mormon zealot—shot and killed a popular Gentile named Worrell. This man, Worrell, called "the Mormon eater," was no less fanatical. Unfortunately, this killing accelerated hostilities. The heavy-handed Nauvoo police kept order within the city and the Legion protected and exacted revenge along the troubled periphery. The pressures on the beleaguered city were continuous and relentless. During the fall of 1845, the anti-Mormons destroyed more than two hundred outlying houses, barns, shops, and granaries. They killed some Mormon men and raped their wives and daughters.

Seeing the violence escalating and getting out of control, and wanting a truce, Young and the Twelve Apostles issued a proclamation on September 24 that declared the Saints would move out of Nauvoo, ". . . as soon as the grass grows, and the water runs." Still, the hostile public sentiment against the Mormons was so great and growing that Governor Ford was worried about open warfare. To make matters worse, government officials were eager to serve warrants on Brigham Young and eight others for harboring a counterfeiting operation in Nauvoo. Young also took seriously rumors that federal troops from St. Louis were planning to intercept the Mormons as they left Nauvoo and destroy them. All of these dark clouds forced Young to abandon his plans for a spring departure. The huge task of abandoning Nauvoo would begin as soon as possible.

Brigham Young announced they would leave in the spring. The Mormon leaders had but two obsessions: finish the Temple for the endowments and prepare the people for migration. It was the second mission, getting ready to move, that consumed Amanda. She joined in the rush to dry more fruit and squash, preserve more pickles, store up on supplies of tea, vinegar, flour, sugar, and every other variety of essential products. The communal environment, with the women feeding off one another's fervor, made this task possible. As they sewed wagon covers and tents, they often claimed visits by the Holy Ghost, related dreams of salvation, and spoke in tongues. Amanda did her best to ignore all of it. She saw that, despite all this religious hocus-pocus, the women got a mountain of work done.

Those men not constructing the Temple worked over-time crafting wagons, ropes, metal tires and chains, axles, wooden yokes, and the myriad other things needed to make the long trek. Never before in America had such a communal effort fashioned so much in so short a time. All the while, the impatient and hostile Gentiles hovered ominously like birds of prey, just waiting for the opportunity to sweep in for the kill. The Saints confronted not only skirmishes, but legal actions as well. All forms of writs issued against the leaders of the Church kept those men constantly wary and always near some protection. With good reason, the Gentile lawmen were hesitant about entering the city itself for fear of bodily harm. They hung around the outskirts hoping to catch some Church official off guard.

While James spent a great deal of time helping build the Temple, William helped in coordinating and directing the migration strategy. As a chilly November wind blew down from the north, James huddled inside at William's table by the fireplace. They were going over the papers showing the figures.

"We've made great progress. Like Zion's Camp, we now have 3,285 families organized into groups of tens, fifties, and hundreds. We have a little over 1,500 wagons completed and some 1,890 begun," William said proudly. "Surely God is pleased with our efforts."

"Surely," replied James. He was thinking how far they had come on the Temple construction. "And, he must be please with our Temple progress as well. The upper rooms should be finished enough to begin endowments by early December."

"Yes, all is going well. I am amazed at how the Saints have bent to the task," William commented. "The work the women are doing is next to miraculous. Ruth tells me that even Amanda has shown great strength and resolve. She's actually been a leader in some of their organizational meetings."

"I must confess, I don't understand that woman," James said shaking his head. "She is so bullheaded at times and then, when I'm about ready to give up, she makes a complete turnabout. Once she makes up her mind to do something, it's done. Although she hasn't said much, clearly she's decided she must make the best of this journey and is putting her back to the task."

"Be grateful, brother. No man understands women. Believe me, I know. The trick, somehow, is to head 'em in the direction you want 'em to go, show a little affection now and then, and hope for the best." William was finding out that not all was bliss trying to keep three women happy at the same time.

It was to the great credit of the Mormons that Nauvoo was unlike any other frontier town. Buildings seemingly grew over night and the quality of the structures that resulted from such activity was unparalleled. There was much to say for the commercial, recreational, and cultural advantages of Nauvoo. One reason for this development, was that Nauvoo had far more women and children than was found in typical frontier towns. Nauvoo was a beehive of activity from its beginning and amazingly, continued to be so almost to the day of abandonment. The Saints built and ran individual homes, farms, businesses, and the Temple as if they would be there forever.

"We got a lot of mouths to feed," James said. They were going over the livestock they planned to take on the journey and the amount of feed required to keep them going. "And, we've got to make sure we have, or can get, enough to last the whole way."

CHAPTER 14

The mental and physical hardships on the everyday citizen-Saint in Nauvoo at this time were great; however, the day-to-day pressures for Brigham Young, the Twelve Apostles and other members of the priesthood during this time were unbearable. As they were trying to sell their property—including the Temple—they also were deciding on their destination and planning for advance parties to prepare the way. They were gathering tithes and avoiding sheriffs and marshals armed with warrants. What's more, they were inspecting the progress on the construction of the Temple, wagons for the trek, and vessels to cross the river. The mountain of paperwork was phenomenal. Then, starting on December 10, the endowments began. The rituals of baptism, sealing, washing, and anointing went on day after day and night after fatiguing night.

They performed baptisms in the Temple basement at an intricate font, held aloft by twelve white wooden oxen. All other ceremonies were in the upper chambers of the building. These ceremonies were elaborate, time consuming, and exhausting. Each person received these rites and there were hundreds upon hundreds of faithful clamoring for these spiritual blessings before the migration began.

James received his endowments early on. As in all cases, his ritual was the same. A priest stripped him of all clothing and then clad him in an exceptional garment held together by bone buttons —no metal allowed. This special item of clothing was a functional suit of long johns that James wore always thereafter. The undergarment protected him from evil. Cuts shaped like the square and the compass—symbols taken from the Masons—adorned the underwear chest-high. There was a slash across the knee. A larger slash across the stomach, symbolized his disemboweling if he would reveal the holy secrets.

Sworn to secrecy and dressed in a white robe, James then witnessed a drama reenacting the creation of the earth and the fall of Adam and Eve. God, Jesus, the Holy Ghost, and the devil all played a part in the allegory that followed the wording of Genesis. In the portrayal, God creates Eve from a sleeping Adam and Eve eats the forbidden fruit from the tree of knowledge (a small tree containing raisins). The person playing the devil crawled around on the floor on their stomach like a snake.

Upon expulsion from the Garden of Eden, the actors playing Adam and Eve donned tiny white Masonic-like aprons painted with fig leaves. Next, James learned certain passwords, grips, and keys and a secret name that would be his in the Kingdom of Heaven. No wonder the Church officials were exhausted. Reserved for men at first, the ritual later applied to women as well, thus increasing the workload tremendously. Amanda politely declined, to everyone's annoyance and no one's surprise.

Despite all the tension within—some self-induced, as a result of the religious and political turmoil inside the city and Church, and a great many from the unrelenting pressures of the Mormon-haters that ringed the city—Amanda had come to enjoy her life in Nauvoo. Contrary to the pronounced goals of the Church leaders to leave the place, for Amanda, there was a sense of stability and permanence about the place. Yes, the destruction of their farm had shaken her terribly, and there were dangerous and chaotic events that seemed to multiply as time went on. Nonetheless, hoping against hope, Amanda purposely wore mental blinders that shielded her from the reality of all that was going on. Her children had blossomed living here. The Westons lacked few physical wants or needs. For the most part, life was good in Nauvoo. It was inconceivable that a combination of religious zeal and intolerance would soon destroy it all.

Serious little Clara had a cluster of friends that alternately bonded and squabbled as little girls are inclined to do. She was only six when the Westons arrived in '41. The uprooting from Double Springs and the uncertainties of the journey to Nauvoo clearly discombobulated this fragile child and for a time Amanda had a genuine concern for her mental well-being. Fortunately, the last five years in Nauvoo stabilized Clara and assuaged Amanda's concerns. Clara was slight of build like her mother and with the same sad brown eyes. Her hair was straight and thick, a rich brown color with red highlights, and usually kept pulled tightly into two large braids. She was not particularly athletic, preferring indoor activities instead. Clara was a typical, well-balanced, healthy eleven-year-old girl. That's all that Amanda could ask for.

Realistically, underneath the facade of normalcy, Amanda had to face that Clara's tranquility was a myth. The effect the flight from Nauvoo would have on her children gnawed at her as she went about her daily routine. She could see clearly that the coming disruption would have many undesirable consequences on the children besides physical hardship. Jeremy would accept and be able to cope with whatever happened, albeit begrudgingly. Clara was inherently incapable of such flexibility.

True to her nature, little Christine would not only accommodate to whatever came, but would find some way to learn and grow by the experience. She was truly amazing and Amanda felt blessed to have such a child. Smart, friendly, exuberant, and voraciously inquisitive, Christine was a joy to have, as her antics and bubbly loquaciousness kept the family constantly laughing. It wasn't so much what she said, as how she said it. Amanda's chief concern with Christine would be to keep this inquisitive child out of harm's way.

Christine was much sturdier in build than either Amanda or James, revealing some of the Dutch stock on Amanda's side of the family. Her light complexion and shock of unruly blonde hair also accentuated her tie to Amanda's Pennsylvania Dutch relatives. Christine had inherited her father's blue eyes, albeit hers were more wide and expressive than his. In short, Christine had the appearance that complimented her personality. She was open, ready, and eager to take on just about anything.

As always, Amanda's paramount preoccupation was the well-being of her children. They were what she lived for. Everything she did, took into consideration the effect it might have on her little ones. She lived in a religiously dominated communal environment that was not to her liking, but since there was no plausible escape, she did what she could to minimize the effects of her doubts on her children. Jeremy knew some of his mother thoughts about the Church, but Clara and Christine did not. Amanda always made sure that she and the children attended the sermons in the Grove, especially when Brigham Young spoke. Of course, there was no escaping the more common "blessing meetings" held in various homes, particularly at William's. The adults that knew of her lack of endorsement of the Church, and that was a relatively small group, would surely talk and whisper behind her back, but such prattle didn't reach the children, and thus they felt little of its effects.

One trait Amanda did like about the Mormons was their acceptance of recreation and relaxation. From the beginning, Joseph Smith believed that social intercourse was beneficial. The puritanical Protestant view that relaxation was a weakness, or even sinful, did not fit the style of the gregarious Saints. The twelve to sixteen hours of work during the summer and ten to twelve during the winter didn't allow for a lot of free time, nonetheless, they used whatever they had with relish. Whether meeting at the apothecary, the bakery, or the tannery, relations were generally cordial while they exchanged news, views, and information. "Walking out" or "riding out,"—walking or riding about town to meet and greet people—was common practice in Nauvoo, as it was in other parts of America at this time. Even though men were often jovial and boisterous, the women were not. Many rules made sure women would not appear to be "unladylike." Ladies didn't beckon to a friend, stare at people, go without gloves, or untie one's bonnet, among other things.

Mostly, sports recreation was for men. Wrestling was one of the more popular sports in Nauvoo, perhaps because Joseph Smith excelled in it and challenged everyone so inclined. Horseracing and foot racing were popular as well. One sport that was essential for any frontiersman was shooting. James was a particularly excellent marksman and won many of the turkey shoots and target or mark contests. William could not come close to his brother in this field of expertise.

The January weather had been particularly kind to Nauvoo—what James and William, and the other tobacco farmers back in Rutherford County called "case weather." By February, however, Mother Nature decided to test the resolve of the new "children of Israel" as they set out for their Zion. On February 4, 1846, Charles Shumway, of the Council of Fifty, crossed the Mississippi and located a campground in the woods at Sugar Creek, Iowa, about seven miles from Nauvoo. Here there was plenty of wood and water, making it a fine place to assemble. Here too, there was relief, however temporary and uncertain, from the growing hostilities back in Illinois.

After Shumway set up camp in Sugar Creek, the beleaguered faithful began their "flight out of Egypt." Day after day, they streamed toward the river. Wagons, livestock, and people all trudged through the muck and slush and lined up at the ferry landing, waiting for their turn to cross. Cold and wet, they manhandled their wagons, loaded with everything transportable that they owned, onto lighters and flatboats and crossed the dangerous, icy-strewn Mississippi. By the time they would leave Sugar Creek, on the February 28, almost three thousand souls assembled in that misery-laden, icy encampment.

Because William was helping to coordinate the exodus that began shortly after February 4, the Westons had to wait as hundreds crossed over the treacherous Mississippi. On the 19th, the day the Westons left Nauvoo for Sugar Creek; it was bitter cold and snowing heavily—a full-blown blizzard.

"I have to tell you, James, I'd sooner face the mobbers than set out with the children in such fierce weather," lamented Amanda. "It's just crazy. Listen to that wind." She was speaking in hushed tones, away from the children.

"Amanda, we've been through this before," he responded in a forceful whisper. "I know you don't want to leave our beautiful home again and set out on such an uncertain course. But we must follow Brother Young, and you know it. Besides, surely you don't want to subject the children and yourself to the fate that the insane bunch of Gentiles have in mind. That would be certain abuse and death with the mood of the mobs hanging outside our beloved city." James was tired of Amanda's resistance to what had to be, though he understood the truth of her concerns. "Let's just do it and not let the children become upset and fearful with any concerns on our part."

"You're right, nobody's worked harder for this day than I have, but I am fearful of what is to come for our children, and for us. I can't help it," she buried her face in her hands started to cry quietly. Despite her resolve, she was having second thoughts now that the time had arrived. The sound of the howling wind easily covered her sobbing from the children who were huddled at the window across the room. The scene outside mesmerized them.

Beyond their two loaded farm wagons, the Weston children saw scores of their neighbors in the freezing morning wind packing their wagons for the journey across the river. A mixture of excitement, fear, and wonder as they viewed the preparations caused their nervous chatter. This situation challenged the imaginations and sense of adventure of the young.

A loud banging on the door, startled everyone inside. It was William. "Come on, James, it's time to go," he said, peering through the partly opened door. The wind and snow whistled through the crack.

"Everyone, get your coats and hats on," Amanda commanded, with a tone of begrudging resignation. "Here, Christine, let me help you," she cooed as she adjusted the seven-year-old's hat. "There you are, all snug and cozy." Amanda patted her youngest on the head and then picked her up in her arms, nestled the little tyke's head into the nape of her neck to protect her from the cold, and walked out the door. James herded the rest of the children out behind their mother and shut the door. Despite what he said to Amanda, closing that door behind him left a sinking feeling in the pit of his stomach. James definitely had mixed emotions about the coming exodus, as well. Everyone did.

"We're all loaded and ready to go," shouted William over the howling wind.

"We're right behind you, brother," answered James. "Come on, Jeremy, you're bringin' up the rear. Keep 'em nice and tight." He smiled broadly at his son and slapped him lovingly on the shoulder. At twelve, Jeremy was big enough and responsible enough to be in command of one of the wagons. For now, though, he had to take a turn at herding the cows and sheep in behind the wagons. He was a large boy for his age and his naturally serious personality made adults trust him beyond his years. Like his father and uncle, he had a strong and tough body developed through many hours of hard work. Unlike the other two, he was not committed to the cause and his body language often conveyed that fact. Everyone but Amanda attributed it to his age.

William and James had outfitted their families with what Brother Parley Pratt had suggested as a minimum for the trip. The brothers were organized and efficient enough, and of sufficient means, to follow Pratt's advice—some families were not. Many families used modified farm or work wagons to make the trip. The Weston brothers left their homes in Tennessee in style with large Conestoga wagons displaying majestic white canvass covers and beautiful dapple-gray horses. Such equipment would be too big and unwieldy for this kind of trip, and the horses would require far too much feed and care.

This time, James had one oak-wood wagon that was four feet wide and ten feet long and pulled by four yoked oxen. Covers were made of canvas, waterproofed with linseed oil. William had three wagons, similarly equipped, to accommodate his three families. James and William each had one riding horse tethered to the lead wagons, the saddles carried their Henry rifles; the colt pistols were at their sides. William also had his Legion saber hanging from one side. There was another horse for Jeremy's use.

Included in the combined livestock of both families were four milk cows, six sheep, and four beef cattle. Loaded aboard each family's wagons, besides clothing, bedding, and few items of furniture, were a thousand pounds of flour, one hundred pounds of sugar, ten pounds of rice, twenty-five pounds of salt, and accumulations of dried squash and fruit, pickles, vinegar, and crackers. They also had packed a tent with poles in each wagon along with two pulley blocks and rope for crossing rivers. Axle grease buckets hung from the rear and tool chests affixed to the sides. A small area was reserved in the wagons so that the smaller children could ride and sleep during the jarring journey, and, somehow, in amongst the possessions, everyone could fit into if necessary. Since the rigs had no springs, nearly everyone preferred to walk rather than ride. In all, there was just about twenty-eight hundred pounds of weight in each of the Weston wagons. William, having three wagons, carried many extra supplies used in common by the Westons. Provisioning themselves for this journey (as well as helping others, like the Johnsons) had nearly exhausted the Weston's rapidly dwindling cash reserve.

The four wagons pulled slowly away from their houses as the wind howled and the snow whirled. Amanda turned her body around, peeked from behind the wagon cover, and wistfully gazed at her home for the past four-and-a-half years. She thought of her beautiful, fertile garden, now lying fallow for winter, the accumulation of furniture, the barn, and all the other possessions she and her family had worked so hard to acquire since their arrival from Tennessee. Gifted to the Church, all this was up for sale for whatever price they could finagle. She did not shed any tears as they seemed to freeze at the ducts, but inside, oh inside, she cried a bucketful. She wondered, how often will we have to go through this for a God that seems unrelenting in his demands for sacrifice? she wondered. How much of our past can we abandon before we lose our identity? The blinding snow was beginning to turn her view into a swirling haze, so, reluctantly she turned her head forward toward the wagon in front and a future of uncertainty and hardship.

The Westons joined a small band of wagons gathering at the edge of the now-frozen river. Jeremiah Johnson and his family owned one of the wagons. Helped by the Westons, Jeremiah's wagon was sturdy and well provisioned. They also had two horses from the Weston stable. Attached to their wagon was a crude wooden trailer that contained a plow, two beehives, a large cooking kettle, two extra saddles and miscellaneous bridles and harnesses. The Westons and the Johnsons would share the supplies on this trailer and the livestock Jeremy herded from behind.

To the contrary, James could not help noticing how ill prepared some of the other travelers were. Many of those assembled seemed to have inadequate clothing, small over-loaded wagons, and few cattle and sheep. They appeared ignorant of what was in store for them and their loved ones. How could that be? James wondered. The Church leaders had been preaching for months the necessity of preparation. Many had waited too long, believing they had until spring to get ready. Some, who couldn't afford suitable wagons and provisions, threw caution to the wind in their eagerness to begin their journey to the Promised Land. For this, they would pay dearly.

William pulled his wagons to the head of the line and James followed. The elders made William responsible for leading this small collection of wagons to Sugar Creek. A man that looked like a walking snowman met him—his long beard, heavy clothes, and boots covered with frozen ice and snow. His walk was mechanical and slow; his body dragged down by the weight of the ice-encrusted clothing.

"It's frozen solid, brother," the man shouted to William. "You can go without fear fer God has paved the way. You'll be met on the other side an' directed whar ta go."

William nodded to the man and then turned to James. "It is indeed providential, brother. We can cross without fear of the soaking I've heard befell so many others. Come on; let's move everyone across as quickly as we can. Pass the word, stay in line, and do not fear the cracking sounds of the ice as we cross. Just keep moving." William shouted through cupped hands against the howling wind.

William, in the first wagon with Elizabeth and Adam inside, waited for James to return. Ruth and Mary Ellen fended their own wagons, each struggling to keep their stubborn oxen in line. This would not be the last time on this long journey that these, and almost all the other women, would be required to perform tasks that under normal circumstances would be difficult even for a man. Fortunately, for Ruth and Mary Ellen, once they got their oxen moving, the fierceness of the storm kept the normally recalcitrant beasts in line.

James motioned to Amanda to wait as he headed down the line of wagons to pass the word. When he passed Jeremy, he saw the dejected look on his son's face. "You all right?" he bellowed. Jeremy nodded his head once. There were too many animals for one boy to handle, but they kept tight together for warmth, heads down and eyes closed tight against the blinding snow. Getting them to move once stopped would be the problem. Jake would help. He was a great herding dog. Jeremy had tied rags securely around Jake's paws to keep them warm. The strong dog managed to move about freely despite the heavy accumulation of ice on the rags. The dog's tongue let off puffs of steam as he panted. His unflagging presence would help Jeremy through the ordeal before him.

"Keep 'em tight against the back of the wagon, son. It won't be long before we are at Sugar Creek," he hollered, patting his boy on the back. Jeremy sensed that was not true, but he felt bolstered by his father's encouragement.

As James passed each wagon, he shouted up the instructions. "When we start, keep movin'. The river's frozen, thank God. Don't fret about the sounds of the ice cracking, it will hold. Just keep movin'," he screamed against the wind. Each driver waved an understanding as he passed by. James saw a mixture of fear and determination on the faces as he went his way. His voice was hoarse by the time he had reached the last wagon. He couldn't believe how exhausting the short trip down and back was. The snow drifted deep and the force of the wind against his body on the return trip was fierce. Finally, he returned to his wagon, signaled to his brother that he had completed his mission. He then grabbed his lead ox's harness and jerked it forward. Slowly, his team inched the wagon forward behind William's wagons. The procession of heavily laden wagons all began to creak toward the rivers shoreline.

The agonizingly slow pace of the caravan against the violent storm tended to disorient Amanda. All about her was whirling increasingly faster, except for the wagons. It was like some dream sequence—the caravan in slow motion and everything else at double speed. The noise was fierce. She turned and put her head through the small hole in the front of the gathered wagon top.

She could hear Christine whimpering inside. "Everything OK?" she hollered back into the darkness. A simple, "Yes," shouted from Clara, satisfied her that everything was about as good as it could get under the circumstances. "Stay close together and keep warm. We'll be across the river before you know it. Clara, check on Jeremy," she commanded.

Clara did as her mother asked. She crawled over the mass of supplies and put her head out the back opening. "Jeremy! Jeremy!" she hollered over the wind. Jeremy was walking like a stick man, with his head down, trudging along behind his herd. The snow and ice were beginning to coat his clothing. He looked up at the sound of Clara's voice, peering over the frozen scarf covering his face. "You OK?" she yelled. Jeremy said nothing but shook his head up and down. "He's OK, Ma," Clara shouted out through the front opening after her return from the rear.

Poor darlings, thought Amanda. They must think we're mad to go out into this weather. *I* think we are mad! We waited so long. Surely, we could have waited until the storm stopped. Why do we have to follow some artificial schedule set up by a bunch of zealots? Would one or two days upset their blessed migration plans? It made no sense to Amanda. She began to long for the warm fire and cozy bed of her home in Nauvoo, even though they hardly had been gone an hour. Madness, sheer madness she iterated to herself. Her mind then went as blank as the whiteout whirling about her. Her oxen trudged methodically behind William's wagons in front.

The river was a mile wide, and they were across without mishap within forty minutes. There was a brief concern as William reached the opposite shore. The guide was nowhere in sight. In the blinding storm, William had led the small train slightly south of the contact point. After all the wagons were across the river, William mounted his horse and set out to find the guide. Within twenty minutes, he had returned with the guide by his side.

"Come on," shouted the tall, skinny man encrusted with icy snow. His boots had accumulated so much frozen ice and debris; he could barely pick them up to walk. Without additional commands, he motioned in a northwesterly direction and trudged off, straight into the wind.

Though the distance was but seven miles between Nauvoo and Sugar Creek, it took the better part of nine hours to make the trip. The journey was interminably long primarily due to the severe headwinds, the blinding snow, and the frozen, rutted, rock-strewn roadway. About halfway, the seventh wagon in the train broke a wheel. The hapless man trudged forward to William's lead wagon, shouting for him to stop. William, James, and the other men in the caravan labored mightily to lift the disabled wagon and replace the broken wheel with a new one. It was an hour before the wagons started to roll again.

Just before the men began the wheel repair, James and Jeremy lifted Jake into the back of the wagon on Jeremy's insistence. He was worried that his friend's paws would freeze standing around. Other wagons contained families huddled together lamenting their misery, but the Weston wagon resounded with barking, laughter, and squealing. Jake played with the girls in the confined quarters—pseudo-biting their arms and legs, licking their faces, and slobbering on their clothes. Overall, however, the wagon train's humans and animals alike were cold and exhausted by the time they reached the campsite.

It was impossible to see the vast number of wagons assembled at Sugar Creek. The whiteout made it impracticable to view anything more than ten feet in any direction. Staggering from exhaustion, the guide motioned for William to assemble the wagon train in the immediate area. They had reached their destination.

History would reveal that when the Mormons evacuated Nauvoo in 1846, walking on ice or transported in boats or ferries, they left in 3000 wagons pulled by 10,000 horses and oxen, 30,000 head of cattle, many horses, and mules and a great quantity of sheep. Loaded in the wagons were hundreds of thousands of pounds of flour, grain, dried fruit, vegetables, beef, bacon, and seeds. The Westons, obviously, were but a small part of this huge undertaking.

Chapter 15

By morning, the storm abated, but the temperatures were still below zero. The blizzard prevented the members of the Weston's wagon train from putting up tents the night before. All huddled together in and among their possessions in the wagons, relying on their collective body heat to survive the night. There was little room. Uncomfortable as it might be, almost everyone slept sitting up—adults holding children. This would be but one night of many where they would have to face such conditions.

Just before dawn, James crawled out of the wagon and surveyed the sea of tents about him. It was bitter cold. Six inches of snow covered the hundreds of wagons and tents that ranged as far as the poor light, fog, and hilly terrain allowed him to see. There was a quiet hush over the encampment, with the exception of the intermittent, muted sounds of snoring, coughing, and the cries of babies. In spite of the hardship, James saw the people were undergoing, it was inspiring to be a part of such a vast undertaking.

"Mornin' Brother James," boomed a familiar voice.

James was in the middle of a long stretch to unravel the kinks from the night's sleep. He stopped and turned his head toward the sound.

He was surprised to see Roy Thomas, who they had first met back in '41 in Fall Creek just before coming to Nauvoo. Big old Roy, the survivor of Haun's Mill, was standing about fifteen feet away beside a dilapidated, snow-encrusted tent. "Brother Roy, good to see you. How in the world did we end up so close just by chance?"

"Bad pennies always show up, my friend. I heard ya fellers pullin' in last night. Musta been a kick crossin the river in that there storm." Roy spat a stream of tobacco juice downwind, some caught on his full beard and instantly froze into a brown mass. Roy often received lectures on the evils of tobacco, but it was one pleasure he allowed himself against all admonitions. "Been ta hell an' back fer this here Church," he would retort. "Cain't believe God an' Brother Smith's gonna care if'n I chew a little tabacca now an' then. Don' smoke it, jus' chew it," was always his response. No one quite understood the distinction he drew, but he'd been doing it so long that it was just accepted.

"How long you been here, Brother Roy?" James asked.

"Five days too long," complained Roy. "Cold as hell is hot an' looks like it ain't gonna change much neither. Cain't wait fer this here gatherin' ta git on the road. Anythin's better'n sitting here freezin' our butts off. Movement, that's what we need, movement." Roy kept flexing his bad knee all during his discourse, trying to restore some circulation back into his mangled extremity.

"Well, for heaven's sake, Brother Roy. How providential that we should camp next to you," William said, climbing stiffly out of his wagon, yawning, and stumbling over to shake hands. The last time they had seen each other was six months ago.

"Welcome ta paradise, Brother William. What say we git a fire goin' so's we don' all freeze ta death?" Most of the rest of the encampment was still sleeping. The majority of those miserable souls slept fitfully throughout the night; still, practically all exhibited that strange human characteristic of sleeping soundly just before it was time to be awake.

The men collected wood from a large pile that was located nearby—which was typical of the encampment's organization. They brushed away the snow from a central location and piled the wood over some kindling Roy had shaved from one of the smaller logs. Soon, the kindling nurtured a larger and warmer fire. Avoiding singed hair, the three men huddled as close as possible around the glowing flames. Similar fires began to glow in various spots throughout the encampment. More would come as the morning light began to penetrate the veil of tents and wagons.

"So, tell us, Brother Roy, what's been goin' on?" asked William.

"A lot a waitin' and whinin'," Roy answered disgustedly. "Some folks been sittin' here since Brother Shumway set up camp. That's more'n two weeks now. Things was gettin' bad here fer a while, I guess. People started gettin' itchy, fightin' one another, complainin' 'bout everthin', an' all like that. Then, ol' Brother Brigham come in ta camp from Nauvoo. He looks around fer a couple a days an' sees what's goin' on. After that, three days ago, he gits his self up on a wagon, standin' tall an' angry, an' starts whippin' everbody in ta shape. Man, woman an' child got a good tongue lashin'. He sets up all kinds a rules an' left no doubt he meant business. Let me tell ya, that feller is one hell a leader. Put on some kind a show, fer sure."

"So how long before we start moving out? Did Brother Young say?" asked William.

"Didn't say exactly. He said they was waitin' fer Kimball, Clayton an' Whitney ta git everthin' back in Nauvoo tidied up—you know, all the Church property an' stuff that we hafta tote along."

"Mornin', boys. Mighty nice to have a roarin' fire to wake up to." Ruth climbed from the wagon and entered the circle of warmth, rubbing her hands over the fire. The cold reddened her nose and cheeks, enhancing her smiling face. Various responses came from the men standing around the campfire. Roy tipped his hat and said, "Mornin', Sister Ruth." William kissed his wife on the cheek.

"Comin' across that river was a miracle; a smooth road of heavenly ice. I tell ya, God is shinin' down his grace on us. I hear crossin' that river when you did in the freezin' water with all them chunks of ice was downright dangerous. Am I right, Brother Roy?" Ruth said, getting her religious twist on events, as always.

"Yer right on that, Sister Ruth," Roy's wife, Amelia, said as she joined the group. Her rumpled clothing moved up and down in unison with the scratching of her amble belly. "We're like the tribe a Joseph fleein' outta Egypt. Brother Brigham is our Moses an' that there mighty Mississippi was our Red Sea."

"A-men," shouted Ruth. "An' that cursed Governor Ford is ol' Pharaoh—stupid an' mean," she added to the analogy, laughing at and enjoying her contribution.

Everyone around the fire agreed that the comparison was fair. Leave it to those two to dream up that one, thought Amanda. She was sitting quietly in her wagon, bundled up with her children and listening to the conversation outside. "Can't see anything heavenly about this fiasco," she murmured.

"That's for sure," answered a dismayed Jeremy.

"Now, son, we both kind of have to keep our thoughts to ourselves," Amanda whispered. "First, we have to make sure the girls are safe and I'm relying on you to help me with that. You and me; we've got to stick together."

"I know, Ma, but that doesn't mean I have to like it."

"I say 'Amen' to that, but we've got to make the best of it. We can't go back. That means we can only go forward, no matter how hard it is or how long it takes. As long as our family sticks together, we'll make it," she cautioned her son.

Jeremy nodded in agreement and understanding.

"That doesn't mean that you and me can't have a private conversation now and then—sort of share our problems. Any time you want to talk, you know you can count on me."

"Yeah, Ma, I know." He reached over and stroked his mother's cheek. Mother and son reinforced the strong bond between them.

Smelly old Jake lie quietly beside the two in the crowded wagon. His head was between Jeremy's legs. His sorrowful eyes glanced upward, studying his master's face. Somehow, he knew not to interrupt the intimate exchange between Jeremy and his mother, but when he saw the conversation was over, he raised his head and began to stir. When Jake stirred, he disturbed everyone in the tightly packed wagon.

"Jaaake," whined Clara as she brushed the big dog's tail out of her face.

"Here, boy," Jeremy said as he loosened the tie holding the canvass cover shut. Jake extracted his body from the tangle of arms and legs and jumped out of the wagon to the ground below. He repeatedly shook his body from side, then went to the nearest wagon wheel and relieved himself.

"Hey, Jake," James called. The big old dog trotted over to James, who rewarded him with vigorous rubbing behind his ears. Jake's tail wagged strongly from side-to-side in appreciation, battering the legs of those standing around. "How you doin', boy?"

"Best keep that there dog on a leash," warned Roy. "Brother Brigham said any dog not on a leash gonna be shot. They been causin' a lot of problems runnin' loose."

"Ain't nobody goin' to put a leash on old Jake," said a voice from the rear. It was Jeremy and his tone and expression left no doubt that he meant what he said. "Ain't no one goin' to shoot 'im either, lessen he wants to get shot," he added.

The adults around the campfire all looked at one another with raised eyebrows. "Somethin' tells me he means it," remarked Roy.

"Well, Jeremy," said William, "Jake's a hero. Bet if I ask Brother Brigham, he'd make an exception for him." Later, William did ask Young, and Jake received a reprieve from wearing a confining leash. No one objected when the big dog with the medal saying, "Hero," dangling from his collar roamed the camp freely. Thus, it would be so for the rest of the long journey.

The word came down—William was to be the captain of a train of ten wagons. As a part of Heber Kimball's Company of 100 wagons, they would be traveling behind Brigham Young's lead company of fifty families (the basic unit of travel). As captain, William was responsible for supervising everything that went on in his train. That task included maintaining discipline, morale, security, supplies, and all work details.

"Brother William, may I have a word with you?" Roy Thomas came huffing up a slope with his bad leg making every step in the heavy snow difficult.

"Of course, Brother Roy. What's up?"

"I hear tell that ya been made captain a this here train. That a fact?"

"That's a fact."

"Well, I been talkin' with our little Fall Creek bunch an' we all agree that it sure would be a blessin' if we all could be a part a yer train.

We know an' trust ya an' have no doubt that ya'd give us the best chance a gettin' through this thing in one piece. Whatta ya think?"

"Well, Brother Roy, I don't have any problem with the idea. Of course, it's not up to me. I'd have to get permission," However, he did have reservations. The "Fall Creek bunch," as Roy had called them, were not the best-equipped wagons on the trail. The Thomas, Jessup, and Adams families were somewhat slipshod in their attention to detail and were like many on the trail, under-provisioned. On the other hand, they were all proven survivors and despite Roy's leg, daughter Naomi's periodic fits (she had epilepsy), and Joshua Jessup's intermittent massive headaches (a lingering effect from his Haun's Mill beating), the families were a healthy bunch. The biggest plus was that they were a known quantity and their loyalty was unquestioned. It would not be a good thing to have just anyone assigned.

"I'll do my best," was William's final response.

William had no problem getting permission for Roy and his group to join his train. Combined with James and the Johnson wagon, the train contained nine wagons. One other wagon belonging to the sisters, Margaret Waters and Josephine Smith, completed the train of ten. Having the responsibility for a pair of older women on the trail was not exactly on William's wish list, but he felt it was his duty.

Therefore, William Weston's train of ten wagons and forty-four people was set and composed of the following families:

Wagon 1: William Weston (38), Ruth (31), and four children—Mary (10), Edith (9), Sarah (5) and George (3).

Wagon 2: Mary Ellen Thompson (27) and two children—John Thompson (5), and Jacob Weston (3).

Wagon 3: Elizabeth Granger (21) and son—Adam Weston (3).

Wagon 4: James Weston (35), Amanda (31), and three children—Jeremy (13), Clara (11), and Christine (8).

Wagon 5: Jeremiah Johnson (40), Mary (36), and sons—Tom (18), and Geoff (16).

Wagons 6 & 7: Roy Thomas (47), Amelia (37) and ten children—Roy Jr. (19), Mary (18), Ruth (16), Mark (14), Joseph (13), Andrew (12), Mathew (9), Naomi (7), Nancy (5), and Parley (3).

Wagon 8: Joshua Jessup (43), Prudence (30) and four children—Joshua, Jr. (9), Michael (7), Mary (5), and Stephanie (3).

Wagon 9: Anthony Adams (34), Annie (27) and two children—Josephine (10) and Roger (8).

Wagon 10: Margaret Waters (62) and her sister, Josephine Smith (60).

William began to inspect the wagons, supplies, and over-all condition of the people assigned to his train. As he suspected, the "Fall Creek bunch" were lacking in provisions and the condition of their wagons and equipment was marginal. Jeremiah and his family he knew were ready and all were healthy. As it turned out, Margaret and Josephine were in excellent health, tough as rawhide, and wholly devoted to the Church. William decided they would be an asset, not a liability, on the long trek westward.

Together, William and James made sure that all was ready for the day they were to leave Sugar Creek. They inventoried food and other supplies, repaired equipment, and instructed everyone on all aspects of the journey, to include hygiene, camp and trail routine, care of livestock, security, and anything else the Westons considered appropriate. When the word to move arrived, the Weston train would be ready. As a part of Heber Kimball's company of fifty, they would follow Brigham Young's lead company. Many of the wagons in Young's company belonged to him because by this time, his family consisted of twelve wives, nine children, and several foster children.

It would be two weeks before the Westons would proceed.

Finally, the word came down—"Pack up, we're movin' out!" At that, the camp became a beehive of activity, heavy with anticipation. Confined far too long, these restless people wanted to start their expedition.

"Here, child, let me he'p ya with that," Margaret Waters said as she grabbed one end of Amanda's folded canvass tent. Everyone was packing up to leave. "Whar's yer men folk? They otta be doin' this here heavy liftin'." She helped hoist the ice-encrusted bundle into the wagon.

"Heavens, Sister Margaret, if I waited around for them to show up,

I'd never get anything done. Jeremy's rounding' up the livestock and James helping William fix something or another of Brother Thomas's. I swan, it's always something." Amanda leaned back against the wagon, panting slightly from the exertion. Her breath formed an icy mist every time she exhaled.

"Ain't that the truth," laughed Margaret. "Josephine an' me figured that one out a long time ago. Nothin' a man can do we cain't. Well, almost nothin'." The old woman's face blushed.

Everyone had been so busy the past ten days getting ready to leave that Amanda had been unable to sit down and talk to either of the sisters. She had met them, of course, and they had been together in group orientations, prayer meetings, and the like. So far, they had only exchanged pleasantries.

Margaret and her sister, Josephine, were very much alike in build. Both were about five and a half feet tall and sturdy. Their hands and faces were weathered and tough and their lean frames belied their strength and tenacity. Neither were particularly good looking, with plain faces, sad eyes, and sunken cheeks, all surrounded by mousy hair. Margaret's nose was larger than her sister's was, but otherwise their features were similar. There was no doubt they were sisters.

Both sisters were always ready with a smile. Their energy was boundless—their work ethic unmatched. They believed they could outwork any man twice their size. Paramount to their personalities was their positive attitudes. Their commitment to the Church was unchallenged. They believed that Joseph Smith was a Prophet and that the Mormon Church was their one true way to salvation. However, they always maintained a healthy, sane outlook that allowed others to believe what they wanted.

"You got time for a cup of tea before I stub out the fire?" Amanda asked.

"Why not? It may be a while afore we git another chance," replied Margaret, as she sat on a nearby box.

Amanda poured the hot mixture into two tin cups and sat on another box near the fire. "Tell me, Sister Margaret, how did you and Sister Josephine end up on this journey all by yourselves?" she asked. Amanda knew Margaret was a widow but other than that, she was in the dark.

"Oh my, that there's a long story." Margaret paused in her drinking and wistfully gazed over her cup. "Jeb—that were my husband—an' me, we joined the Church back in Kirtland, Ohia. Brother Smith were jus' startin' out in them days. Josephine, never married an' was livin' with us at the time, decided ta follow Brother Smith too, an' we been hangin' around ever since."

"Goodness, you've been with the Church that long?"

"Oh yeah, we've been through it all with this bunch. We was there when Brother Smith got tarred an' feathered in Hiram, Ohia, had our house burnt down in Jackson County, Missora, in'34, an' left for Illinois in '38 after Haun's Mill. Jeb caught pneumonia when we escaped ta Illinois—January '39 it was an' cold as ever I seen. Ol' Jeb, he died the followin' month in Quincy." A slight quiver in her bottom lip and her misting eyes showed that she still was hurting after all these years.

"It must have been terribly hard for you, Sister Margaret," said a sympathetic Amanda.

"Yep, well Brother Smith always said that God is always testin' his chosen people ta see if we are worthy. Guess I been tested much as anybody, 'cept maybe the Prophet his self."

"Certainly sounds like you're as worthy as anyone I know."

Margaret laughed. "Darlin', I've a feelin' we ain't seen nothin' yet. Some people been claimin' it's terrible cold here in Sugar Creek. That's the truth; especially fer them that crossed over early. But almost all here's been quiet an' orderly. Some people that ain't seen honest ta goodness privation was complainin' an' bickerin', fer sure. I hear Brother Young give everbody a tongue lashin' an' that was that. Ya jus' wait; this here journey ta the Promised Land is gonna cap the climax. Yes ma'am, this here's gonna be somethin' else, that's fer sure."

"You are so right, Sister; been saying that all along." Amanda said wistfully. "I had so not wanted to go, but had little choice in the matter. If I'd had my druthers, I would have taken my children back to Tennessee, an' that's for sure."

"I gather yer not committed ta the cause?" questioned Margaret.

Amanda flushed a little. "I don't normally make my feelings known to just anybody, but somehow I think you'll understand," Amanda answered.

"Land sakes, Sister Amanda, what's ta understand. Not everbody's as crazy as Josephine an' me. We firmly believe the Mormon Church, with all its faults, is our vehicle ta salvation, but that don' mean it's the same fer everbody," Margaret said.

"I'm glad you see it that way, Sister. Not everyone here is so inclined to accept my viewpoint."

Margaret stood up, put her cup down on the box, and came to Amanda. She grasped both of Amanda's shoulder and looked her straight in the eye. "Don' ya never mind what them others think. Any time ya wanna talk, come see old Margaret, ya hear?"

"Thank you, Sister Margaret, I'll do that." Amanda felt she had made a friend, and God knew she desperately needed one.

CHAPTER 16

"Ya hear that," shouted James enthusiastically, "we're movin' out!"

With a blare of trumpets from Captain Pitts Brass Band, one company after the other followed their leader, Brigham Young, beginning the long journey to the Promised Land.

"Amen, a-men!" cried out a joyous Ruth. "Amen, a-men!" echoed throughout the assemblage.

Even Amanda shared the excitement. Seized with a sense of foreboding, she was, nevertheless, pleased to be leaving this miserable campsite. Motion, she thought, was progress—one more step toward the end of this journey and some semblance of peace in her soul.

It was March 1, almost one month after the first river crossing, and ten days after the Westons had arrived, that the main body of the camp began to pull out of Sugar Creek. Sucking themselves out of the mire of the creek bed, the pioneer Saints headed their wagons for the high ground to the west. It was an impressive sight as thousands of livestock trailed behind hundreds of wagons filled with thousands of men, women, and children. The Camp of Israel, as Brigham called these companies, was on the move and the history along the route would never be the same.

Jake was beside himself. Confined to the campsite, he had been bored and on the verge of trouble for ten days. Because he had free range, he was always nosing into something. Some of the Saints accepted "Jake the hero dog" with open arms—especially the children, who often romped and wrestled with him in the snow. Others were not amused when he would chase their chickens or growl at their tethered dogs. As the camp gathered itself for the long trek ahead, there was an overall feeling of excitement saturating the air. Jake absorbed the mood. He kept running from one wagon to the other, jumping and barking like an excited child. His antics amused everyone in the company and seemed to lift the spirits of those in doubt. The other dogs strained at their leashes, as they wanted to join in the festivities. Eventually, Brother Young's "leash law" fell by the wayside as the trains began to spread out and the need for vigilant dogs increased.

Amanda smiled as she shook her head in mock disapproval. "Jake, settle down!" she shouted. It was like shouting into the wind. Jeremy, of course, beamed with pride. He had the best dog in the world.

Most wagons were pulled by the big lumbering, obstinate oxen. Few of the migrating Mormons, including the Westons, had much experience yoking and driving oxen. These animals, cheaper to buy and to support than horses or mules, were strong, hardy, and forgiving—if you knew how to handle them. Emigrant farmers, like the Johnson's, who had a lot of experience working with cattle, readily learned to yoke and drive these sometimes contrary beasts. Oxen in untrained hands had a tendency to wander off the path, as James and others experienced when they went from Nauvoo to Sugar Creek. Fortunately, at that time, the fierce storm had tempered the oxen teams' propensity to veer any direction but dead ahead.

Such was not the case once the pioneers left Sugar Creek and headed into the open country. Jeremiah and his sons were kept busy the first few days teaching the Weston train how to drive these stubborn animals. They showed them how to stand on the left side of the team just behind the lead oxen and coerce them in the direction they wanted to go by using a whip or a prod and constantly commanding, "gee" (turn right) or "haw" (go left). Jeremy, ever in tune with animals, learned quickly. Just as there were varying talents among the drivers, there was a variety of oxen "personalities" and proficiencies. Young steers did not always bend to the yoke or the commands. Older, smarter bulls knew how to take advantage of greenhorn drivers. Gradually, as time progressed, drivers and oxen each learned their roles and generally carried out the daily grind with a minimum of friction and exasperation.

Getting the large, clumsy wooden yokes on the oxen was another story. Not all the beasts submitted easily to the heavy wooden harnesses and their long ominous horns made many novices uneasy. There were times when a rope tied about the base of its horns and strung through the spoke of a wagon wheel restrained a particularly rebellious bull. One teamster would pull tight on the rope to immobilize the ox while another teamster slipped on the yoke. Here again, as time and routine occupied man and beast over the long trail, such incidents became rare. Each became accustomed to their place in the scheme of things. However, a wise man cared for his teams of oxen by properly feeding, watering, and resting them. Those who did not would suffer greatly as time went by.

From the beginning, a blare of a trumpet and the resonance of the Temple bell carried in the lead wagon started each day's journey. The sounds of the "geeing" and "hawing" and cracking whips of the teamsters became a constant on the trail throughout the long days. So too did the sounds concurrent with the movement of people, wagons, and livestock. Horses' neighs, sheep's bleats, and cows' lows intermingled with the crack of whips, the creaking of wagons, and the clank of metal upon metal. People contributed to the discord by laughing, coughing, singing, crying, shouting, and talking continuously throughout each day's journey. The sounds only began to fade near the end of the day's trip as pioneers and their animals became exhausted. The muted sounds of prayers, songs, and conversations around the nightly campfires drifted from group to group until, finally, the spent wanderers fell asleep.

Amanda had to admit that the endless procession of wagons, people, and livestock was impressive. The shear scope of the movement was overwhelming. From an overall point of view, everything functioned in an orderly, planned, almost militaristic fashion. As with all human endeavors, however, down in the bowels, there was continuous, organized chaos. Sickness, death, equipment failures, and a multitude of problems one might expect with such an endeavor were always bubbling under the surface. Down where the daily struggle of life and death did take place, there was plenty of misery to go around. Sometimes inside, the bits and pieces of each company seemed not to progress at all. Nevertheless, at the end of the day, like a determined turtle, the entire body of migrating Saints crept forward.

Amanda was forever amazed at the resiliency, strength, and bravery of these remarkable people. With few exceptions, their attitudes didn't convey fear or sorrow, just resolution. This was especially true of the women, who carried a major portion of the burden. The multitude of responsibilities and tasks that these pioneer women bore, and the conditions that prevailed in carrying them out, was astonishing. Typically considered political second-class citizens, Mormon women were the backbone of the religion and on the long journey west, they were the glue that held everything together.

Security for the overall assemblage was in the hands of Hosea Stout's company of guards. They posted themselves as outriders to give advanced warning of any danger. Each company and train officer had the responsibility for making sure his people were safe. William had eight men for security rotation. Besides the fathers in every family, Roy Thomas, Jr. and the Johnson boys, Tom and Geoff, were all old enough to pull guard duty and mature enough for William to use in this important function. All the men assigned to security were adept with firearms.

The trace, or trail, they took from Sugar Creek angled northwest along the Des Moines River, up through a settlement called Farmington, and then to a place called Bonaparte Mills. There, some of the pioneers ground wheat at a local gristmill as the main body crossed the Des Moines. For the next ten days, they trudged across the Iowa winter landscape—some days making twenty miles, some only six. Harsh weather set in again and forced the weary travelers to remain in a place called Richardson's Point on a branch of Chequest Creek. Here they stayed for ten days as an incessant rain made the trail impassable. And it was here that some of the first deaths of the journey occurred. As they continued on, consumption, the common name for tuberculosis, became a familiar killer of adults on the trail, as was pneumonia for the elderly. Children were afflicted with ordinary but serious communicable diseases—measles, mumps, and whooping cough—as well as the more deadly scarlet fever and diphtheria. Amanda did everything she could to isolate her children, hoping to protect them from the many health threats. Unsanitary conditions, constant exposure to the elements, and communal living made such precautions sometimes fruitless. Happily, the Westons were sound, healthy children, as were the majority of the other children in the Weston Train.

Finally, the weather improved. Buoyed by the change in the conditions, the Saints coaxed and prodded their oxen out of the rain soaked quagmire and headed them west. The going was slow and slower, as the rainy weather had softened the earth so much that humans and beasts found it nearly impossible to move the wagons forward. As the procession reached the Chariton River, the progress halted again. The prairies that lie ahead were impassable because of the heavy rains. This stop on March 21 through the 23rd, gave the scattered camps a chance to assemble as a consolidated group again. It was impossible to keep the trains together. Each would plod along with their own set of tribulations. Often spread over a three-mile stretch, the column moved like a giant inchworm, the back eventually catching up with the front. The discipline, determination, and dedication of the Saints were incredible.

The Weston train circled with two other trains for the night and began to prepare their camp at a site so muddy that they would sink beyond their ankles as they set up their tents and tended to their other chores. No one complained about the site selection as the earth was the same in all directions—trod to a pulpy mess. Having spent many miserable days and nights at Richardson's Point under similar circumstances, the weary travelers resigned themselves to the continuing dreadful conditions.

Later that night, after prayers, and the children bedded down in the wagon, James and Amanda sat on a wooden bench, propped out of reach of the mud. For once, the sky was clear. An incredible burst of stars illuminated the night. It was frosty, and they huddled together to keep warm.

"You have to admit, James, even though this is the same old sky, this is a long way from our home in Rutherford Springs." Amanda wistfully, looked at the blazing heavens.

"Yes, Amanda," James replied. "It seems like a hundred years ago that we lived that comfortable life, doesn't it?"

"Actually, it seems like a hundred years since we left Nauvoo and it's only been, what, twenty-one or -two days?"

"Yes, twenty-one days."

"And how many miles have we gone?"

"William says eighty."

"Eighty miles," Amanda said, cocking her head to one side making a small sound as she sucked air in the side of her mouth. "And how long do you think it will take us to get to where we're going?"

"At this rate, never," laughed James, causing Amanda to chuckle as well.

"So true, so true," she conceded reluctantly, her eyes watering slightly.

This was the first time Amanda and James had shared a laugh together since leaving Nauvoo.

The grass had not started to grow and inhabitants with which to trade were far apart and seldom where needed. Many animals had to eat bark and small limbs from cottonwood and elm trees for fodder. More well provisioned Saints, like the Westons, fed grain they had brought along to their livestock, although at a reduced amount.

As the days began to add one upon the other, it became obvious to Amanda that the journey ahead of them was going to be even more long and arduous than she had expected, especially for the children. She did everything she could to ensure the safety and well-being of her little brood. However, deprivation, disease, and even death were everywhere. There was no way to shield them from the catastrophic consequences of exposing themselves so openly to the whims of both man and nature. It was true that accidents from shootings, drowning, wagon wheels, livestock mishaps, and the myriad other activities of a thriving community were common back in Nauvoo—but not as noticeable or as often as on the trail. Debilitation and death from disease and disagreements among neighbors were all the daily consequences of everyday life in the city, as well. The stability of home, hearth, and family muted these things in Nauvoo. The trail, with its rigors of living outdoors, traveling in unknown and sometimes unfriendly territory, and being exposed to the worst kind of weather exacerbated all these things.

Life on the trail also subjected everyone to things not common back in the shelter of Nauvoo. Stampedes, lightning strikes, hail, increased attacks from ticks and mosquitoes, fatigue, bad water, and lack of food plagued the Saints as they pushed their way West. Rumors also played havoc. Rumors of Indian raids or threats of Pukes coming up from the Missouri border persistently stoked the fires of fear.

Well provisioned and properly directed as they were, the trail still took its toll on the Weston family. Of increasing concern was the Westons' support for their less capable fellow travelers, mainly the Thompsons and the Jessups. The constant assistance for these families, who were not financially able or smart enough to supply their wagons adequately at the start, began to deplete the Westons' stock of ample provisions. Feed for the livestock was a particular concern.

Amanda noted that Jeremy was even more quiet and withdrawn than usual. She detected a slow, simmering hatred for their lifestyle, and she was worried about his mental and emotional ability to cope. When Amanda tried to discuss this with James, he dismissed the concern. "Jeremy always has been a quiet boy and besides, he's in the beginning of his teenage years. What do you expect?" Amanda knew her son well. They often privately discussed their feelings about the situation, so she knew Jeremy's emotional state was more than just that of being a teenager.

While not close, Jeremy did have a friend, Mark Thomas. Mark, at fourteen, was one year older than Jeremy and yet one or two years behind in intelligence. Like his father, gruff, lame Roy Thomas, Mark was a big, lumbering, pleasant lad who was fun. He and Jeremy had been friends since they first met back in Fall Creek in 1841. Often back in Nauvoo, Jeremy, Mark, and Joseph Smith III fished, swam, and played together. They would sit off to the side after evening prayers and converse about this and that. Amanda was pleased that Jeremy and Mark were still friends.

There was no concern for Jeremy's physical condition as he was developing into a strong, healthy teenager, toughened by the rigors of the journey. Amanda could only hope that God would keep him safe, as she felt he was her main support over the long haul. He was already a major help, especially when it came to tending the animals. As with other creatures, Jeremy had an affinity for the sometimes stubborn but always essential oxen. Somehow, he was able to make them perform where others would fail. He didn't mind tending the big beasts and maybe that was the reason they reacted in kind. Jeremy and Geoff Johnson kept all the train's critters in line.

"Mama, come quick. Sister Josephine's been bit by a snake!" Eleven-year-old Clara was frantic as she pulled at Amanda's long dress. Amanda rushed to the rear of the train toward the sisters' wagon. Sitting on the ground with her back against the wagon wheel, Josephine winced in pain as she held her right leg. Her face reflected her shock.

"Rattler," said Margaret, as she bent over to console Josephine. "Sister Amanda, git Brother Thomas. I need some a his tabacca juice." Without a word, Amanda ran off to fetch Roy Thomas. Margaret pulled down the heavy stocking covering Josephine's leg and exposed the wound that was just above the ankle. Two unmistakable, and by now familiar, puncture wounds were beginning to redden and swell. She made Josephine sit so that her heart was above the wound.

Scrambling up the back of the wagon, Margaret searched for and found a bottle of turpentine. By this time, with Amanda holding on to his arm, old Roy Thomas came hobbling back, wheezing with every step, and nearly swallowing his wad.

"Spit some that there juice rat here," commanded Margaret holding out her hand. Roy did as told and Margaret smeared the juice on top of the snakebite. She then took a rag soaked in turpentine and tied it loosely around the wounded area.

"Ya got any tabacca leaves up front?"

"Yeah, I got some," Roy said.

"Well, I'd much appreciate it if'n ya could git one a yer youngin's ta run a couple down here so's I can wrap it round Sister Josephine's lag wound."

"I can do that," said Roy, but worrying to himself about his dwindling supply. He turned and headed back toward his wagon.

Because she acted so quickly, and because Josephine was in such good health, Margaret helped minimize the chances the rattler's poison would have any dire consequences.

"Sister Josephine yer gonna have ta ride in the wagon 'til ya gits better," said Margaret. It was indeed essential for Josephine to ride in the wagon for a few days to conserve her energy and to keep her leg still.

"Darn nuisance," muttered Josephine bravely, though she was pale and wobbly from the ordeal. "I hate ridin' in that bone-breakin' piece a wood." Josephine and Margaret, in fact, had walked beside their wagon the entire trip, through all kinds of terrain and weather. Josephine struggled to her feet with Margaret's assistance. Together, Margaret and Amanda helped the woman into the back of the wagon. Margaret kept the flap open in order to keep an eye on her sister and planned to walk behind the wagon just for that reason.

"Thank ya, Sister Amanda, fer yer assistance."

"My word," replied Amanda. "I didn't do anything." She was continually amazed at the toughness and resiliency of these two women.

"What happened?" said a breathless and concerned James as he rounded the corner of the wagon. He had been at the head of the train when he got the word there was a problem. "Is it true that Sister Josephine was bitten by a rattler?"

"Yep, an' a mighty big'n too," answered Margaret. "He went a slitherin' off somewhere out thar," she pointed to the area on the left side of the wagon. "We done everythin' we could an' she's restin' now."

"Are you sure it was a rattlesnake? It's mighty early and cold for them to be out."

"Brother James," Margaret said with exasperation, "I guess I know'd a rattler when I seen one, an' that there was a rattler." She defiantly jutted her chin out to emphasize her statement. "Don' care what time a year it is."

"I'm sure you're right, Sister Margaret, I'm sure you're right. You think she's needs more attention?" asked James as he peered inside the wagon at the now sleeping Josephine. "Do you want Sister Ruth to anoint and lay hands on her in the name of Jesus?" he asked.

"No, thank ya. I can handle that as well," was Margaret's blunt reply.

"Seems like Sister Margaret did everything she could. All we can do is pray that there are no complications," interjected Amanda.

"All right. Sorry it happened, Sister Margaret. Let me know if there's anything I can do to help," he said as he headed back up the train.

"Ain't that jus' like a man, always offerin' ta he'p when it's all over an' done with," Margaret said with a chuckle.

"Amen, amen," Amanda said, laughing. "Amen, indeed."

Sister Josephine's encounter with the snake significantly upset Clara. Her reaction was no surprise to Amanda. Clara had always been the frail little girl that Amanda had to protect from the swirling surroundings around her. Clara had never liked change and since the Westons left Tennessee, they had lived in nothing but a world of change. Gradually, Clara came to feel more secure in their home in Nauvoo where the daily routines were more predictable. Amanda noticed an immediate change in Clara's demeanor from the day they announced they would be leaving their home and heading west. Jeremy was aware of Clara's anxiety and helped by constantly soothing her worries by joking about the situation. Their particular relationship eased Clara's concerns in the short run, but deep under the surface, she became more introspective and withdrawn as the journey progressed. Every crisis on the expedition, and there were many, heightened Clara's apprehension. She was constantly wary, often looking around like a frightened doe, taking little comfort in words of reassurance. Clara's vulnerability caused Amanda to be overly protective.

As might be expected, the one child that Amanda had no emotional worry for on the trail was Christine. This unusual eight-year-old had always been able to adapt to almost any environment or situation. Bright blue eyes that danced, blond curly hair that was usually in her face, a smile that displayed even rows of white teeth, and her constant chatter, all added to her carefree attitude and constant quest for adventure. People instantly liked Christine. She was the favorite of the Weston train. The biggest problem Amanda had was keeping track of her. She was constantly looking for the inquisitive and gregarious child. With the many dangers attendant to life on the trail, Amanda was much more concerned with Christine's physical health than she was her mental health. That was some consolation on this dangerous and, to Amanda, ill-conceived journey.

CHAPTER 17

On April 15, at Locust Creek, Brigham Young reorganized the Camp of Israel. He saw that the constant separation of the caravan's parts was detrimental to the overall safety of the whole. Together they were a force; separated they were vulnerable. Also, separated they were unable to take care of the weaker members of the body. However, on the day they resumed their trek, the deplorable condition of the road out of the campsite and the resumption of the rain at noon, soon had the strong and lucky leaving behind the weak and unfortunate to flounder and cope as before. Despite these horrendous conditions, the cycle of life went on as usual—babies were born, people got sick or were hurt, and yes, people died.

So far, the Weston train had been lucky. They only lost some livestock. Three sheep disappeared—one each from the Westons, the Johnsons, and the Jessups. A wolf grabbed and carried away one of the sheep trailing in the back of the train while Jake, the sheep's usual protector, was in the front. Two of the sheep wandered off during a torrential downpour. Hungry wolves surely ate them as well.

Ray Thomas's only milk cow stepped in a hole and broke her leg. The men slaughtered the animal and distributed the meat proportionally throughout the Weston train. William gave one of the Westons' four milk cows to the Thomas family for compensation and milk for their children. William and James also donated one cow, one hundred pounds of flour, ten pounds of sugar, and five pounds of salt to the Church for distribution among the more needy refugees. The Weston brothers kept a wary eye on their dwindling supplies and wondered how they would make the full distance without replenishment. It became obvious; they would not, and this would eat into their rapidly diminishing cash reserves.

Overloaded wagons—many laden with the wrong things—regularly broke or bogged down in the mud.

"Pa, Brother Adams's wagon is stuck again." It was Jeremy shouting to his father through the crescendo of a torrential downpour.

"All right, son," James yelled back, tipping his head in understanding and causing a stream of water to cascade from the brim of his hat. He wearily gave Jeremy a couple of backhand waves, signaling him to lead the way. I'm goin' to have to make that man get rid of some of that furniture, James thought, as he slogged back through the mud and ooze. On his way past Jeremiah Johnson's wagon, he grabbed Tom and Geoff Johnson by the arms and motioned them to the rear. Jeremiah pointed to his chest, gesturing to James if he should come along as well. James shook his head and waved for him to stay where he was. Everyone knew what to do. It wasn't the first time they had rescued a wagon from the nearly impassable trail, and it wouldn't be the last.

As James and the boys made their way to the back, the outline of the Adams's wagon became visible. Anthony shouted encouragement to his oxen team as his long whip cracked above the animals' heads. The weary beasts strained mightily against the yoke to no avail. A mud-smeared, rain-soaked Annie and her two children, Josephine and Roger, tried unsuccessfully to turn the rear wagon wheel mired to the axel in the soft muck—an impossible and dangerous task for a woman and two small children.

James waved off Annie and the children. They thankfully backed away. James then nodded to the three boys who took up positions around the wagon and wheel and in a unified, concerted effort, sucked the wagon wheels out of the mud after three gut-wrenching tries. James slapped the boys on the back as a show of appreciation. Everyone trudged back to their wagons, receiving an unheard "Thank you" and a wave from Anthony as they passed by. It was an effort to suck their boots out of the maddening mud. Spent from the ordeal, they slogged forward, heads down, trance-like, as they had been doing for days. At such times, it was hard to remember that each step brought them closer to the Promised Land.

A few miles later, Adams did abandon a heavy chest of drawers, much to the dismay of his wife, Annie. The treasured chest, sitting forlornly beside the trail, pelted by the rain, received sad glances from occupants of other wagons as they passed by. The chest would not be the only item left littering the trail over time.

God certainly tested the Saints in every way possible. Fanatically dedicated members, like Ruth, took the tribulations in stride—they wore every scar, every setback, and every misery, as a badge of achievement. The harder God pushed, the more they pushed forward. He was merely testing them.

The majority of the flock needed constant reassurance, however. Only through leadership, organization, and discipline could these people survive. To one degree or another, the Mormon leadership from Young on down, was competent and inspiring. The pressures of resolving problems associated with so many lives under such terrible conditions often reached the breaking point, but somehow they met the challenge as the Saints doggedly headed west.

"Come children," Amanda said as she herded her brood toward the wagon for the beginning of yet another day. Her voice revealed her forced, tired resignation. The difficult journey was beginning to take its toll on Amanda. At thirty-one, she looked more like a tired forty-five. The delicate smooth hands that left Double Springs were now calloused and roughened by exposure to hard work and miserable weather. The once happy cheerful face was now drawn and sad; the alert eyes now lethargic. All of this was the result of a great deal hardship, too many disappointments, and too much worry. Amanda was not alone—she was more the norm of the women in this caravan.

However, Amanda's mental and emotional condition was worsening. She put on a respectable front, especially for her children, but every day tested her resolve to see this ordeal through to the end. Often, it took great effort for her just to get up in the morning and face whatever torment lie ahead. The constant threat of disaster wore her down. She gathered up the children and wearily pulled herself into the wagon or plodded alongside.

On the other hand, her nemesis, Ruth, seemed to thrive on the trail. Like some self-appointed itinerant shaman, she roamed from wagon to wagon, exhorting all to keep their faith in God and the Church. She gained strength from each hardship and despite her body showing definite wear and tear, her face glowed with religious zeal.

"That woman's a bit too much," snorted Margaret Waters on an aside to Amanda one day. Considering Margaret was as dedicated as Ruth, her statement spoke volumes.

From Locust Creek, located almost on the dreaded Missouri border, the Saints continued their single-minded trek northwest across the unsettled Iowa prairie. Forging a path through this desolate area was extraordinarily difficult at this time of year. There was no grass to feed their animals and many of these weary pioneers had depleted their corn and fodder before leaving Sugar Creek. Because of this, often the livestock had to eat the twigs and bark of cottonwood and elm trees to stay alive. Such provisions did little to enhance their stamina for the long journey.

The rain had been relentless for three days and the trail reduced to a quagmire of ruts and mud holes from the proceeding wagons. Relentless rainfall also made for dangerous, steep, slippery, swollen stream crossings. Mud clung to man, beast, and wagons in huge clumps of goo. The ascent and descent of steep hills always presented a particular challenge.

"It's gonna take at least a triple team ta get over this one, Brother William," hollered Jeremiah Johnson in his strong Welsh accent. The two men stood in the pouring rain watching the last of the wagons ahead of them bog down. Both men looked left and right to see if this particular hill was the best to go over. As far as they could see, this was the best alternative.

"I think you're right, Brother Jeremiah," shouted William. "While

I ready the teams, you go up ahead and see what's on the other side. I need to know where the best spot is to come up. Don't want to get up there and find I can't get down, ya hear?"

"Yes, brother, I understand," Jeremiah nodded with his rain-soaked hat. The strain of the day-in-and-day-out demanding journey was beginning to show even on the face of this hardened veteran. He had permanent worry lines—the same creases in the faces and under the eyes of most all adults on the trail. "Be back as soon as I can." He turned toward the hill, his boots sucking large clumps of mire as he struggled upward, slipping now and then as he went. Using his hands as balance, he would grudgingly shake off the mud after every encounter with the slush.

This was not the first time they had put more than one team together to pull a wagon up a precipitous hill, but this one seemed to be particularly difficult in light of the high clay content of the mud. Jeremiah was right; this was going to take more than two teams per wagon; and there were ten wagons involved. The older men relied on Jeremy and Geoff Johnson to double- and triple-hitch the teams of oxen. Everyone appreciated their extraordinary talents with animals as they maneuvered the headstrong, tired beasts into position so the men could hook them together. Jeremy and Geoff unhitched and guided two oxen from William's second wagon and put them in the lead. After a great deal of geeing and hawing, pushing and shoving, and cracking of whips, the first wagon was hitched and ready for the ascent. The men tied down everything possible within the wagon while Ruth and the children dismounted and stood together in the rain off to one side.

"Come here," Mary Ellen motioned to them. "Come in here outta the rain." Mary, Edith, Sarah, and George all scrambled up and into the second wagon, huddling together with John and Jacob. Ruth stood in the downpour; defying the swirling rain, her long mud-stained skirt flapping in the cold wind. Might just as well get used to it, she thought. Ruth knew they were all going to have to walk over the hill anyway. It was too dangerous to ride in the wagons.

Jeremiah returned from scouting the hill. "There's no good place ta cross over," he hollered in William's ear, "they're all bad. Best go ta the right of where that last wagon's headed," he pointed. "There's a little knoll about half way down."

William nodded. When he saw the last wagon of the train ahead disappear over the crest of the hill, he motioned to move forward. With Jeremy and Geoff at the head, tugging at the lead oxen, William and James on each side cracking whips over the slipping, sliding, fettered beasts, and the rest of the able-bodied men pushing on the wagon and pulling the mired wheels out of the muck, the wagon slowly began its journey up the hill. William had warned the men on the wheels to stay to one side—the slightest roll backwards could easily pin someone underneath.

It took twenty minutes for the wagon to reach the top. The muddied, spent men caught their breath and looked back down the hill, assessing the slope they had ascended and waving at the huddled families below who were barely visible in the pelting rain. They then turned and looked down the other side—a much steeper incline than that coming up. They could see families from the train preceding them just beginning to regroup. At least three of the wagons had overturned, their contents a jumbled mess with some spilling out into the mud. The men below shouted, pushed, shoved, and strained to upright the wagons while the women scurried about picking up items strewn about the muddy, rain-soaked soil.

"Now *that* is what I *do not* want to happen," William shouted to the panting group assembled around him, as he pointed to the scene below. "Gather round and listen to me. Let's put a brake on the rear." William was referring to the practice of tying a log behind a wagon on a downhill slope, often called a Mormon brake—a dubious technique in such muddy conditions. "I want two teams of oxen in front of the wagon and one in the rear. Rope the rear team so they can help brake as we go down. Nobody, and I mean *nobody*, is to get in front of or near the wheels or the brake. Stay to the sides and keep pulling back on the teams." William stopped for a moment to catch his breath and wipe away the mud and water accumulated on his face.

"Brother James and I will take the lead team. Jeremy and Geoff, you handle the rear team. It's important that you hold them back so their weight helps brake as we go down. The rest of you tie two ropes to the rear of the wagon and pull backwards all the way to the bottom." He paused and looked around the circle of men. "Everyone understand?"

All heads made a positive nod.

"God willin', let's do it!" shouted William, as he saw that the train ahead had cleared away. Comin' up was hard, he thought, goin' down is going to be a lot harder.

After they dragged the log up from below, tied it to the wagon, and everyone was in place, the cluster of miserable men started their descent. There was a great deal of slipping and sliding and "whoaing," grunting, and gasping, but slowly the wagon reached the bottom unblemished. The tired men looked with satisfaction at the wagon, mud-smeared to be sure, but standing upright with all contents secure inside.

"One down, nine to go!" shouted William, turning to plod back up the slippery incline. The look of satisfaction instantly faded as the men realized he was right—it was only nine in the morning and it was going to be a very long day. By the time the crew returned to hitch up the next wagon, an hour and a half had gone by. The returning two oxen stood to one side to rest. That was the routine from there on out. It was obvious there was no way to transport all the wagons over the hill in one day. The train would have to spend the night apart, something no one liked or wanted.

Seems to me it would be a lot smarter to wait until the rain stops and the ground firms up, thought the ever-cynical Jeremy. That it hadn't stopped raining for days—nor would it—was lost on this unhappy teenager. Anyway, as he knew, that was not the way of these Mormons. They pushed ahead no matter what the obstacle. No train wanted to hold up the one behind, even though that was often the case. There were, in fact, trains scattered all over the Iowa countryside, much to Brigham Young's consternation.

Jake's sad eyes looked up at his master. His mud-spattered face had a sympathetic cast, as if he knew what Jeremy was thinking. He whined and nudged Jeremy's leg, letting him know he was supportive. Jeremy patted his faithful dog's head and massaged his wet, soggy ears. No matter how tired he was, Jake never left Jeremy's side as they made trip after trip over the hill.

That night—with the train split half on one side of the hill and half on the other— was one of the more miserable nights the Weston Train had to endure. The rain continued to come down in sheets and a terrible lightning storm struck around ten o'clock, frightening adults and children alike. A cold wind whipped across the water-soaked ground, chilling every living thing. There was no way to build a fire for warmth or to cook food. Most ate squash cakes that had been prepared before and kept dry. People and beasts huddled together for warmth and the companionship that is so necessary to survive such communal misery. All were used to having the train together and missed the feeling of wholeness that offers a sense of protection for the individual.

Amanda couldn't believe it was morning and time to move out again. The gray skies were light enough to let her know that another miserable day was at hand. Begrudgingly, she pulled herself up from her makeshift bed in the wagon. The bedding was wet from all-night rains that had dripped through the wagon covers. Actually, the bedding and clothing had been damp for days. Last night's rain merely aggravated the situation.

Aching from head to toe, she sat trying to pull on her soggy, misshapen shoes that had been wet then dry and then wet so often they were taking on a life of their own. At this point, the feet had to fit the shoes, not the other way around. It would be four o'clock before the men were able to bring the rest of the train over the wretched, slippery, dangerous ridge. For Amanda, an entire day without moving on the trail was a blessing, despite the constant rain. Blessing or no, however, there were many chores to do. Robotically, she climbed down from the wagon and began her discouraging, monotonous, and sometimes unsafe routine. The thoughts of her beautiful, comfortable, and stable life back in Double Springs, Tennessee was a daydream she could always rely on to comfort her in times of depression, but even that was beginning to fade now. Too much had happened and too much was to come. Daydreaming was a luxury she could ill afford.

Chapter 18

By April 24, the wagon trains bogged down again and dotted the bare countryside as far as the eye could see. As he waited for the stragglers to catch up, Young decided to build a permanent settlement at this location near the Grand River. He saw that some of the Saints could go no farther and, he reasoned, countless future companies that followed would benefit from this, the fourth such settlement to be established.

William gathered the men in his train around him. "Brother Young says we can't just sit here and feel sorry for ourselves. Idle hands are the playground of the devil, for sure." He pointed to Roy, Jr. and Tom and Geoff Johnson. "Get your axes and join the group at Brother Kimball's wagon over there," he said, pointing across the encampment. "You're going to cut down trees to make logs. Brother Young has decided to make this another place for future Mormons coming this way to stop." This the young men did without complaint. Anything was better than sitting idle in the damp, cold spring air.

Next, he told James, Anthony Adams, and Jeremiah Johnson to report to a group that would take the logs and make a bridge across a branch of the river. Their experience at assembling such structures before would be especially useful. William, as captain of a train, met with his superior, a second major, to receive the daily critique and any orders from Brigham Young. He then returned to the train to make sure camp was set up properly. Roy Thomas and Joshua Jessup assisted him—both of the old Hahn's Mill survivors were physically not up to the stress the other work details required. Joshua usually went with some of the older boys to collect wood for the fires. Often, Roy gathered up small children and kept them entertained with games and wild stories while their parents labored.

The routine was the same at each location Young chose to establish a base. A trumpeter from the band would blow and the day's work would begin. One crew of a hundred men would begin axing a nearby stand of trees, felling one after the other. Another crew would start trimming and chopping the felled trees into logs that were used to build cabins and, if needed, bridges. Another gang would start digging wells while others fashioned wooden plows. Those with physical disabilities would gather dishes, furniture, and other non-essentials and head off into the nearest settlement to trade for desperately needed provisions. Like swarming ants, they would construct a self-sustaining settlement almost overnight. This remarkable and oft-repeated feat of communal effort always astonished locals and other non-believers, but it also intimidated them and caused them to be jealous. Often, what the Mormons left behind was better than what the non-believers had after years of individual labor.

By the time they departed this particular location on May 11, they left a collection of log cabins, planted and fenced fields, a road, wells, and a bridge over the river. They named the town, Garden Grove. Forty-five miles after leaving Garden Grove, the Saints again stopped on May 16 and started another settlement, Mt. Pisgah. By the end of the month, they had moved westward to where Indian Creek flows into the Missouri River, establishing yet one more settlement called Miller's Hollow. Thus, it was, the Saints forged ahead mile after painstaking mile toward their ultimate goal, leaving established settlements for future travelers to use on their way to the Promised Land.

As if God realized he had pushed the Mormons too far, the rains suddenly stopped. Although the hardships of the trail did not lessen, the spirits of the weary travelers improved. Everyone seemed to smile more often and to have a little more bounce to their stride.

This blessed period of decent weather allowed the soggy ground to dry out and a variety of switch, Indian, and cord prairie grasses to begin growing. With this blessing also came a curse—large numbers of rattlesnakes appeared as well. Horse and oxen noses were particular targets, resulting in many sick animals and some deaths. People were not immune, of course, but were more alert to the danger. Amanda heard that one child in the train ahead had died from a snakebite. Fatigue, poor food, and constant exposure to the elements often made people, especially children, more susceptible to the effects of disease or poison, such as snakebite venom.

Unfortunately, as soon as the weather began to dry, grass fires flared up on the horizon. Whether set by man or nature, this new threat was dangerous. The captains, forewarned of such possibilities, set backfires to stop or divert the on-rushing flames. This action worked, as the treacherous fires swept past them causing no harm. Now, however, the Saints encountered something new—sleeping on charred ground, as soot and ashes from distant fires fell all about them. Within a few days, the rains returned and the grassless ground became even muddier than before.

On May 27, word spread quickly that the United States was at war with Mexico.

"I hope they lose," said Ruth. Her feelings were the sentiment of many of the Saints who had suffered greatly at the hands of the federal government and its biased population.

"Brother Weston," called Brigham Young from atop his horse. "May I have a word with you?" Young reigned in his horse next to William, towering over him—imposing, intimidating, as he looked down.

Bent over greasing a wheel on his wagon, his mind otherwise occupied, William was oblivious to Young's approach. The voice startled him and he jerked up straight. "Oh, Brother Young." He set down the grease can and made a pretense of straightening out his rumpled clothing. "Yes, yes, of course. What can I do for you, Brother?" he stammered.

Next to Young, sitting tall in the saddle of a large brindled horse was a man William knew from the Legion back in Nauvoo—Brother James Brown. Brigham Young slowly dismounted from his horse, removed his right glove, and held out his hand to William. "It's nice to see you again, Brother," he said. "How's your family bearing up under this glorious expedition?"

"Fine, fine. We're all good, Brother." Nervously, William wiped his hand on his clothing before taking Young's hand. He hadn't spoken to Young since he asked for Jake's reprieve from the leash requirement. He was naturally curious. What could Brother Young possibly want from him?

"I believe you know Brother Brown," Young said as he gestured upward toward the rider beside them.

"Yes, I do," replied William, nodding his head toward Brown. Brown nodded back.

"Brother William," Young addressed William directly with full eye contact, "the President of the United States has authorized me to form a Mormon Battalion of 500 men to serve in the U.S. Army and help defend our country against the Mexicans. This is a great opportunity for us to quiet some of our enemies and to generate income for our movement, as well as serve our country in a time of need."

Of course, William knew of the drive to recruit men within the masses moving from Nauvoo and, likewise, was aware of the reasons Young thought this was a great idea. It had been the subject of much discussion around the campfires. He had not thought about joining such a movement, considering his many family responsibilities.

"Within the circles of the officer corps of the Nauvoo Legion," Young continued, "you were considered a superior leader. Frankly, I don't have time to say more than we want you to join the Mormon Battalion in Captain Brown's C Company as a First Lieutenant."

"Well, I ... I am flattered that you would put such trust in me but, I do have substantial family obligations," stammered William.

"I understand, and you are not alone. I realize that this is asking a lot and will entail considerable sacrifice, but we cannot send a body of troops out to represent us and not have good leadership. You, and others like you, are essential for the success of this mission. Unlike some others, you have at least someone to help. I'm sure that, that . . ." Young looked up to Brown for assistance.

"Brother James."

"Yes, Brother James. I am to believe that your brother, who I understand is very capable, will make sure you family is taken care of while you are away. It's a time of great sacrifice for all if we are to reach the Land of Zion. I know I can count on you. Please make arrangements with your family and report to Brother Brown forthwith as the battalion will be moving out on the 20th and there is much to do beforehand." Young remounted his horse with some effort, settled into the saddle, squeaking in protest under his weight, and smiled down at William saying, "You will do well, Brother William. You will do well." He wheeled his horse around, kicked him in the flanks, and with Brown trailing behind rode off to enlist other candidates for the unpopular and confounding mission. Assembling 500 fit men for this operation would not be easy but if anyone could do it, Brigham Young was the man.

"Yes, sir," William said, dazed from the encounter. Young's ability to ask someone to do something and then not wait for an answer was a well-known trait. What he wanted, he got. He was very persuasive and his wrath considerable if he did not get his way. More than one person and group had felt both, and always these encounters had left no doubt as to who was in charge.

Thus, Brigham Young went in and about the encampments from Garden Grove to Mt. Pisgah to Council Bluffs recruiting men for the Mormon Battalion. It was a difficult task. Not only were able-bodied men reluctant to leave their suffering families, their distrust and dislike for a government that had them persecuted and driven from their homes was undisputed. Now, this same government wanted them to fight a war against the Mexicans, who had never done anything to the Saints.

However, these 500 soldiers would be a great asset to Young. Their formation and dispatch to General Kearney in California meant "hard cash" for the Mormon coffers and the transport of 500 men to the West Coast at government expense. In addition, the government gave Young permission to camp on Indian lands and use the grass and timber thereon. Therefore, the formation of the battalion was essential. That it caused great hardship for many families in the caravan was incidental.

"I beg your pardon," Amanda said to James, with her head cocked to one side and a look of utter disbelief.

"I said," James defensively replied, "William has been ordered to go with the Mormon Battalion to fight in the Mexican War." He had dreaded telling Amanda about this situation almost more than he feared the prospects of having to take care of William's families. When William first told him of the circumstances, he had gone weak in the knees. Life on the trail was difficult enough as it was without being directly responsible for the health and wellbeing of William's family, not to mention the leadership of the train and all that it entailed.

"I'm not sure I can do it, Brother," he had commented to William. "Are you positive that you have to go? Excuse me, but that's one hell of a thing for Brother Young to ask."

"Yes, I know, but, little brother, we signed on for this soul saving adventure and know that each of us is but a small part of the whole mechanism that makes it all work. I cannot refuse this order."

"To be honest, I would rather go to war and let you stay home to take care of the families." James was struggling with the whole idea. He had willingly sacrificed much for the Church, but this was almost more than he could abide. William talked the better part of an hour to assure James that he had to do it. There simply was no way out.

Amanda put her hands on her hips and fumed at James. "Surely you jest?" she questioned defiantly. The edge on her voice could have cut through steel. "And let me guess, you," she pointed her finger at him; "you are getting the short end of the stick. *You* have to take care of his menagerie while he's gone."

"Amanda, I have no choice. I like it even less than you do, but I have no choice," James emphasized. "We all have to pull together as a group to pass through this trial of faith, Amanda. I have a duty and with God's help, I will do it as best I can."

"Duty? Duty?" she repeated. "I'm sorry, James, but *we* joined this disaster to supposedly save our souls, not to destroy our family, lose our wealth, and be responsible for a pack of so-called relatives. Five hundred men to go fight for a country that has driven us from our homes and killed our people? Has the whole world gone crazy? No, on second thought, not the whole world—just ours?" Had James been able to see her aura, it was a flaming, beet red.

Amanda was in shock. She had agreed that she would go along with all the privations and hardships of getting to the "Promised Land," because she had no choice. This ... this was too much. Amanda turned and walked away from James. She had to go somewhere and think. They had sucked James into this whole fiasco and, like a whipped puppy, he had given in. For Amanda, it was a case of having to give up ... give up everything she believed in and valued. James stood watching his wife walk away. He felt guilty for putting her in this position. This was just one more ordeal designed by God to test him. It was a test of his faith and he would not fail—no matter what his recalcitrant wife thought or did.

"Excuse me, Brother William, may I have a moment of your time?" It was Jeremiah Johnson, who stood by the front of William's wagon. He held his battered, dirty, old hat in two hands at his waist, nervously fingering the wide brim. His abundant, unruly hair blew about in the gentle afternoon breeze, then and again uncovering the rugged face beneath.

"Of course, Brother Jeremiah, what can I do for you?" William looked up from the harness he was mending.

"It's about Tom," said Jeremiah.

"What about him—is he sick or been hurt?" William noted the look of concern on Jeremiah's face.

"No, no, nothing' like that. It ... it's about this Mormon Battalion business," Jeremiah stammered.

"I take it Tom's been called up to go."

"Yes. Now, I know at nineteen he's a grown man, but I truly worry about him goin' off ta fight some war so far away. Sister Mary is frettin' somethin' terrible."

"I know, I know," consoled William. "I guess you know I'm going as well?"

"Yes, everyone knows. And I was mighty sorry ta hear it, considering all your obligations and everythin'."

"Well, I've resigned myself that I must do Brother Young's bidding if it's for the good of the Church."

"True that is," said Jeremiah. "I guess what I come ta ask is, would you look out for Tom. It would be a great comfort to his mother and me if we knew you made sure he stayed out a trouble."

"It would be my great pleasure, Brother Jeremiah. But he's much younger and stronger than I am—maybe he should be looking out for me," kidded William.

Jeremiah laughed. "You may be right, Brother William. You may be right."

"Tell Sister Mary not to worry. Tom'll be all right. I'll make sure of it."

"Thank ya, Brother William. We'll breathe easier now. And you may be sure we'll help care for your families while you're gone."

"Well, that would be right neighborly of you. Thank you, Brother Jeremiah."

"May God bless and protect you and all the men and boys in the Brigade."

"Thank you. I'm sure he will," said William.

Nineteen-year-old Roy Thomas, Jr. also joined the Battalion. Roy Jr. was not very bright and somewhat uncoordinated, but, all the same, he was an excellent rifleman and he was physically as big and strong as his father. Old Roy grumbled at the loss of a strong back to help with the many chores. That the Prophet selected her boy to go with all those brave warriors thrilled the religious fanatic, Amelia.

It took about a month for Brigham Young to cajole, beg, and order up the 500 men needed for outfitting the Mormon Battalion. There was great concern for the families left behind. Illness, hunger, and other deprivations were common among many, and winter was approaching.

"Are you going to the ball tonight, Sister Amanda?" asked Mary Ellen, innocently. She was referring to a dance planned that evening to honor the men of the departing Mormon Battalion. Under a recently constructed large canopy, William Pitt's Band would provide music for hundreds of dancers.

"I may drop by later," Amanda replied politely, as she patted Mary Ellen on the shoulder.

The ball had been in the making for a couple of weeks and everyone was excited. Amanda was constantly amazed and in awe of the Mormons. Formation of the Mormon Battalion was gut wrenching for many families, as strong men and boys were taken from families during a time of great need, often leaving only their women and children to perform Herculean tasks. Yet, here they were planning a party! Amanda was one of those least affected by the men's departure, but she certainly did not feel like having a party. She just chalked her feelings up to her poor attitude overall and to a broad concern for the hard times ahead. That evening, as the band played, she sat outside the wagon watching the dancers twirl about in the dim light of campfires ringing the canopy. She had no idea where James was. He sensed that her apprehension over this whole Mexican War business would not put her in a festive mood and stayed away. He was right. The one most affected, Ruth, was not happy either, but in true Mormon fashion, she showed nothing but support for the inevitable. It was God's will. Two days later, on July 20, 1846, the Battalion moved out. Both Amanda and Ruth cried, albeit for different reasons.

Not all Mormons left Nauvoo back in the winter of 1846. Nearly 1000 souls were either too poor or too sick to make the journey. They needed assistance and Brigham Young was determined to come to their aid. Word drifted in daily of the plight of these poor saints as each wagon train caught up with the main body. An army of thugs violently forced the remaining Mormons out of Nauvoo and across the river. All of the Gentile's pent-up hatred of Joseph Smith, Brigham Young, and their followers was unleashed on these unfortunates.

The basic nature of humankind stunned Amanda as she listened to these ghastly tales of survival and suffering. She had long ago figured out why outsiders disliked and feared the Mormons, despite the many great and good things the Saints did. Nevertheless, the depth of hatred and the cruelty they exercised displaying these feelings always made her feel sick.

Amanda was aware that Emma and her family remained in Nauvoo after the main body of Saints left. She couldn't help but admire her courage but wondered about the safety and wellbeing of the beleaguered woman and her children. Only later, in mid-September of 1846, did she hear that Emma moved her family to safety in Fulton City, Illinois, 120 miles north of Nauvoo. Amanda was happy and relieved to hear this news. Despite their unusual and tenuous relationship, Amanda felt a kinship with this strange, stern woman. However, she couldn't reconcile in her mind how such an obviously intelligent and knowledgeable person could so easily rationalize the teachings and the actions of her husband.

CHAPTER 19

"Hurry, we're the next to cross!" shouted James. In his new role as leader of the Weston Train, he had little time to become accustomed to the position before Brigham Young ordered a large contingent to leave Council Bluffs and settle on the opposite side of the Missouri River. Earlier, James called all the people in his train together and explained to everyone that they would cross the river and establish a settlement on the other side.

"Why're we doin' this, Brother?" asked Roy Thomas. The trip west had been particularly hard on this old Mormon warrior. A horse had stomped on the foot of his previously mangled leg, causing him now to use a crutch to walk around. This was extremely painful, even for a man used to pain. Besides that, he had contracted a lung infection three weeks ago causing him to constantly cough up phlegm—so much so, that he had to give up his favorite addiction, chewin' tabacca. Instead, he would take a shot of "medicinal whiskey" now and then to cut the phlegm. In short, old Roy was in bad shape and would have liked nothing better than to just stay put for the winter and recuperate. As he said, he was, "Jus' plain wore out."

"Brother Young wants as many of us as possible to move across the river out of reach of any Gentiles that could do us harm," answered James.

"I allow there's gotta be more'n that," retorted Roy between coughs. "There ain't enough Pukes out here ta do nothin' ta nobody."

"Now, Brother Roy, you've been around long enough to know when Brother Young wants us to go across the river, we're going across the river." James tried to muster up as much authority in his voice as he could.

"Yeah, yeah," lamented a disgruntled Roy as he hobbled toward his wagon.

As it was, Roy was right. Young had used formation of the Mormon Battalion as a bargaining chip to receive permission to move as many people as possible across the Missouri to avoid any Gentile misdeeds. The land west of the Missouri was Indian Territory under the jurisdiction of the Bureau of Indian Affairs. However, Captain James Allen, acting on orders from President Polk to form the Mormon Battalion, gave Young permission to make the move. As part of the negotiations for sending the Mormon Battalion, Young established a camp across the Missouri River from Council Bluffs, that he dubbed Winter Quarters. People and wagons immediately started moving across the river on a ferry the Saints had constructed. Some 30,000 head of livestock swam the river.

Ultimately, like many others, the Weston Train made its way across the Missouri with wagons and people on ferries and livestock swimming.

"Words comin' down that we're going to spend the winter here, Brother Roy," James hollered back toward the unhappy old timer. "Looks like you're going to your rest after all."

"Sounds like Brother Young took my advice," Roy yelled back.

"Guess so," answered James.

Roy wasn't the only one who looked forward to the respite. James was particularly pleased to be able to collect his train and establish some order—something not easily done while on the move. They had come only 266 miserable miles from Nauvoo and it had taken them about six months. It was time to pause.

Amanda received the word with mixed emotions. Heaven knows they needed a rest, especially with winter just around the bend. However, she also understood the delay would mean that they would be on the trail that much longer. As she took stock of the toll on her immediate family and the rest of the train, she felt blessed so far. Other than Joshua Jessup, who had contracted consumption (tuberculosis) and Josephine's snakebite, there had been no major illnesses, accidents, or other disastrous mishaps all along the Iowa trek. True, a horse stomped on old Roy's foot, but that only exacerbated an old problem. Quite simply, the Weston Train had escaped the deaths and disasters that plagued many in other trains. She wasn't sure if their train was better organized and well equipped than others or they had just been lucky.

After the crossing, James called everyone in the train together. He had just come from a meeting of train officers who received orders regarding location and composition of their site in Winter Quarters. The task envisioned by Brigham Young seemed almost impossible, but then James long ago had resigned to the fact that "impossible" was not in the Mormon dictionary. Based on the number of people, the Weston Train was to build nine cabins on lots one through nine on Site 27, just off the First Main Street. The organizational skills of Young and his subordinates were amazing, thought James.

"Now listen carefully," James said as the families gathered around his wagon. "We have a big job to do before winter comes." As usual, the massive job of building a settlement of what was to become hundreds of log and sod cabins would be a communal effort. Teams of men would go to the nearby woods and cut and trim trees into logs. Others used oxen and horses to drag the logs to the construction site. Other, more experienced teams would construct the houses.

The struggle for survival for the Mormons meant more than just constructing hundreds of homes before winter. It was part of the Mormon psyche to make sure, no matter how rudimentary, they had schools, places of worship, cultural centers, and police protection. Included in the list of necessities at Winter Quarters was the building of a grist or flourmill on Turkey Creek north of the settlement. Flour and meal from this mill were indispensable to feed the camp during the long winter.

Despite the beaver-like building frenzy all around, it would be the end of August before Amanda would have a reasonably substantial home for her family. Until then, they lived as they did on the trail, a combination of wagon and tent to shield them from the elements. At least it was stationary and avoided the constant striking of camp they endured on the trail. During the hot weather, mosquitoes were a constant nuisance and memories of intermittent fever, or ague (malaria), caused by these pests in Nauvoo concerned everyone. The climate was different but the conditions comparable.

Finally, Amanda stood in the doorway and surveyed the interior of their new home—a small ten-foot square, one-room, cottonwood log house laid cob fashion with a foot-thick roof made of willows, straw, and sod. There was a chimney made of the same prairie sod, a wood floor—a luxury, as many had dirt floors—a plank door, and one shuttered, waxed-cloth window. The walls inside were chinked with mud. Despite it dinginess and size, it was a solid structure that would offer considerable protection against the harsh winter winds that were sure to come. It was obvious, however, that sharing the small space with others in the train would be a necessity, and the thought of months on end of such cramped quarters during the winter depressed Amanda. She foresaw accurately the necessity of having to sleep in shifts if things got tight.

Tears welled up as a wave of despair flooded over her. No matter how hard she tried not to, and how pointless it was to do so, she couldn't hide her dismay thinking how terribly far down on the ladder had they come from their beautiful homes in Double Springs and Nauvoo. She shook her head, fought off the tears, and with pursed lips, rededicated herself to seeing this thing through to the end. How many times had she done this? she thought. Her family depended on her and now was not the time to show weakness, no matter how bitter and disappointed she felt. She busied herself with furnishing her new home with the skimpy, battered items from the tent and wagon. As time went on, she considered herself privileged. Many of those arriving later on would have to live in dugouts carved out of the bluffs or ride out the winter in their tents and wagons.

Members of the rest of the Weston Train, through their combined efforts, had similar structures constructed on their assigned lots by the end of September. Mary Ellen and Elizabeth, and their children, would occupy one cabin—not a happy arrangement but crucial since structures were so precious and their families small. Roy and Amelia Thompson and their brood would occupy the largest structure, a crowded twelve-by-sixteen-foot building. Often throughout the winter, two or three of the Thompson children would sleep with the sisters, Margaret and Josephine, just to relieve the monotony. Similarly, other Thomas children frequently bedded down in Amanda's cabin; especially sensitive Mary Thomas who wanted to escape the overbearing Ruth.

James didn't know the rider that pulled up to him as he worked on his cabin.

"Brother Weston?" asked the man.

"Yes, what can I do for you?"

"I have here a letter from yer brother with the Battalion." He pulled the brown envelope from a saddle bag and handed it to James."

Thank you very much," smiled James. "Can I get you something to drink?"

"No, thank ya. I gotta deliver a whole bunch more." The man whirled his horse about and galloped off.

James sat on a log and quickly ripped open the large envelope. Inside was a letter addressed to him, and two smaller envelopes—one addressed to Ruth, Mary Ellen, and Elizabeth, and the other containing $126.00. He was curious about that amount of cash as he unfolded the letter addressed to him and read:

August 3, 1846

Dear James,

I want to let you know that the Battalion arrived at Fort Leavenworth on August 1 without incident. Here we got arms, ammunition, and effects for our journey ahead. Instead of drawing uniforms, we all took the allowance of $42.00 per man and are sending it to our families and the Church. You distribute the money according to need to my wives, Jeremiah Johnson, Roy Thomas, and to whatever and whomever Brother Young is requesting for the common good.

Tell Jeremiah and Roy that both their boys are fine. They will be toughened grown men the next time they see them.

I hope all is going well. I understand Brother Young has established a Winter Quarters that you will live in until next spring. That is wise. You all will be in better shape for the final journey to the Promised Land.

We have a long, hard, and dangerous journey ahead until we arrive in Santa Fe. Pray for us, as we will for you.

God bless you, brother.

William

It was a busy time for the Mormons in Winter Quarters. The Saints had to prepare for winter and, more importantly, restock, repair, and rededicate themselves for the final leg of the trip next spring. The communal effort meant that if you finished your work, you then helped someone else finish theirs. The more fortunate always helped the less fortunate; the healthy ministered to the sick; the strong lent a hand to the weak. Moreover, regardless the circumstance, everyone had to do whatever Brother Young decided was for the good of the whole.

Remaining in one place was beneficial to everyone, especially the little ones. Children blossomed intellectually and emotionally under stability and routine while their parents regained strength and a sense of purpose. Amanda saw progress in her brood. Clara began to reclaim some color and improvement in attitude. The uncertainly of the trail took a tremendous toll on this sensitive child and Amanda couldn't stop constantly feeling guilty for having to submit her to the vicissitudes of camp life. The soon-to-be-eight, Christine, flourished with the established routine and was to cause Amanda the usual concerns of any parent as she wandered the camp in search of new friends and adventures. Keeping track of this popular child was a full-time chore and constant worry. The maturing, still sober Jeremy looked less tired and troubled. Despite the heavy workload of the camp, he had less responsibility than on the trail. As the summer progressed and then waned, Amanda felt better about herself and her children.

William wrote another letter in October. The Mormon Battalion arrived in Santa Fe after marching 1100 mile, and building a wagon road along the way. Despite the excellent leadership of their commanding officer, Lt. Colonel Cooke, the men suffered from lack of food, improper medical treatment, and forced long-distant marches. They encountered no Mexican forces, only some friendly but thieving Indians. The Weston Train boys were doing well. Everyone missed their families.

Many latecomers straggled into Winter Quarters. Thus, did the poor and destitute Saints swell daily, as did the incidents of illness. The Mormons were cleaner and more orderly than the majority of the frontier communities; but, they did drank from creek water and experienced only rudimentary sanitary conditions—frequently resulting in debilitating cases of dysentery. Seldom did anyone die of dysentery, however. As the winter progressed, the major killers were ague, measles, consumption, pneumonia, and black leg (scurvy), to name a few.

There was a knock on the door. James opened it.

"Brother James, I'm at my wits end," said Prudence Jessup through a stream of tears. "Poor ol' Brother Joshua is coughin' a lot an' spittin' up more an' more blood." She had trucked through the unusually cold, windy autumn evening air and was standing at the doorway of James's cabin.

"Come in Sister Prudence. Come in out of the cold," James said as he gently took her arm with one hand and motioned for her to enter with the other.

Amanda, who was sitting by the fireplace, stood up and came to Prudence's side. "Come, Sister Prudence, sit here by the fire."

"Thank ya, thank ya so much." Prudence walked slowly through the children seated and standing around the cabin and sat in a chair. She was shaking with worry and from the cold walk from her cabin. The fire was warm, but the room smelled of smoke as the sod chimney did not always draw well in a shifting wind. There was also the odor of humans that comes from so many people confined to such a small area for long periods. Prudence paid no mind, as they were familiar odors to everyone living in Winter Quarters.

Once seated, she tried to hold back the tears, but was unsuccessful. "I'm terrible afraid that Brother Joshua's in real trouble," she said between small spasms of crying. "Brother Kimball anointed him an' laid his hands on 'im, but it didn't help none. He said the rest was up ta God. We cain't draw any blood 'cause I don' know nobody who has any leeches. I ... I know Brother Young doesn't cotton ta usin' leeches," she said, "But rat now I'm willin' ta try anythin'. That old yarb an' root doctor, Brother Jameson, was next ta useless," she babbled on. "Brother Joshua won't eat an' he's lost so much weight—oh, so much weight. He looks like a walkin' skeleton," she concluded, placing her face in her hands and openly sobbing. Amanda was standing behind her gently patting her shoulders and glumly shaking her head at James.

James was not surprised. He had seen Joshua just yesterday and noticed that his cheeks were prominent and eyes hollow. When James asked Joshua how he was doing, Joshua complained between coughs that the pain in his right side was terrible and he could hardly walk on his swollen feet. As James knew, these were definite signs Joshua was failing and that death was not far away. Joshua and Prudence knew it too, but forced it from their minds. Their four children recognized that something awful was happening to their father and worried what would happen to them if he died. Consumption struck fear. No one knew what caused it, but everyone knew it was contagious. This put a terrible strain on everyone, especially the rest of the Jessup family who had to share the tiny cabin with Joshua. The hope was that God would protect all others through constant prayer. As spiritual and temporal leader of the train, James was the person who expected to offer comfort and counseling.

"Come, Sister Prudence, let's walk back to your cabin together," James said gently as he took her hands in his. There was nothing to do but comfort her. He was inwardly angry with William for leaving him in this position. William was so much stronger and better at this sort of thing. However, here he was and he was obligated to do the best he could. No one had died in their train since they left Nauvoo and he knew the first death would have a terrible effect on the morale of the others. He also realized that the discussion was beginning to upset his children. He helped Prudence to her feet. They left the room and walked toward the Jessup cabin.

The next evening, after the workday concluded, James assembled all the members of the train in front of the Jessup cabin. Everyone knelt on the hard ground as James led them in prayer, beseeching God, if it were his will, to spare the life of their faithful and beloved friend and father, Brother Joshua. It was not his will as Joshua died the next day. Again, with all assembled, James led the group in prayer as they buried Joshua in a graveyard that was growing in size daily. Brother Kimball was in attendance as well and reflected that he was attending too many of these ceremonies lately. It was now up to James to see that Prudence and her four small children were properly cared for in Joshua's absence. How much more could he take on, he thought. He slid into a state of temporary melancholy. However, God must have answered some of their prayers, as no one else in the Jessup family contracted the disease.

Brother Young was persistent in his push to ready everything for the next and final 1000-mile-journey to Utah. Young originally intended to travel all the way to the Salt Lake Valley in 1846, but the leader of the Saints had to face facts. The lack of preparation of some immigrants, the harsh toll taken in the difficult trek across Iowa, and the loss of manpower in forming the Battalion, convinced Young to wait out the winter encamped on both sides of the Missouri River. Here the Saints would regroup and better prepare themselves for the final push west next spring. The task for the winter was not only to construct living quarters and other structures, but, at the same time, build and outfit wagons sturdy enough for the trek, stock up supplies for those making the trip, and gather other supplies for the sustenance and protection for those remaining behind. They cut and stacked thousands of tons of prairie hay. Bushel after bushel of wild berries were gathered and preserved. They killed, dressed, and salted down or dried wild game. Young's beehive of Saints' backs and hands never wavered in its determination to complete the many tasks before them—he wouldn't let them.

Unfortunately, Amanda's assessment of their train's encouraging luck in avoiding mishaps, diseases, and death was due for another set back. Two months after Joshua Jessup's death, William and Mary Ellen's three-year-old son died. Jacob Weston had always been a fragile child and when he contracted croup, it was too much for his system. The cold temperatures within the cabins were the basic cause. Jacob developed a sore throat, sharp high-pitched cough, hissing-like breathing, and convulsions. On the fourth day, Jacob could not swallow or breathe, quickly causing suffocation and death.

Losing an adult was bad, but losing a child was devastating to the Weston Train. Morale dipped to a new low. Disease and death was nothing new to these hardy people for much of it had occurred back in Nauvoo. Somehow, living together so closely on the trail magnified each loss. It felt like it happened to a member of your own family.

The correspondence between the Westons and William continued intermittently. Another letter arrived from William in which he told how, on November 28, they had their first casualties—a herd of wild bulls attacked the unit. The bulls injured two men before the soldiers drove off the enraged animals. The men called this the "Battle of the Bulls," a joke to all but the injured soldiers.

He told how the Battalion had reached Tucson on December 16. There was a Mexican force located there but they fled when they saw the Mormons coming. The weary men couldn't wait to arrive at their final destination, beautiful San Diego, California.

William bemoaned the loss of his son Jacob and prayed that there would be no more.

CHAPTER 20

Winter came and some 3500 Saints hunkered down and waited out the long days and nights in their makeshift, crowded dwellings. While they were constantly busy just trying to survive and prepare for the coming journey in the spring, the harsh weather, confined quarters, and rampant sickness, wore heavily on these restless people. Nevertheless, their leaders knew that their followers were a hardy, disciplined, and motivated group.

Protecting her children from the rampant sickness that swept through the settlement preoccupied Amanda. It was the same in Nauvoo, but the vagaries of life on the trail and the instability of Winter Quarters made it harder. One of the most prevalent problems was scurvy. Their diet consisted mainly of corn bread, a little milk, salt bacon, an occasional chicken, or piece of beef, and, from time to time, some game meat. They all lacked fresh fruit and vegetables. Whenever Amanda could acquire some—usually potatoes—she gave it to the children. She and James often did without, much to their detriment.

As always, Clara worried Amanda most. It seemed this frail child was always on the brink of illness. Clara's pale color and listlessness was a harbinger. It was no surprise when Clara started to complain that she had a sore throat. Amanda noticed the child had a runny nose, a slight cough, and a fever. These were the symptoms of so many things that there wasn't much that could be done except keep her warm, dry, rested, and as well fed as possible. Many times children had these symptoms and their systems just fought off whatever was knocking at the door. Clara, however, continued to be apathetic and her appetite was waning. On the fifth day, her problem became evident. An itchy rash covered her head and body. Measles! The disease was rampant in Winter Quarters.

Amanda bundled Clara up and took her to the isolation cabin that had been set aside for measles cases. Inside were eight children in varying stages of the sickness. The dingy interior contained beds, chairs, and a couple of mothers tending to the children's needs.

"Oh, my goodness, she does have a bad case," said a tall, boney woman with a tired, drawn face. "Put 'er down over there, Sister." She pointed to an unoccupied cot. "When did she start her rash?"

"Just this morning," replied Amanda.

"I'm Sister Helen Greenleaf an' that's Sister Josephine Baker an' those are our two children over there." She pointed at a boy and a girl curled up on a couple of the beds. "We're on duty now. If you'd like, we can take care of her. All we can do is try to keep the temperature down, make sure she has water, put a little lotion on her, an' don' let her scratch her rash an' make it worse. Most of 'em don't eat anything, but we try to get some soup down 'em when we can." The mothers of the sick children worked in shifts so they could have time to care for their families as well.

"I'd prefer to stay," said a worried Amanda.

"That's good. If you'll stay awhile, Sister Josephine can take a break an' tend to her other children."

"Yes, yes, please do."

"Thank ya, sister," said the weary Josephine as she backed out of the door.

"An' what's yer little one's name?" asked Sister Helen.

"Clara."

"Awright, little Clara, we'll make sure ya get well." Sister Helen patted Clara gently.

"Seems terribly dark in here," said Amanda. She noticed that a blanket covered the lone large window.

"Yes, well children with measles are very sensitive to light so we keep it dark."

"Oh, I didn't know that. I've not encountered measles before. There were a number of cases in Nauvoo every year, but somehow most all the children around us missed catching it. Tell me, how long does this usually last?" asked Amanda.

"Well, all depends on how bad a case the child has—usually, four to seven days. Some rebound quickly, others don't," replied Helen, as she bent over to give a moaning child some water.

"Amanda, is Clara all right?" It was James. He had left for an early morning meeting with the leaders before they discovered Clara was sick. He stood silhouetted in the doorway.

"Well, I guess she'll be all right, but she really has a bad case of the measles right now."

James came over to Clara's bed and bent over to feel her body. She was very warm and continued to cough off and on. "Open your mouth, darlin' so Daddy can take a look." Clara complied slowly. James peered inside. It was difficult to see but tiny white spots lined the inside of her mouth—another sure sign of measles.

"What can I do to help, Amanda?" He took Amanda's shoulders in his hands and looked into her weary face.

"Just make sure Christine and Jeremy are looked after," she replied.

"Count on me," he said, giving her a soft kiss on her bowed head. That was the first time he even touched her in some time. She pondered, why does it always take a crisis for men to show their feelings?

After James left, Amanda sat in a chair next to Clara's bed, staring down at the listless child. Spasms of guilt swept over her and her heart ached terribly. Why in God's name did we bring our children to such a terrible place and put them in so much danger? Shaking her head slightly, she thought, but what's done is done. No sense in wishing for what can't be. Clara could just as well have caught measles in Nauvoo, or even Double Springs. They main thing now was to see that she got well.

For the next couple of days, Amanda was constantly in the measles cabin tending to Clara and the other children. She had been warned that she was going to become ill herself if she didn't take more time off. During her stay, she saw a couple of children improve enough to leave and one more come in. Clara didn't seem to improve at all, but then it had only been two days.

"For heavens sake, Sister Amanda, why didn't ya let us know ya needed some he'p? Jus' found out that li'l Clara was sick." It was Margaret Waters. "There's no need for ya sittin' here all this time when Sister Josephine an' I can do it fer ya. Now git outta here an' tend ta yer family. Goodness, look at ya. Yer a mess. We'll take care of Clara, don' ya worry."

Amanda smiled faintly and blushed. "I guess I am a sight. It would be so kind of you and Sister Josephine." She trusted these two explicitly.

"We've been down weaving baskets fer the past week. I'd rather watch sick li'l ones any day. Now ya go on. Scat!" She used the back of both hands to shoo Amanda out of the cabin.

Amanda took a long look at Clara and headed out the door. For the next couple of days, she caught up on her sleep and long neglected chores. She dropped in every now and then to see how Clara was doing. There was no change one way or the other.

Later, about three o'clock in the morning of the fifth day, a woman knocked on the Weston cabin door. James crawled from under the covers. "Yes," he said as he opened the door. The two began to converse in hushed tones.

Amanda pulled herself out of a deep sleep to hear whispering at the door. "What is it, James?" she asked.

"Amanda," he replied. "Clara seems to have taken a turn for the worse. We should go and check on her." The woman in the doorway kept wringing her hands and nodding her head in agreement.

Amanda and James rushed across the frozen ground to the measles cabin. As they entered, they could hear Clara's labored breathing and increased coughing. There were no doctors in the encampment, so the Saints relied on the ministration of the Church and whatever knowledge they had based on experience and hearsay. Amanda had no faith in the ministrations of the elders and little knowledge of the many illnesses contracted on the trail. She took one look at her daughter;

her heart pounded so wildly she could barely breathe. There was little doubt Clara was in trouble. She was coughing up yellowish sputum in between gasps for air, shaking with chills, and moaning complaints that her chest hurt. Amanda felt her. She was burning up with fever and her skin had a blue cast.

All of a sudden, Margaret and Josephine came rushing through the door. Neither had been on duty that night. "Jeremy says that Clara is worse," said Margaret. "What's wrong with the li'l darlin'?"

"Oh Sister Margaret, I don't really know but I fear she has some real problems," cried Amanda.

"Now, now, let me take a look." Margaret made her way to Clara's bed and peered at the child. What she saw and heard, she didn't like. "Sister Amanda, I'm almost sure it's lung fever." Margaret knew from experience that pneumonia could be a complication of measles, and that was not good.

"Oh my God, oh my God," wailed Amanda, "my precious Clara."

James and Amanda sat by Clara's bed all that day, very frustrated because they did not know what they could do to lessen the child's suffering. They could really do nothing but wait. At four o'clock that afternoon, Clara Weston died. She could no longer sustain her breathing. Amanda collapsed from grief, undernourishment, and fatigue.

It was a cold, raw, wet day when they laid Clara to rest. Amanda sat in a chair under an umbrella, stone-faced; she was too exhausted to stand and too emotionally drained to cry. A perfect day to bury a little girl, thought Jeremy. He stood silently by his mother, shedding not a tear. That was his way. Next to him sat a nervous Jake, leaning lightly against Jeremy's leg, making sure he knew that his faithful dog was there. Jake wasn't quite sure what was going on but he understood that his master was suffering. Panting heavily, his breath created a continuous but fleeting vapor in the cold air. Occasionally, he licked his chops with a loud slurp and gazed upward with his sad eyes toward Jeremy.

After the ceremony, Jeremy took Jake for a long walk, away from the compound. Amanda saw him go and did not worry for she knew that was also his way. He internalized everything and did so alone. Amanda often wished that she could do the same and show so little open hostility, only resignation. Unfortunately, that was not her way.

Before leaving Winter Quarters, Amanda learned that at least 365 people died of various illnesses. Somehow, that large number was small consolation for the loss of her little Clara.

On April 5, Brigham Young's Advance Company began the trek of about 1000 miles to the final destination, the Great Salt Lake Valley. Young had decided that he and a small group would lead the way and mark and improve the trail for others to follow. Thus, a collection of 143 men, 3 women, 2 children, a boat, 70 wagons, fifty-two mules, sixty-six oxen, nineteen cows, seventeen dogs, and some chickens slowly pulled away from the Winter Quarters encampment. Buoyed by this movement, all the Saints rededicated themselves to make ready for their assigned departure. James received word that his train was to be a part of the third company to follow the Advance Company.

The Weston Train, as part of Captain Parley Jacobson's company of 100, finally got the word to move out two weeks later, on April 20. Everyone in the train was eager to renew their journey. Rejuvenated by the arrival of spring and the excitement of starting a new adventure, the children were nearly uncontrollable—laughing, jumping, running, skipping, and playing games of tag. The miseries of the past winter no longer mattered. How absolutely amazing, thought Amanda as she observed the scenes around her. Little exuberant Christine was the most active and noisy of the lot. Naturally, there was a hole in her heart knowing that Clara was not there to join in the fun. Although the crushing sensation she felt was beginning to subside, the pain remained.

Amanda was unable to recover emotionally or physically from Clara's death. She often had periods of depression and had to drag herself out of lethargy to perform the many chores that a wife, mother, and member of the train demanded. Her appetite diminished and when she did eat, she had bouts with indigestion. Of greatest concern, however, was her increasing cycle of chills, fever, and sweating. She knew these to be the sign of the dreaded ague. She was concerned, but the spells were minor, lasting only a half hour or so, and she knew that few people died from malarial fever along the trail. For now, it was her little secret.

Ruth was ecstatic over the movement and kept traversing the train shouting, "Hallelujah!" "God be praised!" "Yes, Lord, we're comin' now!" Despite William's absence, Ruth was tougher and more dedicated than ever. Typical of many of these Mormon pioneer women, the more tribulations they suffered, the stronger they became.

"Why don' that woman shut up?" an irritated Margaret Waters mumbled under her breath. Margaret was equally dedicated to the cause but she performed, as did many in silent strength.

James was increasingly busy making sure everyone was ready for the coming journey. The wear and tear of command, with all of its responsibility for the physical, mental, emotional, and religious wellbeing of those in the train, was obviously not easy. In addition, besides tending to his family, he had the daily-added duty of caring for William's triple brood. He also had to keep a particular eye on Prudence Jessup and her four children since Joshua's demise. Amanda felt sorry for him, but, secretly, took pleasure in his predicament. Surely, all of this should convince him he doesn't need more wives, she thought.

Of singular help to James was the always-dependable Johnson family. Jeremiah, Mary and son, Geoff, went out of their way to make sure they were useful. All felt obligated to William for looking after Tom in the Mormon Battalion. They had always held James and Amanda in high regard for treating them so fairly on the Weston farm.

Almost comical to watch as they broke camp was the Thomas family. There were so many of them and so disorganized that it was a wonder they made the trumpet-call to move out at all. Roy's injured foot and leg pained him constantly. His daily dose of medication (whiskey) seemed to increase in proportion to his swearing. He was little or no help, in fact, at times, a burden.

Amelia's many children seemed no worse for the continued disregard she had for their care. It was accepted in her family that the older children cared for the younger, the weaker, and for themselves. Therefore, the two oldest girls, Mary and Ruth, had to do it all. Like mother hens rounding up their young, somehow they managed to assemble everyone in time for the wagon to leave with the train. Often, bedraggled, half-dressed, sleepy children would reluctantly trail behind the wagon, the youngest hanging onto some one's arm or shirt and some sucking their thumbs. Amelia was around to champion the word of God and to settle disputes. Everyone knew Amelia didn't abuse her children; she just let them grow up "unimpeded."

In the ninth wagon were Anthony and Annie Adams. These dedicated, quiet people seldom caused any problems and always pulled their load of the work involved. Anthony was a workhorse and enthusiastically took on any task assigned. Annie's chronic asthma was debilitating at times but she never used that as an excuse. Wheezing to the point of exhaustion, she somehow kept going. Little eleven-year-old Josephine was equally stoic. Often, however, she had to ride in the wagon because her injured leg gave out.

Bringing up the rear, but always leading in attitude and performance, were the sisters. James could always depend on these two rugged women to keep strays in line, whether human or animal. Jake liked hanging around the sisters' wagon because no matter how scarce the food supply, they always found something for him to eat. Jeremy knew this was one of Jake's hangouts and he didn't mind. He felt equally fond of the sisters. Sympathy, understanding, compassion, and direction were his succor, not food. Jeremy found that with Margaret in particular, he could openly discuss his feelings without fear she would put a religious spin on it, or tell anyone else about his unorthodox attitude. It was Jeremy's job to check the rear of the train to make sure everyone and everything were all right. This gave him many opportunities to visit with these amazing women.

The Jacobson Company followed the trail forged by the Advance Company and others. They made ten miles that first day and camped by a stream from the Little Papillion. Grass for the livestock was plentiful. Other than Mormon teaming the horses and oxen to negotiate a muddy patch of terrain, the travelers encountered no significant difficulties for days. By now, all were adept at this double and triple-hitching technique.

When, on the fourth day, they came upon the Elkhorn River, they were happy to discover that Young had left a cottonwood raft to cross the 200-foot wide, four-foot deep, obstacle. Most livestock swam the river, while wagons and people ferried across on the raft. Oxen pulled the raft across with ropes anchored on both sides of the river. Shortly after crossing the Elkhorn, the vista broadened into a never-ending valley to the north and west. To the south and west, the great Platte River stretched as far as the eye could see, like an endless ribbon of sunlit gold.

As those before them, this company settled down near the banks of the Platte in the evening. It was a captivating sight as the setting sun glistened off the wide, silt-laden river.

"My, this is about as beautiful a sight as we've seen this here trip," commented Margaret Waters to the group assemble about the campfire.

"It is indeed, Sister Margaret," replied Amanda. "It is indeed."

"Heard tell that frontier men always say this here river is miles wide an' inches deep," chimed in Roy Thomas as he winced, rubbing and warming his battered leg near the fire. "Ain't no chance a drownin' in this old water."

The well-read and intelligent Prudence Jessup joined the conversation. "Makes sense—what they call it. Platte means flat or shallow in French."

Always curious about things, Jeremy and Mark Thomas headed for the riverbank to see for themselves. Jake happily ran from side to side, constantly sniffing the grass, ground, and trees to determine what varmint had passed this way before, and urinating on numerous bushes to mark his territory. As the boys reached the embankment, they took off their shoes, rolled up their pants and tip toed gingerly into swift moving, silt-filled water that coursed over the sandy bottom. The water was cold, but refreshing and, as Brother Roy had said, it was only inches deep.

Amanda felt at peace for the first time in a long while as she gazed toward the setting sun shinning off the amazing river and the many freshly leafed cottonwood, elm, and willow trees that lined its banks. Mother Nature has a way of calming and healing the soul at just the right time, she thought. She prayed that this was a sign that the rest of the journey would be more pleasant than the first leg. It didn't register with her, but that night she fell asleep without crying; the first time since Clara died. Her general health had not improved but her spirit was better.

The travelers were now in the broad sunken floodplain of the Platte.

The Indians called this area Nebraska, or Shallow Water. Looking east, cedar-covered bluffs limited their vista. However, to the west, if they could have seen that far, were hundreds of miles of level land. Unlike the first part of their journey across Iowa, this immense plain offered fewer and less challenging physical obstacles. Only occasionally did they encounter steep creek crossings, sloughs, and quicksand fords.

There was little doubt, however, that they had entered into unfamiliar territory—a realm far from the land they considered civilized. During the entire journey, they would only encounter two occupied white habitations, Fort Laramie and Fort Bridger. Indian tribes, on the other hand, abounded. Pawnees, the terror of the Otoes and Omahas; the Sioux, the fear of the Pawnees; and two bitter enemies, the Crows and the Shoshones, all stretched across one part of the land or the other. The Mormons encountered them all, but managed to have reasonable relations with everyone but the thieving, conniving, and sometimes murderous Pawnees. Young passed down the word; remain on the alert. The Saints, including the Westons, resumed in earnest the practice of every man walking beside his wagon with a loaded gun in hand or close by. Wagons traveled in close order and, at night, corralled with wagon tongues pointing out and livestock confined within the circle. The Mormons were justifiably on high alert much of the time.

Chapter 21

For several days, the company had been following the Loupe Fork of the Platte River on its northwest track. They had to cross this troublesome branch to continue westward. The Advance Company had sent back word of some of the problems they would encounter—problems that always challenged the ingenuity and determination of the Mormons. It was April 29 and the company faced one of these problems while surveying a river crossing—quicksand. The leaders searched for the location used by the previous companies, as packing down quicksand made it less treacherous. The more traffic there was the better. The Advance Company had left some rafts, which Jacobson would use to aid them in their crossing. It was late, so he decided to cross the next day.

One worry was a large Pawnee Indian village situated on the south bank of the Loupe. Smoke from fires outside their dome-shaped, earth-covered lodges drifted lazily into the windless evening sky. There were at least 100 lodges in the village. The Advance Company had encountered these same people and sent back word, cautioning oncoming Saints. They stressed being alert. Young had tried to assuage the Indians by offering them tobacco, flour, and other trinkets, but the Pawnee chief felt it was not enough. The chief was adamant about the Mormons not killing their buffalo. Young emphasized to the Indians that they would kill only what they could eat. Meanwhile, he had strengthened the guard to protect the Saint's property. Stealing horses was the Pawnee's specialty, particularly at night. Young's Company would eventually bypass the village unmolested. Messengers relayed all this information to the oncoming companies.

It was now the Jacobson Company's turn to face this same village. That evening, as the weary travelers began to settle down, a group of Indians assembled on the opposite bank of the Loupe, watching the Saints. In due course, forty braves, including a chief, forded the river on foot, spread out, and approached various wagons. Despite the swift current and threat of quicksand, the Indians knew just where to step to cross the river safely.

These were fierce-looking men with painted faces, eyebrows plucked clean, and heads shaved except for a wide strip of hair from the forehead to the back that stood out like a shortened horse's mane. The braves were bare-chested and wore only a breechcloth and moccasins. Most had bows slung across their backs, a few had rifles carried in non-threatening positions. They conveyed signs of a peaceful trade, but the reputation of these notorious thieves spoke otherwise. Every able-bodied man in the Mormon camp was armed and at the ready. The women and children clustered in, around, and under the wagons. Train leaders, including James, stepped out to talk to the various groups of on-coming Indians.

Like pickpockets, the Pawnees learned to distract their victim in one area while robbing them in another. Knives, guns, and other valuables would disappear in an instant. Horses were particularly vulnerable at night. Rumor had it—though never proved—that even small children disappeared.

James conversed with the leader of the group ambling toward the Weston Train. Jeremy was intensely interested and, with rifle in hand, watched James parley. Gradually, he became aware of Jake's low rumbling growl. As he turned, he was flabbergasted to see an Indian squatting down beside their wagon looking at and motioning to Christine who was hiding behind one of the wheels. Standing but four feet from the Indian was Jake, with all hair on end, teeth bared, and saliva oozing from his heavy jowls. The squatting man slowly turned his head toward Jake and stared at the menacing animal.

"Hey you, get away!" shouted Jeremy. He walked over, rifle at the ready.

The brazen Indian slowly stood, not taking his eyes off Jake, and began to back away. A wry smile conveyed more amusement than concern. "How much?" he asked Jeremy, in heavily labored English.

"How much what ... the girl?" snapped Jeremy.

"No, dog."

"You want to buy the dog?"

"Yes, dog."

Jeremy laughed. "You can have him for nothing if you can get him to go."

As if on cue, Jake snarled louder and more ferociously as the Indian looked at him.

"If you want 'im, go get 'im," Jeremy nodded in Jake's direction.

"No, a ... I no want," said the Indian. He had changed his mind. He turned and rejoined his then retreating group.

No trouble ensued that evening, nonetheless, everyone in the camp was nervous from the experience. After prayers, Jeremy told everybody at the campfire of the encounter with the Indian and Jake. The group roared with laughter. Jake sat happily in the midst of the smaller children as they patted him on the head and gave him big hugs. He sensed that he was again the center of attention and rewarded the children with slobbery licks of affection. They scrunched their faces and squealed in delight. Amanda laughed, but held Christine yet tighter.

"No sir, the Indians don't want the Hero Dog," Jeremy said, beaming broadly.

There was a round of laughter and enthusiastic, "Amens."

The water was variable in depth and velocity and required considerable probing and planning before finding a suitable crossing. The swift current nearly swept away more than one animal, including one of the milk cows from the Weston Train. The main thing was to keep moving. Anyone or anything that stood still was soon sinking in the quicksand. Finally, after considerable effort, all crossed safely, and their journey resumed without incident.

The Pawnees, who always seemed to be lurking around the wagon trains, had disappeared the last few days. Since these Indians lived in earth lodges and had gardens, they did not roam far. When one tribe stopped trailing the Mormons, another tribe would assume the watch as the travelers moved into their territory. The Indian's absence was a relief for the Mormons, as the constant shadow of those thieves put everyone on edge. All were beginning to relax when more, but different Indians appeared on the horizon. They made no moves toward the pioneers, but chose rather to keep their distance and observe.

Word filtered back that these were Sioux, who the Pawnees feared greatly. These and many other tribes had a long history of distrust, conflict, and at times open warfare. The Sioux were nomadic Indians that excelled in horsemanship, buffalo hunting, and fighting. That the Sioux seemed peaceful toward the settlers did not make them any less intimidating. No one knew what was on the minds of these strange men.

The Mormon trains progressed slowly westward, the intriguing and seemingly endless Platte River always to their south. Jeremy was always fascinated with his surroundings. He found more comfort and interest in nature and other things outside the train than all the religiously oriented and motivated activities within the train. The Indians particularly held his attention. He wondered constantly about their lifestyle, their thoughts, and their religious beliefs. The stories told by so-called informed or experienced adults seemed more fiction or personal opinion colored by prejudice and rumor than fact to him. That *The Book of Mormon* claimed these people were the descendents of the lost tribes of Israel mesmerized him. If so, why were they so distrusted, so primitive, so unknowing of their ancestral background. Surely, they must have passed down such important stories throughout the centuries. Could it be that *The Book of Mormon* was wrong? He was desperately curious to find out.

For a number of days, the train was stuck by a particularly difficult creek crossing. While the men decided what to do about the situation, the rest of the travelers did what they always do when stalled—catch up. The weather was excellent. When the wagons were on the move, chores suffered, so, stalled wagons during good weather were a blessing. The women were then able to catch up on the washing, mending, baking, and a multitude of other normal, mundane household chores.

Jeremy saw him the first evening the wagons were stuck by the creek. Silhouetted by the orange setting sun, a tall, thin Indian boy stood proudly on a knoll observing the Mormons and their activities. He was motionless; his right arm stretched to the side, his hand holding a bow, one end of which touched the ground. The bow was almost as long as the boy was tall. A medium-sized, skinny mongrel dog sat next to him. The animal was also unmoving with the exception of his head that shifted from side-to-side, as his upturned nose sniffed the air. Neither the boy nor the dog moved as the sun slipped silently behind the distant hills. All during this fifteen to twenty minute period, as he went about building a fire for the evening and other miscellaneous chores, Jeremy kept looking up at the boy. His eyes searched out the silhouette as he pondered what was on the Indian boy's mind. Darkness made the images disappear, but not in Jeremy's mind; the Indian and his dog were in his last conscious thoughts as he fell asleep that night.

Around ten o'clock the next morning, Amanda sent Jeremy out to search for firewood. With Jake happily at his side, the two set out. Jeremy had the family rifle with him just in case he spotted a rabbit or other edible game along the way. They were barely out of sight of the train when, without warning, standing not twenty yards away, was the Indian boy and his dog. Jeremy froze. The dogs began low guttural growls. Locked in this stance for fifteen seconds or so, Jeremy decided to make a friendly gesture. Slowly he raised his right hand, palm out, and shouted, "Hello."

To his shock and amazement, the Indian boy shouted back, "Hello."

Encouraged by this response, Jeremy lowered his hand, told Jake to hush, and slowly moved in the direction of the Indian boy. He cradled his rifle in his arms. The Indian boy reciprocated, silencing his growling dog by banging him with his bow. As they got closer, Jeremy noticed that the boy's skin color was a light brown, much lighter than the Indians he had seen before. He wore a deerskin shirt modestly decorated with red and green beads. Tight leggings covered the boy's long sinewy legs. His skintight hair, kept in place by a strip of leather, ended in two long braids. The Indian boy was also taking measure of Jeremy's appearance as he approached. The boys were roughly the same height and as they came close to each other, their brown eyes locked—not a stare, but a searching look of curiosity.

"You speak English," said Jeremy, "how come?"

"I speak some," replied the boy, in a hesitant, jerky manner. "A man of cross taught me the white man's tongue."

Jake and the Indian dog were now nose-to-nose, eye-to-eye, cautious, trying to reconcile their master's friendly behavior. Being considerably larger than the Indian dog, Jake postured as superior, but this scrappy little cur had seen many battles and wasn't backing down. Soon the two were in the familiar nose-to-end investigation and though still wary, appeared to accept each other on a trial basis.

"My name is Jeremy," said Jeremy, pointing at his chest, "what is yours?"

"I am Chaska, 'First Son Born,' " answered the Indian proudly, slightly puffing his chest.

"Chas –ka," repeated Jeremy. "That's a good name."

"My dog is Nitis, it mean 'friend.' "

"That's Jake." Jeremy nodded his head toward the big dog.

"What mean Jake?" asked the Indian boy.

"It don't mean nothin'. It's just his name." Jake's head came up every time they mentioned his name; ears constantly alert.

Chaska thought that was strange. Every name means something. "Sit," he said, gesturing toward the ground.

Jeremy nodded and the boys sat cross-legged on the soft prairie grass facing each other. They laid their weapons by their sides. Jake and the Indian dog began the game of tag so typical of dogs, chasing, stopping abruptly, eyeing each other, and then, alternately, one running quickly off in a different direction with the other in hot pursuit. As time went on, the competition became friendlier. To the eyes of humans, however, it seemed angrier as the growling and mock nipping grew more intense.

"Why you whites come to our land?"

"We're just passing through on our way to a place far away." Jeremy made a motion with his right hand across his left and pointed to the west. "We don't mean you any harm," Jeremy replied.

"You kill our buffalo."

Jeremy hadn't even seen a buffalo, but he said, "Yes, but like you, only for food." Then, wishing to satisfy his curiosity and learn more about the Indians, he switched subjects. "What tribe are you from?"

"We are called Sioux," Chaska said proudly.

"You speak very good English."

"Not so good. I speak little since man of cross went away."

"Did you also learn to read?" asked Jeremy.

"No, but I know your letters."

Over the course of the next hour, Jeremy and Chaska slowly exchanged information. The boys discovered they were both thirteen years old. Jeremy learned that Chaska was the son of the village headman, a brave warrior. The rest of the family included his mother, and a little sister named Chilam, or "snowbird." He also learned that Chaska lived in a large round tent made from wooden poles covered with decorated buffalo hides. They called these moveable tents *tipis*. Jeremy was only familiar with the earth lodges of the Pawnees. Chaska knew some about how the pioneers lived, mostly by observation, but he was fascinated with Jeremy's explanation of the Mormon religion. He surmised that the communal aspects of Mormonism were very much in tune with the Sioux concept of sharing in the unifying forces of what they call Wakan Tanka. He had no idea what Jeremy was talking about when questioned about the Mormon lost tribe story.

All of a sudden, Jeremy realized that he had been gone from the train for over an hour. Someone would start looking for him soon. He got up and offered his hand to Chaska. "It's been good talking to you, Chaska," he said. "I must go now. Maybe we can meet again soon."

"Yes, it was good," replied Chaska, clasping Jeremy's hand firmly. "Are you now my friend?"

"Yes, I think so," Jeremy chuckled. "What is the word for friend in your language?"

"*Kola*," replied Chaska.

"Then I am your *kola*."

Chaska smiled broadly. "I come again to this place before the sun sets next day. You come?"

"If I can, I will. Goodbye, *kola*."

"Goodbye, friend," Chaska said as he motioned to Nitis with his bow and turned back toward his village. The skinny black and white dog rose and ran off ahead of his master.

Jeremy hurriedly scanned the surrounding area for some firewood. He couldn't go back to the train empty handed. Unfortunately, there was little for him to scrounge. He swept up what he could and headed back.

"That's *it*, after being gone so long?" demanded Amanda.

Jeremy told Amanda about his encounter with the Indian boy. He was so excited about his meeting with Chaska; the words tumbled out one after the other. Jeremy seldom showed such emotion and Amanda was cautiously pleased. "That sounds like quite an experience. But, you must tell your father about this and ask his permission before you go off again, understand?"

"I understand."

"Maybe you should have something to eat and then go out and really find some wood this time, huh?"

"Yes, ma'am," Jeremy answered, still elated at his meeting with Chaska. His mind was cleverly planning what to say at the next meeting. This was a very bright day in the dull routine of a pioneer boy.

Jeremy did talk with James at the nooning. After many questions, James thought for some time. "I guess there is no harm. It's wonderful that you can make friends with an Indian of your own age. But you must be alert. I hear stories of kidnappings by Indians. Make sure you take the rifle and that the boy is alone, and that Jake is with you at all times. And make sure all your chores are done and you're back by evening prayers, hear?"

"I will, I will," said Jeremy enthusiastically. He set about doing all his chores and asked for more. We should let that boy meet with the Indians everyday, thought Amanda.

Jeremy had been thinking. He wanted to give Chaska a gift, but had no idea what. Remembering the Indian was curious about his religion, he decided to give him a Bible. He had received a small Bible for his last birthday. He was not the Bible-reading type. Of course, he was hesitant because he knew Chaska couldn't read, but it was the idea of giving him something different that appealed to Jeremy. Besides,

Chaska knew the alphabet; maybe he could learn to read some of the words with Jeremy's help. That was it, he decided on the Bible.

It had been a beautiful day. The late afternoon sun was heading toward a wide band of cirrus clouds resting atop the distant horizon, promising another stunning sunset for which the prairies were famous. A gentle fluctuating breeze whispered tranquilly in one's ear and made the long prairie grasses undulate with varying shades of green and yellow. As Jeremy arrived, he saw that Chaska and Nitis were already there. A wide grin came across Chaska's face as he spotted Jeremy. Soon the boys were shaking hands, openly delighted they could meet again. Jake and Nitis began their canine ritual, the stiffness of the past forgotten.

"I glad you come," said Chaska.

"I'm glad to be here." The boys positioned themselves cross-legged facing each other as before. "I have a gift for you." Jeremy produced the Bible and offered it to Chaska with two hands.

"For me?" Chaska seemed bewildered as he turned the book over repeatedly.

"Yes, it's a Bible, the book of the Christian religion."

Chaska thumbed through the pages, stopping at various drawings in the book. "I no read."

"Yes, but you know the letters. You can learn. I can help you," Jeremy said as if the two would be together for some time. "See," he pointed to the word on the book cover, "B-I-B-L-E, Bible," he pronounced each letter and then said the word.

"B-I-B-L-E." Chaska slowly traced the letters. "Bi-ble," he mimicked Jeremy's pronunciation and then gave a big smile.

"Yes, yes," said Jeremy enthusiastically.

"This good present. I like." Chaska patted the book gently. Jeremy smiled broadly. Chaska took the quiver of arrows from his back, picked up his bow from the ground, and thrust them toward Jeremy. "You take," he said. Dried deer ligament bound the skillfully made hickory bow for strength. Sharpened flints tipped the ends of the two-foot long arrows.

"No, this is too much," Jeremy said, admiring the workmanship. Besides, I don't know how to use a bow."

"I no read either. You take," Chaska insisted. Both boys laughed.

"Thank you, I will learn to use from you. This is a very nice gift."

Satisfied, Chaska opened the Bible and said, "Now, you show how to read."

For the next half hour, Jeremy began the difficult task of teaching Chaska various simple words. He began by reviewing the alphabet, which to his surprise, Chaska knew quite well.

Both boys were absorbed in the book when Jake began his slow rumbling growl. Jeremy looking up and over Chaska's shoulder, saw an Indian man atop a white horse approaching them. Jeremy's look of concern and Jake's growling made Chaska look back over his shoulder.

He turned his head back toward Jeremy. "No worry, he my father." The boys rose and Chaska turned to salute his father. The man gracefully dismounted the undersized horse. This horse, like most Indian ponies was unattractive. Indian horses were fast, durable, maneuverable, and, because they grazed only on whatever grasses were available, lean. Jeremy noted the man was dressed like Chaska, but wore a more heavily adorned shirt. He had two red paint slashes under his eyes and a large eagle feather protruding from the back of his hair. He carried a plains rifle casually in his right hand and displayed a steel head tomahawk in his leather belt. His father's admonition to make sure he was alone with the Indian boy loomed largely in Jeremy's mind. Despite Chaska's assurances, he was worried.

Chaska began talking to his father in both words and sign language. Despite his size, dress, and armament, the father's demeanor was friendly. His brown face was kind; his dark eyes sad. "This my father, Matoskah. That mean 'white bear,' " Chaska said proudly. Matoskah gave a cautious smile and then proffered Jeremy a large hand as his eyes scanned Jeremy's face. They shook hands warmly as Matoskah nodded his head slowly in approval.

Chaska showed the Bible to his father, explaining what it was and that it was a gift. Matoskah examined the book, looked puzzled, but finally nodded his head in consent. He then addressed Chaska at length, in both words and sign language, pointing often to Jeremy and in the distance toward the direction of the Mormon trains. Looking back at Jeremy, he briefly studied his face as if making a decision. Matoskah then pulled off his neck and over his head, a necklace made of rawhide threaded through a large buffalo tooth. He placed the necklace in Jeremy's hands and spoke to him in Sioux.

"He say, 'Be brave, and have long life.' "

Jeremy was overwhelmed. "Thank you, thank you," he said, staring down at the necklace.

Matoskah said a few more words to Chaska, leaped easily onto his horse, raised his rifle in a salute to Jeremy, and rode away. Soon he disappeared over the adjacent grassy knoll.

Relieved and still stunned, Jeremy said, "I like him. He seems like a very nice man."

"He good man, but strong warrior. He headman in village. He like you. He say your people no problem. That good."

The sun was creeping toward the horizon again and Jeremy realized he had to go. He thanked Chaska again for the bow and arrows as he picked them up appreciatively. Chaska held up the Bible and repeated, "I like." The boys agreed that they would meet again next evening so Jeremy could help Chaska with his reading and Chaska could show Jeremy how to use the bow and arrow. On his way back to the train, Jeremy thought heavily about this day's adventure. It dawned on him that he would be lucky to have another day to meet. The wagons could move out at any time. He also decided that he would not tell anyone about meeting Matoskah and put the necklace in his pocket. His father might not let him come back for another visit if he knew about the Indian chief.

As it turned out, the boys did meet the next day. They cemented their relationship, exchanged their specific knowledge, and learned more about each other's culture. Chaska explained that humans, buffalo, and all other animals came from mother earth. Jeremy wondered how that squared with Genesis in the Bible and with Joseph Smith's view of where the Indians came from. He hungered for more, but that was not to be. He told Chaska that they were leaving in the morning as all of the wagons had crossed the difficult creek. The Mormon leaders were eager to resume their journey. Both boys were sad that their meetings would end but swore their friendship would go on forever.

Within hours of leaving the creek area, the routine of the long journey resumed. The company traveled for two days without any particular mishaps or incidents. They sighted a few Indians in the distance, but Jeremy knew they were not his friends. Their unique hairstyle identified them easily as Pawnee.

On the night of the second day, a monumental thunderstorm unleashed its fury on the weary travelers. The storm had been brewing all day as thick, dark clouds tumbled in from the northwest. The Saints did as always under these circumstances—gathered up all their livestock and huddled together in their wagons and tents. The lightning and thunder created a deafening clamor when combined with the heavy rainfall. Between the noise and fighting the rain seeping into the wagons and tents from the incessant pulsating squalls, sleep was impossible. By two o'clock in the morning, the storm had passed. Man and beast were thankful and all fell into a much-needed sleep.

When the bugle sounded for everyone to rise in the morning, there was a collective groan. Everything and everyone was soaked. As they shook off accumulated water and packed their rain-soaked gear, something became evident—horses were missing.

"Pa," said Jeremy, "ol' Benjamin's gone!" Benjamin was the horse Jeremy rode most.

"What, are you sure?" asked James.

"I've looked everywhere and he's not here. Guess the rain fixed it so's we couldn't hear the clappers." Jeremy was alluding to wooden noisemakers tied to horses and cows in order to keep track of them.

"Indians know how to cut them off." James disgustedly held up a muddied clapper.

As it turned out, six horses where missing from the company. It became obvious to everyone that Pawnees had snuck into the camp during the storm and made off with the horses. Loss of so many valuable animals was a severe blow and the Saints were heartsick. Reconciled to their loss, and resolving to be more watchful, the travelers resumed their trek.

It was only an hour later when the cry of, "Indians!" was heard from a scout along the southern flank. Men grabbed their rifles, preparing for the oncoming Indians looming in the distance.

"Wait!" yelled Jeremy. "They're Sioux, not Pawnees." He ran out in front of the group of men mounting their horses. "They mean no harm."

"How do you know, son?" hollered James.

"Just wait and see, Dad," Jeremy pleaded.

The mounted men all paused and looked hard at the approaching Indians. Gradually, it became obvious that there were only two Indians, despite the number of horses.

Jeremy ran forward as he shouted excitedly, "It's Chaska and his father!"

"Jeremy, wait," commanded James, but the boy was gone, running and waving his arms at the coming Indians. The men followed at a slow trot, their rifles at the ready.

Unbelievably, it was Chaska and his father, Matoskah. They were herding six horses, including Benjamin. Jeremy ran up to the father and son, laughing and reaching up to Chaska. Chaska slid down from his horse and the boys embraced.

"Your horses?" asked Chaska.

"Yes, yes, how did you find them?"

"We saw Pawnee with horses. They come from this way," he pointed at the train.

By now, James and the other men from the train reined up. They were dumbfounded at Jeremy's relationship with the two Indians.

"Pa, this is my friend Chaska. That," he pointed to Matoskah still sitting proudly on his horse, "is his father, Matoskah. They've brought our horses back."

James saluted the brim of his hat and nodded toward the unsmiling Matoskah. "Thank you," he said. Matoskah nodded back.

"They got 'em back from the thievin' Pawnees," Jeremy said proudly with his arm around Chaska's shoulder. "This man," he pointed up at Matoskah, "is the headman of his tribe and a great warrior. But he is a friend to the Mormons."

By now, the men had dismounted and were claiming the horses. One after the other nodded at Matoskah and said, "Thank you." All were still confused as to how Jeremy was such a close friend with these Indians.

"Your friend," James pointed at Chaska, "he speaks English?"

"Yes," replied Chaska.

"Good. Please tell your father that we thank him for his kindness."

Chaska conveyed the thought in sign and words. Matoskah replied that it was what Sioux do for friends. Chaska relayed that to James.

"Is there something we can do for him in return?"

"Yes, do not kill too many buffalo."

"Please tell him, that is a promise." Seems like an easy promise, thought James. I haven't even seen a buffalo.

Satisfied that the meeting was over, Matoskah nodded his head at James. He then reached down to Jeremy, placing his hand on his head, and, as interpreted by Chaska, said, "Goodbye little friend." He motioned for Chaska to mount his horse.

"Goodbye friend," said Chaska, as he embraced Jeremy.

"Goodbye kola." They both fought hard to stop the welling tears, for such a display would be unmanly, especially at thirteen. However, both knew this would be their last meeting and that saddened them beyond any appearances of masculinity.

Without another word, Chaska grabbed the horse's mane and pulled himself effortlessly onto the animal's back. Father and son saluted the Mormons with upraised arms and rode off. Jeremy and the others stood silently watching the Indians ride away. Chaska looked back once and waved at Jeremy before disappearing over the horizon.

"Well, that beats everything," said one of the men.

"God sure was lookin' out for us on this one," stated another.

"No, Jeremy was lookin' out for us." James proudly patted his son on the shoulder.

Later, everyone hounded Jeremy to explain how he came to know the Indians and become such fast friends. He explained the story behind the necklace, which he now wore proudly. There was little doubt he was a hero around the camp. No one thought to ask what happened to the two Pawnees caught stealing their horses. In the end, did it matter?

CHAPTER 22

Amanda began to find the daily routine increasingly difficult. She tried desperately not to let her illness consume her, although the debility was unbearable at times. Despite her condition, she would drag out of bed and run through her chores like an automaton. She seldom participated in prayer meetings and discussions—she was too tired, too sick, and finally too uninterested. No one seemed to notice. It was a toss between whether she was less interested in the subject matter or too exhausted to care. All of this was so unlike her as she had always kept a hand in what was going on in order to protect her family.

Amanda told no one of her affliction, but she often discussed her state of generalized malaise with Margaret Waters, who always had a sympathetic ear and reasonable ideas for coping. Strong old Margaret often had seen the signs of exhausted resignation when the mind and body no longer operate in unison. Critical sickness under these conditions is like the sword of Damocles hanging over one's head. It was only a matter of time before the blade falls.

James was too busy to spend time with his frail wife and, besides, Amanda had noticed something else—James sneaking into Elizabeth Granger's wagon late at night. At first, she was livid. The thought that her husband was consorting with his brother's wife—third wife or not— was unbelievable and unacceptable. The old Amanda would have charged in like a bull, defending her territory, and castigating her errant husband. Instead, she leaned against the wagon and cried. Between sobs, she reasoned that she had not been a good wife to James for some time. In addition, her attitude toward Mormonism was definitely an embarrassment to her devout husband. In the end, what did it matter? With 500 or so vibrant men of the Mormon Battalion absent, James and Elizabeth's tryst was just one of many. She internalized this personal tragedy, confiding in no one. Had she known that James's infidelity was common knowledge in the Company, her humiliation would have been greater.

Jeremy was often his mother's refuge for sanity and solace, as she was his. He frequently sat by her side and they talked. Their conversations covered everything from religion, to nature, to history, to love, to life on the trail, but never about his parent's relationship. She found him to be more understanding than many his age and was impressed with his constant quest for knowledge of the world around him. She felt sorry that he had had so little time with Chaska. It always seemed that Jeremy was leaving behind a friend—Jake in Double Springs, Joseph Smith in Nauvoo, and now Chaska. His bond with the Indian boy was of short duration, but she was amazed at its intensity. Mark Thomas was an occasional refuge, but they were not close. It was more a friendship of convenience for both boys. Thank God, he had his faithful companion and inseparable friend, loveable old Jake

The various trains in the company rotated positions from time to time. It was the Weston Train's time to bring up the rear—to eat dust, as they say. The position was particularly bad now as many grass fires had burned over the ground, resulting in the usual dust mixed with unusual ashes lazily floating to the rear of the trains. At times, it was difficult to breath. Exacerbating this situation were menacing clouds of dust rolling in from enormous herds of roaming buffalo in the distance. The grazing of these great shaggy beasts also meant a shortage of feed for the Saints' undernourished livestock.

Mostly, the Jacobson Company followed the ruts and other trail signs created by the companies ahead. Their additional passage helped create what Brigham Young wanted—a road from Nauvoo to the Great Salt Lake Basin. Young did whatever he could to help those behind him. For example, the Advance Company left progress makers to let the followers know how far they had come and to encourage them to keep going. The first marker the Jacobson Company passed was a cedar post that had the following inscription, "From Winter Quarters, two hundred ninety-five miles, May 8, '47. Camp all well. Wm. Clayton." The Jacobson Company passed this marker on May 22 and they found many more throughout the rest of the long trek. This simple connection with their leader always buoyed their spirits.

The weather was perfect for traveling—cool and clear. Days and nights were thankfully uneventful since passing the first marker. The Weston Train moved forward in the train, right behind Captain Parley Jacobsen's lead train. A man named Roy Henson was out front of the company, acting as point. Suddenly, he appeared at the top of the upcoming ridge, rode hastily toward the company, and reined in next to Jacobson and James. "Brother Jacobson, sir, there's a whole bunch a Injuns 'bout two miles past that there ridge." He turned in his saddle, pointed in the direction, and continued, "And I do mean a whole bunch ... maybe fifty ta seventy-five. They got a chief ridin' in front with a lotta feathers hangin' from his head."

"Where's there's buffalo, there's Sioux," Jacobson said resignedly. "God knows we've seen enough signs of buffalo for days now. That many mounted warriors could mean trouble." Jacobson looked up at the late afternoon sun and squinted. Think we should call it a day and form up here?" he asked James as he made a circle with his hand toward an adjacent flat area.

"Yes, probably wise to do so, Brother," replied James. Just once, I would like to finish out a day without some blasted trouble, thought James disgustedly. He turned his horse about and started passing down the word to circle the wagons and collect the livestock.

"Brother Henson, grab somebody else and go back out and keep and eye on those Indians. Let us know what they're up to," ordered Jacobson.

"Yes, Sir," answered Henson who galloped off to find his younger brother. The two then started toward the Indians at a full gallop.

It wasn't long before they were back. "They're headed this way, about a half hour or so," said Henson.

"There's more'n a hundred of 'em," chimed in Henson's excited brother.

"Let's round up everyone we can with rifles here, Brother James. We need to show them a strong front while I parley," said a nervous Jacobson. He was the leader and had to show courage under pressure. He had always been able to do that before, but it looked like this encounter would be a true test of his leadership.

The frightened women and children took refuge in and under the wagons. The Company had Indian scares and some contact previously, but nothing quite this imposing. The shear number of warriors was frightening everyone. Margaret and Josephine, and many other women, armed themselves and made sure that ammunition was readily available for their men folk. A small number of men spread out around the perimeter of the encircled wagons to make sure no Indians snuck up from the rear.

The Mormons' hearts sank as the Sioux warriors came over the crown of the ridge a few hundred yards away. The number was intimidating for sure, but the effect of the painted faces and battle dress, the many feathers adorning their heads, shields, and horses, and the array of weapons was even more menacing. The Indians brought their horses to a halt; a line silhouetted against the clear sky. The chief, whose headdress flowed down below the flanks of his horse, boldly came forward. An equally menacing warrior whose headdress was a small but intimidating buffalo head accompanied him. The chief's rifle was stowed in its scabbard. The men stopped a few yards in front of the Saints.

The Indian with the buffalo head shouted in broken English, "Who your headman?"

Jacobson stepped forward. "I am Captain Jacobson. We come in peace."

"Our great chief, Enopay, say you must stop. Go no farther."

"We are Mormons, a peaceful people. We just pass through to another land."

"Our great chief, Enopay, say too many before you, you must stop."

"Maybe your chief would take something for our safe passage through your lands," probed Jacobson.

The interpreter talked briefly with the chief who shook his head negatively.

"Our great chief, Enopay, say no. He say you kill buffalo. He say you make way for more of your people. He say you go back now."

How did the chief say all that with one shake of the head, thought Jacobson. Obviously, he had made up his mind before their meeting. Jacobson was puzzled as to how to proceed.

All during this exchange, Enopay, meaning "brave," sat perfectly still, stoned faced, and observant. His eyes searched the band of armed men before him. Then, his wandering eyes stopped and he stared directly at Jeremy, who had snuck up into the ranks of the men with his rifle and bow. The chief raised his right hand and pointed at Jeremy as he mumbled a few words to his interrupter.

"Our great chief, Enopay," intoned the Indian, "he say where boy get buffalo tooth around neck?"

All eyes fixed on Jeremy and his necklace. Jeremy's mouth became dry and his knees shook as he realized he was the center of attention. Summoning all his courage, he stepped forward. James was stunned.

"I am a friend, a *kola*, of the headman, Matoskah," he said boldly.

The surprised chief repeated, "*Kola*, Matoskah?" He looked at his interpreter and asked him how this could be. Obviously, they knew the name Matoskah and it carried weight.

"How this possible?" asked the Indian interpreter. "Matoskah great warrior. He kill many men."

"Matoskah is my friend. He gave me this," Jeremy said as he held up the buffalo tooth, "and his son, Chaska, gave me this." He held the bow in front of him. "Matoskah is also a friend of the Mormons. He gave us back our horses stolen by the Pawnee." Jeremy was losing his apprehension the more he talked. "Matoskah said to me, 'Be brave, and have long life.' "

The Indian with the buffalo headdress told the chief all that Jeremy said. The two men talked back and forth at length. The chief kept asking questions and looking from his interpreter to Jeremy and back with each exchange. They were having a hard time reconciling their knowledge of Matoskah, the great and feared warrior, with what Jeremy told them. Finally, the conversation was over. The chief looked long and hard at Jeremy and then he nodded.

"Our great chief, Enopay, say you may pass through our lands." The interpreter spoke with his best authoritative voice.

"Please thank your great and wise chief," said a relieved Jacobson.

Jeremy locked eyes with the chief and placed the bow held in his right hand over his heart as a salute.

The chief clasped his hands in front of his body with the back of the left hand down and said, "*Alsechta*," meaning "peace." Of course, none of the Mormons knew this. They just took the gesture as friendly. The chief took one more look at Jeremy, nodded slightly, turned his horse abruptly to the rear, and galloped off toward the confused gathering of warriors. The interpreter followed. The entire body of Indians then disappeared as quickly as they had come.

There was a collective sigh from the Saints and their hearts began to pound normally again. Then there was a great cheer for Jeremy. They lifted him on their shoulders and praised him without restraint, all of which embarrassed Jeremy greatly. He was glad when the clamor subsided. Jake ran around barking wildly, rousing the other dogs into a frenzy. James was amazed at his son's mature performance and their good luck at his associations with the fierce Sioux warriors. Of course, Amanda was elated, and hugged and kissed her son, first on one cheek and then the other. Once again, Jeremy was the talk of the Company. Margaret Waters suggested to the Weston Train at the evening prayers that they strike a medal for Jeremy with "hero" inscribed on it, just like Jake's. The two did somehow always come through when things got rough.

"Thank you, but no," said Jeremy. "One hero is enough. Besides, I think I'll wear this instead." He held up the buffalo tooth.

"Amen, and amen," was the response as they all clapped enthusiastically.

There were few secrets amongst this tight knit group of weary travelers. Nearly everything said and done became fodder for conversation. Amanda seldom trafficked in gossip, but she listened intently. She was more than aware that though highly dedicated and motivated, the Mormons were, nonetheless, human. There were good people and bad, strong people and weak, likeable people and disagreeable ones, highly motivated people and lazy good-for-nothings. In other words, the daily interaction that began in Nauvoo was no different from anywhere since the beginning of humankind. The same was true on the trail, except that forced closeness and constant movement aggravated each situation. Nerves were a little more on edge. Some happenings were serious, but often they were humorous.

For example, Joseph Jenkins in another train within the Jacobson Company had a cluster of chickens but no rooster. He had observed that Elias Horn, in an adjacent train, had three roosters. Jenkins made a deal with Horn to buy a rooster for one dollar. Three weeks later Jenkins brought the rooster back and said he wanted his dollar back because the rooster had done nothing but chase other roosters in the company—not one chicken. Horn refused to give back the money. That feud had been going on for three months with no resolution in sight.

Another, more serious matter was the Davis-Harrison disagreement. Both men claimed to own the same lamb. It was easy to identify cattle, horses, and goats; sheep were not so easily discernable—especially lambs. The families from each wagon were adamant in their belief of ownership and took to stealing the hapless animal back and forth. The crescendo of disagreement finally reached Captain Jacobson's ears. Jacobson listened as both sides passionately argued their case.

Finally, Jacobson closed his eyes and raised both hands, palms out, indicating he had heard enough. He mused for a while as if giving this great thought. At last, he said, "Kill the lamb and divide the meat."

"No, no," cried the children from both sides, "don't kill 'im." Seeing the distress on their children's faces, the adults on both sides agreed.

"All right, since neither side can prove ownership, you must share the lamb. The lamb will go from one family to the other every other week. Brother Davis, your family starts today and you will turn over the lamb to Brother Harrison next week when the assembly bugle blows, and so on. Any questions?" He scanned the faces in front of him.

They hesitated as they thought it over but finally they agreed.

Brothers Davis and Harrison shook hands and Davis's children picked up the lamb and walked away, making semi-hidden faces at the Harrison children.

Thank God, I only have to decide on lambs and not babies like Solomon did, thought Jacobson. He walked away shaking his head and muttering to himself. I suppose I'll have to go through this again when it comes time to slaughter the animal, he lamented.

Seldom did Jacobson engage himself in disputes that involved the potential use of firearms. One occasion that Amanda, and everyone else, knew about was when the Reverend Jesse Simpson threatened to shoot old Roy Thomas, or was it the other way around? Never were two men more unalike than Jessie and Roy. The congregation still referred to Brother Simpson as "Reverend" out of respect for his position before joining the Mormon movement. He was the minister of a large Methodist congregation in Boston when he converted, shaking the church to its foundation. A small, thin man, with a whisper of a gray moustache and an ample shock of white hair, he spoke quietly until aroused by certain passages in the Bible. He was well educated, having graduated from the Divinity School at Harvard, and though not wealthy, considered himself among the elite in Nauvoo. His wife was equally sophisticated, as was his only child, Stephanie.

The decision to pick up and leave Nauvoo for an ill-defined destination was difficult—a true test of his newfound faith. Jessie lost a great deal financially and, in his eyes, much of his hard-earned dignity. Serving the masses was not the same as living with the masses.

As the story goes, one target of Reverend Simpson's distain was Roy Thomas. Now, everybody knew about Roy and his peccadilloes, and Amelia and their ten children. Let's just say, the Reverend didn't consider the Thomas's in the same class as the Simpson family. So, when in his eyes things got a little too cozy between fourteen-year-old Mark Thomas and his thirteen-year-old daughter, Stephanie, Simpson was not pleased.

One evening, the youngsters sat atop a log just outside the circle of the campfire. They were sitting shoulder-to-shoulder and talking as they watched the moonrise in the evening sky. The Reverend came up from the rear, grabbed Mark by the collar, and stood him up. The boy was as tall as the man and probably weighed about the same.

"Come with me, young man," he barked as he pulled him back toward the wagons.

"*Daddy*!" protested Stephanie. She stood by the log, hands on hips, indignant.

"Excuse me, sir, but take yer hands offin me," objected Mark. He pulled the Reverend's hand loose. "I'll be more'n glad ta come with ya but don' touch me none," he warned.

Roy was sitting in a chair near the fire, sipping his "medicine", and rubbing his leg as usual. He looked up and saw the reverend and Mark heading his way. "What's up Rev," he asked. Obviously, the Rev's upset about somethin,' he thought.

"I want your son to stay away from my daughter," spewed out Simpson.

"Why, what's he done?"

"I didn't do nothin', Pa. Me and Stephanie wuz jus' talkin'."

"Well, that right, Rev?" challenged Roy.

"Doesn't make any difference what they were doing, I don't want that son of yours anywhere near my daughter. Understood?" Simpson said defiantly.

"Sounds high'n mighty ta me, Rev. My son not good enough for the likes a ya?" Roy stood up, towering over Simpson.

"Got nothing to do with it," countered Simpson, cowed but defiant. "Just keep him away or somebody might get hurt."

"Somebody might get hurt!" roared Roy, "Ya little varmint. I outta let Mark knock ya around a little. I've squashed piss ants bigger'n you. Now git outta my face afore I shoot yer ass." Roy grabbed his Winchester from the wagon.

Well, the story of that encounter ricocheted around the company and brought a great deal of laughter. Jacobson thought it was funny too but, as the company commander, he had to make sure this went no further. He called the two men together and lectured them on the principle of getting along.

"Fine by me, Brother Jacobson, but I shed blood fer Brother Smith a long time ago when *he* didn't back down from nothin' or nobody. Just remind *Brother* Simpson a that and tell 'im ta mind his place. He ain't no better'n me."

With some urging, Roy and the Reverend eventually, though reluctantly, shook hands and went their way. Jacobson, mentally crossing his fingers, considered the matter over. Mark and Stephanie continued to see each other, although with a great deal more discretion. After hearing the story from Margaret, Amanda laughed heartily—the first time in a long while.

CHAPTER 23

Every Sunday during the trek west, the Saints observed the Sabbath as a day of rest and recuperation for the saddle-weary riders, foot-sore walkers, and bone-jarred wagon riders. It was also a day of rest for the drained horses and oxen pulling the wagons. Unless it was deemed necessary, there was no hunting or fishing on the Sabbath. Church services and meetings occupied the majority of any Sunday, but everyone caught up on many neglected chores, as well.

The Jacobson Company faced yet another river crossing, although not a difficult one for these experienced travelers. The Weston Train successfully crossed the obstacle and was in an assembly area waiting for the rest of the trains. They were to make camp there that evening. Because it was early afternoon, and the day before the Sabbath, Jeremy got permission to take Jake and explore the immediate area for some small game. The main admonition was not to wander too far from the train. The boy was not concerned; he knew Jake would alert him of any trouble ahead. Jake loved these little excursions and ran from side to side sniffing everything in sight, tongue flopping about, and with the dog equivalent of a grin on his face. Jeremy was happy just to getaway on his own.

The two walked for about a quarter of an hour. Jeremy saw him first, in the distance; a man slouched over on his saddle, his horse plodding slowly over the prairie grass, coming in their direction. Jeremy stopped, stood tall, and studied the approaching figure. Jake took notice and sniffed the air and, staring in the direction of the horse and man, he emitted a low, rumbling growl.

Slowly the man rode toward Jeremy. The man was white, although a very dirty one. "Quiet, Jake," said Jeremy as the traveler reined in his horse a few yards away. Reluctantly, Jake obeyed but remained alert. Jeremy noted that the man was about average size. He had rugged, trail-worn features, long scraggly brown hair and beard, and sharp penetrating blue eyes—very tired, blood-shot, sad eyes.

"Howdy," said the man in a weak, weary voice. He wore a big floppy hat, a long buckskin coat, cotton shirt, jean cloth trousers, and leather boots and gloves. Dirt and dust from the trail encrusted everything, including his saddle, saddlebag, and his horse. To Jeremy, he looked old—even older than his father.

"Howdy," replied Jeremy. He lowered his rifle to his waist, sensing the man was no threat, even though heavily armed. Jeremy saw a gun belt with a pistol (turns out he had two), a rifle in his saddle scabbard, (turns out he had four), and a bowie knife strapped to his boot. "You a gun fighter?" Jeremy asked bluntly.

The man chuckled weakly. "Nope, you one?" He nodded toward Jeremy's rifle.

"Nope." Jeremy's face reddened slightly and he lowered his rife a little more.

"You one a them Mormons?"

"Yep."

"Suits me, I like Mormons. Good, clean, God-fearin' folks."

"Glad you think so," replied Jeremy. "Looks like you've been on the trail quite a spell."

"'Bout two weeks. Come up from Fort Laramie. Had a little Injun trouble on the way. Don' suppose I could git some rest an' grub at yer wagon?" The man shifted slightly in his saddle.

It was then that Jeremy noticed the bloodstain on the man's left shoulder—a bullet wound. No wonder he looked so beat up. "You shot, mister?"

"Yep."

"Well, you best follow me so my ma can take care of that."

"Thank ya. Name's Ezekiel," said the weary man.

"I'm Jeremy."

"Glad ta know ya, Jeremy." Ezekiel winced as he put his glove up to his wound. Now that he had found refuge, all the determination needed to push this far drained from his body. He felt dizzy, slumped more in the saddle, held the horn with both hands, and dropped the reins.

Jeremy picked up the reins as they fell from the man's hands, and slowly led the weary horse and wounded man back toward the train. There was a buzz of conversation as people at the wagons shaded their eyes and pointed in Jeremy's direction. Jake ran ahead barking wildly, as if to alert everyone about his involvement in the drama.

"Who you got there, Jeremy?" asked Margaret Waters, as Jeremy approached the wagons.

"Name's Ezekiel," replied Jeremy, "and he's wounded."

Ezekiel raised his head, gave a weak smile, and attempted to dismount, but he passed out. A host of arms aided him down onto a tarp spread on the ground.

"My word, I guess he *is* wounded," said Margaret. "He's got a bullet hole in 'im. Quick, Sister Josephine, git me my medicine kit."

Amanda looked concerned. "Jeremy, where did this man come from?"

"Out yonder," replied Jeremy, pointing in the general direction. "He just rode up from out of nowhere."

"Well, take the saddle off his horse, and water and feed that poor thing," said Amanda. She then assisted Margaret in taking off the stranger's dirty coat and shirt and washing down the wound area. They looked at each other quizzically as they took off and set aside the gun belt. Ezekiel had lost a lot of blood and he was very pale, but he was strong as an ox and responded positively to the gentle treatment.

Ezekiel started to come around. "Thank ya, sisters," he said weakly. "Don' never mind about the hurt when ya take the slug out. I can stan' a lot a pain an' it ain't the first time. Save the slug 'cause I collect 'em." Two other nasty body wounds attested to that statement.

"Don' have ta be so brave, mister. I'm good at this. What's yer name, ag'in?" asked Margaret.

"Ezekiel. My friends, an' I ain't got many, call me Zeke. You get that there bullet out an' yer my friend, sister."

"Well, Ezekiel, this ain't gonna be pretty, but it'll be quick as I can." Margaret was not bashful in her probing and Zeke generated no more than a low moan in the process. True to her word, the slug was out quickly.

"Here, give me some of them bitters," she pointed at Roy Thomas's medicinal whiskey stored in his coat pocket.

Reluctantly, Roy fumbled around until he produced the pint-sized bottle and handed it to Margaret. She pulled the cork out with her mouth and then poured a little in the wound.

Ezekiel winced. "Don' waste that stuff, sister," he gasped. At this point, he was near exhaustion and relaxed with relief that the worst was over.

"He's right," agreed Roy, "don' waste that stuff."

"Oh, hush, Brother Roy," Margaret said as she set about stopping the flow of blood and patching the wound.

"He's one strong man," exclaimed Amanda.

"That he is," replied Margaret, "that he is."

It was late in the afternoon and the sun was beginning to dip in the boundless horizon. Margaret and Amanda were discussing where to make room in one of the wagons for their patient. Margaret insisted that there was much more room in their wagon so that is where he would go.

Jeremy and Jake were sitting on the ground next to Zeke as he dozed and regained his strength. Jeremy had built a fire near the man to keep him warm.

"What's them two talkin' about?" Zeke wheezed, startling Jeremy. He hadn't realized the man had come around because his eyes remained shut.

"They're tryin' to figure out where to put you up for the night."

"No they ain't. Hey sisters," he bellowed to the women. "Don' ya bother none. I'm gonna sleep where I always do, rat here on the ground."

"Ya'll do no such thing, Zeke," retorted Margaret, bending over him and looking him squarely in the face. "Ya just had a bullet dug outta ya and'll catch yer death if ya sleep on that there cold ground."

"What's yer name?" Zeke asked Margaret, returning her steadfast gaze.

"Sister Margaret."

"Well, Sister Margaret, you an' me got off ta a pretty good start, an' I thank ya. But let's not ruin our relationship by insistin' I do somepin I ain't gonna do. I got me a little tent in my bedroll an' I *always* sleep in it with my saddle as my pilla."

"You are one stubborn man," Amanda said, as she stood over Zeke with her hands on her hips.

"That I am, sister. An' what's yer name?" he asked Amanda politely.

"I'm Sister Amanda."

"She's my mother," Jeremy said proudly.

"Well, Sister Amanda, ya got one fine boy there." He nodded in Jeremy's direction. As he spoke, he saw before him a small sad woman who was once very attractive but had not weathered the trail well. Zeke was an excellent judge of people and it was clear to him that despite some failing health and spirit, this was an intelligent and very determined lady. She could go the distance, he thought. "I don' mean no disrespect, but I'm usta pretty much doin' what I want. Seems ta me that me sleepin' here on the ground causes nobody problems, an' that's what I want."

"Your right, Zeke, it's no problem, unless, of course, you die in the middle of the night. Then it's a big problem."

Zeke laughed. "Still no problem, ma'am, ya'll just pack up an' leave. Even the buzzards gotta eat some stringy old human flesh now an' then."

"Not funny, Zeke, but you have your way. Just don't wake me in the middle of the night moaning if you get cold. Jeremy," she looked at her son, "put up Zeke's tent and fix it the way he wants." She then turned to Zeke and asked, "What's your last name, by the way?

"Ain't got one," he replied.

"You don't have a last name?" asked a puzzled Jeremy

"Nope, ain't got no mom an' pop or any other kin I knowed of."

"Everybody has a ma and pa," said Jeremy.

"Oh, somebody had me, that's fer sure. But, I never knowed who it was an' I've pretty much been on my own since I can remember."

"That's terrible," lamented Jeremy.

"Oh, it ain't so bad. I seen some kids that have parents treat 'em real bad. I'd rather be on my own. Not ever' body's lucky as you," he concluded, as he gave Amanda a big smile and a wink.

James had been at a company meeting getting orders for the next day's journey during the time of Zeke's arrival. When he returned late, he was surprised to see a strange man sleeping under a small tent next to his wagon. As he called the Weston Train together for the evening prayers, Jeremy filled him in on the presence of Zeke. He had many questions for this new arrival, but that would have to wait until morning. As was the custom, by eight thirty, everyone bedded down for the night.

The night passed and Zeke slept soundly. There was no moaning to keep Amanda awake, only Zeke's incessant and thunderous snoring. She thought, now there's a man that has a tolerance for pain unlike anyone I've ever known.

Sunday was a time to relax, but not to lower one's guard. Young had warned everyone that the Pawnees would be far more likely to steal their horses than to harm anyone. They preferred to make such raids at night when everyone was asleep and the guards most vulnerable. It was a hard lesson the Jacobson Company would learn again this night. Four horses disappeared. Fortunately, for the Weston Train, none was from their families. They only had six horses and one colt to begin with. Unfortunately, for the families that did lose a horse, there was no Matoskah to bring them back.

"That's the best breakfast I've et in many a moon," beamed Zeke as he patted his stomach in satisfaction. He was sitting up now and the color had returned to his face.

"There's more if you want it," said Jeremy. He was mesmerized by this strange man.

"No, no, I had plenty. Tell your ma I said thanks. What's all the fuss about?" Zeke asked, as he observed the Saints chattering among themselves about the Indian raid.

James approached Zeke and heard the question.

"Indians stole four horses last night," he answered. "Oh, I wasn't here when you came in. I'm Brother James Weston, Jeremy's father and captain of this train. I understand your name's Ezekiel."

Zeke nodded affirmatively, "Sorry ta hear 'bout the horses."

"Yeah, well, we have to be more alert. So, Ezekiel, tell me how come you ended up way out here by yourself with a bullet hole in you?" challenged James.

"Let me tell ya, it wern't planned. I jus' come back from Californi where I dropped off some settlers. That's my job, takin' wagon trains across this big ol' country. This was my fourth trip. Everbody wants ta go west, not east, so I have ta come back by meself most times." Zeke paused, drew in a deep breath, and winced as he rubbed his injured shoulder. "Never had a problem before, 'cause I'm pretty good at spottin' Injuns early an' keepin' outta their way. But a day ago, two stray bucks I didn't see ambushed me. Believe you me; they had me between hay an' grass out in the open like that."

"Sounds like a bad situation, for sure," interrupted James.

"Yep, killed one a 'em with this here," he nodded at his rifle, "when they come chargin', but the other one got me in the shoulder. Knocked me clean off my horse. When that there buck come up ta see if'n I was dead, I rolled over a plugged him rat between the eyes with my pistol. Pawnees, they was. They don' usually act like that."

"That's quite a story," remarked James. "You're lucky to be here."

"Yer rat about that. If it weren't fer ol' Jeremy here, I might be buzzard meat fer sure." He reached over and affectionately messed up Jeremy's hair. Jeremy blushed.

"There's a couple a rifles in the bedroll on my saddle. Took 'em off'n them Injuns. Ya can have 'em if'n ya want—I got plenty."

"Well, thank you," James said, surprised. "The train can always use more weapons. That's mighty kind of you, Ezekiel." In a friendlier, less challenging tone, James continued, "I hear you don't claim a last name. Is that right?"

"Never got none, so I don' claim none."

"Well, if you have to have only one name, Ezekiel is good as any. You know what it means?'

"Nope."

"It means, 'God will strengthen.' Ezekiel was a Prophet in the Old Testament. There are stories that say he was responsible for bringing some people back to life."

Zeke pondered that one. "Nobody ever told me that before. Kinda looks like ol' Jeremy is more like Ezekiel than me."

"That may be true," James laughed. Still hesitant, he asked, "Where do you work out of?"

"St. Louie usually. There's a bunch a people that want ta go out west. They got no idea what's ahead. Half of 'em don' even know how ta shoot a gun. It's a big challenge gettin' 'em across, let me tell ya."

"Any of them Mormons?"

"None I run in ta," answered Zeke. "Most Mormons come from Illinois. Besides, they's too well organized ta need my kind a he'p."

"Well, we'll be heading out again in the morning," James said as he stood, put on his hat, and adjusted his clothing. "You can come along 'til you feel better, if you like, even though it's heading in the wrong direction."

Zeke rubbed his beard in contemplation. "Ya know, I might jus' do that. I'd be a dumb ass ta head out by meself in my condition. Them damn Injuns would get me fer sure. I could go far as Fort Laramie with ya an' see if I can pick up some settlers in trouble there. Besides, might be I could help ya'll out along the way. I know what's comin'."

"Fine Zeke, but you've got to follow our rules and our schedule. That includes no drinking, smoking, chewing, and *swearing*." James emphasized the swearing.

"Well, I don' do three outta the four anyways, so I guess I can live with that." Zeke extended his hand. "I'll work on the fourth one," he said as he winked.

James shook Zeke's hand firmly, grinned, and nodded his head once in agreement. He surmised that this stranger was no threat and could even be an asset.

Jeremy smiled broadly. He liked this rugged individual. Having Zeke along would make life more bearable and interesting, he thought.

As he rested and recuperated, Zeke spent the day observing the Mormons' actions on the Sabbath. There was much praying and other church-related activities, but he thought them to be about the busiest people he ever saw on what was to be their day of respite. Rest on the trail was an illusory concept.

The next day, May 3, the Jacobson Company wagons, following Brigham Young's lead, stayed on a course north of the Platte River. The Saints had enough of a challenge on the trail—especially now that they were in Indian country. They didn't need to venture south of the river where they could run into other trains of pioneers, some having a dim view of the Mormons. With some justification, the Mormons believed there was also more disease south of the river, especially the dreaded ague.

Interestingly, the land, the weather, and the flora and fauna suddenly changed from that experienced since leaving Winter Quarters. The land was flatter than they had seen before and, with the exception of certain areas, much of the grass transformed into a short curly variety called buffalo grass. There was a steady breeze and it was drier than before. Lips and hands chapped easily. The cry of wolves, seldom heard previously, became commonplace and put everyone on edge, especially Jake. There was also an increase in the number of deer and antelope flitting across the land, as well as prairie dogs burrowing under the ground. As the weather turned colder, there was little doubt that they had now entered the beginning of the western part of this vast country.

Day after day, the Saints trekked westward. Following the tracks of many wagons that had gone before them, they kept close to the familiar Platte as they gradually climbed from the flat treeless plains toward the elevated tablelands of the West.

"I'm riding old Benjamin," Jeremy said to Zeke as they rode side by side. "What's your horse's name?"

"Horse," replied Zeke.

"Horse? What kind a name is Horse?"

"Good as any. He don' care none. Once had a dog name a Dog 'til he was kilt by a rattler."

"A horse named Horse and a dog named Dog. You're a strange man, Zeke."

"Suppose so," offered Zeke, "I jus' like ta keep things simple."

It was obvious to James that this man, Zeke, had a strong hold on Jeremy. The two were constant companions. They talked continuously as Zeke rode his horse with Jeremy walking beside him, or both walking or riding together. Zeke did the majority of the talking, with Jeremy asking many questions. James marveled at Zeke's stamina considering his wound. His constant gesticulations suggested that whatever pain he experienced was of no consequence. There was a concern, however—what kind of things might an obvious vagabond gunman be telling his son?

Curiosity finally made James rein in his horse and join the two as they rode along together. "What are you two jawing about today?" he asked.

"Pa, Zeke really knows a lot about this country. We've been talking about the land, the Indians, the plants, the animals, and a whole lot more," replied Jeremy enthusiastically.

"Where'd you acquire all this knowledge, Zeke?" James's interest was piqued.

"The school a hard knocks, Brother James. Been livin' an' travelin' this here country fer the better part a ten years or so. When yer on yer own, it pays ta know everthin' you can about yer surroundin's just ta survive."

"Makes sense to me."

"Like that plant over there," Jeremy pointed to a cluster of yellow flowers on the ridge. "What're they called again, Zeke?"

"Golden Alexanders," Zeke replied.

"Yeah, Golden Alexanders. Zeke says you can cook those flowers and they're good to eat ... if you like vegetables."

"Didn't know that," commented James. He was impressed. "Sounds like something we should know, that's for sure. Well, I best be checking on the rest of the train. How are you feeling, Zeke?"

"Good, good. Jeremy keeps my mind off the hurt with all his questions." He knocked Jeremy's hat to one side with a friendly shove.

"Later," James said as he rode back toward the end of the train. *Looks like I don't have anything to worry about there,* he thought. *In fact, looks like we can definitely use old Zeke and his knowledge before we arrive at Fort Laramie.*

CHAPTER 24

Because of weather, trail conditions, accidents, and other unanticipated circumstances, the Jacobson Company wasn't always able to follow a set routine. Even so, Brother Jacobson tried his best to enforce a routine set in accordance with Young's ideal order for traveling and camping.

Every morning of travel, the bugle sounded at sunrise. Everyone arose—some willingly, many reluctantly—and prayed before leaving their wagons and tents. The pioneers ate breakfast, packed their gear, corralled, yoked, and hitched up the draft animals, and completed everything else required to make ready for the day's journey. At the sound of another bugle, the wagons moved out by no later than 8:30 am.

Depending on the terrain, weather, and the availability of feed and water for the animals, the wagon train rolled on at about two miles per hour for a day's trip of six to twelve miles. Most children and adults preferred to walk beside the slow moving wagons because riding on the hard spring-less wagon seats was quite uncomfortable. Walking also reduced the load the oxen had to pull.

The weary travelers took a nooning break in the middle of the day and oxen and people rested. While the livestock grazed, the Saints ate their dinner—usually something cold, like sea biscuits, called hard tack, or corn meal mush and milk. Refreshed and fed, the entourage would hitch up and continue the day's journey. By the end of the day, the livestock was corralled, campfires made, supper eaten, tents assembled, and preparations made for bedding down for the night. Often, members of the trains would gather around a fire, tell stories, and sometimes sing. At the sound of a bugle, James, and other train masters, would lead their trains in prayer and pass out the instructions for the next day. Everyone was ready to retire by eight thirty or nine o'clock.

Varying amounts of disorder existed every day within every family, wagon, and train, depending on relationships, health, degree of need, and the vicissitudes of the trail. To the distant observer, if there was chaos, it appeared organized. Inch by inch, foot by foot, mile by mile, the wagon trains continued forward on their relentless quest for the Promised Land. The routine had a sameness to it, with long stretches of boredom. However, everything from Indian threats, stampedes, bad weather, deaths, and the many other occurrences that prevailed along the trail, often disrupted what would otherwise be a mind and body-numbing day.

Amanda had recovered from yet another bout with ague. She felt tired and very weak. The ground was relatively smooth and so she opted to ride in the front seat of the wagon. It was a beautiful day, a bit chilly, but clear and sunny with a mild breeze. The sounds of the moving wagon train were all about—wagons creaking, animals plodding, horses whinnying, hawks screeching overhead, people talking, children laughing and crying, and on and on. All of this was but subliminal background noise for Amanda as she sat musing about nothing, just taking in the rays of the sun and the moment of peace.

"Penny fer yer thoughts."

The voice made Amanda twitch. It was Zeke walking beside the wagon. Actually, he had walked there for some time, unnoticed by Amanda.

"Oh, my word, you startled me," she said, putting her right hand over her heart.

"I'm sorry, I don' mean ta bother ya none."

"That's all right, Zeke. You're never any bother."

"Mind if I come up in the wagon an' chat with ya a while? I'm not much for walkin'."

That's a lie, she thought. He's walked a hundred miles just since he joined us. She moved to one side and patted the bench. "No, not at all. As a matter of fact, I'd like some company."

Zeke hiked himself into the wagon and sat next to Amanda. He took off his hat and placed it in his lap. Squinting up at the sun, he said, "Beautiful day, ain't it?"

"Yes, it is. I was just thinking that a moment ago. We don't get many like this, do we?"

"No, an' we probably won't get many more."

Amanda and Zeke were ill at ease. This was their first one-on-one conversation without others around. Their proximity made both nervous and it was difficult to talk.

"I have been looking at all the wildlife as we go by. The noise of the wagon train stirs up quite a bit. Trouble is, I don't know what a lot of them are. Are you familiar with the birds here on the prairie?" It was a superfluous question as she heard from Jeremy about Zeke's vast knowledge of plants, animals, Indians, and other aspects of the open road.

"Some a 'em," replied Zeke.

"Look, over there," she pointed to a brown and black bird with a bright yellow breast sitting atop a rock, "what kind of bird is that one?"

Zeke peered in the direction Amanda pointed. "Oh, that there's pretty common here. That there's a Meadowlark, a Western Meadowlark."

"We had Meadowlarks back in Nauvoo, and even in Tennessee, but they didn't look like that. How come you know so much about the animals and birds and such in this area, Zeke?"

"Well, when yer alone an' liven outta the saddle as much as I have, ya pay attention ta the animal an' plant life. Got nothin' else ta do. Learned most a it from the Injuns. Much as I hate some a 'em sometimes, they know everthin' 'bout where they live. Their lives depend on knowin' such stuff."

"You're a fine student and teacher, Zeke." Amanda was impressed with his knowledge and gentle ways.

After an awkward pause, Zeke looked at Amanda and said, "Ya know ... I been meaning ta talk ta ya 'bout somethin' fer quite a spell. Maybe now's good a time as any."

"Oh, really, now what would that be?" Amanda turned her head sideways and looked at Zeke. She was very curious.

"Well, me an' Margaret ... I mean, Sister Margaret, been noticin' that ya ain't exactly up ta yerself now and then."

"Oh, you an' Sister Margaret been 'noticin', huh?" she parroted Zeke. "And pray tell, what you been 'noticin'?" There was an edge to her voice.

"Ya know me, Sister Amanda, I ain't one ta beat around the bush none. We, Sister Margaret an' me, been thinkin' ya kinda got a touch a the ague." He averted her eyes when he said the word. Amanda was silent. After a moment, he raised his head and looked directly into her eyes. His deep blue-eyed stare gave her no room for denial. She looked away and down and began a useless attempt to hold back tears.

Amanda's lower lip quivered as she dabbed her eyes with a small hankie she withdrew from her sleeve and muttered, "I'd hoped no one noticed."

"Sister Amanda, yer a brave an' beautiful woman, one a the strongest I ever knowed, but there comes a time when ya need help. All them people out there that love ya wanna help. Ya cain't just go on actin' like nothin's wrong. It's gonna catch up with ya soon, an' ya know it."

"I know, I know," she answered, resigned to the disclosure. "I just don't want to be a burden to anyone and I sure don't want to worry my children."

"Well, yer in charge. Me an' Sister Margaret ain't gonna say a word 'til ya do. If ya need any he'p at any time, jus' say so, ya hear?"

"Zeke, you have become a true friend of the family. I really appreciate the way you have adopted Jeremy. He so needed some guidance and you've given him a lot. Thanks so much," she said, as she kissed him on the cheek.

Zeke actually blushed. He stammered, "A ... Jeremy's a great boy, an' I like 'im a lot. I never told nobody before, but I had a little boy oncet that woulda been about his age."

"Oh, Zeke, I never knew. Whatever happened to him?"

"Well, he an' his mother was kilt in a Injun raid 'bout twelve years ago. I been on the road ever since. Guess I jus' let Jeremy kinda take his place. Just don' tell nobody about this, especially Jeremy."

"You have my word, and I'm so sorry," Amanda commiserated.

"Thank ya, it ain't nothin' now, but yer family is special ta me. I don' want nothin' ta happen' ta any a ya, understand?"

"You are one of the kindest, best men I know, Zeke. We are all blessed to know you."

"Likewise," Zeke replied, as he climbed down from the wagon. Reaching up, he shook Amanda's outstretched hand. "Ya'll take care now, understand?"

"I will, Zeke, I will," she said with a wistful smile. Left alone with her thoughts again, Amanda now had to think about when and how to tell her family of the ague.

The days passed, and Amanda wrestled with her "little secret." Increasingly, since her encounter with Zeke, Amanda noticed that other members of the train were beginning to look at her questioningly, and felt that maybe they were coming to some other worse conclusions. She owed it to her family that they find out first and from her. After prayers one evening, she called James to one side and confessed her problem.

"Amanda," James said tenderly, "I have suspected for some time that was your problem. Your chills and fever have not gone unnoticed, you know."

Amanda was confused. "You have 'suspected for some time' and never even ask me what was wrong? Why?"

"I don't know ... I ... just felt you would tell me when you wanted to," he stammered. When asked so bluntly, he really didn't know why he had not pursued the subject before. It was just another indication of how much he and Amanda had grown apart during this long journey. Amanda knew that was the reason, as well.

"I'm truly sorry, Amanda, that I have not been more attentive. And, I'm sorry you have such a serious illness. We'll do everything to help you. Just say what you need. I know there's not much we can do—maybe some bleeding."

"No, I'll have none of that," Amanda snapped. "It hasn't been too bad and we both know people that have had ague that lived for many years with only occasional problems."

"That's true, but conditions of the trail don't help. You've got to take care of yourself. I will make sure you have a lightened load."

"No, again," said Amanda, "unless I'm down and out, I will pull my load. There are too many people suffering far worse than I am for me to be treated like somebody special."

"Whatever you say, Amanda." James knew better than to argue with this determined woman. "When are you going to tell the children?"

"Tomorrow sometime, when I feel up to it."

"Tomorrow, it is," James agreed. He pulled her toward him tenderly and though she resisted slightly, hugged her gently. He felt a wave of guilt over the deterioration of their relationship since leaving Nauvoo and knew that he was primarily responsible. Yes, he realized that some situations, like William's departure, had control of his life, but he also knew that he had done little to meet his wife's needs under trying circumstances. Amanda cried softly in his embrace.

There was little wind, so the dust from the wagon wheels and the livestock's hoofs hung around the train in a stifling, aura-like cloud. Otherwise, it was a beautiful morning with huge white cumulus clouds billowing in the bright blue western sky. The sounds of the trail were but a muted background noise to Amanda, who gathered her children around her as they walked. The pace was so slow that even short-legged Christine had no problem keeping up.

Amanda wasn't sure where to start. After chatting idly about the day, she set about explaining why she was not feeling well these days. "They call what I have, ague," she explained.

"What's that mean, Mommy?" asked Christine.

"It means that every now and then I will have some bad days. One minute I will feel cold and the next minute hot, and I'll be sick for a few hours."

"I've heard of ague before," said Jeremy, "there's no cure, right?"

Amanda put her arm on his shoulder. "That's true, son, but it's not as bad as so many other sicknesses."

"You're not going to die, are you?" asked serious Christine.

Amanda chuckled reassuringly. "No, no, darlin'. I just wanted you to know so you wouldn't wonder what was wrong when I do have a spell."

"I knew you had something," said Jeremy. "I asked Zeke, but he told me that maybe you were just tired from the long trip. I knew he was lying, but I let it go."

"Oh, you've always been so smart, Jeremy. Anyway, I want all of you to help me out with the chores if I slack off, ya hear?"

"Sure, Mommy," Christine said. Jeremy just nodded his head in agreement, as he gave Amanda that singular admiring look they had exchanged so often.

That evening, Amanda revealed what many previously figured out—she had ague. "Ain't no big thing," said Margaret Waters, "I've knowd some that lived with the Illinois shakes fer years. Pain in the rear fer sure, but not somethin' our Amanda cain't handle. Come on now," she continued as she gave Amanda a big smile and a reassuring hug, "it ain't catchin'." Everyone smiled and gave Amanda words of comfort and support. Amanda felt better that evening as she went to bed. No longer hiding her not so well kept "little secret," gave her comfort and peace.

Unlike the previous days, this day gusty winds swirled the dust of the trail about, covering everything with a fine grit. The trail itself was reasonably maneuverable; the Advance Company and others had improved stretches as they went along. James was continually amazed at the vitality displayed by those in the lead as they forged ahead, all the while improving conditions for those to follow.

"That's Grand Island," Zeke said, pointing south across the Platte. "That there place's got a lotta deer; also got a lotta Injuns from time ta time. But I can take a couple a men over and see what we can find, if ya like."

"No, no ... it looks inviting," remarked Captain Jacobson, "But we been warned to stay this side of the river."

The hunting party sent out earlier had not been successful, so the thought of deer just across the river was tempting. Jacobson was beginning to rely on Zeke for advice and to lead any hunting forays—if Zeke couldn't find any suitable game, no one could. The Company proceeded to a location previously used by other companies, just this side of where the Wood River emptied into the Platte. Here, they camped for the night.

Jeremy pitched the family tent next to Zeke's small tent. This was the routine now. James usually slept in the tent with Jeremy while Amanda and Christine slept in the wagon. Occasionally, one or two of the Thomas girls spent the night in the wagon. Jake invariably placed his large smelly body between the two tents or under the wagon.

The moon was shining brightly and all was quiet, but something caused Jeremy to stir. It was the low rumble of Jakes growl. Jeremy then became aware of the nervous shifts and noises made by the cows, sheep, oxen, and particularly the horses.

"What is it, boy," whispered Jeremy.

"Somepin's outside the corral, an' he knows it," whispered Zeke from the other tent.

All of a sudden, Jake got up and headed outside the circle at full speed. Jeremy, Zeke, and James all scrambled to their feet. Zeke and James grabbed their rifles. The moon was sufficiently bright for them to see the problem. A lamb had wandered outside the circle and was facing two large white wolves. Jake didn't bark but silently and speedily attacked the nearest wolf. The battle was on. The wolves, each about the size of Jake, began fighting this brazen attacker. The noise was ferocious and aroused everyone in the company. Zeke and James were armed, but there was no opportunity to take a shot as the entangled animals snarled, scratched, and bit one another with unrelenting ferocity. It was vicious, mortal combat.

In one swift movement, Jake compressed the larger wolf's throat between his powerful jaws. He violently tore at his victim, while ignoring the other wolf's attack on his back. As one wolf fell dead to the ground with a terrible gurgling scream, the other wolf stopped his attack on Jake, turned, and sped off into the night, his tail between his legs. Jake stood exhausted, looking down at the dead wolf. He was bleeding profusely from multiple wounds on his face, back, and hindquarters.

Jeremy sped to the side of his dog and was shocked to see the damage. "Oh Jake, oh Jake," he cried as he put his hands on some of the wounds to stem the blood flow. Soon, everyone was crowded around and expressing great concern over Jake's condition. Together, James and Zeke picked up the huge injured dog and carried him back to the circle.

Sister Margaret rushed to the dog's side as the two men lowered the spent, wounded dog onto a piece of canvass. She began to treat the wounds that were bleeding profusely and soon stopped the serious flow. Jeremy cradled Jake's head tenderly in his lap. "Hope them wolves ain't got no diseases," Margaret said, as poured some of Roy Thomas's medicinal whiskey on the wounds. "This should help keep the infection down," she added. Jake cringed at every application but did not make a sound. With sad eyes, he looked into his master's face for reassurance. It wasn't long after that the wounded, exhausted animal was asleep under a warm blanket and the crowd began to disburse. Jeremy lay down beside his loyal friend and Zeke covered them both. It took a while for everyone to settle down.

Thus, Jake added another chapter to his storied life as a champion. Within a few days, he was up, limping somewhat from a sizeable gash on his right rear leg. The scars were many and large and only served to remind everyone that once again, Jake was the "Hero Dog." This was particularly true because, somehow, the lamb had escaped any harm during the deadly encounter.

"Amazin' dog," Zeke said shaking his head in admiration. "Best ever I seen." Obviously, Jake had won another convert.

It was May 9. The word had come back from the Advance Company to be on the lookout for the great shaggy buffalo that up to now they'd only seen outlined in the far distance. As the Weston Train, the lead train in the company this day, came over a rise, Jeremy was the first to spot them—a huge herd far off to the northwest.

"Look, Ma!" he shouted excitedly, pointing to the distant mass of grazing animals. "There's gotta be a thousand of 'em." Jake had actually alerted Jeremy to the sight. His keen smell and sharp hearing had detected the herd. Now that he had sighted them, he was going crazy, excitedly running back and forth, and barking wildly. This is what made a big dog's life worth living.

Everyone came running to the north side of their wagons as the word spread back through the company. Exclamations of awe mingled with excitement as the full dimensions of the herd came into view. Over the next couple of hours, the wagon train plodded forward, coming steadily closer to the big, brown mass of grazing buffalo. He figured that everyone would eat well that night on fresh buffalo meat, rather than the difficult-to-digest salted meat they had become accustomed to ingesting. As if reading his mind, a rider from Brother Jacobson came forward and approached James.

"Brother Weston, yer suppose ta lead a group a men and kill some a them buffalo so's we can feed ever'body in the company tonight."

"Thank you, brother," James replied. "I'll do just that."

"Brother Young said not ta kill any more'n we can eat," the rider warned as he rode off. James grabbed his rifle from his saddle holster.

"Ever kill a buffalo?' asked Zeke, sitting on his horse a few yards from James, one leg propped over the saddle horn, whittling on a stick with his bowie knife.

"Nope," replied James as he checked his rifle and ammunition, "never even seen one 'til now."

"Mind if I give ya some pointers? They ain't that easy ta put down, lessen ya knowed how.'

"You killed any before?"

"My share."

"So, tell me what I need to know," tested James.

"Well, first, ya can use that pea shooter awright," Zeke said, pointing at James's Hall Rifle, "but it's gonna take a lot a shots an' ya gotta be lucky. What ya need is somethin' like this." With dramatic flair, Zeke withdrew a long octagonal-shaped-barrel rifle from a deerskin scabbard on the right side of his saddle. "This here's a Hawkins. Cost me a arm an' leg back in St. Louie, but it's got a lead ball that'll kill a buffalo at 200 or more yards with one shot if, ya hit 'em right."

"Now there's what you call nail driver—a fine weapon, indeed." James balanced the weapon in his hands and admired the craftsmanship. He knew Zeke had a Hall sheathed in the other scabbard. "You said that you have to hit them right. So, where do you aim?' he asked, pointing the long rifle at the vacant distance.

"Jus' about any place in the upper forward body. Don' aim fer the forehead. That's like shootin' in ta an adobe wall. That'll jus' make 'em mad."

"Sounds like you ought to be doing the hunting in place of me. How about it, you feel like showing us how instead of just telling me?" James didn't see any sense in letting all that experience go to waste.

"It'd be my pleasure," answered Zeke with a broad grin.

Riding out to the side of the wagon, James whistled to Jeremiah and waved him to the front. As Jeremiah came abreast, James told him to keep the train moving while he and Zeke went forward to hunt. Joined by six other men with rifles, the group galloped off toward the herd of buffalo.

Sure enough, many shots rang out, but as Zeke predicted, the inexperienced hunters only managed to stampede the fringe of the herd. However, before the raid was over, the hunters killed three buffalo cows, each weighing about three quarters of a ton. One enraged bull charged the novice buffalo hunters and nearly gored a couple horses. Only the men's excellent horsemanship saved them. Two of the kills were from Zeke's long, single load, buffalo gun. Multiple shots from many rifles downed the third. Gonna pick out a lot a lead out a that one, thought Zeke, as he looked down at the many oozing bullet holes.

Skinning and dressing a buffalo was also a new experience for the Saints. Despite the still tender wound in his shoulder, Zeke gave the men pointers as he demonstrated with his sharp bowie knife. In addition, as he worked, he explained the best way for them to hunt buffalo in the future. Everyone was impressed and appreciative. They gave him one of the hides for his contribution. The other two went to Captain Jacobson for distribution as he saw fit.

As the Weston Train lumbered on alongside the distant throng of buffalo, a malodorous breeze wafted from the shaggy beasts. The smell was nauseating, but a bigger aggravation came when the Saints realized that the buffalos' close-cropped grazing left little for the Mormon cattle, sheep, and oxen to eat. In addition, small little insects called buffalo gnats were more than a nuisance. The bite from one of these little critters was worse than a mosquito. However, on the plus side, Zeke pointed out that the plentiful dried dung, known as buffalo chips, could be used in place of wood for fires—a blessing, as trees were far from plentiful on the open plain.

That evening, everyone gorged on the delicious buffalo meat. It was sweeter than beef and just as tender. Unfortunately, for many, the after effects were very uncomfortable. The digestive tracts of the Mormons were not used to the fresh meat and diarrhea struck with vengeance. Thus, the vast herds of buffalo were both a blessing and a curse to these nomads. Zeke had no such problem. Years on the plains made him immune to almost everything—excluding bullets.

"Ta the mother a my best friend, I give ya my buffalo hide an' hope it keeps ya warm when ya hit the cold mountains." Zeke smiled at Amanda and pointed to the hide draped over the wagon wheel. She looked so pale that he was sure she could use it more than anyone else in the train. Besides, he liked this fragile, determined little woman. She had a certain air of independence he didn't see in the rest of the Mormons, except maybe Jeremy and crusty old Margaret. Them's three of a kind, thought Zeke.

"Well, thank you, Zeke. I'm overwhelmed. I've never even felt a buffalo hide before," she said, stroking the shaggy pelt gently.

"Buffalo kilt this time a year don' give as good a fur as one's kilt in winter, but it's better'n nothing'. I'll teach Jamie boy here how ta scrape it, salt, it an' dry it so it'll be nice an' soft fer ya when it comes time ta wear it." Zeke beamed—he was obviously pleased with himself.

"You're very kind, Zeke." Amanda blushed. She was not used to such kind gestures, especially from a stranger. What a prize her son had picked off this God-forsaken land she thought.

CHAPTER 25

"Pa, Zeke wants to take me out and see if we can shoot us a deer. I got all my chores done. Is it all right, if I go?" Jeremy and Zeke had been on many walking tours and discussed many things, but they had not yet gone out to hunt.

"I don't see why not, as long as you're careful. Make sure you're back by prayers, you hear?" Jeremy knew well how to handle a rifle and, by now, James was confident in Zeke's ability and sense of responsibility.

Jeremy came running to Zeke, sitting by the wagon whittling on a stick. "Pa said it's all right," he said, with a big smile.

"Well then, gather up yer horse an' saddle an' let's go." Zeke stood, put his knife away, dusted off his pants, and started saddling his horse.

As Jeremy was saddling up, Amanda saw what he was doing and that he was very excited about doing it. "What's going on, son?" she asked.

"Zeke an' me are goin' hunting."

"Pa know?"

"Yep."

"Well all right, but you be careful," cautioned Amanda.

"Maaa," whined Jeremy, "I'm with Zeke."

"Well, you still be careful, and take care that the horse doesn't step in one of those prairie dog holes and break a leg."

"Ma, you worry about the darnedest things," Jeremy said as he kissed his mother on the cheek and pulled himself into the saddle. "I'll be careful, promise."

Amanda stood by the wagon with her arms folded and watched her son and Zeke ride slowly away from the encampment. They were both talking and gesticulating as they went. He's growing up so fast, she thought. He'll be fourteen in July, but he's already had the experiences of a grown man. Don't know why I worry about him, especially with Zeke. I guess that's just what mothers do. A tear slowly made its way down her cheek. She could tell that she was about to have another one of her ague attacks. They seemed to be coming more often, lasting longer, and taking a greater toll. Starting to shiver uncontrollably, she looked around to see that no one noticed. Agonizingly, she pulled herself into the back of the wagon and covered up with every available blanket and coat. She drank a cup of composition tea—a mixture of bayberry, ginger, cayenne, and cloves.

Jake hated it when Jeremy commanded him to stay put. He couldn't understand why Jeremy would leave with his horse and rifle and not take him. As they rode off, Jake kept sitting then standing, barking, panting, and licking his chops, but he stayed put. Zeke told Jeremy that they were going to do some serious hunting and they didn't need Jake running around scaring all the game away. Zeke promised that he would go out with Jake and teach him how to be a superior hunting dog, but today was not the day. As the days went by, Zeke did teach Jake how to behave on a hunt. In fact, he did better—he taught him how to help in the hunt.

"What we huntin' for, Zeke?"

"Anything we can eat, but I hope we can bring in a deer, or if we're really lucky a pronghorn."

"What's a pronghorn?"

"Most folks calls 'em antelope, but they ain't, really."

"I saw one of them once ... at least I think I did. I saw it and then like a flash, it was gone. Brother Roy said it was an antelope."

"Yep, they're purdy fast, but, ya can still shoot one if ya know how. Only we gotta see one first."

"What's it look like?" ask Jeremy.

"Oh, it looks somethin' like a deer, but smaller. They only weigh 'bout 100 pounds an' stan' 'bout three feet or so at the shoulder. One reason ya don' see them is 'cause they usually see ya first with them big eyes of theirs. Their name comes from the big 'ol horns they got up front—kinda curved inward." Zeke demonstrated with his hands from his head.

The man and boy walked now, with their horses trailing behind. The rolling terrain was treeless, and covered with tall prairie grass that swayed in the gentle breeze. Suddenly, behind a knoll to the right, a large brown animal bolted away. Four stiff-legged jumps and the animal disappeared over a crest. Zeke had raised his rifle, but the speedy creature vanished before he could aim.

"Damn, we gotta be more alert," said an exasperated Zeke.

"What was that?" asked Jeremy.

"T'was a Mule Deer."

"How'd you know, it was gone before I got a good look."

"Well, did ya see how he jumped with all four legs hittin' at the same time as he took off?"

"Yep."

"That's the way Mule Deer run off," explained Zeke. "Rest a the deer just high tail it. Too bad, he were a big one. Let's sit a spell. That fella probably scared off everthin' aroun'. We'll wait'll it settles down some." Zeke picked out a spot on the grass and lay down on his back with his legs crossed at the ankles, hands linked behind his head, and hat over his face. He exhaled a big satisfied, "Ahh!"

Jeremy quickly emulated his friend. Only he lay down with his hat on and his face up, gazing at the billowing clouds floating across the bright blue sky. Their horses grazed quietly nearby. The grass was soft and smelled wonderful. The sun felt good.

"Zeke," said Jeremy.

"Yeah."

"You believe in God?"

There was a pause. "Cain't say, nobody ever ask me before."

"Well, I'm asking you."

Another pause. "Don' know. Never been convinced there is or there ain't," Zeke finally said. "Don' think much about it."

"Well, I'm always wonderin'."

"You? I thought ya was a good Mormon boy."

"Bein' a Mormon has nothing to do with if there's a God. I was a Baptist before. I'm the same boy now as then but now the Baptists want to kill me. If there's a God, why would He let that happen?"

"I don' know, son," replied Zeke, "yer over my head."

"I been thinkin'. Maybe people made up God instead the other way around."

"Why's that?"

"'Cause everybody seems to have a different idea about who God is and what he wants us to do. If there's a God, seems he'd have the same rules for everybody. If *I* was God, the rules would be the same," added Jeremy firmly.

"Well, ya ain't God," said Zeke. "So, I guess ya best foller the Mormon rules now."

"I don't have a choice, but I don't have to like it."

"When ya git growed up ya can do what ya want, I guess."

"I can't wait," said Jeremy with finality. It felt wonderful to be able to talk to someone about such feelings and not worry about the impact. Zeke was truly a good friend, thought Jeremy.

"We best quit wonderin' an' wishin' an' git back ta huntin'," Zeke said as he rolled over to his hands and knees and then stood up. Jeremy followed and the two meandered toward their horses.

About a half hour later, as they were starting over a rise, Zeke suddenly squatted, motioned with his hand for Jeremy to get down, and put his finger to his lips commanding him to be silent. The horses had stopped back behind another rise and were quietly eating grass.

"A pronghorn," he whispered, pointing over the knoll ahead. Still whispering, he said, "Be very quiet an' crawl over yonder behind that rise over thar —he pointed off to the left. When I signal ya, take off yer hat an' slowly raise it so's it peeks over the rise. Make sure ya do it slowly. When I nod, wave the hat back an' forth very slowly, over an' over. Got it?"

"Yeah, but why?"

"Tell ya later. Now git," Zeke nodded toward where he wanted Jeremy to go.

After Jeremy was in position, Zeke motioned for him to raise his hat. Jeremy did so. Then he nodded for him to wave the hat back and forth. Jeremy complied. Zeke then stood slowly, with rifle aimed, and fired. The pronghorn fell instantly.

"You got 'im, Zeke! You got 'im!" Jeremy screamed repeatedly, as ran toward the dead animal. "How you know to do that?" he asked in wonder, as Zeke walked up to the fresh kill.

"Oh, it's a trick an Injun taught me." He kneeled down beside Jeremy and the dead pronghorn. "These fella's is fast, but they's also mighty curious. He was more interested in yer hat than in me. Ya heard that curiosity killed the cat? Well, I guess in this here case, curiosity killed the Pronghorn." He laughed at his own joke.

Zeke slit the throat of the Pronghorn to let it bleed and preserve the meat. Then, together they hoisted the animal across the back of Jeremy's horse, behind the saddle. It was a big one and was not easy to hoist as dead weight. Once in place, Jeremy kept looking down at the large horns. "Those are beautiful, Zeke. Suppose I could keep 'em?"

"Don' see why not. They'll remind ya always a yer first big kill."

"I didn't kill 'im, Zeke, you did."

"No, *we* did. We're a team—remember? Couldn't a done it without ya wavin' that hat," he lied.

Regardless, the "team" was very popular when they arrived back to the wagons. The Weston Train ate well that night and had plenty to share with another train. Even Jake got a big bone; easily forgetting the earlier slight.

It was June 5 and someone shouted, "Look, there's Chimney Rock." Everyone scurried to the left side of the wagon train to see this well-known and anticipated attraction. There, located to the southwest, in the middle of a treeless plain, rose this recognizable landmark. The isolated land mass was about a mile in circumference at the base and 300 feet high and had a shaft of rock protruding from the middle that shot up another 120 feet. The Indians called it elk penis; the more reserved pioneers said it looked like a chimney. No matter its name, it was impossible to ignore.

"Don't look more'n twenty mile away," said one man. It turned out to be much more. The clear air, especially against a cloudless sky, made distances difficult to judge. Many hunters found their shots fall short of their prey because of this illusion.

Reaching this landmark was an important milestone. At this point, the Jacobson Company had traveled 450 miles from Winter Quarters. The Platte Valley had been infinite and exhausting. The Saints were now entering a geological transition between the monotonous plains and the higher, drier mountainous country ahead. There were numerous, easily forded creeks and in between, water was plentiful from shallow wells—some dug by earlier Mormon companies. The countryside contained more bluffs, rocks, and rough terrain. The plant life also changed to include such things as Indian Soap Weed, or yucca, and cacti with prickly pears. Besides the always present rattle snakes, there was now an abundance of lizards scurrying everywhere. Bald eagles soared high above while jackrabbits scurried about.

No matter the terrain, the weather, the sickness, or any other of the many adversities, the Saints' spirit as a group never faltered. Amanda was right—the Mormons were an amazing people. Brigham Young had instilled in his followers the need for socialization as well as spiritualization. Nauvoo grew and flourished because there was a strong sense of community and social cohesion besides their religious commitment. The Saints carried that same spirit with them on the trail. Ingrained into the fabric of these people were music, singing, and dancing. The nightly campfire was for prayer and issuance of orders, but also for entertainment. Often fiddlers played and people sang songs. It was a way for the weary travelers to rest, unwind, and forget the hardships of the day's journey. It was also a way to bond with one another.

Despite the many problems that beset the Mormons along the trail, and the fact that not everyone was properly prepared to make such a trip, these people were far superior to most of the pioneers headed west at this time. By typical pioneer standards, they were equipped and armed better than other travelers, and the well-organized Saints had a chain of command that kept order and looked out for the least of their flock. Perhaps the most overwhelming difference was their motivation.

The Mormons had a goal beyond land grabbing and gold digging. They were going to set up a completely new heaven on earth—the Promised Land. This journey was the road to their salvation.

Past Chimney Rock, everyone then became captivated by the geological wonder to their north and west—Scotts Bluffs. The massive collection of sandstone cliffs and caverns that rose sharply from the surrounding landscape looked like a giant castle surrounded by a fortified city. The Indians called it "*ma-a-pa-ti*"—hill that is hard to go around.

That night, as they settled down around the campfire and completed their evening prayers, the question of how Scotts Bluffs got its name came up. Zeke waited a bit, looked around to see if anyone knew, and then volunteered.

"Well, I can tell ya what I heard, if'n ya want."

"Yes, Zeke, tell us what you know," cajoled Jeremy. His awe of Zeke never waivered.

"Yes, yes, tell us," chimed in the other children. The adults all nodded their approval. There was nothing like a good bedtime story around the campfire.

"Different people got different stories," started Zeke. "This is what was told ta me." He paused to collect his thoughts. "Ever since the '20's, besides Injuns, mountain men roamed these here bluffs," he looked up and his head and eyes followed his hand as it swept across the massive terrain. "Seems that back in about '28, there was a party a three such men comin' down the upper part a the river, when their canoes got turned over an' floated away. They hung on ta their rifles but their powder was ruint. They was stranded up in them mountains an' couldn't hunt nothin' ta eat."

"What'd they do?" asked a wide-eyed Christine.

"Mostly they ate roots an' berries, but they was mighty hungry after a while. They walked fer days when one a the fellas, name a Hiram Scott, got sick an' couldn't walk no more. By now, they was near starvin'. While they was lookin' fer berries, they seen a fresh trail made by white men. If they hurried, they might be able ta catch up an' git some he'p. But Hiram couldn't walk none an' they was too weak ta carry him. What a ya think they done?"

All the children mumbled between themselves. "They yelled real loud so the other men could hear 'em," offered seven-year-old Nancy Thomas.

"Nope, too far away," came the quick answer.

"They built a fire ta let the others know they were there," said Anthony Jessup.

"Nope, they didn't have no time. Besides, they was headed in the wrong direction an' wouldn't see no smoke," answered Zeke.

"I know, I know," shouted Mark Thomas, "they left Hiram behind and ran after the other men for help."

"Yes siree, yer right on that," Zeke said, nodding his head, "that's exactly what they done. Problem was, they didn't tell 'ol Hiram. They pretended ta go look fer berries an' jus' didn't come back." There was a hushed gasp among the children. Mormons would never do that they thought to themselves.

"Did they catch up?" asked Jeremy.

"They sure did an' they was saved. Thing was, they didn't tell nobody about ol' Hiram being back there. They said he was dead already."

More gasps ensued from the audience.

"But, that ain't the end a the story. Them same mountain men was walkin' in that area the followin' summer when they come on ol' Hiram's skeleton. They knowed it was him 'cause a the clothes hangin' on the bones. But whar they found 'im was *sixty miles* from whar they left 'im before. Poor ol' Hiram crawled all that long way by hiself before he died. Anyhow, ever since then, people call this here area Scotts Bluffs. Seems like that's only right, don' ya think?"

There was a chorus of "Yep's," and nodding heads.

"You sure that's a true story?" asked a dubious Jeremy.

"Nope, jus' what I heard," answered Zeke with a sly smile and a wink.

On the following Monday, as the Company moved out from Scotts Bluffs, it started to rain—a drenching, cold, windy rain that seeped into every crack and crevice. However, the black, boiling clouds were fast moving and quickly the rain became intermittent and then, just as quickly, became nothing. Rained just enough to soak everyone, thought Amanda disgustedly. Her negative thinking was short lived, however, as the sun burst forth and a bright blue sky and gentle breeze followed. That would be the weather pattern for days afterward.

The wagons crossed a swift-moving, clear-water creek. A number of beaver dams littered winding water. Zeke looked from one side to the other. "Ya got any fishin' gear?" he asked Jeremy.

"Sure do."

"Well, git it out an' tell yer pa that me 'n you's goin' fishin'. We'll catch up with 'em in a short while."

"You see some fish in there?" asked Jeremy, swinging his head from side to side. He didn't see anything.

"Sure did, now git before we lose this chance."

Soon, Jeremy and Zeke were walking up the stream on its jagged downstream course toward the Platte. "This here's a spring fed crik an' it's gotta have some good eatin' fish in it."

In about one and a half hours, Zeke and Jeremy were trotting back toward the wagon train, both with large triumphant grins. That night the Weston Train feasted on three large spotted trout, one two-pound dace, and two three-pound suckers. What a relief, they didn't have to resort to boiled beans and hard biscuits that night. In the Weston Train, Jeremy wasn't the only one that thought Zeke was a wonder.

For the next five days, the Jacobson Company persisted westward, despite the constantly changing weather and terrain. The pioneers preceding them left an easy-to-follow trail across the dry barren pebble-strewn soil. Slowly, the landscape took on a subtle change, becoming hilly and timbered as they approached the eastern slope of the Rocky Mountains. Plants that were familiar from back east, such as dandelion, pigweed, and peppergrass, mixed in with southernwood and cacti covered with prickly pears. Jeremy loved the slightly tart taste of the prickly pears, although he found it irritating to have to remove the needles—even more irritating if he didn't remove them all. Trees were becoming more numerous along the banks of the Platte. The outline of the Black Hills west of Fort Laramie gradually appeared on the horizon. Finally, the Company reached the banks of the North Platte opposite the fort itself. Here, on June 16, they made camp. They were now 543 miles from Winter Quarters and 809 miles from Nauvoo.

CHAPTER 26

"What's this place all about, Zeke?" asked James as he, Zeke, and two other men waited for a Fort Laramie flat boat to take the supply wagon across the Platte. Captain Jacobson had asked James and two other men to cross the river with a wagon, acquire some needed supplies, and scout out the situation at the fort. Jacobson knew that this is where previous trains, including the Advance Company, crossed because traveling north of the Platte was no longer feasible. Zeke invited himself along. This was familiar territory for him and, just maybe, was as far as he was going to go with these Mormons.

"Well, when I first come here back in '35, it were called Fort William after a fella named William Sublette who set it up. Weren't exactly no fort 'cause there weren't no walls or army or nothin'. Then in '41, American Fur Company man, name a John Sarpy, took it over. He called it Fort John, an' put up a bunch a adobe buildings, most a what ya see over there now."

"How come they now call the Fort Laramie?"

"Don' rightly know, 'cept them there's the Laramie Range, even though most everbody calls 'em the Black Hills." Zeke pointed toward the rising plateaus to the west. Actually, the mountains and the fort took their names from a French Canadian named Jacques La Ramée who traveled that area and had the misfortune of getting himself killed by the Indians.

Fort Laramie was just that, a collection of adobe buildings sitting on top of a bare, gravely, low-lying mesa, between and overlooking the confluence of the Laramie and North Platte Rivers, some two miles away to the east. Over the years, it had become an important way station and trading post for westward pioneers traveling north and south of the Platte. As the years passed, it would become even more important for the immigrants, especially during the gold rush days.

As the boat, with the Saints' wagon aboard, made its way across the river, James continued to question Zeke. "Who's in charge here now?"

"Fella by the name a Jim Bordeaux runs the place fer the Fur Company."

"We likely to find any trouble here, you know, Mormon-hater types from Missouri?"

"Well, all kinds come through here. Most are decent God-fearin' types, but there's always a fair share a scallywags an' mean critters hangin' around ta see what they can get fer nothin'. Gamblin', drinkin', brawlin', an' stealin' is what they do best. But there shouldn't be no trouble. Bordeaux takes kindly ta Mormons an' besides, gun fightin' an' brawlin' ain't exactly good fer business, ya know. Jus' keep yer money hid an' yer rifle close by anyway." James noted Zeke had both pistols strapped on underneath his long buckskin coat.

As they landed and unloaded the wagon from the ferry, Zeke nodded in the direction of the main building. "While ya'll are tradin' an' buyin', I'm gonna see if thar's anybody needs shepherdin' outta here ta anywhere west."

"Sure, no problem. We'll let you know when we're ready to take off, in case you want to come back," said James.

"Oh, I'm coming' back. Ya don' think I'd let ya have my horse an' saddle fer nothin'," do ya?" Zeke yelled back over his shoulder. "Besides, I gotta say goodbye ta Jeremy an' Amanda." He disappeared inside the building.

James shook his head. What a man, he thought.

After about an hour, James and the other two Saints busily loaded their wagon with the provisions they had bartered and purchased. They paid scant attention to the group of scruffy men, six in all, who stood on the side, leaning against hitching posts and sitting atop barrels. Two whittled on nondescript pieces of wood; one tilted his head toward the sun, with his eyes closed, soaking in the rays. The other three stood around studying the Mormons with a menacing glare. Two of the men were smoking roll-your-owns; the rest were chewing tobacco, periodically spitting to one side or the other.

"Hey," said the biggest, meanest-looking of the bunch. "Hey," he repeated. "Ya'll Mormons?"

James turned, faced the man, and replied, "Are you talking to us?"

"Hell, yeah, who'd ya think I'm talking ta, yer horse?" The other men snickered. "Well, are ya Mormons or not?"

"Well, since you put it that way, yes," answered James, straightening up to his full height.

"Ah, I really didn't have ta ask. We knowed ya was Mormon bastards from the start. Now, tell ya what yer gonna do, unless ya want all them wives of yer'n cryin' out their eyes, yer gonna get back on that there ferry an' paddle yer way back 'crost that river."

James responded, "We're all finished here anyway. We don't want any trouble, mister, so, just as you say, we'll head back now." He motioned for the other two to climb into the wagon as he grabbed the reins of the horses.

"Whoa, whoa," yelled the fierce man. "I said *ya'll* git. Didn't say nothin' about that there wagon an' them horses leavin'."

"I don't think so," said James. He dropped the reins and moved toward the wagon for his rifle.

All the men stood at once and stared at James. Hands were on hips, guns in their holsters, but at the ready. "Stop whar ya are. Yer a little slow in the head. Do ya think ya can take all us?"

"He don' have ta, Amos. I see yer up ta yer same old stupid tricks."

"Well, as I live an' breathe, Ezekiel. I thought ya was dead 'long way back."

Unnoticed by all, Zeke had walked up behind the wagon and stepped out to confront the men. He had pulled his coat back, revealing both guns still in their holsters.

"So, tell me Ezekiel," challenged the man called Amos, "Since when did ya become a Mormon lover?"

"Ya two in the wagon, git down an' go over yonder." Zeke pointed away from the area. "Ya too, James."

"Zeke, it's not worth it," pleaded James.

"*Now*, James!" he commanded. James and the men did as told. Zeke never took his eyes off the hooligans in front of him. "It's like this, Amos, I ain't so much a Mormon lover as I am a man who cain't stan' Mormon haters."

"Ya goin' ta stan' there an' tell me yer willin' ta get kilt over them three?" Amos nodded in the direction of the three Saints.

"Yep."

"Look, Ezekiel, we got six guns, uh ... no, seven," he patted the second weapon at his side as he grinned broadly. "Ya willin' ta go ag'in seven guns?"

"Yep"

"Ya always was a cocky son-of-a-bitch, but I didn't think ya was stupid."

Spectators later said they couldn't tell who drew first, but by the time the thunderous noise abated, the horses settled down, and the smoke cleared, Amos and one of his cohorts lay dead; two others stood, holding their wounds. The remaining two checked their bodies, amazed that no bullets found them. Zeke crumpled to the ground with four bullets imbedded in him.

James was horrified. He ran to Zeke's side, turned him over, and started to cry. "Zeke, Zeke, what have you done?"

Bordeaux came running out from the administration building, as the crowd started to gather. "What the hell is goin' on here," he demanded. In the confusion, the four remaining Amos men quietly slipped into their saddles and rode away before anyone noticed. The crowd talked all at once to Bordeaux, giving him an account of what went on—some were partially accurate and some just made up.

Kneeling beside Zeke, James put his ear down to the dying man's face. With foamy blood oozing from his mouth, Zeke whispered, "Damn ... bad endin'." He coughed. "James, ... tell Jeremy he can have my horse, an' saddle, an' pistols." Zeke coughed again. "I really love that boy, ya know?"

"I know, Zeke," James said as tears dropped and intermingled with Zeke's blood.

Zeke emitted more blood from his mouth and weakly continued, "Ya keep my rifles, awright?" James nodded. "An', Brother James ..."

"Yes, Zeke." James put his ear closer to hear Zeke's weakening voice.

"Bury me the hell on the other side of this damn river." That was the last statement Ezekiel uttered.

Numb with shock and grief, James struggled to pick up Zeke's body and put it in the wagon. The other Saints rushed to his side to help.

"I'm truly sorry this happened," said Bordeaux compassionately. "I take it Ezekiel was a friend of yours?"

"That he was," answered James with his bottom lip quivering.

"Well, I've known Ezekiel for a good number of years. He was a little rough on the outside, but he was a fine man inside. A lot better then than that sorry bunch," Bordeaux said, looking in disgust at the bodies of Amos and his cohort.

"Yes, he was the best."

"This sort of thing doesn't happen here very often. You make sure you tell your people that Fort Laramie is safe for Mormons. I met your leader, Brigham Young, when he passed through back a spell. We got along just fine because we both hate that old Missouri governor, Boggs. Yes, sir, your kind of folk can come here any time and Jim Bordeaux guarantees their safety. You tell 'em that, will you?"

Like you took care of Zeke? James thought, but he said, "Yes sir, I will, Mr. Bordeaux." James gave a snap of the reins and headed back toward the flat boat. Zeke's death hung over James like a black cloud, compounded by the realization of what this would do to his son. How am I ever going to explain this to Jeremy? How could he explain something that he didn't quite understand himself? Zeke had worked his way into the hearts of many in the Company, especially in the Weston Train.

The flat boat slowly made its way across the river. A subdued murmuring crowd of Mormons stood waiting anxiously on the shore. It was some distance across, but they had heard the shots and seen the commotion on the other side. It was obvious that the returning men on the ferry were somber—they were not talking and their heads hung low.

"There's only three of 'em. Somebody ain't comin' back," said a man who stood taller than the rest. No one could see the body lying on the deck.

Jeremy's instincts made him think the worst. He saw that Zeke's floppy hat was not atop any of the men standing by the wagon. Surely, he wouldn't have stayed on the other side without his horse, he thought.

"Oh, my God, somebody's been shot. There's a body on the deck," cried a woman as the boat got closer. When the boat docked, it became obvious it was Zeke's body. The crowd rushed forward, clamoring for information, amid increasing expressions of grief. James and the other men picked up Zeke's body and carried it ashore. They laid it gently on the ground. Everyone was now rushing toward the small group. Women were wailing; children were screaming.

"For God's sake, Brother James, what happened?" asked Jacobson, pushing his way through the crowd.

As the throng hushed, James told how Zeke had given his life defending them from the vile crooks at the fort. All the while he was telling what happened, he kept looking around to find Jeremy. Within earshot of the crowd, Jeremy stood apart, around the side of a wagon. He was in absolute shock, so much so that he was near fainting. His head was pounding, his stomach was in knots, and his heart had a terrible ache. Jeremy had never experienced anything like this before in his young life. He was so dizzy that he grabbed the wagon wheel and slowly slid to the ground in a limp sitting position. He began to sob uncontrollably. Amanda, who had been frantically searching for Jeremy, finally spotted him slumped near the wagon. She ran to his side, sat down beside him, and cradled him in her arms. Neither said a word as she tried to console her devastated son by burying his head in her bosom and hugging him tightly, rocking gently back and forth.

The next day, everyone in the Jacobson Company turned out for Ezekiel's burial. All the women and children were crying—some softly, others openly. The men stood around with their hats held in their hands, heads down, somber faced. The realization of Zeke's death was beginning to dawn on Jeremy as he stood next to the body. He was not crying; there were no tears left. Besides, he reasoned, Zeke would be embarrassed if I stood here like a slobbering baby.

"Lord," intoned Jacobson, "Brother Ezekiel was not of our faith, but he embodied the very essence of what we believe. He was kind, generous, and helpful. He gave his very life to protect our brethren. We ask that You receive him with open arms in heaven for surely there has never been anyone who deserves it more. Amen." There was a chorus of "Amens" among the many sobs. Normally, Brother Jacobson would have gone on at great length, but he detected that no one was in the mood for that. For some reason, this strange, crude man had won a unique place in everyone's heart. Zeke was a man of few words and it seemed only appropriate his burial ceremony should be the same.

The men of the Weston Train, Jeremy, James, Roy Thomas, Anthony Adams, and Jeremiah and Geoff Johnson, lowered Zeke's body into the freshly dug grave. Once at the bottom, they pulled the ropes free. Jeremy stood looking down at his friend's body. Sensing his master's grief, Jake whined softly and nudged Jeremy's leg. Jeremy slipped the necklace with the buffalo's tooth given to him by Matoskah from his neck and tossed it down into the grave. "Goodbye, Zeke," he said. Then he turned and walked away. The sound of shoveled dirt followed him.

For three days, the Jacobson Company ferried their wagons, livestock, and other possessions across the Platte in the chartered flatboat belonging to Fort Laramie. It was a long and tedious process, with much wasted time for those waiting on both the north and the south sides of the river. As promised, the Mormons were welcome at the fort. Bordeaux went out of his way to accommodate the Company. He claimed that they and all the other Saints that came through on their way west were orderly, polite, and clean. That was not true of many of the pioneers that visited the fort. The transition finished on June 19 and Jacobson used the next day, the Sabbath, as a day to assemble and reorganize for the long journey ahead. It was a welcome and enjoyable day, apart from swarms of grasshoppers that streamed across the camp.

The next day, now south of the Platte River, the Saints began to see another change in the landscape. Chokeberry bushes and cottonwood trees followed the river while cedar and pine trees appeared on rugged cliffs. There were steep, sandy inclines that made ascent extremely difficult and that required wheel locking and rope restraints necessary. Despite these encumbrances, the Company made twelve miles that day. They were very experienced travelers at this point.

Since crossing over to Fort Laramie, a number of wagon trains from Missouri began to appear on the trail. The Saints were obviously wary of these westward-bound pioneers, even though the Missouri trains were usually much smaller in number of wagons. As the Jacobson Company settled in for the first day, a train of Missouri pioneers pulled in behind and made camp. At this time, the Weston Train was bringing up the rear and so, when all had settled down, they were within a short walking distance of the Missouri train.

From the sounds emanating from the rear, it was obvious this was a rowdy bunch. As dusk settled in, four men from the Missouri train came forward. From their stagger, laughter, and loud talk, it was obvious they were drunk. James stood at the back of Margaret and Josephine's wagon, guns at the ready. Roy Thomas, Jeremiah Johnson, and Jeremy lingered at the side of the wagon with their weapons. Jake stood beside Jeremy, emanating an occasional low growl. James's experience at Fort Laramie was obviously fresh and his trust level was at zero.

"Good evening, gentlemen," James said as the men came within a dozen feet. "What can we do for you?" The men stopped with some difficulty, staggering and bumping into one another.

"Oh," slurred one scruffy looking fellow, "we jus' come ta shay howdy ta our fella travelers."

"Yeah," muddled another as he laughed and nearly fell over, "we jesh wanna shay howdy." All the others laughed raucously. One took a swig from a bottle, spilling some on his filthy shirt.

"Maybe you should call it a night and head back to your wagons," James said, nodding his head to the rear, "we don't cotton to any partying here."

"Now that ain't very friendly," said the man with the bottle. "You

Mormons suppose ta be friendly an' nice." He smiled a crooked, malevolent smile, "Maybe yer still pissed we kicked yer butts at Haun's Mill, uh?" The other men laughed raucously.

Before James could react, Roy Thomas stumbled forward and placed his shotgun barrel on the drunken man's forehead. The man was wide-eyed and dropped the bottle to the ground. "Ya think that's funny, ya Mormon-baitin' bastard? I should blow yer head off!" Everyone froze. The air was electric.

"Roy, Roy, he's drunk," shouted James. "Put the gun down. He's not responsible."

"Responsible, my bad knee. He best git his sorry ass back ta whar he come from or I'll blow 'im back." Roy was red-faced and tense—ready to explode.

"He don' mean nothin', he's jus' had too much whiskey," another Missourian said. "Come on, Joseph, git back here." He tugged at the thoroughly frightened man.

James stepped forward, put his hand on the barrel, and slowly lowered the end of Roy's shotgun from the man's forehead. "Let it go, Roy," he said gently.

Roy scowled at the man. One last momentary stare and he turned away and hobbled back to his wagon, swearing beneath his breath. The Missouri men turned and walked away. The confrontation had made them much more sober than when they came. One man turned back and held up his hand. "Sorry," he said to James. James's shoulders slumped, his nerves frazzled. One more crisis over, he thought. He wasn't sure how many more he had left in him.

Chapter 27

The Saints would meet many more pioneers from Missouri along the trail. Practically all these Oregon-bound travelers behaved poorly compared to the Mormons, but they also just wished to arrive at their destination in one piece as quickly as possible. Some were unfriendly but not hostile; the majority was affable and cooperated with their fellow travelers, no matter their religious beliefs. The temperament of the other pioneers they ran into along the trail was the least of the Mormons' problems; terrain, weather, equipment failure, and sickness would beleaguer them the rest of the way.

After Zeke's death, Jeremy became depressed. He did not want to be on this damnable trip to begin with and he lost nearly everything important to him along the way. Everyone from his friend Jake, back in Double Springs, Joseph Smith, Jr., in Nauvoo, Clara in Winter Quarters, Chaska, and now Zeke, had entered his life, brought joy, however briefly, to his world, and then, for one reason or another, departed, leaving him with a great sense of loss. He would be fourteen-years-old next month and though he had physically grown strong and had the experience of someone twice his age, he was emotionally still a boy. He did not yet understand that such incidents were the stuff of a normal life, especially on the frontier. He had always handled setbacks by becoming more withdrawn and taciturn and Zeke's death pushed him farther in that direction. He was near despair.

Amanda saw this happening and was beside herself with recrimination. Margaret Waters watched as well. One evening, as everyone was huddled around the campfire singing hymns, Margaret spied Jeremy sitting on a knoll by himself, away from the camp. He was staring off into the darkened distance. Quietly, Margaret ambled over to Jeremy and stood by his side.

"Mind if I join ya, Jeremy lad?" she asked.

Jeremy was somewhat startled, not having heard her approach. "No, not at all, Sister Margaret." He stood and pointed at a place for her on the mound.

Margaret sat with considerable effort and breathed a long sigh as she looked off in the distance. Jeremy resumed his seat.

"Sometimes I jus' git tar'd a all them people. Same thing ever night. Makes ya wanna scream, don' it?"

"Yeah," replied Jeremy. "I thought I was the only one that felt that way."

"Nonsense, boy. Ya'd have ta be crazy not ta git fed up with this trip."

"Well, this trip *is* driving me crazy."

Margaret looked over at Jeremy. "Yeah, well I been a noticin' that ya seem down in the mouth lately. What's eatin' at ya?"

"Everything," he answered curtly.

"*Everythin'*—my word, that's a heap a hurt. I'm bettin' that Zeke's dyin' brought most a this on, huh?"

"It didn't help none," Jeremy said, his eyes slightly watering.

"I gotta admit, that was a terrible thing. Made everbody hurt, but especially ya, bein' as close as ya was."

"Yeah."

"Yep, yer hurtin' a lot, but did ya ever think yer hurting is causin' somebody else a lot a pain?" asked Margaret.

Jeremy looked up at Margaret. "Like who?"

"Like yer ma, that's who. An' that poor woman, bein' sick an' all, ain't got enough strength ta git through the day, let alone be worryin' about yer problems."

Jeremy looked down at his lap, thinking.

Margaret continued, "Yer gonna be what, fourteen soon, rat?"

Jeremy nodded his head.

"Well, that's near a grown man. Maybe ya should put yer hurts in yer pocket fer a while an' tend ta yer ma. She's got hurts ya never heard of an' she needs yer he'p. What ya think?"

Jeremy paused for a moment and then looked Margaret in the eyes. "You're probably right, Sister Margaret. I'm not the only one with hurts."

"Now that's talkin' like a real man," Margaret beamed, placing her arm around Jeremy's shoulder and giving him a squeeze.

"Thanks, Sister Margaret," Jeremy said with a genuine smile.

"No thanks needed," Margaret replied as she struggled to stand. Jeremy jumped up and assisted her. They both strolled back to the campfire. Jake spotted his master and trotted out to meet him. Jeremy stroked his dog's nose tenderly.

Jeremy walked over behind Amanda who was sitting on a stool. From behind, he bent over and kissed her on the cheek.

"My word, what's that for?" said a surprised Amanda.

"For nothing," replied Jeremy with a broad smile as he patted her shoulder. He looked across the fire at Margaret who had seen his gesture of affection. She smiled and nodded her approval. That boy'll be awright, she thought.

"Ya mean we have ta cross back over that blasted river ag'in?" Roy Thomas said, shaking his head in disgust.

"Looks like," James responded.

"Why in tarnation did we cross it ta begin with?"

"Don't know, but I'm sure Brother Young had his reasons. Besides," continued James, "he left us a beautiful ferry boat to cross with ease." James was referring to a substantial boat the Advance Company had constructed and left behind. Three men stayed behind to run the ferry that aided all the Mormon trains following. It was also a great source of income for the Saints as they charged other non-Mormon pioneers for its use. The ferryboat was made of two twenty-three-foot-long, six-inch diameter, cotton wood log canoes, joined by five-foot-long crosstimbers. Short upright wooden posts attached to each corner and a rudder affixed to the rear completed the structure. This crude but effective ferry could readily float a loaded wagon across the rapidly flowing, 100-yard-wide river.

The river they were talking about was their old friend, the North Platte. At this point, the river curved southwest towards its source, forcing all travelers to cross over to the west bank. In addition, at this point the late spring runoff and snowmelt still glutted the river with fast-moving water, making the crossing difficult and dangerous. It took the Jacobson Company three days to ferry everyone across. All were safely across by July 2, Jeremy's fourteenth birthday. Margaret and Josephine gave him a sweater both had been knitting since leaving Winter Quarters. Amanda and James presented him a bowie knife that James had acquired while trading at Ft. Laramie. At fourteen, Jeremy now owned Zeke's horse, saddle, and two pistols, a rifle, an authentic Indian bow with arrows, a newly acquired bowie knife, and a loyal affectionate "hero dog." By any standards measured on the trail or back in Nauvoo, Jeremy was a wealthy young man

The countryside before crossing the North Platte had been some of the best the Jacobson Company had encountered. Vast pine tree forests covered the highest hills. Some of the inclines were steep and difficult to climb and descend, but water and grass were plentiful and the livestock significantly benefited. Black-tailed deer and antelope were abundant. Occasionally, their old friend the buffalo provided them meat that their systems now tolerated with ease. Black bears and the scary grizzlies were common, as were Horney Toads and the bothersome and dangerous rattlesnakes. Wild onions and edible mushrooms were plentiful. It was definitely one of the more pleasant stretches of their long journey.

However, a few days past the river, everything changed. The land was barren, sandy, and destitute of grass. There was little wood, as trees were scarce and only sage and thorny little shrubs grew. The greatest disadvantage though was the lack of potable water. Many of the streams in the area were so foul the oxen would not drink due to the salty taste and rotten smell. To make matters worse, bogs mired the livestock as they came forward to drink from whatever potable streams they found. Mosquitoes swarmed day and night, making life miserable for humans and beasts alike.

The mosquitoes took their toll on Amanda. Often, during an ague attack, she barely had the strength to shoo them away or enough feeling to know they were even biting. James, Margaret, and Jeremy constantly checked to make sure she was under the mosquito netting. She often thrashed about during the fever stage, exposing herself to the merciless pests. Most of the time, despite her debilitating weakness, Amanda was still able to do her chores, say her prayers, and tend to her children.

Since the talk with Margaret, Jeremy was particularly attentive to his mother. For some reason, the seriousness of her illness had not registered before. He was too concerned with his own feelings. He could easily see that she was battling many problems once he took notice and he felt ashamed that he had been so insensitive not to see them previously. This was a particularly adult perspective for a teenager.

On this day, the travel had been a particularly difficult. Just before the nooner, a nasty, fast-moving rainstorm with frightening flashes of lightning and deafening claps of thunder ripped across the wagon train. There was no way to prepare for such an event—you just hunkered down and made the best of it. Progress was torturous under these conditions and with no orders from the front, the train lost inertia and came to a standstill on it own.

Amanda fully recovered from one of her ague bouts that night so she felt better than usual. Her spirits were high. The storm registered less of an irritant to her than were the mosquitoes forced under the tent or into the wagon by the tumult outside. She spied Jeremy running for cover.

"Hey, Jeremy, come in and sit by your old mom." Amanda made room on the wood trunk just inside the canvas covering the back of the wagon.

"Gladly," Jeremy answered as he poured the water from his hat brim and climbed into the opening. He sat next to his mother and looked at her face as water streamed down his nose. "Howdy," he said with a big smile and a crinkle of his nose.

"Howdy," she replied with a happy glow on her face. She gave her son's broad shoulders a tight, affectionate hug with her left arm.

"This here storms a pain in the butt," he said with disgust.

"It is indeed, but I kind of like it. It gives me a chance to be with my boy, whose growin' bigger, stronger, and *away* from his mama. You've got too many chores and important things to do now and I miss our old fat chewin' times together."

"Yeah, I know, so do I."

They both sat quietly and mulled over the circumstance.

"Ma, do you think we're ever going to get to wherever the heck it is we're going?" said a pensive Jeremy.

"That's a mighty good question, Jeremy, a mighty good question. Sometimes it seems like we're going nowhere, doesn't it?"

"That's for darn sure."

"But you've had some pretty unusual adventures and met some interesting people along the way, haven't you?" She tried to put a positive spin on what both considered a disaster.

"Yeah, but a lot of hurt as well."

"I know, I know. You truly miss Zeke, don't you?" She knew the recent hurt was what he was lamenting most.

"More than you'll ever know," Jeremy sighed.

"Well, I miss that character too, terribly. But I look at it this way, son; I feel blessed that I got to know him at all, even if it was a short while. He gave me a different outlook on life. And, Jeremy, maybe you don't see it, but you're a better man for having known him."

"I suppose you're right, but that doesn't make up for losing him."

Amanda nodded her assent and then took Jeremy's face between her hands and looked deep in his eyes. "I hope you know how much I love you," she said softly. "You're the light of my life."

"I know, Ma, and you are mine," Jeremy replied tenderly as he held her hands in his and kissed her on the forehead. The two sat silently, side-by-side holding hands, gazing out at the swirling rain for almost a half an hour, until the storm subsided.

Amanda treasured this moment. Although they had always been close, they had never expressed their feelings quite so openly. It seemed different, more heartfelt, now that he was older.

The Advance Company and some of the Missouri trains, in the

course of their move forward, had removed many large rocks and cobblestones from the trail. However, there were stretches that were still rugged and steep. This was hard on the wagons. Inevitably, an axel broke on one of the Thomas's wagons. James sent Jeremy forward to tell Brother Jacobson of the predicament. Soon, Jeremy returned, shaking his head.

"Brother Jacobson says they can't stop here. There's water and grass seven miles ahead and they're going on. He said Brother Thomas will just have to fix his wagon and catch up."

James nodded his head in understanding. Wasn't Roy's fault, he thought, but why does it always have to be him. He couldn't hide his agitation. They had spare axletrees but replacing a broken one was a major chore and old Roy was in no shape to help. By now, all the Weston Train wagons stopped and everyone gathered around looking down at the broken axle.

"Brother Anthony, Brother Jeremiah, and Brother Geoff," James said, pointing to each as he spoke, "you all stay behind and help me change out this axle. Brother Roy, have you got a spare?"

"Yeah, it's in the bottom a the wagon somewhar."

"All right, we'll find it. You take all the other wagons and follow the Company. Jeremy, you go along and help Brother Roy. We'll change it out and catch up later," James instructed.

"Thank ya Brother James. I sure appreciate it," Roy said as he began to hobble forward to James's wagon in the front. "I'll make sure we git camp set up."

It was well after dark before James and the other men pulled into the campsite. They were tired and hungry. No one complained; it was just another day on the trail.

The Jacobson Company trudged through a land of small salt-water lakes, sandy trails, little wood for fires, and scarce grass for feed. On July 5, they reached the pure Sweetwater River. Here, there was still no wood, but grass was plentiful along the banks. A short distance to the north of the west bank of the river, a prominent domed-shaped rock captured everyone's attention. Dubbed Independence Rock back in 1830, this attraction exhibited the painted or scratched-on names of the many trappers, emigrants, and other travelers that had camped nearby. Jeremy added his name to the collection.

The next day the train passed through Devil's Gate. For thousands of years, the Sweetwater carved this 100-foot-wide gap with perpendicular cliffs on both side. It was an impressive chasm, indeed. After that, another day of bleak and barren terrain faced the travelers as they crossed three creeks and ran into steep river embankments. Thus it was, the Saints continued to travel westward across land devoid of buffalo, but with plenty of antelope and, of course, the miserable mosquitoes.

The trail now showed the effects of heavy traffic. It was no longer a case of following the just the tracks of the Advance Company. Many wagon trains from Missouri and other eastern locations occupied the landscape—all fighting for water, grass, and wood as they trudged toward their western goal. Often, the fellow travelers aided one another with trading, medical assistance, and equipment repair, but the Saints usually had to eat trail dust, scrounge for feed and fuel, and from nearby trains, listen to mountains of profanity and witness unruly behavior; much detested by the Mormons.

One particularly beautiful evening after a long hard journey, the Saints made camp by an ample, clear-running stream; banks abundant with rich green grass for the tired oxen and plenty of wood for fires. They were happy because it was Saturday. That meant they would be spending the Sabbath at this pleasant location. The cloudless sky and moderate temperatures on the backside of the divide bode well for the next day. Their joy was somewhat tempered as a Gentile train of about forty wagons slowly assembled downstream of their encampment. There was a collective groan amongst the Mormons.

"Don't seem as ornery as most," remarked Brother Jacobson. He and James stood surveying the newcomers as they made camp. "They have a moderate look about 'em."

"That's true," replied James. "I make them to be Quakers. Think we should go over and say hello?"

"No need," Jacobson said pointing to the three men headed their way. "Looks like they're sending a delegation over."

"Hello to thee, friends," said one of the approaching men stiffly "We hope our camping downstream does not bother thee." The man was large, well built, conservatively dressed, and, under his wide-brimmed hat, exhibited a full shock of white hair that matched a perfectly trimmed beard ringing his weathered face. He had no moustache. "My name be Williamson, Joseph Williamson," he said proffering his hand. This was a face of character, thought James.

"And I am Brother Jacobson. You're more than welcome," replied Jacobson, returning the handshake warmly. By the dress and language, these men were indeed Quakers, he thought.

"I guess thou art of the Mormon religion, true?"

"That is correct and I assume that you are Quakers."

"We are, indeed, the Religious Society of Friends. We're headed for the land called Oregon to establish a colony where we can farm, raise our families, and live in peace."

"And we are in search of the same near the Great Salt Lake in Utah," replied Jacobson. "You are more than welcome to camp where you are. Perhaps, after we all settle in, we could let our people socialize. Though we travel in groups, it's lonely on the trail, as you know."

"Indeed it is, friend. It is not our practice to mingle, but I know ye Mormons to be God-fearing and well-behaved and our people do have need of such intercourse," answered the Quaker. The man then nodded stiffly, turned, and walked away. His compatriots followed.

"Strange people but maybe we'll get some peace and quiet after all," James said to Jacobson as the men departed.

"Remember, we are strange to many, Brother James," admonished Jacobson.

"Thou art correct, Brother Jacobson," said James, with a bit of humor. "One must remember that when we look and laugh at monkeys, they are looking back."

CHAPTER 28

That evening, the Quakers and the Mormons intermingled in both campsites. The Friends were stiff and formal and felt uneasy with the openly gregarious Saints. Carefully, tactfully, each side probed the other for beliefs and experiences. The Mormons knew little of the Quakers, so they had a great curiosity about these extraordinary people. Both sides asked many questions and, in the spirit of seeking knowledge, countered none. The Friends, with their belief in religious tolerance for all, were mentally more open to understanding than were the highly indoctrinated Mormons. However, their collective reticence with outsiders made it harder for them to communicate.

The children from both camps eagerly played together, less encumbered by thoughts of social constraints or religious tenets. Even here, the Quaker children were always conscious of their watchful parents' eyes and glares for behavior deemed inappropriate. The teenagers warily eyed one another but gradually found subjects of mutual interest they could discuss. Jeremy, in the Quaker camp, was avidly interested in these different people. At first, he stood back and observed, feeling a slight bit above the idle chatter. However, all that changed when he saw Margaret.

Margaret was the name of a beautiful flaxen-haired girl of fourteen who sat aside one of the campfires. The light from the fire highlighted her small, alluring face framed in a dark gray bonnet. She had engaging blue eyes separated by a slightly upturned nose, suggesting aloofness. Ample dimples accentuated lips that were almost too sensual for a girl her age. She had a diminutive frame that sat proudly, her hands folded loosely in her lap, and her legs crossed at the ankles. To Jeremy, she looked like royalty. The overall effect caused him to be weak in the knees, dry in the mouth, and generally disoriented. He stared unabashedly at Margaret Hammond until she became aware of his attention and looked directly into his eyes. When she gave him a nod and a slight smile, his usual self-confidence disappeared. He was, in a word, smitten.

Somehow, Jeremy managed the courage to thread through the crowd and approach Margaret, trying to look as casual as possible.

"Hello," he said, his voice fluctuating somewhat due to his age and influenced by his nervousness. He bowed slightly and smiled.

"Hello to thee," replied Margaret. She was coy and flirtatious; something her parents would not have approved.

"Uh, do you mind if I sit down?" he asked, pointing to a vacant spot on her bench.

"Please," she replied, her open hand indicating the same spot on her right. She moved just enough to make room.

Jeremy sat next to her, not knowing how to orient his body or what to do with his hands. He folded them in his lap. Then he unfolded them and reached across his body, offering his right hand. "My name is Jeremy, Jeremy Weston."

"Nice to meet thee Jeremy, Jeremy Weston," she teased. "I'm Margaret Hammond." She placed her hand in his. They shook much longer than needed. Jeremy couldn't believe the effect this had on him. He had never felt like this before. He sat there dazed, looking into her face.

After a second or two of uncomfortable silence, she withdrew her hand and said, "And what brings thee way out here in the wilderness, Jeremy Weston?"

"A ... I don't know. I'm here because I don't have a choice. My parents made me come. What about you?"

"I hadn't thought of it that way," she answered pensively, "but I guess that's why I'm here as well."

"If you had a choice, would you take off and go somewhere else?"

"Why, heavens, I wouldst have no place to go if I wanted to."

"Well," said Jeremy becoming braver and confident now that the ice was broken. "I would go away in a second. I have a little money saved up and I own a horse, a saddle, two pistols, a rifle, and a bowie knife," he said proudly. "And, oh, I have my dog and best friend Jake, too. He'd go with me."

Margaret's eyes were wide, her mouth slightly open as she listened intently. "Thou art serious? Thou wouldst leave thy family? Where wouldest thee go?"

"I wouldst go to Tennessee." He mocked her language. "Why do you talk using thou and thee and thy? I've never heard that before."

"I don't know," she retorted, pouting somewhat, "that is the way of my people. We have many things that are not of others. I have never known any different."

Jeremy put up his right hand in front of him, "Oh, I didn't mean to make fun of you. I like it. It's ... a ... very ... unusual. But I like it," he added quickly. "Truly."

"Not a problem," she said soothingly, "but why wouldest thou leave?" His moment of braggadocio caught her attention.

"I guess because I don't believe in everything the Mormons think and do," he said boldly.

Margaret was surprised. "Why? Aren't thou a Mormon. Aren't thou a Christian?"

"Oh, I guess I am." He detected the alarm in her voice and face. "It's just that there are so many rules and things that don't make sense to me," he tried to explain.

"But thou art only a boy of what thirteen, fourteen, fifteen?" she probed.

"Fourteen," he said defensively, "so what? Does that mean I can't think for myself?"

She smiled with a slight tilt of her head. "I am fourteen also." Then seriously, "But I wouldst never presume to go against the faith of my family and friends, even if I were to leave."

"That's probably because you're a girl. Boys look at things differently." Jeremy slightly puffed his chest to emphasize the point.

"That's not true," Margaret said defensively, again showing a slight pout.

Jeremy and Margaret suddenly became aware that the community gathering was ending. Margaret heard the voice of her mother calling her name.

She rose and offered her hand again. "It was nice meeting thee Jeremy Weston. I must go now."

Jeremy stumbled awkwardly to his feet and grasped her hand. "We'll be here at this place tomorrow. Can we meet again?" he asked hopefully.

"Yes, why not. That is, if thou don't run away during the night," she teased.

"I promise," he smiled, raising his right hand.

Margaret turned and walked away. Just before disappearing behind a wagon, she turned, smiled, and nodded in his direction. Jeremy stood there mesmerized. Their meeting and handshakes occupied his thoughts long after everyone was asleep. Only when the sun came up the next morning did he realize that he had finally drifted off to sleep.

The next morning, Jeremy gathered a bucket of water from the nearby stream and placed it near the wagon. Amanda was busy stoking the fire to prepare the morning meal.

"Good morning, Ma. How art thee?"

Amanda stood erect and looked at her son, her head tilted to one side. "I'm fine this morning, Jeremy," she lied as her bones ached from stem to stern. "And why art thou talking like the Quakers?"

"I don't know, I kind of like it, it's special."

"Oh, I see," she smiled.

They both resumed their chores. Amanda noted a particularly lightheartedness in Jeremy's voice and quickness in his actions. Both were unusual at this hour. "What makes you so chipper this morning?" she asked.

"Nothing in particular," he fibbed. There was a pause and then he said, "I met a girl last night."

"Did you now," Amanda said as he turned her head sideways toward Jeremy. "And what's so exceptional about *this* girl?"

"Oh I don't know. She's just kind of different. I really like her," he added.

"Well, all the Quakers are different, son," she teased as she laughed to herself. This was the first time Amanda ever noticed Jeremy to have an interest in any girl.

"I didn't say I liked *all* Quakers. I just like this one."

"Is she pretty?"

"No, she's beautiful." Jeremy reddened at his comment.

"I see," said Amanda, shaking her head knowingly. "Are you going to see her again?"

"I hope so."

"Just remember, son, these people are very different from us and we'll be parting soon. Having a 'like' for someone who is so different can lead to some hurt," counseled Amanda.

"Oh, Mother, it's not like that," Jeremy flushed.

Amanda knew budding puppy love when she saw it, but had no real concern due to the circumstances. Time, however short, would prove Amanda mistaken.

The Sabbath is a busy day with all the minor chores to catch up on and attendance at Church services and business. It was the same for the Quakers. Though separated by the two camps, Jeremy and Margaret were able to surreptitiously wave or nod to each other at various times throughout the day. At one point, Margaret beckoned Jeremy to meet her at a tree located between the two camps. There, quickly, she asked him if he could join her family for dinner that evening. Amanda watched some of this activity, noting that Jeremy managed to position himself to be in full view. More importantly, she was able to see the girl that had captured so much of Jeremy's attention. What a beauty she is, thought Amanda. She saw instantly why Jeremy was so infatuated.

Amanda was not surprised when Jeremy came to her and asked if he could go to Margaret's wagon for dinner. He said that her parents had invited him.

"Of course, but you must take something. Here, they might like this." Smiling, she handed him a freshly baked loaf of bread wrapped in a clean cloth. "And make sure you're back before evening prayers."

"Thanks, Ma. You're the best." He gave Amanda a kiss on the cheek. She noticed he had gussied himself up with his face shining brightly and hair slicked down. He ran excitedly toward the Quaker camp.

"And mind your manners." She called after him.

"I will," he said, "promise."

After Jeremy reached the outskirts of the Quaker camp, he slowed down to a more decorous walk. He had no problem finding her wagon, having seen Margaret in and around it all through the day. Margaret spied him coming and came out to meet him. Many inquisitive eyes were on the two as they politely shook hands and then walked toward the Hammond wagon. As they approached, Mrs. Hammond looked up from stoking the fire, and Mr. Hammond peered over his glasses from the book he was reading. Two look-alike young girls sat off to the side. All were dressed in dark colors and in great modesty.

"Mother, Father, this is Jeremy Weston. Jeremy, this is my mother," Margaret said freely. Margaret knew her mother wouldn't have any problems meeting Jeremy as they had been discussing the meeting throughout the day. Her father was another story.

"Welcome, Jeremy," Mrs. Hammond said extending her hand. Jeremy hesitated and then quickly took Mrs. Hammonds hand.

"Thank you, ma'am. Oh, here's a gift," he stuttered. "It's fresh baked by my mom," he said proudly.

"Well thank thee, Jeremy, and thank thy mother. That is most kind." She opened the cloth, smiled, and shook her head appreciatively.

"And this in my father," Margaret nervously introduced her father.

Jeremy came up to Mr. Hammond and held out his hand, "My pleasure, sir," he said feigning boldness.

Mr. Hammond put down his book and rose, towering over Jeremy. He was a man of imposing stature, weighing over 200 pounds, and standing six-foot, three-inches tall. After briefly looking Jeremy over, he offered his hand. His bearing was intimidating but his manner was one of a gentle giant. "Thou art welcome in our camp, Jeremy." Both Jeremy and Margaret let out a sigh of relief. Mrs. Hammond laughed inwardly, amused at their reactions.

"Oh, and these are my sisters, Jane and Judith," Margaret said. The girls had been standing nearby evaluating Jeremy as any ten-year-olds would. They were twins and showed signs of being as beautiful as their older sister. "Hello, Jeremy," they sing-songed together, tittering, and coquettish. Their father glared at them and they stopped, casting their eyes downward.

"Hello, girls," replied Jeremy, reddening slightly.

Mrs. Hammond was an imposing woman in her own right, with a lean, large-boned frame that reached five-feet-eight in height. Like all of the Quaker women, she was clad in a simple gray bonnet, long gray dress, black shawl, and a drab green apron. She moved gracefully as she began dishing out the food in tin plates. She handed Jeremy a plate and said, "Sit thee here, next to Margaret, Jeremy." She winked at her daughter. The twins giggled, the father scowled, and they instantly sobered.

Once everyone settled down, a moment of silence prevailed over the meal. Quakers had no common grace, only their individual thoughts. Mr. Hammond spoke, "I understand from Margaret, thou art a wealthy lad." He raised his eyebrows and nodded his head, turning the statement into a question.

"I ... I ... wouldn't say wealthy," stammered Jeremy, embarrassed at the question.

"Well, I'd say a lad of fourteen with a horse, a saddle, a rifle, two pistols, and a bowie knife was pretty well off. Oh, yes, and a friendly dog, I hear."

"I was given most all but the dog by a very dear friend who died," Jeremy countered, flushing slightly.

"I am, indeed, sorry to hear of thy gain through someone's loss," said Mr. Hammond sincerely. "And where is thy friend, the dog?"

"Oh, Jake," Jeremy smiled broadly, "he's back at the wagon. You don't want that big mutt here. With all this good food, he would be slobbering and begging all over the place." Everyone laughed.

With the ice broken, the rest of the evening's conversation ranged from life on the trail to some of the differences in the beliefs and actions of the two groups encamped on the edge of the stream. Even though Jeremy found the family somewhat serious, there was much laughter as well. Jeremy and Margaret slipped fond glances at each other whenever they thought no one was looking—Mrs. Hammond caught them all.

The twins snuggled up near Jeremy from time to time; Margaret chased them away with a look of irritation. Mr. Hammond smoldered at the twins' actions. Jeremy and Margaret had no time together alone, but they felt satisfied with the closeness of their bodies and the acceptance of the group. Time went by quickly and soon the meal was over and the call for evening prayers intoned. Jeremy's feet seemed not to touch the ground as he rejoined his family for the evening prayers. The smitten lad hardly knew what he was saying, mouthing only words.

"Where ya been, Jeremy," teased Christine.

"Out," replied Jeremy. He winked at his mother and headed for bed. Again, Jeremy would be awake long after everyone else was asleep. Margaret's face and figure filled his thoughts. Once again, Jeremy was at peace with his world—he had found another friend.

CHAPTER 29

The next few days passed uneventfully as the Jacobson Company crisscrossed the winding Sweetwater River time after time, following the trail of the Advance Company and many other pioneers headed west. Soon they came to Sulphur Spring—a strange place with sulfurous and pure water, and turf that covered a solid body of crystal-clear ice. To the delight of the women, they found large quantities of pure potash on the edges of these springs. They gathered and saved as much as they could to raise bread dough. They also gathered up abundant quantities of high quality salt and saleratus, or baking soda. These items were always scarce on the journey and never available in the quality found here. The women soon found the saleratus of such high quality they had to use less or it turned their bread green.

There was a chill in the air and snow on the ground during their gradual assent up the eastern slope of the Rockies. Water and fuel were not abundant but adequate as they camped near creeks, white popular groves, gooseberry bushes, and fields of white clover.

"Yer gonna need that there sweater we knit ya, Jeremy," said Margaret.

"You're right," Jeremy smiled as he pulled the garment from underneath a pile of clothing.

Everyone was digging down into the trunks in their wagons to find their winter wear. Coats and gloves would be a necessity as they crossed the top of the pass, even though it was only the first part of July. Amanda was thankful for the wonderfully warm buffalo skin that Zeke had given her. Under Zeke's tutelage, Jeremy had tanned the skin to perfection.

"Would you look at this, my water pail froze over last night," complained Ruth. The wind coming down from the ice and snow in the mountains was particularly cold that night and water and milk froze before morning. This would not be the last time this happened before they reached a lower altitude on the other side of the Divide.

"We've got to reach the South Pass before we start heading down to warmer weather again," said James.

"And when do ya think that'll be, Brother James," asked a grumpy Roy Thomas. Cold weather always bothered his bad leg.

"I'm guessing that we'll be there by Friday and spend the Sabbath on the downhill slope." In their daily meetings, Brother Jacobson passed on what information he had about the upcoming trail to all the train captains. Having the Advance Company blaze the trail for them and passing information back by riders or guideposts was a great benefit. The organization of the Mormons continued to be a huge advantage, especially when compared to the loosely organized Gentile pioneers. This constant flow of information helped reduce speculation, rumor mills, and grumbling. The trail was difficult enough; not knowing what was going on made it worse. Brigham Young learned this lesson early on, back in Sugar Creek.

No one saw buffalo for some time, so the main source of meat was antelope, along with an occasional rabbit. James, with Zeke's long rifle, Jeremy, who had become an excellent shot, and Jake, the experienced hunting dog, were the primary hunters for the Jacobson Company. Although their hunting feats often could not feed the entire company, their success meant they were regularly out hunting rather than performing the many other communal chores demanded of everyone else. If they shot more than they could carry, as was often the case, Jake would run back to the train barking and lead a couple of mounted men back to the kill site. The hunting trips also gave James and Jeremy time together to bond. James became more and more impressed with his son's physical and mental maturity. It was hard to believe he was only fourteen.

"Pa, is Ma going to get any better?" Jeremy asked, as he rode side-by-side with James. The two were on another hunt. Jake was running from side to side in front of the two slowly moving horses, his eyes always alert, his nose constantly sniffing the air, and his tongue flopping loosely from his mouth. Jake was never happier than when he was on one of these outings.

"Most people who get ague can live with it for many years," James answered. "Being on the trail is a big problem for her though. But, she's a strong woman. I'm sure she'll be all right."

"I don't know. She seems to be getting weaker and weaker." Jeremy slowly shook his head and frowned. He had been more concerned lately as Amanda had developed a cough along with her other symptoms. The two rode in silence for a while.

"Can't help but notice that you've taken a fancy for some Quaker lass. She's pretty. What's her name?"

Jeremy reddened slightly and ducked his head. "Margaret ... a ... Margaret Hammond."

"Is she as nice as she looks?"

"Oh yes, she ... she's perfect ... with her manners and everything, that is."

"Is she a good Quaker, mind her parents, and live according to their rules?" James teased.

Jeremy gave an exasperated exhale as he slowly shook his head positively. "All of that."

"Even so, son, I've been watching and you must be careful. The Friends have ways strange to our beliefs and even if they are good, honest, God-fearing people, you could find yourself in a bit of a pickle if you were to maybe do something like fall in love." James looked directly at Jeremy, nodded his head, and raised both eyebrows as emphasis. "You understand what I'm saying, son?"

Jeremy blushed at the word love. "I understand." Changing subjects, Jeremy asked, "How long do you think we'll be before we all get to wherever it is we're goin'?"

"Can't say exactly, but Brother Jacobson said we should be there sometime during the second week of August."

"More'n a month more, uh?" Jeremy added up the weeks in his head. That was discouraging he thought.

"Afraid so," replied James. "Shh, hush," James said suddenly, holding up his hand and bringing his horse to a stop. Jake had come to a standstill and pointed his nose off to the right. The hunters slowly and quietly dismounted and crept up behind a large bush. There, not more than forty yards in front of them, was a large pronghorn buck, quietly grazing on clover. The buck's ears were up and alert, but the white tail was down and the wind was in their favor. The animal was unaware of their presence.

Crack! The sound of the James's rifle resounded across the valley as the buck staggered and then dropped. There would be more meat for the Jacobson Company that evening. The excitement of killing another antelope was still there, but nowhere near that of his first kill with Zeke. Jeremy still had those beautiful horns stashed in the wagon. Someday, he thought, he would display them on the wall in his house and tell his children and grandchildren about this and many other wonderful adventures with his dead friend.

Monday morning, at 8:00 a.m., the Saints packed up, forded the creek, and headed west, winding within the shadow of some high bluffs. Even though well marked by the Advance Company, the trail was difficult, with arduous ascents and descents. It was often essential to lock their wagon wheels in order to slow the wagons on steep slopes. A couple of wagons broke down, but with typical Mormon efficiency, they were soon repaired and the Saints were on their way again. The next few days' march was exhausting for the teams of oxen and the pioneers as well. The Friends fared no better as they trailed behind the last Mormon wagon.

Jeremy was delighted that the Quaker train of wagons followed the Mormons. He had heard that the Friends' leader, Williamson, and Brother Jacobson had come to an agreement; the Quakers would follow the Mormons on the daily journey until they reached the Fort Bridger. Williamson decided not to take the Sublette Cutoff at Parting of the Ways. Most all travelers destined for Oregon would head northwest on the Sublette Cutoff, but Williamson decided to take the longer route because the Friends needed supplies for the final push to Oregon. The two camps seemed to integrate well, both respecting the orderly lifestyle of the other. The Friends particularly liked the protection afforded by the friendly Mormons. Like the Mormons, the Quakers often met harassment from unruly pioneers, especially those from Missouri. Unlike the Mormons, however, the pacifist Friends would not fight back.

This arrangement was perfect for Jeremy and Margaret as they were able to meet often. Both sets of parents kept a careful eye on the two and wondered where this relationship might lead. Realizing their children—and they did consider them children—were very young, both knew that fourteen was a dangerous age. Feelings may very well cloud reality, and the reality was, while they all occupied the same space, the Mormons and the Quakers lived in two different worlds.

The next day, James, Jeremy, and Jake headed out again from the group to see what they might shoot to increase the meat supply. After cresting a craggy knoll, about three miles from the train, they were astonished and delighted to see three buffalo grazing in a small, grass-covered dell below. It had been quite a while since they chanced upon these shaggy beasts.

"Where'd they come from?" asked Jeremy in astonishment.

"Don't know and don't care," answered James as he maneuvered his horse into position. An experienced buffalo hunter at this point of the journey, James quickly dispatched two of the buffalo with Zeke's buffalo gun. The third ran off in a cloud of dust. Jeremy galloped back to the main body. It would take more than a couple of riders to skin and bring back the meat from this kill and there was no way Jake could convey that idea.

As James stood guard over the slain buffalo, he was surprised to see the outline of three Indians appear over a rise about three hundred yards to the west. He noted that the Indians had blankets covering their shoulders; thinking that was strange since the temperature during the day was not cold enough for such attire. Nervously, he watched the three men as they sat on their horses looking at him without movement. The distance was too far for him to see the men clearly, but the feathers in their headbands stood out against the bright blue skyline and he saw they were riding without saddles. After fifteen or so tense minutes, the Indians suddenly turned their horses and rode away. James was much relieved when Jeremy returned with a body of Saints. Jake was running happily in front of the group, barking wildly.

James related the sighting of the Indians to Brother Jacobson when they returned. The concern at this point was not for any assault but as always, for the protection of their livestock. About this time, the Quaker leader, Joseph Williamson rode up from the rear. Jacobson iterated James's experience and their concern.

"Not to worry, friend," said Williamson with a big grin. "They be but Missourians trying to scare us from better pasture ahead. Tis nothing but a trick we have become used to already."

"Thank you for that news, friend. If that's the worst we get from the Missourians, I'll be glad for sure." Jacobson laughed loudly. The Saints were much relieved and pressed onward until they found the good campsite the Gentiles tried to conceal.

"Tell me, Margaret, why is it you Quakers are so easy on everyone else and so hard on yourselves?" asked Jeremy. The Saints and the Friends had again camped in close proximity. Jeremy and Margaret took advantage of the situation, sitting in plain view on a large rock between the two camps.

"What do thou mean?" said Margaret.

"Well, you don't allow music and singing and dancing, and you don't like reading novels and watching stage shows, and your dress is so very plain. You have so many rules that it seems like a hard life to me. But you don't care if the Mormons or anyone else do all these things."

"Well, we believe all people have an inner light that tells them what to do. God speaks to every one of us directly. We cannot judge others. Every Friend chooses to follow the rules. If they do not, then they are not of our beliefs," answered Margaret. "That is our way."

"So you choose to follow the rules whether you like them or not?"

"Of course. Don't thou follow the rules of the Mormons? If thou don't follow the rules, then thou art something else ... someone else."

"I follow only because I don't have any choice. I think maybe you are the same."

"That is not true, Jeremy. I *want* to follow the rules," Margaret said emphatically.

"Followin' the rules and wantin' to follow the rules are two different things to me. Someday, when I'm grown up, I'm going to make up my own rules."

Wisely, Margaret counseled, "Everyone must always follow somebody's rules, Jeremy." She paused and then, with skepticism showing on her face, questioned him. "So, thou willest choose to leave thy people?"

"Yes," Jeremy shook his head seriously, "if I have to."

"That is sad," concluded Margaret. She couldn't imagine leaving her people and their ways—ever.

As both the Mormon and Quaker trains halted for the noon break, Margaret was enthralled with what she saw at the edge of the surrounding woodland. Beautiful purple flowers, known as Fairy Slippers, were interspersed among the trees. She wandered from the wagons intent on collecting a bunch of the flowers for her mother. As she gathered up one after the other, she slipped behind a huge bolder and was hidden slightly from the camp's view.

"My, ain't ya a purdy little thing," slurred a large, unkempt, man as he grabbed her arm. He came on so unexpectedly Margaret was completely surprised and so frightened she was unable to scream. The smelly, drunken man drew her close, his shaggy, long red beard brushing up against her face. "Bet yer sweet as ya are purdy." He leered down at the trembling Margaret.

"Bet you're not going to find out, mister. Let her go or I'll blow your head off." From his vantage point at the Weston wagon, Jeremy saw Margaret enter the forest but he also saw the man lurking behind the rock. Short on time and unable to say anything to anyone, he grabbed one of his pistols from his saddlebag and raced forward, motioning to Jake as he lit out.

"Whoa there, sonny boy, that's a mighty big gun fer a young'n like ya." The man pulled Margaret in front of him. "Ya might just hurt somebody else if yer not careful."

"Let her go *now*," Jeremy demanded, leveling the pistol at the man's head. "I'm a very good shot. Besides, if I don't get you, my dog will."

It was then the man became aware of the low rumbling sounds behind him. He looked back over his shoulder and his eyes widened as saw Jake standing behind him, ready to attack, saliva dripping from his snarling mouth. Instantly he pulled his hands away from Margaret, who ran toward Jeremy and cowered behind him.

"No harm done, boy. I was just havin' a little fun. I'll jest mosey on back ta my camp." The chagrined man started backing away to one side keeping his eye on Jake. Jeremy's pistol still pointed at the man, with the hammer cocked.

"If I see you anywhere near our camps again, I'll have my dog tear off your face," Jeremy said in as stern a voice as he could muster.

"No problem." The man sidestepped off toward the edge of the woods. Once he felt it was safe, he turned and walked briskly away, looking back a couple of times to make sure Jake wasn't following him.

Jeremy un-cocked the pistol and slipped it in the back of his trousers. As he turned toward Margaret, she put her arms around him and hugged him tightly. "Oh, Jeremy, I was so scared." Tears began rolling down he cheeks.

"Shh, it's all over," Jeremy relished the nearness of their bodies. He held her gently, patting her on the back.

"What in heaven's name is going on here," demanded Mr. Hammond. He had looked up from chopping wood and seen Jeremy standing with the raised pistol. He could not see Margaret or the man hidden by the rock. He did notice a man disappearing in the woods as he came up.

Jeremy and Margaret parted, both looking embarrassed. "Oh Papa," cried Margaret as she ran to her father and hugged him tightly. "Jeremy saved me from a terrible man who grabbed me before I knew he was there."

"What were thee doing out here by thyself?" demanded Mr. Hammond.

"Just collecting flowers for Mama."

"I saw the man behind the rock, grabbed my pistol, and ran as fast as I could to help her. I didn't have time to call for help," said Jeremy, feeling he had to explain why just he was there.

"That was a mighty brave thing to do, lad. I thank thee for thy action."

"Oh, I'd do anything for Margaret, Mr. Hammond. Besides, Jake was here to help if I needed him." Jeremy pointed at Jake standing nearby, his big tongue hanging to the side as he panted happily, jerking his head up at the sound of his name.

"Well, I thank thee too, Jake." Mr. Hammond walked over and stroked the big dog behind the ears. Returning to Jeremy, he offered his hand, "Thank thee again, Jeremy." They shook hands firmly. "Now, Margaret, darling, thou best gather up thy flowers and bring them to thy mother."

The news of the encounter quickly spread through both camps. Parents reinforced to their children the rule not to wander off alone from the wagons. Everyone praised Jeremy for his quick action. Brother Jacobson, James, Jeremy, and two other men mounted their horses and rode off toward the traders' campsite.

"That's the one," Jeremy said as he pointed to the red bearded man sitting on a log next to the fire. The three traders stood up nervously as the mounted Mormons surrounded them.

"What ya done now, Manny?" demanded one of the traders as he glared Manny's way.

"Ain't done nothin', Roy," replied the edgy Manny, his eyes darting from one rider to the next.

"I suggest you men pack up your gear and head out *now*," demanded Brother Jacobson. "If we so much as see you around our camp we'll shoot you on sight. Understood?"

"Yes sir, we understand," replied Roy. "We're headin' east with our loads so ya won't see us ag'in." He motioned to the other men to start packing as he kicked dirt into the fire. "We'll be gone in two shakes," he added.

The Mormons stared down at the hustling men for a few minutes and, upon Brother Jacobson's nod, they turned their horses around and galloped off toward their campsite.

"Damn you, Manny, yer drinkin' gits us in trouble no matter

where we go," screamed Roy, as he slapped Manny across the face. "Yer dumber'n a mule." The three men packed their gear and headed east. Roy was still grumbling to Manny as they rode off.

CHAPTER 30

It was a particularly hard day on the trail, steep, rugged, and strewn with rocks. Wagon wheels caught in the many cracks and crevices. Those like Amanda, who were ill, had to dismount from the wagons and either walk or ride horses; the wagon gyrations were just too brutal. Last night had been cold, the water and milk again freezing. Gradually the weather warmed and the road smoothed as the train reached the summit of the South Pass and entered the gradual ascent of a great rolling prairie some fifteen or twenty miles long. Foot-high sage bushes abounded. The sick and infirm climbed back into their wagons as the road smoothed. By the end of the day, the weary Saints and Friends were camped along the banks of the Sweetwater River where there was plenty of grass and fresh water.

"How come you never ask anything about my religion?" Jeremy and Margaret were sitting side-by-side on a fallen tree facing the river.

"Why should I?" Margaret said. Oh no, she thought, he's in another one of his religious moods. Jeremy was constantly wondering and questioning his own beliefs more than hers. "What thou believest is thy concern, not mine."

"Does that mean you don't care about what I believe? You don't seem to even care about what you believe."

"Jeremy Weston, that is simply not true. I do care about both." Margaret was indignant. "It is just the Quaker way not question what others believe."

"Well my religion bothers *me*. We Mormons have been run out of town, even killed, because of what we believe. A lot of what we believe is a secret, to us kids anyway. How am I supposed to believe what I don't know or understand?"

"So too have the Quakers been persecuted. It's just because we're all different, Jeremy."

"Well. I don't like being different. Seems to me it's a whole lot of trouble to be different and sometimes downright unhealthy."

"Jeremy, we have to trust our parents. They love us and want the very best for us." Margaret put her hand on Jeremy's shoulder, tilted her head, and looked him in the face. "Right?" The touch of her hand calmed Jeremy.

"You know I really like you ... a lot," said Jeremy.

"And I thee."

"What are we going to do when we reach Fort Bridger?"

"I don't know. I don't think it's our choice, Jeremy. We are only fourteen, only children."

"I am not a child," Jeremy barked. He stood up defiantly, his arms crossed.

Margaret lowered her head, pursed her lips, and said nothing.

Realizing he had upset her with his harshness, Jeremy backed down. "I'm sorry, Margaret, I didn't mean to yell. It's just that I am confused. Sometimes I feel like a man and sometimes not. But I do know that I have very strong feelings about you and don't want to lose you."

Margaret reddened slightly and hung her head even lower. This impetuous boy flattered and confused her.

It was obvious she had strong feelings for Jeremy too, but was more levelheaded in understanding their situation. A fourteen-old-girl was innately more mature than a boy was at the same age.

The call for evening prayers floated toward the couple. "Well,"

Margaret said nervously, "I ... I've got to go. I will see thee again soon, yes?"

"Oh yes," replied Jeremy. He had uncrossed his elbows and was fidgeting with his hands.

"God be with thee, Jeremy," Margaret said as she turned and walked away. The walk turned into a dainty run as she neared her campsite.

"And with thee," Jeremy called after her. Why is it I always seem to make a fool of myself? he thought. Jeremy had become a very befuddled lad since meeting Margaret. It was understandable. He didn't realize it, but this was the first time he had been in love.

The Jacobson Company, following the well-traveled trail, came to a fork in the road—one heading west and the other south and west. A guide board posted by Brother Willard Richards of the Advance Company indicated it was 297 miles back to Fort Laramie. Brother Young had selected the left hand trail, as did Brother Jacobson. It took four days for the Saints to reach the Green River after crossing barren desert terrain yielding nothing but wild sage and grass root. Swarms of mosquitoes were their constant companions. They forded both the swiftly moving, muddy Little Sandy and Big Sandy streams. The experienced travelers found navigating under these conditions of little consequence. However, a major problem began to rear its ugly head—a sickness called mountain fever. Almost a third of the company was afflicted with throbbing headaches, muscle and joint pain, nausea and vomiting, followed by high fever. No one knew the cause. The mysterious ailment seriously impaired the company's progress. Amanda, in her weakened condition, turned out to be the worst case.

"Ma, how are you feeling?" Jeremy crawled into the dimly lit, tightly packed wagon to check on his mother. He did this often during the day. Amanda did not bother to raise her head. She turned her face toward him and smiled faintly; sallow, sunken eyes betrayed her true condition.

"Much better, darling. I don't think I'm going to do any dancing tonight, but I am doing fine."

Jeremy knew better. "Is there anything you need?"

"Other than an end to this miserable journey, no." Both gave a small knowing laugh.

"Amen to that," said Jeremy.

"But, son," she slowly raised her hand to his face, "something else is bothering you. I can tell. You have had a bedraggled look for days now."

"I'm fine, really," Jeremy quickly but unconvincingly answered. He certainly did not want to cause his mother to worry.

"Is it that girl ... Margaret?"

"Well, I am a bit confused about her, yes," he answered.

"And . . ." Amanda nodded her head waiting for an explanation.

"Well, I really like her a lot and in a few days we're going to be at Fort Bridger."

"Oh, I see. That will be the parting of the ways." Amanda needed no explanation. She had seen this coming for a long time. "Surely you knew that day would come. How does Margaret feel about it?"

Jeremy looked away and shook his head. "I'm not sure. I know she likes me but she seems to care more about not hurting her parents. Her religion is important to her, too."

"Those are good qualities, Jeremy. Sounds like she has a level head on her shoulders. You do realize that you are both only fourteen years old?"

"Yes, I know," said an exasperated Jeremy. "I guess I just don't understand why I can like someone so much and not be able to be with her. It's not fair."

"Love ... yes, love," Amanda emphasized at his quick glance, "can be a difficult thing. The problem is when you are in love it is hard to think straight."

Jeremy ran his hand over his face and gave a frustrated sigh. "It seems like every time I like someone, they're taken away."

"Yes, Jeremy, you have lost a lot of friends through no fault of your own. But, son, that is the way of life. Part of growing up is having to face such realities. What kind of person you are depends on how you handle such hardships." She could tell that he was too young and immature to comprehend fully what she was saying.

"Maybe all that is true, but I don't have to like it."

"No, you don't, but you do have to accept that which you cannot change."

"Well, when I get older, maybe I can do something about it."

"Jeremy, I'm sure you will," Amanda said reassuringly. "Here, give someone who truly loves you and will never leave you, a big hug." She held out her arms.

Jeremy embraced his mother and whispered in her ear, "You are my one true friend."

Tears welled in both of their eyes as mother and son reinforced their extraordinary bond.

The Green River was another one of the seemingly insurmountable obstacles the Mormons had to overcome in order to reach the Promised Land. The river was a 180 feet wide, fifteen feet deep, swift moving impediment to reaching their goal. The Advance Company made their job easier, however, leaving behind two rafts, each twelve feet by twenty-four feet rigged with oars and rudders. They ferried the wagons across and made the horses and cattle swim. The crossing took three days, somehow without mishap. Both Mormons and Quakers labored side-by-side until all were across. The days were hot and the mosquitoes unbearable.

All during the time it took to complete the crossing, Jeremy and Margaret were able to meet often. Margaret noted a slight change in Jeremy's attitude. He was uneasy in their relationship, although his ardor was undiminished. Females always sense these things. Males, especially boys, are oblivious to such nuances.

"My father says it may be only four or five days before we reach Fort Bridger."

"Yes, I know," Jeremy said nonchalantly.

"I will be most sad when that happens, how about thee?"

"Margaret." Jeremy looked Margaret in the face, his eyes slightly watering. "I will be more than sad. My mother says that I *more* than like you; she says that I love you," he blurted out.

"Well, thy mother says so, uh, what say thee?"

"I ... I don't know. I guess so. I've never been in love before. All I know is that I feel different when I'm with you—different than ever before." This was uncharted waters for Jeremy. All his life he did everything so that he could feel like and become a man. Girls had always been a nuisance and a passing interest, at best. Now all of a sudden, there was this beautiful girl that made him think of little else.

"Jeremy, I feel the same. I'm not sure it is love because I have never been in love either. Are we old enough to be in love?"

"I don't know, I guess so. Why not?"

"The problem is, we're not old enough to be on our own," lamented Margaret.

"The main problem is that you're a Quaker and I'm a Mormon, even if we *were* old enough," blurted Jeremy.

Both fell silent. There was truth in what Jeremy said. Try as they might to ignore that fact, it was always there overshadowing everything else

Finally, Jeremy said, "Well, if it is love, then I guess I love you no matter what. I am very mad that I can't do anything about it. It doesn't seem fair."

"I guess I love thee too, Jeremy. No matter what, I will always hold a place in my heart for thee."

The two young lovers' eyes locked as they conveyed their feelings to each another. The other problem confronting this situation was that they were never out of sight of one camp or the other. Physical contact was out of the question as both of their parents knew the dangers of the early teens and were constantly on the alert. Understandably, Jeremy's first love produced disillusionment and frustration.

The next few days, the Mormon and Quaker trains traversed the countryside without a major unpleasant incident. Mountain fever was rampant in both camps. Nevertheless, the pioneers pushed forward. They encountered a variety of landscapes, some with adequate feed and water, some not. Usually, they made camp on the banks of two tributaries of the Green River—Hams Fork and Blacks Fork. Swiftly churning muddy waters characterized the majority of these creeks and streams, but the travelers forded all with relative ease. The days were hot and suffocating from the dry dust churning from the wagon wheels and livestock. The minute the sun disappeared, the air from the snow-covered mountains gave everyone a chill. Shrubbery was mostly growing near the banks of the rivers and streams, but there was an abundance of tallow weed, wild flowers, and flax strewn about the countryside. The main large game for hunters was antelope and there were large quantities of fish—a welcome supplement to their diet.

The caravan passed by a number of Indian lodges occupied by the families of trappers and hunters that had taken squaws as wives. Many children played in and around the lodges and waved happily as the wagons passed by. Brother Jacobson's lead wagon entered the grounds of the small trading post called Fort Bridger, situated on one of the islands created by three principle channels of Blacks Fork. A typical frontier wall surrounded the lodging quarters and offices, opening onto a hollow square. On the north, there was a large enclosure for livestock. A strong timber gate helped protect the fort from wild beasts and unfriendly Indians. A few Snake Indians, friendly to Whites, milled about two large log houses, the main structures.

"How do, Brothers?" hailed a man in a wide-brimmed hat. He knew instantly that they were Mormons. The man was over six-feet tall; his rawboned, powerful frame moved with agility and confidence. He had gray eyes, abundant brown hair, and a personable smile. "Welcome ta Fort Bridger. Major James Bridger's my name, though most call me Old Gabe."

"Hello to you Major." Brother Jacobson offered his hand, "It is my pleasure. Your fame has spread far and wide."

Indeed, many knew that Bridger and other mountain men had roamed throughout the western third of the United States for many years. While trapping in late 1824, Bridger came upon the Great Salt Lake, that, at the time, he thought was part of the Pacific Ocean. It was commonly believe that he was the first White man to see the lake. This, of course, made him of great interest to the Mormons.

"And this is my friend, Joseph Williamson," said Jacobson as the Quaker walked up from behind.

"Welcome Mr. Williamson," greeted Bridger in his typically hospitable manner. "I must say, I don' often see Mormons an' Quakers traveling together. In fact, I don' see many Quakers at all."

"Tis true, there are many more Saints on this trail than Friends, who take the northern bypass. I trust thy friendship is extended to both?"

"Indeed, indeed it is. We welcome men of all stripes, red an' white. All that is requested is civility an' some form a trade." Bridger smiled broadly.

"We easily fit into both categories," said Williamson.

"Well, now, Mormon trains have passed through already, including yer leader, Brother Brigham Young. All have set a high standard fer responsibility an' fairness in trade, an' not a one has caused any problems. I cain't say that about some a the others, especially some a the ruffians comin' out a Missouri."

"And none shall cause a problem, Major Bridger. Your business should be blessed with many more trains of Saints to come," said Jacobson.

"So I understand," replied Bridger. "Please, there's plenty of room fer all yer wagons so set up camp as ya like. We got all kind a supplies an' other services like smithin'. So, make yerselves at home, gentlemen. Let me know if I can be of assistance." He strode off waving and smiling to everyone as he headed toward his office.

Both trains found an ideal campsite about a quarter of a mile from the fort. There were many streams filled with fish and banks plush with rich tall grass. Cottonwood and ash trees abounded. Roy Thomas was sitting on the ground, his back leaning against a wagon wheel; his head tilted back facing the sun, his eyes closed.

"Enjoying yourself, Brother Thomas?" said James as he approached Roy.

"You bet," replied Roy. "This here sun feels great on my beat up old lag."

"I'm sure it does. Isn't this a wonderful spot?"

Roy looked around and took in the beauty of the surrounding countryside. "Yep, wouldn't bother me none if Brother Jacobson said this is as far as we go. Where we're headed cain't be no better'n this."

James chuckled. "You know, Brother Thomas, I think if we put that to a vote, it would be 100 percent in favor. Of course, I don't think Major Bridger would think much of it, not to mention Brother Young.

And I don't think we want to face either one of those fellas. Best you rest up for the final push. The sooner we start the sooner we get there." Physically and emotionally worn out from the trip, many Saints, some of whom were sick, began to wonder if all this effort was worth it.

"Yer right, of course, but no harm in wishin'," Roy sighed.

For the next two days, the Saints and the Friends repaired their equipment, restocked their supplies, and rested their livestock and themselves. The charismatic Bridger entertained James, Brother Jacobson, and other leaders in the train around the campfire. He had many tales to tell about his adventures throughout the untraveled west and he loved telling them. Jeremy sat on the periphery and was enthralled. Some of Major Bridger's stories reminded him of Zeke and his many tall tales.

Everyone's attitude always seemed to improve any time the company took time off from the road. Amanda, confined mostly to riding in the wagon, was particularly relieved. It did wonders for her body, still plagued with mountain fever and malaria, to stretch out on the motionless grass and gaze up at the boundless sky.

"How are you today, Ma?" asked the constantly attentive Jeremy, as he stretched out by his mother on the grass.

"Fine, Jeremy, fine. It does my old bones good to leave that infernal wagon."

"Is there anything I can get for you?"

"No, thanks, son. I'm just content to lie here and rest while everyone else does the work."

Jeremy knew that his mother must really be wearing out as she was never happy doing nothing while everyone else was busy.

"So, have you said your goodbye to Margaret yet?" Amanda watched daily as her son's manner grew gloomier the nearer they got to Fort Bridger. He was not as lighthearted after their little get-togethers as he used to be. It didn't take much to understand why.

"No, they're not leaving until the morning," Jeremy lamented.

"I know it is difficult for you to go your different ways. I really am sorry that you have to go through this. Everyone always remembers their first love as something special."

"Was Pa your first love?"

Amanda chuckled. "No, heavens no," she sighed. Her expression was one of looking back in time.

"Well, who then?" Jeremy's interest was piqued.

"Oh, I was about a year older than you are, back in Pennsylvania. His name was Ned and I really thought I loved that boy. He acted like he loved me too."

"Did you ever kiss him?"

"What kind of question is that?" Amanda feigned shock. "Well, actually yes—once."

"Well, what happened?"

"Oh, he left me for another girl. I was crushed—cried for a week."

"That must have been terrible for you."

"It was," Amanda sighed again, "but I got over it. And you will too. At least Margaret is not leaving you for another boy," she chuckled.

"I guess you're right. But, she is leaving and that really hurts me."

"I know, son. I'm sorry for that."

"It's all right; it's not your fault." Jeremy reached over and gave his mother a kiss on the cheek.

Jeremy could hear the rain tapping lightly against his tent. In the distance, there was an occasional roll of thunder. It was morning and time to awaken. Typically, as a teenage boy, it was not his favorite time of day. Today was worse, though, as the Mormons and the Quakers would be going their separate ways. Margaret would actually be leaving him on this dark and dismal morning. He had tried to prepare for this day but there was no way to do so. Despite the inevitability of their separation, he dreamed the impossible. Quickly, he pulled on his boots, grabbed his hat and coat, and ran toward Margaret's wagon.

The Hammond family was up and almost ready to go. Jeremy skidded to a walk and approached their wagon.

"Good morning, Mr. Hammond," he said, bowing his head, "and to you, Mrs. Hammond."

"Good morning to thee, Jeremy," replied Mr. Hammond.

"I've come to say goodbye to you all." Jeremy eyes searched for Margaret.

"She's in the back," Mrs. Hammond said, smiling and nodding to the rear of their wagon.

"Thank you," Jeremy replied as he quickly walked to the rear.

He rounded the corner and saw Margaret trying with some difficulty to push a bundle into the back of the wagon.

"Can I help?" he asked as he took hold of the bundle, pressing close to Margaret's body.

"Oh, Jeremy, thee startled me." She breathed heavily and turned to face him. Their noses were within inches, their eyes locked.

"Were you going without saying goodbye?" he whispered.

"No, of course not," she whispered back.

The rain fell gently on their faces.

"I will never forget you, Margaret."

"Nor I thee."

Jeremy kissed her full on the mouth and then turned and ran away. Margaret stood alone in the rain, astonished by what had just happened.

"Are thee all right?" asked her concerned mother, who came back to check on her daughter after seeing Jeremy run away.

"Yes ... yes, I am fine," said Margaret, still in a daze.

"He's a fine boy. We're all going to miss him," consoled Mrs. Hammond.

"Yes, we will." Margaret wiped a tear from her rain-soaked cheek.

CHAPTER 31

The two-day layover at Fort Bridger gave James a chance to take stock of his train—equipment, livestock, and people. Considering the miles traveled, the diversity of weather conditions, the amount of sickness and accidents, the number and variety of encounters with animals, Indians, and rapscallions, and, yes, even death, the Weston Train was in fine shape compared to some others.

The last word from William reassured everyone that he, Roy Thomas, Jr., and Tom Johnson were all safe in San Diego. James wished fervently for William's early return to resume his family duties. It seemed to James that Ruth, without William's steady hand, exercised less control over her children and increased her religious fervor almost to the point of fanaticism. Mary Ellen Thompson and her three children had been an asset to the operation of the train—the children were well behaved and Mary Ellen always helpful and positive. Elizabeth Granger was an asset and a liability. Their "secret" close relationship had begun to wear thin and though Elizabeth was always discreet, James knew the only way to cleanly break off the relationship was for William to return.

Jeremiah and Mary Johnson, Margaret and Josephine, and Prudence Jessup were the kind of people needed for success—steady, reliable, hard working, and faithful. James could always count on these five in a crisis. None had been seriously ill or inclined toward accidents—except for Josephine's snakebite. Anthony and Annie Adams were a little strange at times but never caused James any problems. Fortunately, they remained reasonably healthy and pulled their load throughout the trip.

Roy Thomas was, well ... a pain at times and a drain on James's patience. He always did whatever he could, considering his physical affliction, but not without constant grumbling. It was just his way and his many humorous idiosyncrasies always seemed to balance his complaining. His wife, Amelia, was the typical hard working, dedicated Mormon wife who always did what was ask of her. The only complaint for James was her seeming lack of interest in corralling her ten children.

Of course, the Weston Train also had its tragedies. Joshua Jessup had died of tuberculosis that he had contracted in Nauvoo. Moreover, they'd lost poor little Jacob Weston to croup and his beloved sweet Clara to measles. At this point, James considered Amanda a casualty, as well. He saw her physical condition degenerating daily and her indomitable spirit waning. He felt particularly bad about Amanda, because not only was she his wife, but also because his ardent desire to reach the Promised Land contributed to her condition.

As the Jacobson Camp packed up and headed west, following the trail traveled by the advance companies, they bid farewell to the Quakers, who struck out northwest toward their final destination in Oregon. The Saints would reach their destination at Salt Lake, some 150 miles from Fort Bridger, long before the Friends would pull into their final resting site 900 miles away. James took consolation in this and passed back his feelings as the trains separated. "Take comfort in knowing we will reach the Promised Land long before our Quaker brothers find their final destination."

Jeremy strained, nearly riding backwards in his saddle to catch a glimpse of Margaret. Finally, he saw her walking beside the family wagon. She spied him and waved a hankie that was the recipient of a copious number of tears. Jeremy waved back. The two lost sight of each other as the Quakers' train disappeared around a bend. Jeremy turned frontward in his saddle, his shoulders and head slumped forward in sadness for he knew he would never see Margaret again.

As if God were putting the Mormons through one last test of faith, the closer they got to the Great Salt Lake Valley, the more difficult the terrain became. They were only a few days out from Fort Bridger and had negotiated some of the steepest terrain of the entire trip. Precipitous rocky ascents and near perpendicular descents made locking wagon wheels a common practice. At the end of an exhausting journey on the fifth day after leaving Fort Bridger, the Saints arrived at Red Fork Canyon. The travelers knew this unusual canyon by reputation, as its narrow passage way and distinctive echoing characteristic were excitedly talked about throughout the camp. The journey was difficult as the vertical slopes of the canyon were so close and crooked, and the creek so deep and rapid, that there was barely room for one wagon to pass. However, the canyon's echoing reputation was well founded. The dissonance of sounds reverberating throughout the chasm was as disquieting to the animals as it was entertaining to the travelers. Wagon wheels creaked, groaned, and rattled like carpenters hammering on wood. Cattle lowed and nervously listened to the return of their plaintive cries. Children and adults alike delighted in hearing their yelling resound repeatedly throughout the ravine. A simple pistol shot sounded like a cannon. Finally, the Saints emerged from the beguiling canyon and camped amidst abundant feed and water.

As the train settled down and made camp, it was still a couple of hours before darkness. James decided to try his luck hunting in the surrounding mountainous environment.

"Come on, Jake," James called as he shouldered his rifle and headed away from the wagon train. The big dog sprang to his feet and happily ran toward James. He knew instantly from James's attitude and the shouldering of the rifle that they were gong hunting. Zeke had trained Jake well. He loved hunting and had proven himself useful many times. He was particularly good at tracking down and subduing wounded game, like sheep, deer, and wild boar. No matter the size or ferocity of the quarry, he always seemed up to the task. Therefore, when invited to go hunting, he was always ready. With only a momentary glance back wondering why Jeremy wasn't coming along, he gleefully headed out with James. Jeremy was aware of the hunt; he had chores to do and was caring for his ailing mother.

The evening was crisp and clear. James hoped that he would be able to shoot something worthwhile within a short distance from the path of the wagons. He was in the mood to bag something as big as a deer, but if he did so, it meant going back to the train to fetch help. One man carrying such large game was impossible. That's when Jake became particularly useful for at the command, "Jake, stay!" he would stand guard over the kill and make sure that no scavengers, like wolves, coyotes, or buzzards would begin to gnaw on the prize before it could be recovered by men from the wagon train. Alternatively, when James didn't feel like making the trek back to the wagons, he would command, "Jake, go!" As he had for months, Jake would scamper off and bring riders back.

James's boots sought out smooth spots and clearances between jagged rocks as he made his way up the mountainside. He was constantly on the alert as he peered around and between the large pines that were interspersed with mesquite bushes and saw grass. Silent and determined, he climbed upward until the wagon train was lost from sight. Jake ran from side to side, expertly picking his way among the many obstacles, silent and watchful. The only sound he produced was from his mouth as he panted. His giant tongue flopped side-to-side in his mouth, dripping saliva, and his tail wagged happily back and forth.

The two hunters picked their way through and up the rugged terrain about a mile without as much as a cottontail rabbit coming into view. The landscape suddenly turned into a sharp precipice as James rounded the bend of the mountain. The view was breathtaking with steep canyons and rough mountains intermixed for miles against a backdrop of billowing white clouds and blue sky. James paused to take in the magnificent view, the wondrous blending of colors, the scent of pine as it wafted on the gentle breeze, and the hushed silence of the vastness spread before him. A lone eagle screeched forlornly as it soared over the empty space below. It was awe-inspiring—one of those moments that forces a man to reflect on the immenseness of nature and his insignificance by comparison.

Before him was a natural path about four feet wide, with a small shrub-dotted ledge above on the left and a steep abyss on the right. The view was spectacular; however, the prospects for game were limited in this direction. He was about to turn around and retrace his steps when he heard a noise and caught a glimpse of movement around a sharp bend in the path. Was it a mountain goat, he thought? Slowly he crept forward with his rifle at the ready, hugging the mountain on his left, and peering around the bend. Whatever it was in front of him was moving in the opposite direction. His curiosity pulled him cautiously ahead. After all, it could just as easily be a mountain lion as mountain goat.

As James rounded another sharp bend, he came into full view of a brown, furry cub bear. With that discovery, he froze. He hadn't seen a grizzly up close before, but he had heard many stories about disastrous encounters with these huge beasts. Everyone knew not to mess around with the cute cubs because the mothers defended their offspring ferociously. James didn't have time to assimilate all these thoughts before the mother bear, weighing about 300 pounds, entered the picture. Upon seeing James, the grizzly rose up on her two hind feet in a towering, aggressive stance and emitted a loud, spine-shivering roar. The huge beast bared large, yellow teeth shrouded in puffs of breath and spittle between roars. Her long claws struck menacingly at the air in front of her.

In his dread, James couldn't remember what he was supposed to do if he encountered a grizzly—stay put and shoot, or run. Despite their large size, these huge animals are extremely agile and fast, reaching speeds of 35 to 40 mph—running was not wise. Before he had a chance to decide, the bear decided for him. She charged him full speed. James instinctively dodged the oncoming beast by stepping back around the mountain bend. He almost tripped in the process. The bear swiped at James with her large paw, that, fortunately, the rock wall partially deflected. James felt a searing pain shoot through his left shoulder as the claws tore through his outer clothing. He grimaced, grabbed his shoulder, and flattened himself against the rock wall, shielding the bear from his view.

At that moment, James became aware that the bear's roar had changed. It was more intense and frantic. The deafening growl of the bear mixed with that of another ferocious creature. James could hear much shuffling and scuffling—obvious sounds of a major battle. Cautiously, he peered around the edge of the rock wall. There, to his astonishment was the bear grappling with a ferocious Jake. Jake had jumped from the ledge above and clamped his huge jaws tightly around the bear's nose and one eye. No matter what the bear did, including standing up and ripping at Jake's underbelly with her razor sharp claws, the Hero Dog hung on. Then to James's horror, bear and dog disappeared over the edge of the precipitous cliff, locked one to the other in their death struggle. Suddenly, there was silence.

James stood frozen in disbelief. Slowly he crept forward and peered over the edge of the cliff. There was no sight of Jake or the bear as the rocky precipice ended some three to four hundred feet below, shrouded in a mist that hung in the tops of giant pine trees. The beauty and silence returned to this panoramic view, marred only by the knowledge of what had just occurred. James could not believe that Jake was gone. That loveable, big, old dog had always been there when anyone needed him. Granted, Jake was a pain at times but even when he was in trouble, he had a charm that one couldn't help but forgive him. Oh God, thought James, how am I going to tell Jeremy?

James took one last look over the canyon edge, as if doing so would bring Jake back. He shook his head and sighed, rose wearily to his feet, inspected his wound, shouldered his rifle, and headed back down the mountain. The bear cub whimpered behind him as he left the path. He felt a momentary concern for the defenseless cub. He knew the cub would die a slow agonizing death from starvation without its mother or, more likely, be killed by some hungry predator. However, there was only enough room in his heart for one tragedy, so he trudged on, leaving the cub behind.

As James came within view of the wagon train, his mouth became dry and his legs shook. His injured shoulder was just now beginning to throb. He was suffering from the shock of having been injured by a mammoth beast and grappling with the loss of Jake. Mostly he kept rehearsing what he would say to Jeremy. How many times am I going to have to bring this boy bad news, he thought. He approached his family wagon and, as if on cue, Jeremy spied him, noticing William's torn shirt and bloody, injured shoulder.

"Pa, what happened?" As James came into view, Jeremy rushed to his side.

Hearing the commotion, Amanda shakily climbed down from the wagon. "Oh my God, James, are you all right?"

Others in the train started to gather around as a weakened James sat on a nearby fallen tree trunk. The realization of what had happened began to sink in and he was ashen in color and felt woozy. Ruth saw that James was injured. She came running with bandages and a bottle of whiskey to help sterilize any wound. As Amanda carefully removed his tattered shirt, James winced. Actually, the wound, with three clearly defined claw marks, looked worse than it was, for the slashes were not deep.

"Biggest bear you ever saw," James told the crowd. "He almost got me, but for Jake."

It was then Jeremy became aware that Jake was not around. He had a sinking feeling in the pit of his stomach. "Where ... where is Jake?" he asked tentatively.

"Son, that dog lived up to his reputation. He attacked that bear head on to keep him away from me." With a quivering voice, James proceeded to tell the story of how Jake died as Amanda and Ruth bandaged his wound. "I'm so sorry, son, but you would have been very proud of that old boy." James put his right hand on Jeremy's shoulder, knowing that there was no way to consol his son.

Typically, Jeremy said nothing. Crestfallen, tears filled his eyes as he kept shaking his head in disbelief. Some of the other smaller children sobbed as they began to realize that old Jake was dead. Everyone was in shock. Jeremy walked away, some distance from the train, and stood motionless as he stared off into the distance toward the mountain range where Jake had made his last stand. There would never be anything or anyone to replace that magnificent friend. In a short span of time, this young lad had lost two of his best friends and companions, and a girl he loved. With these loves and losses, Jeremy was growing up too fast.

The Mormon trains preceding the Jacobson Saints had cleared the all but impassable trail well. This made easier their journey to Big Mountain Pass—the last obstacle before the Promised Land. A constant excited buzz prevailed among the weary travelers, as they knew the end of their long struggle was at hand. Renewed strength flowed through tired bodies and even the sick seemed to rise above their illnesses. Somehow, even the long-suffering oxen felt the excitement and quickened their step.

Amanda, however, was near her emotional and physical end. The last few miles had been excruciating. As the oxen lumbered onward, every motion of the slowly moving wagon magnified the pain in her aching body. She coughed constantly, had a throbbing headache, a persistent fever, and aching bones. The mountain fever she contracted twenty days before compounded her serious case of malaria. She drifted in and out of delirium. Jeremy was by her side, soothing her fevered brow with wet cloths; worried about her obviously grievous condition. It was beyond his comprehension that he could lose not only another friend, but also his beloved mother.

The sounds of, "Hallelujah! Hallelujah!" from the wagons ahead lifted Amanda's spirits for a moment. With Jeremy's assistance, she strained to sit up and peer over the edge of the wagon for her first view of the goal so long sought after. Finally, the rocks parted and she was able to survey the vast landscape before her. Although the lake was not visible from this location, the Great Salt Lake Valley spread out below; its flatness emphasized by the ruggedness of the surrounding mountains.

"Thank you God, thank you God!" screamed Ruth above the level of the cheering pioneers. Tears of joy flowed down her cheeks as she ran hugging and kissing one person after another.

"My God in heaven," Amanda wailed, as she scanned the inhospitable, arid terrain and sterile-looking lake countryside that lie in the distance. "Have we come all this way, lost our children and our fortunes, suffered so greatly, for this?" The greenery of Tennessee and her beautiful gardens in Nauvoo appeared before her eyes. She slumped back into the wagon and sobbed uncontrollably. As the last remaining strength drained from her mind and body, she tried, but could not, make sense of it all.

Amanda could not visualize the raw promise of the enterprise that was taking place—the industrious city, the magnificent Temple, the many Mormon towns and settlements that would stretch from Salt Lake, north into Idaho and as far south as Mexico. Despite all odds, these passionately driven people would accomplish their mission. They, indeed, had passed the severest of tests, their crucible of faith. All this was to be lost on Amanda. The frail, ailing, dispirited woman, who had endured so much, died quietly in the creaking wagon as it descended into the Promised Land. Jeremy sat sobbing by her side. Life had dealt him another blow. He had now lost his "one true friend" who said she would never leave him.

Back in January, the Mormon Battalion had marched into San Diego, General Kearny's headquarters for the Army of the West. This was to be the Battalion's final destination in the war against Mexico. The general praised the Mormons for what he called the longest military march in history. They had not one encounter with the enemy but their perseverance and dedication under such dreadful conditions gave General Kearny reason to praise them in the highest order back in Washington.

Only twenty-two men died from disease and other natural causes during the entire campaign. Before their release from duty, many of the men helped in civil works projects. One significant project the Mormons worked on was Fort Moore erected near a small town called Los Angeles. The fort was one of the first U.S. military installations in California. Surprisingly, eighty of the Battalion reenlisted in the regular army for another six months. One of those men was Roy Thomas, Jr. The structured lifestyle of the Army was ideal for this "slow thinker" and the repetitive nature of the Army's physical routine helped overcome his uncoordinated ways. He would become a career soldier. Jeremiah and Mary Johnson's boy, Tom, was an exemplary soldier who never left William's side. Eventually, Tom would make his way to Salt Lake for a reunion with his beloved family.

William mustered out of the Army in San Diego on July 16, 1847 and reunited with his family in Salt Lake two months later. He became a prominent Mormon leader and eventually had ten wives. James would realize the promise and help in the building of a distinct new world by establishing a community fifty miles south of Salt Lake. He would have three wives. The indomitable Christine, who thrived in any environment, matured into a dynamic Mormon wife and mother. Nonetheless, like her mother, she would insist on a monogamous marriage.

When he turned sixteen, Jeremy packed his saddlebags, tied his pronghorn prize to his saddle, and astride Zeke's stallion, Horse, headed east, traversing back along the Mormon Trail. He journeyed to Fort Laramie, where he visited Zeke's grave. Here, on the lopsided cross, Jeremy took his bowie knife and carved, "Jake – Hero Dog" next to Zeke's name. Ultimately, Jeremy ended up in Virginia. There he lived with his uncle, Thomas Weston. Surviving the arduous years of the Civil War, Jeremy eventually married, had two children, and became a prosperous tobacco farmer, as his father once was. The pronghorn trophy hung proudly over his mantel. Jeremy held no religious beliefs for the rest of his life.

THE END